Colonial Daughter

Heather Garside

Colonial Daughter

Heather Garside

Yarraman Press, 2017

Yarraman Press,
PO Box 275,
Capella, QLD, 4723, Australia

www.heathergarside.com

Authors Note: All characters in this novel are fictitious, with the exception of the French priest, Dean Murray, who actually did minister in Rockhampton at the time of this story.

Although in most cases I have made every effort to be true to the geography and history of the area, I have taken liberties with the area on the Dawson River where I have sited Lloyd Kavanagh's property. Although Bauhinia Downs did (and still does) exist, its boundaries did not extend as close to the river as I have described.

Chapter One

Central Queensland, 1873.
'They can't make me go to England!'

There was no-one to hear her but the black crow watching with beady eyes from a nearby gum tree. Seething with helpless frustration, Louise Ashford crumpled the letter into a ball and stuffed the pages inside her sleeve. It was just like her autocratic father to direct her future without thought or care for her wishes.

Clutching at the gate with trembling hands, she pressed her face against the sun-bleached timber and inhaled its homely, comforting scent. With the Queensland sun beating upon the nape of her neck, her parents in England seemed more remote from her than ever.

It would be autumn in England now, the leaves turning gold and brown, then falling to be raked and burnt in blazing bonfires. The air would be cold and bleak with the biting promise of snow. 'Home' her parents still called it, even after twenty years. To Louise it sounded a grim, forbidding place, despite their descriptions of green fields and hedgerows and the balmy Devonshire summer. She suspected their memories might be as short as those same English summers.

Beyond the gate, perhaps half a mile away, a dust-pall hovered sluggishly above the trees. Cattle bellowed in the stock-yards, dogs barked and men shouted and Louise longed to be participating in the activity. It had been the same back at Banyandah.

Sometimes she'd been allowed to ride out to watch the cattle being brought in; sedate excursions with a groom or a governess and her younger sister. Her father, her brother and half-a-dozen stockmen had been in charge of the herd, amid the noisy confusion of cracking stock whips, bawling cows and clouds of floating dust. And she had to sit her mount and watch them. Harry Ashford's daughters didn't demean themselves by working with the men.

Louise straightened abruptly at the rumble of iron wheels on the dirt road, the soft clop of horses' hooves and the jingle of harness. She struggled for composure as James's wife Mary drove up in the buggy, her daughter Sarah seated beside her with a picnic basket at her feet.

'Louise, I was wondering where you were.' Mary's slender hands were gentle on the buggy reins, drawing up the buggy pair with practised ease. 'I'm taking morning tea to the men. Would you like to accompany us?'

'Of course, Cousin Mary.' She hardly felt like being sociable, but the cattle yards as always drew her like a magnet. Louise opened the gate and closed again it behind the vehicle, then lifted her skirts in one hand to step up to the rear seat of the Abbot double buggy.

'You seem upset.' Mary clicked up the horses. 'Is it your father's letter?'

She nodded. 'He says I must come to England with Charles. He's written to Charles and instructed him to collect me, so it seems there's no way out of it.'

Mary glanced over her shoulder. 'I wish I could be in your shoes, Louise. I know James has prospered here, but oh dear, I miss the green of England and family and friends...it broke my heart to leave it all behind.'

Louise gritted her teeth, sensing an implied rebuke. 'I'm not close to my family–and if you knew them better, Cousin Mary, you'd understand why. Charles is the only one I saw much of, as a child. And the colonies are my home in the same way that England was yours. I'm a Cornstalk, a colonial and I love the bush.' She tossed back her long dark hair. 'I remember visiting Sydney in July and I hated the cold, wet winter. I'm sure England would be far worse.'

There was a hint of compassion in Mary's voice now. 'You've no choice but to accept your father's wishes, my dear. You're only eighteen and your place is with your family. We love having you here, but we can't intervene in this. And I'm sure Charles won't be dissuaded.'

Louise bit her lip. She knew Mary was right. She'd been allowed to stay behind when her parents travelled to England, but it was different now that her father had inherited the family estate and intended to remain there. She'd adored her elder brother as a child, but the gap between them had widened with the years. Charles could be as merciless as her father when he chose.

Mary drew the buggy to a halt under a shady ironbark tree a discreet distance from the yards. It wouldn't be prudent to go closer, for the smell of singed hide and the bawl of bellowing calves made it obvious the men were branding–not a fit spectacle for the delicate eyes of a lady.

Lindsay, Mary's youngest son, was the first to join them. He'd escaped his studies to help with the mustering and as he happily set about gathering leaves and wood for a fire, Louise marvelled that this was the same lad who continually procrastinated and fiddled in the school room. Once the billies had boiled, Cousin James and his two elder sons joined the ladies beside the buggy. The stockmen took their pannikins of tea and slabs of cake before retiring to a respectful distance.

'Hush,' Mary admonished Lindsay and Sarah, who were chattering excitedly. 'Run away and play while we adults talk. Louise has some news to tell you, James.'

'Oh? What's that?' James looked up from his tea and smiled at Louise in a friendly, quizzical fashion.

Despite her bad humour, she found herself returning his smile. James was a quiet, courteous man who bore no resemblance to her own family. He was short and fair, while most of the Ashfords, including herself, were tall and dark. The contrast in personality was equally marked: perhaps that was why she liked him so much.

But her mood darkened as she related her news. 'The mailman brought a letter from Papa. My grandfather passed away in June, but it seems my Uncle George, who was to have inherited, succumbed to a tropical illness in South America. This means Papa is now Squire of Fenham Manor.' Bitterness constricted her throat, sharpening her tongue. 'My parents are ecstatic, despite their grief for poor Grandpapa. Unfortunately they now expect me to join them in England.'

James's smile faded. 'It is only right that you should do so, Louise.'

'Perhaps England won't be so bad,' Jack, the eldest boy, commented quietly.

Louise glanced at Jack, a gangling twenty-year-old in dirty shirt and breeches. His bashful admiration had both irritated and gratified her at first, but his confidence seemed to be growing of late. 'They'll never allow me to return here.' Suddenly she was close to tears, clenching her fists in frustration. 'Oh, damn Uncle George for dying on us!'

'Louise!' Mary's eyes widened. 'Such language from a lady!'

'I beg your pardon.' Louise would have reacted sullenly to a similar reprimand from her mother, but she had much fondness and respect for Mary. And she was only too aware of the Barclay men watching her in astonished fascination. It was fortunate the younger children weren't listening.

Mary broke the awkward silence. 'It's only natural that your family wants you with them. I'm sure they miss you, Louise.'

'Miss me?' Louise made a derisive sound in her throat. 'You don't know my parents well, Cousin Mary. I'm sure Papa has hardly noticed my absence and as for Mama... She expects me to be her companion now, but she forgets that I seldom saw her as a child. We were raised by nursery-maids and governesses.' Her fingers curled into fists of frustration. 'I didn't know what a proper family was until I came to stay with you.'

Mary's eyes softened. She looked at James, who took a sip of tea before replying in a careful tone. 'I'm sorry, Louise, but I think you'll have to make the best of it. I felt your father wasn't anxious to leave you with us in the first instance, so I won't interfere in this now.'

That was certainly true. It was only a chance meeting between her father and James that had led to the invitation, for the cousins hadn't seen each other in years. James Barclay wasn't so well up in the world as the Ashfords and her father had been offended by James' suggestion that Louise act as tutor to his two younger children. But Louise had been determined, thinking it an adventure. She liked children and preferred to believe she would be a useful addition to her cousin's household.

It had turned out even better than she'd expected. She enjoyed tutoring Sarah and Lindsay, but the closeness and camaraderie of this simple family had somehow exposed the cold arrogance of her own. Now her mother's idle lifestyle, pursuing the social round of races, charity balls and afternoon teas, seemed shallow and trivial.

She looked up as Mary spoke.

'Think of it as an adventure,' her cousin's wife said bracingly. 'A chance to travel, to see another country.'

Louise shuddered. 'Four to five months at sea–I'll be miserably sick. I'm a dreadful sailor.'

Mary's face turned grim. 'You'll manage, Louise. It's the children who suffer most. We had two little ones when we sailed from England–Jack was three. He survived but his younger brother didn't.'

Chastened, Louise bowed her head. 'I'm sorry, Cousin Mary. I didn't know.'

She was silent then, but her resolve hadn't weakened. If the Barclays were unsympathetic, she'd have to make her own plans.

Later that afternoon, when her lessons with Sarah were finished, Louise walked to her favourite spot by the Dawson River. It was her habit to sit here and read or daydream in leisure moments. Today she was unable to relax. She stood at the edge of the water and tossed pebbles into the still green depths, trying to plan her next move.

There was only one solution. If she couldn't remain with the Barclays, she must disappear. Lose herself where Charles couldn't find her.

Her work with the Barclay children had given her some experience as a governess. The position was a step down on the social scale, but she enjoyed useful work and it offered her the chance for the adventure she craved.

She spent the afternoon forming plans and discarding them when obstacles arose. She knew her biggest stumbling block would be Charles, who would do his best to pursue her wherever she went, but gradually an idea formed in her mind.

At last, when the shadows of the river gums stretched long across the water to the opposite bank, she scrambled up the slope and returned to the homestead to bathe and change for dinner.

James Barclay had settled on the Dawson only five years before and his simple slab home with shingle roof compared poorly to the grand house at Banyandah. The run itself was still largely unfenced, though James and his sons were working hard to remedy that. In the meantime it was a challenge to control the half-wild cattle which led them a reckless chase at mustering time.

Now, as Louise arranged her hair for dinner, she reflected how this pioneering lifestyle appealed to her own restless spirit. Her coming-out in Sydney last year hadn't been a success. At a time when it was fashionable to be small, plump and fair, she was tall, dark and slender, the strong Ashford features which looked so well on Charles somehow less becoming to a woman. Few men had shown an interest in her and those who did had bored her, much to her mother's exasperation. The attention she enjoyed here, where unattached women were outnumbered by men four to one, had come as a pleasant surprise.

Tonight, on impulse, she changed into one of her more sophisticated gowns. She hadn't worn it since leaving Banyandah. The fabric was a striking, green-striped taffeta, with a boned, close-fitting bodice. A flounced overskirt was swept back to bunch and drape over the horsehair bustle at her waist. The skirt finished in a long train which annoyingly persisted in catching on splinters in the slab floor.

Sarah and the older boys gazed at her admiringly as she joined them at the table in the dining room, but Mary raised her eyebrows.

'What is the occasion, Louise?'

Louise smiled and shrugged. 'I thought I'd best re-accustom myself to dressing for dinner. I suppose I shall have to do a lot of it in England.'

She tried not to feel guilty about the lie. If her plans worked out, she wouldn't be wearing glamorous gowns in the immediate future.

Tonight, as always, the fare on the Barclays' table was tasty but simple. A beast had been killed the day before so there was fresh meat and vegetables from the homestead garden. Mary's fowls provided eggs and the house cows kept them supplied with milk and butter. A cowboy looked after the milkers and the garden, but the only house staff employed were a housemaid and a cook. Mary Barclay seemed to enjoy helping with the cooking and the lighter household duties–tasks that Mrs Ashford considered far beneath her dignity.

After everyone had retired from the dinner table Louise sought the solitude of her bedroom. The room actually belonged to Jack, but he'd moved in with his brother for the duration of her stay. She suspected he had a crush on her, but perhaps having his privacy restored would compensate for any regret he might feel at her departure.

She walked through the French doors onto the rear veranda, settling on one of the canvas squatter's chairs and staring out into the starry night. There was a thin sliver of moon in the east, just rising above the tops of the trees. A cowbell tinkled in the distance and further afield a beast bellowed once. A sudden rustle in the garden made her heartbeat quicken. Brown snakes called for constant vigilance, but she told herself it was probably only a harmless lizard. Then a step on the veranda had her turning swiftly, her pulse fluttering. The family seldom ventured out here at night.

It was Jack. He smiled at her hesitantly. 'I thought I'd find you here. Do you mind if I sit with you?'

He looked ill at ease and Louise wasn't cruel enough to refuse him. It had obviously taken all his courage to seek her out. 'Of course not. I was just enjoying the night air.'

Jack crossed the narrow veranda and settled on the edge of it, his back resting against one of the posts, his arm lying on his up-drawn knees. 'It's bad luck that you have to go to England.'

She nodded, glad to have an ally. 'Do you blame me for wanting to stay here, Jack? England sounds so crowded and oppressive, besides being cold and rainy and smoky. I know I wouldn't be allowed to do the things I most enjoy and of course I'd be expected to snare some distinguished gentleman for a husband.'

Jack looked disconcerted. 'Doesn't the prospect of marriage appeal to you?'

'Not particularly. And an English marriage would ensure I couldn't return here.' She stared morosely past him, knowing her father would choose her husband for her, or attempt to do so.

'Louise.' Jack's voice was barely audible. 'Would you consider marrying me instead?'

'Oh, Jack!' Her heart gave a sudden, alarmed lurch. She hadn't expected this. 'I couldn't–'

'Why not?' He scrambled to his feet and moved to her chair, pulling her up to face him. 'That way you could stay here. You like it here, don't you, Louise?'

'Of course I do, but—'

'But what?' She could sense his nervousness and excitement as he continued to hold her arms. 'I'm terribly fond of you, Louise. Father's doing well here and we'll be building a proper house soon. In another ten or twenty years we'll be as well off as you Ashfords, just you wait and see!'

His eagerness bolstered her confidence, made her feel in control. She'd never been held by a man before, in the romantic sense, yet she felt less naive than the obviously inexperienced Jack. Having Charles as an older brother had seen to that.

One day she'd come upon Charles in the stables at Banyandah, engaged in illicit activity with a female servant. To a thirteen-year-old girl, it had been a shocking and disturbing sight, reminding her of the mating animals her mother tried to prevent her from seeing. The maid was later sent away, the servants whispering she was with child. Louise hadn't realized at the time that Charles was probably the father and of course he hadn't admitted responsibility. She often wondered what had happened to the girl and felt guilty that she'd done nothing to help her. Perhaps if she'd told her parents what she'd seen…

'I don't care how much money you have, Jack. But I hadn't thought of marrying you. We're cousins, after all and Papa wouldn't be in favour of it.'

'Louise,' he whispered in entreaty. Suddenly he was closer than she'd realized. His hands slid up her arms and he bent his head to kiss her mouth, once and then again. 'I know I'm not much compared to those titled gentlemen your father probably has lined up for you in Devon, but I would take good care of you.'

'Jack!' She pulled away. His lips tasted of the cabbage and boiled onions they'd eaten at supper and she resisted the urge to wipe her hand across her mouth. 'I'm fond of you, but even if that was enough for me, it wouldn't weigh with Papa.' Their fathers might be cousins, but their families were poles apart. 'Anyway, Charles will be coming to fetch me once he has our passage booked and he isn't likely to be impressed by any plans of ours. You don't imagine he would sail without me?'

Jack released her with obvious reluctance, disappointment and a trace of resentment edging his voice. 'I'm sorry. I hadn't thought of it that way. Is he so relentless, your brother?'

She laughed lightly. 'Yes, he is. I don't think you'd like him.'

He moved away from her and resumed his stance beside the veranda post, staring despondently at the dark blur of the flower bed bordering the house. Louise watched him, biting her lip. It was clear she'd hurt him and she regretted that. If she loved him, she supposed, she'd have fought for him. But she wouldn't marry for convenience.

Perhaps Jack was too unworldly for her. By upper class standards he wasn't particularly cultured or well educated. His gauche shyness made him unexciting to her, accustomed as she was to men like Charles.

Louise drew up her skirts and petticoats and rose to her feet. Jack turned from his contemplation of his mother's garden to help her but she was quick to shrug his hand off her elbow. 'I think we should both go in, Jack.'

'So that's it, then? You'll be going to England?' He'd moved between her and the door and was barring her way. Louise hoped he wasn't about to kiss her again.

'Unfortunately I see no alternative.'

He finally stepped back, allowing her to precede him through the door. As they joined the others, who were enjoying a singsong around the piano, the younger Barclays greeted them with inquisitive glances. James and Mary made no comment on their absence, inviting Louise to add her voice to the others while Jack retired silently to the corner, a glum expression on his face. Perhaps it was as well she would be leaving them soon.

On retiring Louise smuggled several newspapers and journals to her room and began leafing through them. At last, in an issue of the *Morning Bulletin*, she found the address of a Rockhampton employment agency. She set about writing a letter to them, advising of her urgent need of a teaching position, preferably in the western districts of the colony.

She described her eight months of experience in the Barclay household and listed her personal accomplishments. These included the genteel arts of music, drawing, painting and embroidery, as essential to the education of a refined young lady as the three Rs. Adding another twelve months to her age for good measure, she signed herself, 'Miss Lucy Forrest'. Lucy was a convenient derivative of Louise and Forrest seemed an imaginative alias, neither too obvious nor too unusual.

Finally she set about forging a character reference from her cousin, copying his handwriting from a letter he'd sent her before she came here. She practised his signature on a scrap of paper before adding it to the reference and placed both sheets inside an envelope which she addressed to the agency. Her problem now was to find an opportunity to post it.

That was only the beginning, of course. The success of her plan depended on the agency finding a place for her before Charles arrived to collect her. Hopefully her preference for the western districts would work in her favour. Most governesses were reluctant to venture into the newly settled areas, with all the associated dangers and discomforts of pioneering life. Charles would have to set his affairs in order at Banyandah before his departure and engage a manager to run the property in his absence. A passage to Portsmouth would have to be obtained, which could mean a wait of several weeks. At the worst she could take her courage in both hands and simply flee, whether she had a position to go to or not. She would manage somehow.

The next day was Sunday. Louise heard that one of the men was riding to Gainsford to spend his day off there. Since she happened to know this particular stockman was barely literate, he was the ideal person to post her letter. He was unlikely to note the forwarding name and address.

When she saw him leaving, she left the house and hurried after him, waving the letter in her hand. 'Tom, will you post this for me in Gainsford? I finished it last night and when I saw you riding out …'She left the sentence unfinished, smiling at him with as much charm as she could muster.

'Why, certainly, miss.' He returned her smile and tucked the letter safely in his shirt pocket.

The next three weeks passed with excruciating slowness. Yet another Tuesday arrived, accompanied by the mailman with his packhorses. Louise was in an agony of suspense. There was nothing for her, not even a word from Charles. But on the Friday afternoon a visitor arrived, an Indian hawker with a loaded wagonette. His stock was extensive, consisting of articles of all descriptions: dress materials, patent medicines, books, kitchen utensils. He was a glib, persuasive fellow with ingratiating manners and perhaps hoping to win Mary's favour, he'd collected their mail from the post office in Gainsford.

After he'd gone Mary thumbed through the mail, passing a letter to Louise. 'Here's one for you.' She paused, frowning at a second letter. 'What is this one? "Miss Lucy Forrest, care of Mr J. Barclay." Who on earth is that?'

Louise forced a laugh and reached quickly for the letter. She was prepared for this. 'Oh, that's for me. I submitted a piece to the Morning Bulletin, using a pen name.'

Mary looked surprised. 'I didn't know you wrote.'

'It was just a poem. They've probably rejected it.'

Louise excused herself and hurried to her room to read the letters. First she opened the envelope addressed in Charles's bold handwriting.

My dear Louise,

I have booked our passage to sail from Keppel Bay on the first of the next month. I shall be arriving to collect you on the twentieth.

Hurriedly she consulted her calendar–that was Tuesday, only four days away!

I hope my letter precedes me and that I find you packed and ready. I trust Cousins James and Mary are in good health.

Your brother,

Charles.

If it hadn't been for that God-sent hawker, your letter wouldn't have preceded you, brother dear, Louise reflected grimly. A fine mess I'd have been in then.

She picked up the second envelope and turned it over for a moment, suddenly afraid to open it. It was from the agency, of course. Supposing they had been unable to place her yet? What then?

She mentally shook herself and tore it open, dispensing with the paper knife. This letter also consisted of a single sheet only, but it was more closely written than the first and she scanned it quickly. She realized she'd been holding her breath when, after the first couple of lines, she released it in a sharp gust of relief.

The agency had secured a position for her with a family who lived near the township of Banana. They required a governess to teach four young ladies in reading, writing, arithmetic, music, drawing, painting, embroidery and needlework. The family, a Mr and Mrs Greenwood of New Haven, offered a comfortable wage and living quarters and the governess would be treated as a member of the family. The agency had taken the liberty of booking Miss Forrest's seat on the coach out of Westwood on Friday the thirtieth, three weeks away and had written to inform her prospective employers of her arrival date, enabling them to meet her in Banana. Mr Greenwood would pay her outward fares.

A combination of fear and excitement bubbled up inside her. Banana! It was supposed to be a busy teamsters' town, somewhere south of Gainsford, she thought. And these people lived out of town, so what were the chances of Charles finding her there? It seemed fate was with her after all.

Chapter Two

Louise decided Sunday would be her best chance of making an escape. With no church close enough to attend, the Barclays always passed their Sabbath with prayers and visiting their neighbours.

She made her apologies after breakfast, pleading a sore throat and a headache. The headache was genuine, if the sore throat wasn't. The previous night she'd been unable to sleep, her mind racing with her plans and increasing apprehension. Mary must have been convinced by her wan face and shadowed eyes, as she accepted her excuses without question.

Louise watched them off from her bedroom window: James, Mary and the two children in the buggy, the older lads on horseback. Suddenly she realized she might never see her cousins again and her throat constricted. They'd been good to her, all of them, and they deserved better than this deceit she was about to practise on them. But she squared her shoulders, pushing her remorse aside. She would need to call on all her resourcefulness and a large measure of luck if she was to succeed in eluding Charles.

When the others were out of sight she reached for Jack's valise from the top of the wardrobe. It was perfect for her purpose since it was designed to be carried on horseback. Wiping the dust and cobwebs from it, she began to pack.

She chose two of her plainest daytime dresses, underwear, stockings and a pair of button-up shoes for everyday wear. Then she hurried to the little storeroom where she knew the men kept their swags. They frequently camped out when mustering and she'd seen Ed carry them there. Selecting one from the pile, she paused.

On a rack behind the door were several rifles. A rifle would be awkward to carry, but on the shelf beneath in its case was an Adams five-shot revolver. James had shown her how to load and fire it, in case of an Aboriginal attack. Grabbing the gun and cartridges, she carried them and the swag to her room. She stowed the revolver and ammunition in her bulging valise, then unrolled the swag to add a few extra items: tooth-powder and brush, soap, towel, hairbrush and nightgown. She would be uncomfortably short of clothes, but there was nothing she could do about that.

Adopting a casual air, she left the house to stroll to the saddle room. Here she found a quart-pot and a split sugar-bag which the men sometimes used to carry rations, and wandered back to the kitchen with them hidden in her skirts. It was the cook's day off and only a maid was on duty in the kitchen. Busy drying dishes, the girl looked up at Louise in obvious surprise.

'Please go to the men's quarters, Sally and ask one of them to bring the horses into the yards for me.' At the girl's questioning look she added easily, 'I'm feeling much better now. I've decided to follow the others. Mrs Barclay said to do so if I wished.'

'Very well, Miss.' Sally set off obediently and Louise abandoned her languid manner, stuffing the sugar-bag with the necessary provisions for a couple of days. She'd no idea how long it would take her to reach Banana, but she hoped to be able to buy food from teamsters or station homesteads en route if she fell short.

She carried everything to the back garden and stowed it all under a shrub. There was no-one about to see her. She returned to her room to change into a riding habit and riding boots. Finally she sat to write a letter to James and Mary. This proved to be the hardest task of all and she was interrupted when the maid knocked on the door.

'Hopkins has run the horses in, Miss and he wants to know which horse Miss wants him to saddle for her.'

Louise looked up from her letter. 'Tell him to saddle Shadow, the bay Galloway. Ask him to bring him to the gate and tie him there, if he will. I shall be along presently.'

She resumed her letter, trying to still the trembling of her fingers. She'd suddenly realized the magnitude of what she was doing and her heart raced. She was about to leave the sanctuary of this house to fend for herself on the road, sleeping beneath the stars with only a revolver for protection. And she knew nothing about this family at Banana. But she'd gone too far to back out now.

At last she finished the letter and read it through uncertainly. She hoped that James and Mary wouldn't think too badly of her.

Dear Cousin James and Cousin Mary.

I hope you will forgive my reprehensible behaviour in taking leave of you like this and in making free with your possessions. I know it is poor thanks for the kindness you have shown me during the past eight months, but I am determined not to go with Charles and I understand that you could not intervene to help me.

I was careful to choose a horse that should not be too sorely missed. I shall take good care of Shadow and one day I may be able to return him to you. I have left ten pounds in payment for him, together with a further fifteen to cover the cost of the swag, saddle and revolver. I hope the loss of them does not cause you too much inconvenience. You may do as you wish with the possessions I have left behind.

You need not fear for my welfare. I am going to a family who require a governess and I have enough money to support myself for some time. When Charles arrives, please tell him not to waste his energies in searching for me. He is most unlikely to find me.

The months I have spent here have been the happiest of my life. Please accept my gratitude. I wish I did not have to leave you like this and I deeply regret any distress my actions may cause you. Please extend my goodbyes to all the family and I trust that Lindsay and Sarah do not neglect their lessons.
Your affectionate cousin,
Louise Ashford.

She folded the pages with a small sigh and wiped a trickle of moisture from her eyes. Sealing the letter in an envelope addressed to 'Mr and Mrs James Barclay', she propped it on her dressing table. Then she spared a final glance at the room where she'd spent so many contented hours, gathered up her riding gloves and hat and walked briskly outside to her waiting horse.

Not wishing to be recognized, Louise gave a wide berth to the camp of a teamster with his bullocks and loaded wagon as she crossed the river. She skirted the town of Gainsford, its single street almost deserted on this day of rest. The town had been built at the junction of three roads and lacking a map to guide her, she could only guess which way to travel. But she'd already decided not to go east to Westwood, since Charles would be arriving from that direction in two days' time. Since she knew Banana lay somewhere to the south, surely the southbound route to Bauhinia Downs must point her in the right direction.

It was lunchtime when she rode away from Gainsford, but her churning stomach rebelled at the thought of food. Besides, there was no time to eat. It was imperative she be well away by nightfall. She carried water in a canteen strapped to her saddle and Shadow had drunk at the Dawson crossing, so he would tolerate a dry camp tonight. The October weather was warm but not hot enough to cause him real distress.

After several miles the lancewood and rosewood ridges opened into better grazing country timbered with box, gum and broad-leafed ironbark. Louise rode steadily, sometimes trotting and cantering, then dropping back to a walk to allow Shadow to gain his wind. Speed on this first day was crucial, but she'd achieve nothing by overheating or exhausting her horse.

She tried not to think of the future, hoping the sickness in her stomach would disappear if she concentrated on her surroundings. The bush seemed to envelop and soothe her, the silence broken only by the steady rhythm of her horse's hoof beats and the occasional carking of a crow, mingling with the rustle of leaves in the breeze. She enjoyed the gelding's smooth, easy paces at the trot and canter, but she was forced to use her heels and the whip when she drew him back to the walk. Shadow's problem wasn't so much general laziness as an unwillingness to extend himself at that gait.

Louise found herself regretting the spurt of conscience that had prompted her to choose the Galloway over one of the Barclays' favourites. She should have taken Mary's big grey Cavalier, whose mouth was gentle and whose free, long stride was a delight to ride. But no, she couldn't be so callous, for Mary thought the world of her Cavalier. At least they wouldn't miss Shadow.

Shadow's redeeming points were his quiet nature and puny size, enabling her to mount the sidesaddle with the aid of a log or a stump. He was an attractive horse with obvious breeding, but his mouth had been spoiled at breaking, making him dangerous to gallop in the timber after cattle. Louise wasn't concerned with this failing at the moment, but his reluctance to walk out and his inclination to jig-jog were frustrating. She was tired and irritated by the time she made her solitary camp by a dry gully a couple of hours after first dark.

She'd avoided the usual watering stages, skirting the camps of teamsters and other travellers. A woman riding alone would provoke undue attention. At the very least she might be recognised or reported on to Charles and at worst there were plenty of unscrupulous types in the bush. She refused to dwell on the possible dangers, but set up camp some distance from the road, in a clump of bull-oaks and stringy-bark where she felt comparatively safe.

She'd watered Shadow again at a stagnant, shrunken pool in one of the creeks she crossed. Now she hobbled him out to graze and set about building a small fire. Although she'd never done this before, she'd watched the men often enough. With relief she watched the dry leaves and twigs flare into life and soon there was a small blaze to set her quart-pot beside.

When it had boiled, she added tea leaves and sugar and ate her frugal meal. By this time she was hungry enough to enjoy the dry bread and salt meat. The tea was refreshing, not as strong as the men usually made it, hot and pleasantly sweet.

Unable to spare any of her precious water for washing, she wiped her plate and her fingers clean with a clump of dry grass, unrolled her swag and brushed out her hair before braiding it for the night. Reassured that Shadow was still grazing nearby, she loosened the lacings on her corset and took to her swag fully dressed.

During her childhood she'd often longed to camp beneath the stars as the men folk of the family did. But after an hour of restless tossing and turning, Louise thought wistfully of a soft, feather mattress, clean sheets next to her skin and the security of four walls about her. A lone mosquito droned persistently about her face, although there had been no rain for months. The bones in her corset dug into her ribs and when she rolled to her side, the hard ground pressed into her hip bone.

The night noises she enjoyed listening to from her cousins' veranda sounded different now. A curlew wailed mournfully and a pair of dingoes howled nearby, making her spine tingle and her stomach muscles tighten. Although she knew the wild dogs were unlikely to attack her, she scrambled out of the swag and threw more wood on the fire.

Eventually the dingoes moved on and she awoke shivering just on dawn, the two blankets in her meagre swag barely enough to ward off the chill of the spring night.

Her body ached all over and her eyelids drooped with weariness, but since she was awake, she decided to make an early start. Shadow would travel better in the cool of early morning. She fanned the dying coals of last night's fire into a blaze and put her quart-pot on to boil, before setting off after Shadow. It was still dark but she could hear his hobble chains jingling nearby as he grazed. He nickered when she called him and readily submitted to the bridle.

Louise pressed her cheek against his, gratified by this small show of appreciation for her company. Her confidence rising, she led him back to the camp and saddled him. She ate quickly and packed her belongings, fastening them securely to the saddle. As the eastern sky lightened, she mounted with the aid of a fallen log and regained the road before setting off at a brisk trot.

Her sore muscles protested at being back in the saddle, making it impossible to sustain the pace of the previous day. Luckily Shadow was shod, or he would probably have been footsore by now. After a couple of miles she eased back to a walk, shifting her tender buttocks in the saddle.

Long before the wagon came into view, a teamster's voice and cracking whip heralded its approach from the opposite direction. Louise concealed herself behind a clump of wattle as the team crawled past; twenty-two red and roan bullocks yoked two abreast, the wagon piled so high with bales of wool, she marvelled the load didn't topple. Oblivious to her listening ears, the bullocky cursed freely. She blushed and squirmed, wondering if his embarrassment would equal hers if she were to show herself.

She was less fortunate in dodging two male travellers on horseback. As she rounded a bend in the road there they were, riding towards her. It was too late to hide. They stared hard at her as she came abreast of them, but she held her head high, looking stiffly straight ahead and guiding Shadow to the furthest edge of the road.

When they raised their hats to her, saying, 'G'day, Ma'am,' she nodded, murmuring a barely audible response. She continued her way, at first not daring to look back, but when she did she saw them reined in on the road, gazing after her.

As she rode on, she worried about the encounter. Hopefully they'd be long gone before Charles came searching.

Coming upon good water in a creek at eleven o'clock, she decided to stop for lunch. Since she'd made good time, she unsaddled Shadow and left his reins trailing so he could graze. She rested after her meal and lulled by the warmth of the sun, dozed off to sleep. When she woke, the sun was past its zenith and she was heavy-eyed and listless, but she hastily re-saddled Shadow and continued on her way.

Another ten miles brought her to the Bauhinia Downs homestead, situated with a scrubby rise to one side and a fall of open country rolling to a creek on the other. To the west an unusual, knobby hill rose abruptly from the open downs. Instead of travelling due south, the road swung westwards after leaving the homestead. It seemed she had no alternative but to ask for directions and hoped this wouldn't give Charles a further clue to tracing her.

Spotting a figure near the horse-yards, she rode to intercept him. The bearded stockman turned to stare at her in obvious surprise, but he saluted her courteously, raising his cabbage-tree hat.

'G'day, Ma'am. Are you visiting someone at the homestead?'

'Actually, no.' She took a deep breath, trying to still the tremor in her voice. 'I'm travelling to Banana, but I'm not familiar with the roads. Could you give me directions, please?'

'*Banana*?'

Confronted with that startled tone, her heart did a quick flip-flop and her stomach churned. 'Is that a problem?'

The man shrugged. 'Well, it's only about sixty miles, as the crow flies'–he pointed to the east–'but there's no road that way, not from this end. You'd have to follow the road all the way through Gainsford and Westwood and back again. Have you come from Springsure?'

'Yes,' she lied, her thoughts whirling in panic. How fortunate that he hadn't seen her approach on the Gainsford road. She smoothed her hand along Shadow's mane, but closed her fingers into a fist when she saw how badly they were shaking. 'Could you find someone to guide me? Travelling all that way by road is out of the question. I must be in Banana by a certain date.'

She saw him hesitate and added quickly, 'I could pay.'

Louise could almost read his thoughts. A young lady riding alone was a puzzle in itself, her possession of money and an upper-class accent only adding to it. But so long as he was prepared to help her, his opinion scarcely mattered.

He was silent for a moment as if considering the options. 'I hardly know whether to mention this, but there's a fellow camped here with a mob of cattle. He's droving them to his place this side of Banana. On the Dawson, that is. He's only got two men and one of them is sick. It doesn't seem fitting'–he frowned doubtfully–'but he's a sound young chap. I know him well enough. It'd be a slow trip, going with the cattle, but shorter than going by road. He'd look after you and see you got to Banana safely, I dare say.'

A glimmer of hope helped settle her roiling stomach. 'When is he leaving?'

The stockman shook his head. 'Don't know. Depends on his man, I suppose. He got here yesterday evening and the fellow was crook then. Apparently he's worse today. Kavanagh won't be able to wait long, though. He'll have to get the cattle on the move again.'

'Could you take me to see him?'

'Well,' he hesitated, 'perhaps it'd be better if I took you to the big house and handed you over to the housekeeper, Mrs Black. I'll talk to Kavanagh and he can come up and see you later. You'll have to stay here the night, whatever happens. The boss is away but the housekeeper will look after you.'

Louise nodded gratefully as the tension eased out of her. Such was bush hospitality, to extend this much courtesy to a stranger. A proper bed and a bath would be most welcome. She glanced down at her crumpled, travel-stained riding habit and winced, wondering what sort of picture she must present.

She could see the man's intense curiosity struggling with his natural reticence. She hoped his curiosity would lose the battle, but it wasn't to be. As he escorted her to the house he asked diffidently, 'How do you come to be travelling all alone, Miss? It's pretty risky for a woman.'

She forced a light, dismissive laugh. 'Oh, it's not so very dangerous. I've been avoiding other travellers and so far I haven't met with any trouble.'

'Are you armed?'

'Yes, I have a revolver.'

'I'd keep it handy, if I was you.' His voice held a note of grimness. 'There aren't many ruffians about who'd dare to touch a lady, but these roads are pretty lonely and there'd be no-one to help you if you ran into trouble. Don't you have family?'

'My parents are in England. I was governessing for a family in Springsure and I'm about to take up a new position near Banana. My name is Lucy Forrest, by the way.'

He raised his hat. 'Sam Naylor. Pleased to meet you, Miss Forrest. You'd have been much safer taking the coach to Westwood and connecting with another coach to Banana there. I'm surprised the family let you travel this way.'

'I had to leave in a hurry, Mr Naylor. I couldn't wait for the coach.' Make of that what he would; he couldn't ask more questions without being intrusive.

He gave her a sideways, speculative glance but said no more, leading her towards the homestead. Once there he dismounted and helped her out of the saddle. He sent a maid to find the housekeeper and introduced her when she arrived, briefly explaining Louise's circumstances. 'I'll talk to Kavanagh now. See if he can take the young lady with him.'

'I don't think much of that idea.' The housekeeper turned to Louise. 'Miss, if you're willing to go droving, you're braver than I am.'

She was a large, grey-haired woman with beefy arms and a waistline that bulged in spite of her corset, but her face was kindly. 'Get Miss Forrest's bag for her, will you, Sam?' She turned back to Louise. 'You must be wanting to wash.'

'I'd love a bath, thank you.'

Mrs Black escorted Louise to a spare bedroom and had a maid bring in an iron bathtub which she filled with warm water. Fortunately the housekeeper asked no questions, only venturing the information that Mr Naylor was the head stockman and was in charge in the owner's absence.

Left alone, Louise made the most of her bath. Afterwards she donned one of her two dresses and brushed out her hair. Her muscles still ached, but at least she felt clean and respectable again.

Waiting in the sitting room, she picked up a recent edition of the *Brisbane Telegraph*. She'd scarcely begun to read of an expedition by a Mr Dalrymple to explore the north coast of Queensland when Mrs Black appeared at the door.

'Mr Kavanagh's waiting on the veranda.'

Louise followed the housekeeper to find a man sitting on the railing, swinging his riding boots idly against the slats. He slid to his feet as she approached, politely removing his battered hat and setting it against the post as Mrs Black made the introductions. He was a rough-looking stockman with tousled sandy hair and dirty clothes, quite tall and slim but otherwise not particularly prepossessing. Unlike most bushmen who sported flowing beards, he was merely unshaven with a week or two's growth of whiskers giving him an unkempt appearance. Mr Naylor had referred to him as young, but Louise hadn't guessed quite this young. Looking at his stubbled face she realized he was probably no older than her brother Charles.

'Naylor says you're travelling to Banana,' Kavanah said, once the introductions had been made. His eyes were alight with friendly curiosity. 'There must be better ways of getting there than going through the scrub with a mob of cattle.'

Louise shrugged. 'The other option is out for me, I'm afraid. It's too far and I don't have that much time.'

'Hmm. You'll never find your way on your own. I don't want to refuse to take you and have you getting lost on my conscience, but do you think you'll handle a droving camp? It's no Sunday picnic.'

Did she really want to spend several days in the company of this unkempt individual? She reminded herself of Mr Naylor's recommendation of his character and hoped he was more respectable than he looked. Right now she couldn't afford to be choosy.

She summoned a smile. 'I'm tough and determined, Mr Kavanagh. I've not been droving before, but I'm a competent rider and I'm accustomed to cattle. I should be most grateful if you'd allow me to accompany you.'

He eyed her in silence for a moment. She stiffened under his scrutiny, but at last his gaze shifted.

'I'll say yes, but I hope I don't regret this. When do you want to leave?'

'In the morning, I'd hoped.'

The young drover frowned. 'That depends on Thompson, my man. He's crook and he seems to be getting worse. Unless he improves in a hurry we won't be going anywhere.'

Alarm shot through her body. 'What's wrong with him?'

'Dysent'ry,' he supplied shortly. 'I'm going to ask Mrs Black if there's anything she can do for him. She's pretty good with sickness, I hear and the station has a well-stocked medicine chest.'

'Dysentery! But he could die. He must at least be bedridden for a couple of weeks.'

Kavanagh seemed unmoved by her dismay. 'I don't think he'll die. He hasn't got it that bad. But if there's no sign of improvement soon I'll have to go on without him–see if I can find someone else to help me with the cattle.'

'That won't be necessary. I can take your man's place.'

He smiled, his eyes travelling idly over her. 'I don't think you know what you're letting yourself in for, Miss Forrest.'

Louise bristled. 'Perhaps not, but I have mustered cattle before.' Thank God that was true–James Barclay had occasionally allowed her to help bring in a quiet mob of cattle. 'I'm not afraid of hard work and I promise I won't let you down.'

'Oh, I dare say. But we'll wait until I can get another man, all the same.'

Her throat tightened as she imagined Charles hot on her heels. 'But we *must* go–I can't wait here. It's out of the question!'

Kavanagh's eyes narrowed. 'What's the hurry?'

She tried to dissemble. 'These people are expecting me–the family that I'm to go to, that is.'

She'd betrayed too much of her urgency, she realized. He gave her a disbelieving stare. 'I think there's more to your story than you're telling, Miss Forrest.'

Louise averted her head, biting her lip in a tacit refusal to answer any more questions. He didn't press her, suddenly saying, surprisingly, 'All right, then. We'll go tomorrow morning, if I can talk Mrs Black into looking after Thompson. But it won't be an easy job, you know, taking cattle through all that scrub between here and the Dawson. There's five hundred head of young cattle and that's plenty for three men to handle, let alone a woman riding sidesaddle. And there's the night-watch, too. Divine and I can't cope with that on our own.'

Her stomach quivered but she straightened her shoulders, looking him in the eye. 'I'll do my share,' she assured him firmly.

Ten minutes later Lloyd Kavanagh mounted his horse to return to his camp at the station water-hole. He'd consulted with Mrs Black and had received her permission to leave the sick man in an empty hut where he could stay until he was recovered. The housekeeper had promised to tend him and Kavanagh felt confident he was leaving the man in good hands.

He thought about the girl, wondering what she was up to. She was game, he had to give her that–either game or stupid. He hoped it wasn't the last. She looked the competent, independent type and he'd based his decision on that. For all their sakes he'd better be right. With five hundred head, miles from anywhere in the brigalow, she'd bloody better not let him down. Controlling the cattle in the thick scrub would keep three of them busy. He couldn't afford to mollycoddle her.

He'd questioned Sam Naylor about her earlier and Sam had shrugged and laughed. 'Hell, I'm no ladies' man. You'll see for yourself, soon enough. But I wouldn't advise you to go getting any funny ideas about her, even if she does go gallivanting about the countryside on her own. She talks and dresses like a silver tail. I wouldn't be surprised if she's got a lot of important male relations around somewhere. Besides, I told her you could be trusted, so don't make a liar out of me.'

'I won't.' Kavanagh grinned. 'I daresay we'll be too busy with the cattle to think of romance.'

Now that he'd seen her, he thought the prospect of romance even less likely. If Miss Forrest had looked the troublesome, flirtatious type he wouldn't have taken her with him, no matter how persuasive she was. Tall, thin and haughty; that was his first impression of her, and she was certainly a swell. She probably wouldn't lower herself to wipe her boots on him. Nevertheless, he would keep his word to Naylor and try to look after her, allowing for his other responsibilities.

But he strongly suspected the next few days wouldn't be easy for any of them.

Chapter Three

The housekeeper woke Louise at four o'clock the following morning. Within fifteen minutes she was in the kitchen, dressed in her clean habit and sitting to breakfast at the rough wooden table. It was the first time ever she'd eaten in a kitchen, or so early in the morning. Her stomach was churning and the thick slab of bread and jam seemed to stick in her throat. But she forced it down, knowing her next meal might be many hours away.

With Mrs Black's help, she carried her belongings from her bedroom to find the young drover waiting outside with two packhorses and a youth of about sixteen. Kavanagh greeted her politely in the half-light, introducing the lad as Cecil Divine. Divine's broad hat cast his face in shadow, but she could see he was thin and shaggy-haired. He mumbled a response to her acknowledgment without meeting her eyes and held the horses as Kavanagh set about adding her belongings to the two pack-saddles. Her valise was awkward, but Kavanagh seemed patient enough and eventually got it all settled to his satisfaction.

She was grateful to find that Sam Naylor had bridled and saddled Shadow for her, avoiding further delay. She turned to thank him and then extended her charm to Mrs Black, expressing gratitude for her hospitality. Sam Naylor helped her into the saddle with a bemused expression, his pipe hanging slackly from his mouth. Louise suppressed a smile. Somehow, she thought, he didn't quite know what to make of her.

The head stockman had sent one of his men to see them on their way for the first few miles. As they rode to the stockyards where the cattle had been held overnight, Kavanagh and the other man, Richards, talked. They discussed the season, the prospects of rain and the condition of the stock. Louise rode her horse beside them, listening with interest, discovering the cattle had come from a property near Springsure.

'It's pretty dry over there at the moment,' Kavanagh said. 'They're selling off their young cattle. I've had a fair season on Myvanwy and I'm not fully stocked yet.'

'How've they been to handle?' the Bauhinia Downs man asked.

Kavanagh gave a short laugh. 'They're all right now. For a start they were a bit touchy, though. They rushed on us the first night and we lost a couple, but a few days on the road soon settles them down.' He glanced at Louise, smiling. 'Have you seen a cattle-rush, Miss Forrest?'

'No. I'm not sure I wish to, either. Are you certain they won't rush again?'

'You can never be sure of that, 'specially with young cattle. I just hope they don't, since we're so shorthanded.'

There was an awkward silence for a moment. Richards and young Divine averted their eyes, obviously wondering how she would handle a stampede and Louise felt they were wishing her elsewhere. Kavanagh continued his conversation with the Bauhinia Downs man, his manner in contrast relaxed and easy. She was grateful that he didn't appear to share their misogyny.

At the stockyards Kavanagh dismounted to open the gate. He stood beside it to count the cattle as they surged to freedom, while Louise and the other men remained on horseback to contain them. The cattle were a good, even line of Shorthorn steers and heifers, reds and roans with the occasional white. Considering the season and the distance they'd already travelled, they were in remarkably good condition. Despite his youth it appeared this young cattleman was a capable drover–for Louise had listened to the men's talk enough to be aware of the common mistake of hurrying stock and walking the flesh off them.

The cattle responded obediently to the steadying horsemen and were soon travelling eastwards, striding out at this early hour. The packhorses and the half-dozen spare mounts trotted ahead of the herd, their heads turned to home. Kavanagh had informed Louise that two of the saddle horses would now be available for her use. This was fortunate, as it was Shadow's third day under saddle and he was in need of a rest.

Louise, directed to stay at the rear of the herd, held her horse in check. The animals required no pushing at this stage. She'd always possessed a lively, though frustrated interest in stock and in the management of Banyandah. As a child she'd hung on every word of her father's stockmen, listening avidly whenever her father and Charles so forgot themselves as to mention station affairs in the hearing of their womenfolk. In consequence she'd acquired knowledge out of proportion to her practical experience and she was glad of it now as she set about proving her ability to Kavanagh.

When they halted for their 'dinner camp', as the men referred to their lunchtime meal, he gave her a look that she hoped was approving.

'You weren't lying.' He'd taken food and eating utensils from one of the pack-saddles and now they waited for the billy to boil while the lad watched the mob. Richards had left them sometime earlier, but most of the cattle were content to rest in the shade, requiring little supervision on Cecil Divine's part. 'You must have handled stock before.' He gave her a bold grin. 'I'll tell you, when I saw you this morning in that fancy riding habit you had me worried. But you're making out all right. Don't push 'em, though. We'll have to let 'em feed along this afternoon.'

Louise smiled sardonically. 'Whatever you say, sir. I'm grateful to have your approval.'

He gave her a sideways, amused glance as he took food from an old flour bag and began to prepare their meal. She watched with interest as he cut thick slabs of cold damper and sliced a piece of dark, slimy-looking corned beef. She suppressed a shudder but resolved not to complain. After all, what had she expected? Droving fare was plain at the best of times and this man was obviously used to rough living.

It was blessedly cool here, under the shade of a sprawling bauhinia tree. Louise had already noticed that it was in bloom and now she picked one of the bright red flowers from a lower branch, curiously turning it in her fingers. Under other circumstances she'd have pressed the flower in a book, but reminding herself that she wasn't here to study nature, she cast it aside and returned her attention to her companion. Kavanagh seemed content for the moment to be quiet, but his silence was an easy one, unlike Divine's constraint.

If the food was unappealing, she was agreeably surprised at the improvement in Kavanagh's appearance today. He almost looked presentable. He'd obviously washed last night, exchanging the dirty clothes for clean ones and he'd also shaved, leaving only the side-whiskers that extended to the line of his jaw. His features without the stubble were surprisingly attractive–thin, brown and strong, with a light dusting of freckles.

There were crow's feet at the corners of his green eyes, a legacy of the Queensland sun along with the freckles on his nose. The lines seemed premature in one so young, but added character and charm to a smile that was quick and engaging. She supposed he would set hearts fluttering amongst girls of a certain class.

She gave herself a mental shake, wondering why she was even looking at him. Strapping he may be, in his striped Crimean shirt and stockman's moleskins, but the gulf that separated them was wider than she could begin to imagine. He wasn't the sort of company she was accustomed to keeping. She would do well to remember that.

In spite of this resolution she found by the end of the meal that they were talking companionably, mostly about cattle and horses. Divine, who had left the resting cattle to eat with them, stared sullenly into his pannikin and uttered not a single word, returning to his vigil as soon as he'd finished his meal. As he rode off Louise commented on the condition of the herd and Kavanagh nodded, taking a pipe from his pocket and tamping tobacco into the bowl.

'They were better than I expected, seeing how dry it is around Springsure. And I've nursed them along pretty well.' He held a burning stick from the fire to his pipe and puffed vigorously, looking at her through narrowed eyes. 'Talking of Springsure, who were you governess for there?'

The question took Louise off balance. She paused a moment to gather her wits before improvising hastily. 'A Mr and Mrs Jones. Do you know them?'

'What's his first name?'

'George.' Heavens, these names were imaginative.

'No, don't think I've met him. Where do they live?'

'In the main street.' This had to be safe enough, since there had to be a main street, although she knew nothing of Springsure. 'Next to the hotel.'

He looked askance at her. 'There's three hotels, you know.'

His tone was indulgent, as if he thought her a little stupid. She flushed, stung into recklessness. 'I'm talking about the Grand,' she retorted defiantly. With any luck there *could* be a Grand Hotel– there seemed to be one in almost every town in the colony. If not, that was just too bad. Who did he think he was, asking so many questions?

He was staring at her with a strange expression on his face. 'There are three hotels in Springsure,' he repeated softly. 'The Commercial, the Springsure and the Shearer's Arms.' He paused, watching her keenly as he drew on his pipe. 'I don't think you've ever been there in your life!'

She turned away in confusion, aware of her high colour. She said nothing and after a moment he asked deliberately, 'Where the hell did you come from, then?'

'Gainsford,' she retorted, with some dignity. 'Not that it's any of your business.' Thank God the boy had returned to the cattle. Suddenly it had occurred to her that Kavanagh was likely to know the Greenwoods at Banana, since he lived in the same district. He may as well be told the same story as they, which was only part of the truth after all. 'I was acting as governess for the Barclay family, of Sherborne. Have you heard of James Barclay?'

He nodded, regarding her with lively curiosity. 'What's the idea of this yarn about Springsure, then? And why on earth didn't you go back through Westwood? Surely James Barclay's not the sort of bloke to let a girl go traipsing about by herself with bugger-all idea of where she's even going?' He stopped and cleared his throat. 'I beg your pardon. Excuse the language.'

His interrogation, coupled with that unpleasant word, was becoming offensive. His lack of respect was mortifying, but she was a fool to have encouraged him in the first instance. 'I would prefer not to discuss this, Mr Kavanagh. I asked you to escort me to Banana. That is all you need to know.'

He stared at her, his expression challenging. It appeared he wasn't easily intimidated. 'Did they throw you out, or something?'

She glared at him, heat rising to her cheeks. 'No, they did not! For your information, the Barclays weren't aware that I was leaving.'

On reflection, that information would have been better kept to herself. Kavanagh looked at her suspiciously, his eyes very keen and hard. Perhaps he suspected her of being caught out in some misdemeanour, such as stealing–which wasn't so very far from the truth–or...

His eyes dropped to her stomach, so fleetingly she could almost have imagined it. But it was enough to make her remember the maid who'd left Banyandah after becoming entangled with Charles.

She jumped to her feet, all burning humiliation, and gathered the remains of her meal. Some of the cattle were drifting off to graze, which gave her a good excuse not to linger. Kavanagh began to pack the food and Louise went to her horse, looking about for a possible mounting block. Then she realized he was there beside her, holding out his hand for her foot. She wanted to brush him away, but there was no suitable log or stump in sight, so she was forced to subject herself to his touch.

As he hoisted her into the saddle he asked, 'How'd you come by the horse, then? That's Barclay's brand on the near shoulder, isn't it? 6JB?'

'I bought him,' she said shortly, wishing she could swing into the saddle like a man. 'I paid ten pounds for him, which is rather more than he's worth.'

'From Barclay? Why would he sell you a horse if he wasn't a party to you leaving in such a hurry?'

She settled her right leg around the horn of the saddle and arranged the skirt of her habit before turning to face him, looking down at him with all the arrogance she could muster. She resented these impertinent questions and it irked her that under normal circumstances he, a mere stockman, wouldn't have dared to cross examine her so. 'Would you believe that Mr Barclay had no idea he was selling him?' she asked coldly.

There was a pause while he comprehended that. Then he burst out laughing. 'By Jove, that's rich. Looks like I'd better keep a good eye on my gear when you leave, or I might be missing half of it.' The greenish eyes were alight with mischief. 'Was it your light fingers got you into trouble with the Barclays, then?'

How dare he make fun of her! Hot blood rushed to her head, overriding discretion.

'Unless you apologise for those remarks, Mr Kavanagh, I'll leave you here and now and hope to God you lose every single head of these damned cattle in the scrub.'

He started and sobered instantly, taken aback probably as much by the ferocity of her response as by her language. It was hardly the standard vocabulary of a young lady. As her anger cooled–which it always did very quickly once she'd vented it–she began to wish she'd spoken more temperately. One of these days she would learn to guard her tongue.

He touched his hat. 'I'm sorry, Miss Forrest. It's none of me business how you came by the horse, or why you left the Barclays. Forget I ever asked you.'

It wasn't the most gracious apology she'd ever received, but he sounded sincere. In the circumstances she hardly knew how to respond, so she said nothing, merely inclining her head slightly before turning her horse away.

On reflection she was pleased that she hadn't seemed to forgive him too easily. He was far too impudent and it would pay to keep him at a distance in future.

They travelled the herd about ten miles that day, mostly through brigalow scrub which accentuated how shorthanded they were. It was difficult to keep the mob together when it was impossible to see all of it at the one time, while a beast could lurk in a thick clump of scrub and be unseen by a rider passing a few feet away. However young, half-grown cattle lacked the independence of mature animals and a couple of times an overlooked beast came trotting up behind the mob, anxious to rejoin its mates.

As they neared the waterhole in Zamia Creek where they would make the night camp, Kavanagh asked his two assistants to help him 'string' the herd out, so he could count them. Louise was very surprised to learn the tally he arrived at was identical to what he'd counted out of the yards that morning.

The waterhole was a fair-sized one and was surrounded by hundreds of cattle tracks and scattered piles of dung. Yet it was now deserted by all but an emu crouching at the water's edge, dipping its long neck to drink, and a mob of whiptail wallabies which swiftly fled their presence. Louise watched them bounding away, balancing effortlessly on their long tails as they cleared fallen timber and veered nimbly through the brigalow.

After watering the cattle they held them on an open creek flat, settling them for the night. Louise stayed with the cattle while Kavanagh and Divine went off to set up camp. She watched from a distance as Kavanagh unloaded the packhorses while Divine, as horse-tailer, hobbled all the horses out to graze, with the exception of one, which he saddled. She knew that would be the night-horse, kept in readiness for the first watch. Kavanagh busied himself with the cooking, and presently called her in to eat while Divine went on first night watch.

Dinner was delicious–damper, still hot from the camp-oven, spread with dripping and treacle–an appetising contrast to the bitterly salty meat they'd eaten at lunchtime.

Divine went off on first night-watch, leaving Louise sitting with Kavanagh by the fire. The silence stretched between them. At last sheer boredom tempted Louise to break it.

'I'm beginning to realize how shorthanded we are, Mr Kavanagh. Five hundred cattle and a mob of horses is a handful for three in this sort of timber. Why haven't you another man?'

She'd wondered if Kavanagh was harbouring a grudge at her earlier outburst, but now he grinned, looking vaguely embarrassed.

'I did, at the start. Trouble was, he couldn't stomach taking orders from someone younger than he was and we ended up having words. That was the finish of him. He reckoned he was going off to join the Palmer River gold rush. I wish him luck, because he'll need it up there, amongst the cannibal blacks and the Chinamen.' His tone was dry. 'I would have been better off keeping me mouth shut, because useless or not he was better than no-one. It's the Irish temper–gets me into trouble.'

She had to smile. He was likeable when he turned his sense of humour against himself. Certainly it was preferable to having him direct it against her. 'So you're Irish? I suppose Kavanagh's an Irish name.'

'Yes, it is. But I'm only half Irish. Me mother was Welsh. Me first name–Lloyd–is Welsh.'

Irish and Welsh–to Louise, with generations of unadulterated English breeding behind her, the combination sounded exotic. Not that he looked exotic, at all. He was certainly not dark as she imagined the Welsh to be.

'I'm afraid my heritage is comparatively boring,' she offered. 'My parents are both English.'

'Do they live here in Queensland?'

'They used to. My father has property near Rockhampton, but early in the year they travelled to England to visit my grandfather before he died. Now my father has inherited the family estate in Devon and won't be returning.'

He looked curious. 'Why didn't you go with them?'

She shrugged. 'I love Australia. England sounds so forbidding and...stifling.'

'But isn't this a bit of a comedown for someone like you? The way you talk and the way you dress–you seem like a swell. Were you born here?'

'Yes, I was.' She smiled, deciding not to take offence at his terminology. 'Can't you tell? My mother says my accent is *so* colonial.'

He seemed to find that amusing. 'No. I couldn't tell. To me you sound like a Pommy through and through.'

'How strange, when I can't detect either the Irish or the Welsh in your speech.' In this pioneering country where British and Irish immigrants were barely outnumbered by the native-born, his broad Australian accent was conspicuous.

'Oh, that's not surprising. Both Ma and Dad were born in New South Wales. Me grandparents came out from the Old Country. Me Dad's parents were what you might call "Assisted Immigrants".' He cleared his throat. 'Assisted by the law.'

She stared at him nervously. 'Convicts, do you mean?'

He gave a callous-sounding laugh. 'Yeah. Grandpa and Grandma Kavanagh were both transported for stealing and I won't pretend they were victims of circumstance. They were a rough and ready old pair. Grandma and Grandpa Griffiths came out of their own free will. Grandma Griffiths was a respectable servant girl and she was the only one worth very much.' He scratched his jaw thoughtfully. 'Well, I'm not sure about Grandpa G. He was supposed to be a decent cove, but he died before I was born.'

He stood up, dusting the dirt from the seat of his trousers. Abruptly he changed the subject. 'You can go on the next night watch. You'd better get as much sleep as you can. Divine'll wake you up when he comes in. Sing to the cattle, let 'em know you're about. There's nothing more likely to spook 'em than have someone sneak up on 'em.'

He dumped his swag on the opposite side of the campfire and set about unrolling it. Louise eyed him warily. There were plenty of convict descendants in the Colonies, but she'd never before heard anyone freely admit to being one of them. Was he trying to shock her? Most people were ashamed of such ancestry, trying to cover it up at all costs; particularly if they had risen to a position of importance in their community. Those of poor origins had a chance to succeed in Australia as they never could in Britain. If Lloyd Kavanagh had already established himself as a grazier at his age, he must be among those who had the ability to prosper.

That didn't guarantee his respectability. Nighttime made her vulnerable and his earlier impudence had unsettled her.

But in other respects, he had behaved as a gentleman. So far he'd respected her privacy and had made it easy for her when it could have been difficult. Surely she was safe with him? Just in case she took out the revolver and loaded it, then placed it next to her pillow within easy reach.

She was too tired not to sleep, in spite of the discomforts that plagued her. Her skin itched with perspiration and her clothes and hair were gritty with dust, but she rolled herself in her swag and slept as one dead. The last thing she remembered was listening to the lad's whistling as he circled the drowsy herd. Then Divine was leaning over her, shaking her awake.

Struggling bravely from sleep, she climbed out of her swag and hastily pulled on her boots. Divine helped her to mount and, looking back, she saw him fall into his swag without even loosening his belt.

Louise's first experience of night-watch was an ordeal. Her eyelids drooped with fatigue and her body ached from the long hours in the saddle. She took Kavanagh's advice to sing to the herd, although she felt foolish serenading the unappreciative cattle. But it did relieve the tedium and help her to stay alert. She hoped only that her companions were too busy sleeping to listen.

After breakfast the next morning Louise packed her belongings and, as she rolled her swag, retrieved the revolver she'd hidden under her pillow. Carefully unloading it, she looked up to find Kavanagh watching her.

'Do you know how to use that thing?'

She flushed, not wanting him to know she'd doubted her safety. 'Yes, I do. Mr Barclay showed me.'

'Well, I hope so, because I don't want one of us getting shot by accident. Yourself included. You won't need to protect yourself in this camp.'

She smiled at him soothingly, the night's fears seeming ridiculous in the light of day. 'It isn't that I don't trust you, Mr Kavanagh. I'm just not accustomed to sleeping in the bush.'

He shrugged. 'Sleep with it if it makes you happy. Just be careful of the damn thing!' His expression lightened and his eyes twinkled. 'Did you buy that off Barclay too?'

She smiled back at him, determined not to let him ruffle her this time. 'Yes, I did. Without his knowledge, of course.'

Laughing, he shook his head at her, then gathered up her swag and carried it over to the waiting packhorse. He quickly strapped it to the pack-saddle, his mind already obviously on other things.

Today he'd saddled one of his own horses for her. Kavanagh held the chestnut mare while he helped her to mount. 'She hasn't been broken to the sidesaddle but she's so quiet, I'm sure she'll be all right." As she settled the skirts of her habit he added, "I think you'll find her a better ride than that horse of yours. Barclay has a reputation for horse-breeding, but I can't say your nag lives up to it. He might be a thoroughbred, but he's a hard-mouthed brute. It's a shame–someone must have ruined him along the way. Doesn't look like he can walk much, either.'

Louise bristled inwardly, some perverse reaction making her fly to the defence of the horse she'd been so out of charity with earlier. Nag, indeed!

She smiled coldly. 'At least he's quiet and good-natured and no trouble to catch. Personally I prefer a horse to have looks and breeding.'

This was spoken with a significant glance at the big, rawboned creamy that Kavanagh had tethered nearby, a common-headed gelding with a coarse black mane and tail. The horse had tried to avoid capture that morning and then had stood trembling, the muscles along his belly and thighs taut with nervousness, while Kavanagh bridled and saddled him.

She hadn't seen evidence of Kavanagh's self-alleged Irish temper before, but the smile in his eyes quickly faded at her scathing words.

'Why, you...!' He dropped her mare's rein as if it burned him and swung away to his own horse, snapping, 'Dynamite mightn't look much, but when it comes to cattlework he'd piss all over that bloody thoroughbred of yours!'

He mounted abruptly, startling the nervous animal into a forward lunge. Yet he found the saddle effortlessly and rode away with the agitated gelding sidestepping and chomping at the bit, leaving Louise bristling with indignation.

Kavanagh continued to avoid her for the rest of the morning. Louise told herself it was a good thing, if that was the language he planned to use. However droving cattle was dull work without that ready sense of humour and even the unwelcome curiosity to break the tedium. It seemed he was proud of his big creamy horse, whatever his lack of pedigree. Once her temper cooled, she began to regret that superior, snobbish remark. But his crude outburst made an apology difficult.

At lunchtime Louise watched Kavanagh dismount in the shade of a stunted brigalow, wondering why it should be up to her to put an end to hostilities. She approached him anyway, soothing the big creamy horse with her voice when he would have sidled away. Her hand stroked his rough neck as she studied Kavanagh's averted cheek.

'Mr Kavanagh, I'm sorry if I offended you this morning, but I shan't tolerate being spoken to in that fashion.'

Kavanagh turned quickly from loosening the girth and glanced at her. 'I'm sorry about the language.' He had the grace to look ashamed. 'But you should've expected that when you decided to go droving with a rough cove like me.'

'No doubt. But if I try not to antagonise you, will you attempt to speak civilly?' She tangled her fingers in the gelding's coarse mane and surprised herself by adding, 'You're right, of course. Old Dynamite might be no oil painting, but I suspect in cattle-sense and stamina he'd surpass many well-bred horses.' She looked up at him and her mouth quirked. 'Listen to me. Any more of this and I'll be grovelling.'

'That I can't imagine.' Kavanagh laid a hand on Dynamite's tense rump as he moved around him, unbuckling his quart-pot from the pouch attached to the dees of the saddle. He turned to her with the blackened quart-pot in his hands, the humour back in his eyes and gave her a lingering, crooked smile that did something strange to her stomach. 'But if you want to get along with me, just remember one thing. Criticize me if you like, but don't criticize me horse.'

Chapter Four

Lloyd Kavanagh hadn't known a girl like Lucy Forrest before, but he wasn't about to let her intimidate him. He supposed she was used to lording it over people like him, but at the moment he was the boss and he didn't plan on letting her forget it. Fortunately the episode with the horse seemed to have brought them to a better understanding.

They might almost have been alone, so much did Cecil Divine keep out of their way. Lloyd pitied the lad's shyness but was amused at his endeavours to avoid Miss Forrest. Divine volunteered to watch the cattle while the others ate, and consumed his meal alone while Lloyd took his place with the mob. At midday the stock sought respite in the shade from the humid heat, leaving their drovers free to relax. While Divine sat in self-imposed isolation, Miss Forrest unbent enough to engage Lloyd in conversation.

She was as lonely as he was, he realized, and not nearly as stuck-up as she'd first made out. He discovered she was curious about his origins and he found himself telling her things he rarely volunteered to anyone. He supposed that was what the company of a comely girl did to a man.

'My dad had a small cattle run near Grenfell, in New South Wales,' he told her, noticing the sheen of moisture on her clear skin. She hadn't once complained about the heat, despite the dark, close-fitting jacket she wore. 'He's still got it, as far as I know, if he hasn't gone broke on it. It was wild and woolly, uncivilised country when I was a kid and most of the people around there were pretty wild and woolly to match.' He rubbed his chin, hearing the disparaging note in his own voice. 'Including me old man.'

'What do you mean by that?' Her grey eyes were alert and interested, flattering him to continue.

He shrugged. His father had been an abusive drunk, but he wasn't about to tell her that. 'It was bushranger country. I grew up on stories of Ben Hall, Frank Gardiner and Johnnie Gilbert. When I was a kid I wanted to be a bushranger meself, but when Ben Hall was shot down I reckoned there had to be better ways of making a living.'

'So you decided to be a cattleman instead?'

He grinned. 'First up, I decided to leave, but I didn't get to be a cattleman straight away. I got a job on a sheep station further up the Lachlan and the owner, Mr O'Donnelly, tried to set me on the straight and narrow.' He remembered the wild boy he'd been, angry at his father's beatings and his smile faded. 'O'Donnelly was a real decent old bloke–he took me under his wing and was more of a father than me dad had ever been.'

He hadn't intended to betray his bitterness, hadn't wanted or asked for the concern in her eyes. 'Wasn't your father good to you? What about your mother?'

Lloyd drew breath, trying for a more neutral tone. 'Ma did her best, but she was always overworked. She was supposed to have been something before she married Pat Kavanagh. He was a real no-hoper.' Why was he telling her this? He hadn't talked about his father in years, but now he'd started, he couldn't seem to stop. 'He never made anything of that place he had. I was the oldest and once I was big enough to run over to me grandmother's house I didn't stay there much. Old Grandma Griffiths had more of a hand in bringing me up than me own mother did.'

'Your mother's mother?'

He nodded, the pressure in his chest easing as his memories took a more welcome turn. 'She was a wonderful old lady. She taught me to read and write, which was just as well because I never went to school. Not that Grandma'd had much education herself – she'd just picked up a bit here and there. She was a coalminer's daughter, but she'd worked as a lady's maid.' He'd always known he was her favourite; perhaps she saw that he was more Griffiths than Kavanagh, for all that he looked like his father. 'It was after she died that I left home.'

'So she'd lived close by?' Miss Forrest sipped delicately from her quart-pot. It could have been a china cup at a ladies' tea-party.

'Yeah.' He plucked a stalk of dry grass and chewed it, remembering a tiny cottage smelling of home-baked bread and biscuits, comforting fare for a boy who was always hungry. The peace and quiet had been comforting too, in contrast to the frayed tempers and crying kids at home. 'After me grandfather died she came to live on the selection, in a little hut about a mile from the main house. It was right on the creek, near a waterhole where I used to go fishing. It was a nice spot. Grandma had a big garden there and she was pretty-well self-sufficient, right up to the time she died.'

'What about your father's parents?' She set the quart-pot down and leaned towards him, her eyes alight with interest. 'Were they still alive?'

He found himself watching the rise and fall of her breasts under the dark stuff of her jacket and dragged his gaze away before she noticed. 'The two old lags?' He snorted derisively. 'Yeah, they were alive, but I only saw 'em once or twice, which was enough. They lived in Bathurst.'

Her mouth twitched. 'You don't seem to think much of your family, Mr Kavanagh.'

'If you'd met them, you'd know why. It wasn't just because they were ex-convicts. They were pretty rough, I can tell you.' He stood up and held out a hand to help her rise, knowing he'd told her more than enough for one day. 'Come on, we'd better get these cattle moving.'

Louise mused over Kavanagh's revelations, surprised how much his story had touched her. That glimpse of an unhappy childhood tugged at her emotions, bringing a new sense of empathy for him. Their backgrounds were totally different, yet they both seemed to be escaping their families. She admired him for trying to make something of his life despite a dubious upbringing.

Not that there was anything distinguished about his present occupation. She'd been quick to discover the romantic image of the drover belonged only to fiction. The routine of the days was dull and monotonous, with Kavanagh's company at mealtimes the only bright spot. The nights she positively hated, when, with her body aching with exhaustion, she had only the hard ground to lie on and a few brief hours of sleep.

Kavanagh told her it was normal to have at least four men to share the night-watch, with one of these men acting as cook and another as horse-tailer. With only three of them to share these tasks the load was heavy, particularly for Kavanagh who was responsible for the greater percentage of them. It was he who took the longest watch before sunrise, when the cattle were at their most restless. It was also he who prepared their meals while Divine attended to his duties as horse-tailer. He'd seemed stunned when Louise told him she'd never cooked in her life.

But the biggest trial for Louise was the lack of hygiene. Generally it was easier to wipe their eating utensils clean with a clump of grass, than wash them at the muddy edge of the waterhole in the green, fouled water they were forced to drink. Opportunities for bathing were rare, especially when privacy was a necessary factor. Louise supposed bushmen must learn to tolerate their own body odour, but, in the fashion of the fastidious Queen Victoria, she was accustomed to bathing as often as every day in the hot weather. Her brief efforts at mustering hadn't prepared her for working and living without respite amidst the heat and dirt. Her hair was snarled and stiff with dust, while her body felt grimy and sticky, the smell of stale perspiration mingling unpleasantly with the odour of horses and cattle dung.

Yet there was little she could do about it. She hadn't the time or the means for a proper bath, so she had to content herself with the knowledge that the men were just as dirty as she was.

On the third day out from Bauhinia Downs, they had a dry stretch of about twenty miles to cover. It was a stifling, hot, still day, the sky pale and hazy with heat. It was no weather for driving cattle. They pushed the animals hard in the cool of the early morning so there would be time to rest in the hottest part of the day. One roan heifer became overheated, her lolling tongue streaming saliva, her gait stiffened.

'Leave her behind,' Kavanagh told her when Louise approached him for advice. 'She'll probably catch up tonight.' He swung his horse away to head a wayward steer, then yelled, 'Watch out!'

A swarm of wasps flew at them, buzzing angrily, their disturbed nest concealed amongst the leaves of a brigalow sapling. Kavanagh's horse leapt away in response to a well-placed spur, but Louise was slower to react. She cried out as the stings pierced her skin like red-hot needles and thumped her heel against the mare's ribs, urging her into a gallop. At a safe distance she dragged the horse to a halt, rubbing her smarting cheek and upper arm.

'Are you all right?' Kavanagh drew his mount alongside, his eyes glinting with sympathy. 'Did the wasps get you?'

Louise nodded, gasping.

'Here, I'll put some water on it.' Without dismounting Kavanagh unbuckled the canteen from his saddle and kneed his horse close, splashing water on her cheek. Louise's mare shied away and he leaned across to grasp her rein with the other hand. 'Did they get you anywhere else?'

'Yes.' She rubbed her arm, indicating the spot and he slopped water from the canteen, soaking her sleeve. His knee pressed against her leg as his strong hand restrained the fidgeting mare. Louise tried to ease away, uncomfortably aware of the improper contact.

His eyes narrowed and he loosened her rein, moving his horse away. 'It'll sting for a bit, but you'll be all right.'

'The water helps.' Louise looked down in confusion, wondering if her cheek was red and swollen. 'Thank you.'

When they took their 'dinner-camp', Kavanagh looked up at her quizzically as she sat on the opposite side of the fire. 'How are you feeling? Your face looks a bit bunged-up.'

Louise's cheeks heated. It wouldn't be so bad if she could see for herself, but without a mirror she had no way of knowing how awful she looked. For some reason she found herself minimizing her pain. 'I'm much better now. Thank you.'

He grinned sympathetically. 'The first time you've run into wasps? Sorry, I was the one who stirred 'em up and you got the brunt of it. Lucky you got away as quick as you did.'

His concern only made her feel foolish that she hadn't spotted the wasps herself. She changed the subject–she'd discovered she preferred to be the one asking questions. 'How far is it to your selection now?'

'Another day. We'll be there tomorrow night, all being well.'

'How did you become a landowner, Mr Kavanagh?'

He didn't reply immediately. He crouched before the fire, shaking tea leaves from a small bag onto his palm. Using the same bag to protect his fingers, he grasped the handles of his quart-pot, lifted it from the flames and tipped the tea leaves onto the bubbling water. 'I'd been in the carrying business for a few years, hauling from Westwood to Banana. I had horse teams and I did pretty well with 'em. They're faster than bullocks, though you'd never get an old bullocky to admit it.' He smiled briefly and Louise envisaged the crusty old bullockies belittling a young upstart teamster with his horses. 'Once I had the money I took up the lease for Myvanwy.'

'That's an unusual name.'

'I named it for me Welsh grandmother.' He added two handfuls of sugar to the tea and reached to break a clean twig from an overhanging branch, using it to stir the brew. 'Thought I owed her that much.'

She smiled, wondering how many young men would bother, in similar circumstances. 'Is it a large property?'

He tapped the side of the quart-pot, encouraging the tea leaves to settle. 'It's fifty square miles, with five miles of river frontage. There's plenty of permanent water and good flats for grazing. I've always wanted land and cattle of me own.'

Louise observed him silently, calculating his age. What had he said yesterday–he'd left home in '65 and he'd been fifteen then? That would make him twenty-three now, the same age as Charles. He'd achieved much in a few short years. There was a toughness about his face and an air of self-reliance in his manner which no doubt came of having to make his own way in the world. The three days' growth of beard on his jaw mingled with the grime of the droving camp to make him look older. She remembered how differently he'd looked when he was washed and freshly shaved.

'What about you?' He broke into her reverie. 'Why are you having to earn your living, then? I thought girls like you stayed at home with their sewing. Won't your father send you money?'

She shook her head. 'I'm afraid I'm out of favour with Papa at the moment. But I enjoy teaching children. A life of idle luxury becomes boring eventually.'

He gave a short huff of a laugh. 'Teaching is one thing, but what would your Papa say if he could see you now?'

Louise smiled. 'He'd succumb to one of his rages and keep me under lock and key for the rest of my life.'

'Yeah and I can't say I'd flaming blame him,' Kavanagh muttered dryly, digging in one of the pack bags for food.

She had a sudden urge to confess all, to tell him who she really was. It was ridiculous, for she had no reason to trust him with her secrets.

Only later did she wonder how different things might have been for them, if she had.

At dusk they came through Kavanagh's boundary and onto the waterhole in Roundstone Creek. Louise's heart lurched as she spotted a group of Aborigines camped beside the water, crouched around their cooking fires. There were perhaps fifty of them, men, women and children and nearly as many dogs; flea-bitten, half-starved animals, cringing at the edges of the group in anticipation of discarded scraps.

The cattle milled nervously, lifting their heads at the strange scent of people and dogs. Louise was about to seek Kavanagh's reassurance when she saw him ride ahead to talk to the natives. She clung to the rear of the herd, well out of the reach of boomerang or spear.

Her revolver was rolled away in her swag, where it was difficult to retrieve at short notice. She'd heard of the massacres at Hornet Bank, on the upper Dawson and at Cullin-la-Ringo, north of Springsure. The last of the two had taken place only twelve years before, with nineteen white people murdered, including women and children.

Most recalcitrant tribes had since been subdued, but even so, fear parched her throat. How could she sleep tonight, knowing the rider on night watch would be too busy with the cattle to guard the camp? Kavanagh carried a rifle on one of the packhorses and another revolver strapped to his saddle, but firearms were only effective if one was awake to use them.

Kavanagh spent almost half an hour with the Aborigines while Louise and Divine watered the restless cattle. Eventually they settled them for the night on a stretch of clear ground, on the opposite bank to the natives' camp. This was despite an argument with Divine who was reluctant to select a campsite without his boss's direction. Bad positioning of the herd meant danger to men and animals in the event of a rush, but Louise was too tired and hungry to wait any longer.

'We can always move them if we have to.'

Divine looked sulky but obeyed her without further protest.

When Kavanagh returned, he didn't even comment. He looked preoccupied and appeared surprised when Louise asked if the Aborigines were friendly.

'Yeah, they seem to be. I haven't seen this mob before– apparently they're from the Wadja tribe. They've come from the Expedition Range, but they've all broken up and scattered now. Doesn't seem like they've had much contact with whites. A bit of Pidgin was the best I could get out of 'em.'

'How did you manage to talk to them, then?'

He shrugged. 'Oh, we got by. I've picked up a few words here and there and there's always sign language. At least this mob seems to have kept to their old ways, instead of hanging around the stations for their flour and tobacco.'

'I wish I could see their camp at close quarters. Are you sure they aren't hostile?'

He shook his head. 'Most of the blacks around here have learnt to keep on the good side of us. I'll take you over there if you're game, but I warn you they're just about naked.'

She looked away quickly, heat washing her cheeks. There was an awkward silence and she stole a sideways glance at him. He was playing with his bridle reins, his face expressionless, but she had the feeling he was laughing at her. Bristling inwardly, she turned in her saddle to look at the blazing campfires. 'What are they cooking over there?'

'Wallaby, goanna, a few yams. They offered me a bit of goanna. It was pretty good, too–a nice young, fat one.'

Louise swung back to him, horrified. 'You didn't eat it?'

'Why not?' He was grinning openly now, obviously enjoying this. 'I've tried it before. It's not bad tucker, a bit like fowl.'

'So, while we were battling with the cattle, you were sitting over there, yarning and eating goanna.' Her voice sounded waspish even to her own ears.

'True enough.' He was still grinning. 'You should see the way they do their cooking. None of this skinning and gutting business. They chuck 'em on whole, the skin burns off and the gizzards dry up into a hard little mass in the middle. Saves a lot of trouble.'

She knew he was taunting her and she lifted her chin, not about to be bested. 'You'll have to show me. To use your vernacular, I'm game to go over there if you're game to take me.'

He chuckled. 'If you put it like that, how can I say no?'

After their evening meal Kavanagh walked with her to the natives' camp. As they approached, Louise picked out the men folk squatting on their haunches around a dying fire while the women crowded, chattering noisily, in front of one of the gunyahs. Suddenly all conversation stopped and a couple of the men, presumably elders, came forward to meet them. They were naked as Kavanagh had described, except for a twisted grass belt about the hips from which another clump of grass hung to serve as a scanty loincloth.

It was the first time Louise had seen aAborigines in their natural state at close quarters. She hardly knew where to look. She was used to the half-domesticated tribes who hung about the stations and who were supplied with clothes by their white benefactors. Louise fixed her eyes on the black faces, trying to hide her embarrassment from her companion. Although he kept a straight face, she suspected he was still laughing at her.

The two elders drew them into the circle about the fire and Kavanagh handed out plugs of chewing tobacco, before filling and lighting his own pipe. Louise, awkward and ill-at-ease, followed little of the following conversation. She turned her head to smile at the women and children hovering curiously in the background. That one smile was enough to make them scattter, giggling nervously.

One of the men, who she gathered was called Wollamba, spoke Pidgin English and seemed to be the interpreter of the party. When at last Kavanagh rose to go, the aborigine pointed towards the west where a bank of heavy clouds hung low in the moonlit sky.

'A big-feller storm bin come longa sun come-up,' he observed. 'Plenty big-feller thunder, lightning, Wollamba bin think.'

Kavanagh's gaze followed his pointing finger and Louise sensed his anxiety. The extreme heat threatened to build into an electrical storm. This was unwelcome news to anyone overlanding stock and she'd earlier heard him ask Divine to keep extra night-horses. Apart from the obvious dangers of lightning, wind and hail, a storm was likely to panic both cattle and horses.

As they returned to their camp Kavanagh said, 'I don't like the feel of the weather myself. It's been so flaming hot. I'll rig the fly up now, in case we get some rain out of it. If it starts to look threatening, I'll help Cec with the cattle. You stay out of it, Miss Forrest.'

She didn't protest. At least his concern with the weather had put an end to his teasing.

Lying awake in her swag, she watched while Kavanagh set up the tarpaulin he'd referred to as the "fly". Her thoughts returned to the near-naked women at the Aboriginal camp. He'd seemed quite unconcerned by their exposed breasts and buttocks and she supposed he was accustomed to seeing them that way. She remembered the vague, whispered stories she'd heard of white men gratifying themselves with the lubras, paying the black women's husbands in tobacco, clothing, foodstuffs or alcohol for services rendered. The thought sickened and disgusted her and she wondered if her young companion had ever participated in anything of the sort.

Surreptitiously she watched him as he shifted gear under the tarpaulin and was pleased to see him take to his swag once he'd finished. She lost the battle to stay awake, but was roused by the storm onwards of ten o'clock. In the faint glow of their dying campfire she could see Kavanagh pulling on his boots. Surely he couldn't have sought himself a woman and returned to his bed in that span of time.

Not that his morals were any concern of hers, of course. It was merely intolerable to think of any man behaving with such lack of respect for her presence.

Chapter Five

Lloyd stared at the night sky and swore silently. A mass of black cloud swirled above them, obliterating the moon and stars. Lightning flashed incessantly to the west and south. He judged the storm to be a quarter of an hour away at most. Although he couldn't hear the cattle above the wind or see more of them than a vague mass outlined in the lightning flashes, he sensed they were stirring restlessly. If they rushed tonight the girl would be a hindrance, an added responsibility, rather than an asset to him. If he'd had any sense he'd have left her at Bauhinia Downs.

He turned to fire instructions at her. 'It'll be here any minute—you'd better move under the fly.' Shoving his hat on his head, he threw a couple of logs on the fire. 'I don't think there'll be much rain in it, but you never know. Keep an eye on the mob though, won't you? This is the sort of night they could go. If they do rush, be ready to run.' He gestured towards a large box tree not far from their camp. 'Get behind the tree if they come this way, climb it if you can. Whatever you do, don't try an' help us. It's no job for a woman riding sidesaddle.'

He didn't wait to hear her reply, quickly saddling and mounting the horse he'd tethered nearby. His stomach knotted as he noticed the cattle milling in agitation. Young animals like these, without the steadying influence of breeding cows, were particularly prone to panic.

Lloyd sought his young assistant in the dark and paused to exchange a few words with him. He could barely make out Divine's features, but he caught the frightened gleam of the whites of his eyes and heard the tremor in his voice.

'Do you think it'll be a bad one, Lloyd?'

'It's looking that way.' Lloyd's voice was grim. 'You been caught in a storm with a mob before?'

Divine mumbled the negative. 'Do you think they'll rush?'

'I bloody-well hope not.' A rush was no picnic at the best of times, but with only this inexperienced lad and the girl to worry about, it could end in disaster. At the quick sickening of apprehension, he thrust his thoughts aside. He'd heard of men who cracked-up on the droving camp, unable to cope with the unrelieved tension of handling half-wild bullocks that sometimes rushed night after night in succession. These weren't touchy bullocks, only well-handled youngsters he'd become almost sentimental over in the days since he'd taken delivery of them. But if he was worried, could he blame his young offsider for feeling a bit panicky?

He tried to sound reassuring. 'Don't worry, Cec. They should be all right, but if they do go, keep with 'em until they've steadied down and then we'll try to get 'em ringing. Turn the lead in towards the tail and keep 'em going in a circle.'

He sensed rather than saw the boy's nod and left him to it, smiling grimly. Here he was playing the father-figure, the man of experience, at all of twenty-three.

The storm was almost upon them. Jagged forks of lightning, incessant and vicious, tore open the darkness of the night while the thunder exploded loudly in its wake. The wind whipped up great clouds of dust and leaves, forcing Lloyd to close his eyes against the grit and shield his face with his arm. But there was as yet no rain and nor did he expect it. This was one of those dry electrical storms that go hand in hand with drought and heat.

Busy holding the cattle, his nervousness was pushed aside. At least the darkness was no longer an obstacle, for the lightning flashes crowded and overlapped each other in merciless succession. It was as much as he and Divine could do to hold the animals together. He almost began to wish he'd called upon Miss Forrest after all.

He was turning back a breakaway heifer when he saw the sudden streak of flame. His ears pounded with the simultaneous thunder-crack and the crash of splintering timber. Something hard hit his arm, tearing the sleeve, but although he registered the impact the pain didn't follow until a moment later. By then he had no time to think about it, for the mob had broken in unison, galloping at an angle towards the creek, sweeping Divine along on its outskirts.

Lloyd was riding his favourite, Dynamite, and he was glad of it, for there was no horse to equal him in the dark. As they raced to wheel the lead, the gelding cleared obstacles his rider hadn't seen and as always if allowed his head dodged trees and low branches unerringly. Lloyd thought each moment must be his last, but miraculously when Dynamite stumbled into a shallow depression and partially lost balance, he recovered and quickly regained his stride.

The rush wasn't a severe one and already the cattle were slowing. Lloyd was able to overtake the leaders before they reached the creek and turn them back on themselves. Divine had extricated himself from the mob and was close behind him. They had them ringing nicely when he noticed a third rider out of the corner of his eye, galloping almost as recklessly as they. He knew it could only be Miss Forrest, riding sidesaddle on her hard-mouthed bay gelding, but he had no time to do anything about it then. It was perhaps half an hour later, when the worst of the storm was past, before they had the herd firmly under control and he could afford to protest.

He'd meant to be diplomatic, but he was exhausted and generally in a bad humour. His comment reflected that in spite of himself. 'I thought I told you to stay out of it if they went!'

She stared back at him defiantly. 'I know you did, but what was the use of that? You were obviously having difficulties.'

'We would've managed,' he retorted shortly. 'I could've done without the extra worry of trying to keep an eye on you. It gave me the cold shivers seeing you galloping about in the dark in that blasted sidesaddle. And on that blasted horse!' he added for good measure.

She didn't reply, but another distant flash of lightning illuminated her pale, tense face. Her lower lip trembled and she looked close to tears. Lloyd was immediately overcome with remorse

Abruptly he leaned towards her. 'Here, are you all right? You'd better get off for a bit.' He slipped from the saddle and moved to her stirrup to catch her in his arms. He held her for a moment, long enough to feel her shaking. Now that he came to stand on them, his own legs were none too steady–the unremitting tension and all the hard riding of the past hour had taken its toll. And his injured arm burned like a hot brand.

'Do you want to sit down?' he asked her gently.

'No, I'm all right now.' Despite the reassurance her voice sounded tearful. 'It was just the storm–I thought the camp was about to be struck, or blown away. And when that tree was hit–I didn't know what to do.' Her voice quavered. 'I'm afraid I almost panicked. But Shadow had pulled away–I had to catch him–and then it seemed only sensible to help. After all, it was I who insisted we leave without your other man.'

He'd never heard that note of uncertainty, even contrition, in her voice before and his heart contracted. He had to admire her courage, for she wasn't stupidly unaware of the danger as he'd at first thought. A rush of emotion overtook common sense and he hugged her impulsively. The movement made him wince and he let his arms fall away.

'Is there something wrong? Are you hurt?'

'Just me arm. A lump of wood hit me when that tree was struck.'

She dropped Shadow's reins and swiftly examined the wound. It was too dark to see much, but Lloyd knew his sleeve was rent almost in two and what was left of it was soaked with blood.

'Oh, Lloyd!' Her fingers fumbled with his sleeve. 'It's been bleeding–is it very painful?'

Her use of his Christian name was disconcerting, almost distracting him from the pain. 'It is a bit, but I'll survive.' He stepped back. 'I haven't got time to do anything about it now. These cattle will need a couple of us to hold them for the rest of the night and if anyone needs a spell it's Divine. He hasn't been off his horse for hours.'

'Yes, of course.' She bent to pick up her horse's reins. 'I'll help you. You'd better tell Divine to go to bed.'

When the dawn came, it revealed more destruction than any of them had realized. Shattered pieces of timber, some two or three feet long, had been flung from the lightning-stricken tree in a radius of a hundred yards. Close to the camp, another small tree had been uprooted by the wind and fallen branches were scattered around. The fly was blown almost from its moorings and hung limply from one corner. But most significant of all, in the spot where the cattle had camped before the rush, was a dead steer. It had apparently been killed by a flying piece of wood.

Lloyd joked, 'Lucky that bit of stick didn't hit *me* on the head, or I'd have been a goner, too,' but Miss Forrest frowned at him and told him it was no laughing matter.

She seemed surprised that he wasn't more upset at the loss, but in reality he was considering himself fortunate. When he counted the mob out, he was only the one beast short, with the only other injuries a lame shoulder and a crushed hip. The rush hadn't been crazed enough to result in the usual casualties of broken legs and animals trampled to death.

'A man's bloody lucky,' he said to Divine. 'I think someone must be looking after me this trip–whether it's the Good Lord above or what.'

Perhaps Lucy Forrest had brought him luck. Despite his earlier misgivings she'd proved her worth with the cattle. She'd certainly saved a long delay at Bauhinia Downs, or the problem of finding a replacement for Thompson, who might not have been fit to travel for some time. And God knows she'd brought a bit of pleasure to an otherwise dreary trip.

The Aborigines, camped on the other side of the waterhole, didn't appear to have suffered unduly from the elements. Their flimsy-looking gunyahs were obviously stronger than they appeared. Kavanagh had almost forgotten them in the greater urgency of the storm. It was lucky the cattle hadn't rushed over their camp.

After they'd breakfasted, Louise was finally allowed to attend to Kavanagh's wound. The torn edge of his sleeve had congealed to a long gash on his upper arm. Kneeling on the ground beside him, she bathed away the dried blood with water from the billy. He clenched his teeth and winced several times as she worked. Louise watched his tense expression in concern.

It was disconcerting to find she enjoyed being this close to him. She noted his ruffled fair hair and the beads of perspiration on his skin, the lean, unshaven jaw and the firm, well-shaped mouth. She remembered the way he'd held her last night, albeit so briefly. Over the past few days she'd become accustomed to his touch, thanks to the sidesaddle, and there was a kind of pleasurable familiarity about his closeness that was seductive.

Finally she bandaged the wound with a strip torn from his only clean shirt. 'Be sure to keep the dirt out of it, now, so it doesn't become infected.'

He shook his head, smiling. 'I've had worse than this before and never got more than a bit of fever.'

'It will heal more rapidly if you keep it bandaged.' She spoke briskly, knowing she must put distance between them. 'I don't want all my good work going to waste, Mr Kavanagh.'

His face changed and he seemed to retreat a little. 'You ought to be a nurse, Miss Forrest. You're good at this.'

'Another Florence Nightingale? I don't think so. I'm not that saintly.'

He rose to his feet, smiling briefly. 'No, I daresay you're not. But thank you, anyway. It's feeling better already.' He shoved his hat on his head and turned to his horse. 'Come on, we'd better get a move on before it gets too hot.'

Lloyd was frowning as he joined Cecil Divine with the cattle. He tried to concentrate on the job in hand, but it was difficult when his mind couldn't get past the memory of gentle fingers on his skin and female warmth bending close. His careless words to Sam Naylor came back to mock him. Now he had to stop himself from mooning over the girl, stop his eyes from lingering on her face and hair and that slim body he'd once thought too thin. Strange how it had begun to haunt his dreams at night. There was a responding warmth in her that he wouldn't have believed possible just three days before. She'd put distance between them this morning, but he knew she wasn't indifferent to him.

She was so unlike the other girls he'd known. Was it only because he'd been in the bush too long that he'd come to fancy her? It had to be more than that. The shared laughter and talk lured him as much as anything else. After her earlier standoffishness, her friendship and those brief glimpses of softness and sympathy drew him like a moth to the flame.

Perhaps the result would be the same and like a stupid bloody moth he'd end up with his wings singed.

After leaving Roundstone Creek and the Aborigines behind, they forced the reluctant cattle up a rocky jump-up, as Kavanagh referred to it. It was a steep incline thickly timbered with rosewood, lancewood and wattle, which levelled out to a tableland, but gradually dropped again to the flat floodplain that bordered the Dawson River. This was more fertile country timbered with silver-trunked gums and ironbark.

At this time of the year the river had ceased flowing and was reduced to a string of waterholes in a wide, deep channel bounded by tree-clad banks. It seemed strange to Louise who'd travelled so far, that she was now, according to Kavanagh's reckoning, no more than seventy miles upstream from James Barclay's homestead, on the same mighty Dawson. Lloyd Kavanagh's stock had drunk from the very same water she'd fished and boated on earlier in the year.

They watered the cattle before driving them to the half-completed stockyards on higher ground. In the morning they would be cross-branded with Kavanagh's brand before finally being turned out to graze.

The living quarters stood about half a mile downstream, on a slight rise above the river. Louise wasn't sure what she had been expecting, but not this crude hut, its walls hand-hewn ironbark slabs, the roof sheets of stringy-bark. Two similar, smaller buildings, the meathouse and the harness room, stood nearby, shaded by a big gum tree.

After they had turned their horses into the paddock for a well-earned rest, Kavanagh escorted Louise into his home. The first room was fairly large, serving as a kitchen, dining and living area, with an open fireplace for cooking and a beaten ant bed floor. Basic furniture consisted of a slab table, a couple of kerosene cases in place of chairs, a shabby dresser containing a few pieces of cracked and chipped crockery and more comfortable-looking chair with a handmade wooden frame and hessian seat.

Kavanagh looked awkward for the first time since she'd met him. 'It's not much,' he admitted, 'but it's a roof over me head and it'll do until I'm in a position to build something better.'

He strode across the room and held aside another strip of hessian curtaining a doorway. 'This is the bedroom. You can sleep in here tonight–Cec and I will throw our swags in the other room.'

Louise joined him at the doorway and peered in. This was a much smaller room, again furnished with kerosene cases, an old battered chest of drawers and a stretcher bed built of saplings and hessian.

Louise pressed past Kavanagh and went to feel the mattress. It was horsehair and prickly to the touch, yet looked gloriously inviting after sleeping so many nights on the hard ground. Kavanagh followed her and dragged the blankets from the bed, tossing them into the furthest corner of the room. He took two clean ones from the chest of drawers and laid them neatly on the mattress.

'The others were due for a wash.' He smiled apologetically. 'No sheets. Will this be comfortable enough?'

'Thank you, it has to be better than sleeping on the ground. I don't believe I shall ever become accustomed to it.'

'I daresay you won't have to. Unless you plan to take up droving for a living.'

She caught his eye and found herself returning his infectious grin. 'I hardly think so. Though now that it's over, I can appreciate the experience.'

'Not many ladies would say that. Not proper ladies like you. Me Irish grandmother would have been used to worse.'

'Certainly, I won't compare it to prison.' She noticed a scrap of mirror wedged in a crack in the wall and walked over to check her reflection, wincing at the grubby, wild-haired baggage who stared back at her. There was a small red lump on her cheek where the wasp had bitten her. 'I suppose if your Kavanagh grandparents were "rough and ready", as you phrased it, that must be an inevitable result of living under such terrible conditions.'

'Perhaps. You must be thinking I'm in no position to criticize, seeing the way I live.'

'I'm not here to make judgments, Mr Kavanagh. I'm too much in your debt for that.' She swung away from the mirror, deciding her appearance would have to wait. 'I'm sure I've left myself open to harsh judgments, which I hope you haven't made about me.'

His colour rose, reminding her of some of their earlier conversations. 'The truth to tell is, I don't know what to make of you.'

She moved to the door, wishing she hadn't started this discussion. 'Let's leave it that way, shall we?'

Everything was relative, Louise realised. Once she would have found Lloyd Kavanagh's living conditions impossibly primitive. But they were vastly better than a bush camp. Even the lavatory out the back was an improvement in comfort and privacy to squatting behind a tree, and his thoughtfulness as a host couldn't be faulted. Without being asked, he heated water over the fireplace and made a bath for her in a round iron tub in the bedroom. He provided her with a rough, clean towel and homemade soap and left her to wash.

As she undressed, Louise was uncomfortably aware that only a thin sheet of hessian protected her privacy. She'd grown to trust Kavanagh, but being alone with two males in this unusual situation made her feel exposed. Uneasily she wondered if they were thinking of her in here, mentally picturing her as she removed her clothes.

The homemade soap was slow to lather, but after several days without, any sort of bath was a luxury. When at last she was clean again, she dressed in one of the print dresses from her valise and combed the knots from her wet hair. She surveyed her reflection in the mirror, noting how brown her face was. Her lady-like white skin was a thing of the past.

She felt herself blushing as she re-entered the other room. Divine was nowhere to be seen but Kavanagh looked up at her quickly from the fireplace, his eyes seeming to take all of her in, from her demure dress to her tidy hair. Her colour intensified and she joined him to peek into the simmering pot, trying to hide her embarrassment.

He had salt beef, jacket potatoes and onions boiling in a large camp-oven, while a second camp-oven presumably held a damper. A blackened kettle full of water stood ready to hang over the fire for brewing tea.

His approving smile sent a surge of warmth through her body. 'Do you mind watching this while I clean up?'

Twenty minutes later he reappeared from the bedroom in clean, respectable clothes and with the four days' stubble shaved from his face. The fresh, wholesome smell of soap replaced the odour of horses, dust and sweat. He looked better than she'd thought possible. She swallowed and dragged her gaze away, knowing he was aware of her scrutiny just as surely as she'd been aware of his a short time before.

Until this moment, she hadn't realized how good-looking he was. She tried to picture him in the cutaway coat, waistcoat, bow-tie and fashionable narrow trousers that Charles appeared so distinguished in, knowing he wouldn't possess such garments and probably wouldn't be comfortable in them. Yet there was something in his personality that intrigued her more than clothes or good looks ever could–something vibrant and quirkily humorous, even the touch of impudence that had infuriated her at first. As if to illustrate her thoughts, he threw a teasing grin at Divine, who had just come through the door.

'How about it, Cec? Are you going to use the tub?'

The lad, perching himself on a kerosene case in the furthest corner of the room, shook his head vigorously. 'Aw, no, I'll be right. It's getting a bit cool for it, I reckon.'

Kavanagh winked at Louise but merely said, 'Suit yourself,' before carrying the tub outside and depositing the water on the ground. Louise hid her smile. Judging from Divine's grubby appearance he must belong to the school who considered an all-over wash once a month quite sufficient. But at least he'd rinsed his face and hands and combed his hair. Such details hadn't concerned her in the bush, but it was surprising how quickly her old fastidiousness had returned now that she was once again sitting to a table to eat her meal.

Divine was more withdrawn than ever within four walls, leaving her and Kavanagh to dominate the conversation. Louise floated on a wave of exhilaration, the words bubbling out of her. She laughed at very little, aware of little else but the man sitting opposite her. If only this interlude didn't have to end. If only she didn't have to face going to a houseful of strangers, to be very likely treated with the disdain most families showed their governesses.

Kavanagh was the first to mention her immediate future, bringing that tiny corner of dread to life. 'I'm sorry I won't have time to take you to New Haven tomorrow, Miss Forrest. Cec and I will be most of the day branding these cattle. Are you in much of a hurry?'

No, I'm not in a hurry, she thought. But she didn't say it aloud.

'What is today? Friday, isn't it? The Greenwoods are supposed to be meeting me next Friday, on the coach. So there is certainly no urgency. However I don't wish to impose on your hospitality any longer. If you give me directions, I could make my own way.'

'No need to do that. I'll take you Sunday morning, if you can think of a good reason for turning up a few days early.'

'I shall think of something.'

He laughed drily. 'I bet you will. You've certainly spun me enough yarns–I just hope you convince them better than you convinced me.' He turned to the lad. 'Cec, I hope you've got a short memory, because you're going to have to forget that Miss Forrest was ever with us. Hear?'

The lad looked startled at Kavanagh's emphatic tone. He nodded his head vigorously. 'I won't say nuthing to nobody. I'm no gabster.'

They both had to laugh at that. 'No, Cecil,' said Louise. 'That is one thing it would be difficult to accuse you of.'

Chapter Six

Louise was too exhausted to notice the dubious comforts of Lloyd Kavanagh's makeshift bed. Recent habit had her waking early, but when she entered the main room of the little shack only Cecil was present to greet her good morning.

'Lloyd's gone over to the neighbours,' he informed her diffidently. 'Said he'd be back for breakfast, though.'

Since Divine seemed to have the preparations for the meal well in hand, Louise decided to relieve him of her unwelcome presence and went outside.

She wandered a little way down the track that led to the river, pausing where another road branched off and headed downstream. Noticing fresh horse tracks turning that way, she guessed that this must be the direction Kavanagh had ridden. She perched on a fallen log and gazed towards the river, enjoying the pleasant warmth of the early-morning sun on her bare head. She lapsed into a peaceful daydream, more pressing worries for the moment forgotten.

The sound of a horse roused her and she turned to see Kavanagh approaching. He was accompanied by two big yellow kangaroo dogs who gambolled ahead at the sight of her, alarming her with their raised hackles and stiff, faintly wagging tails until a word from their master brought them to heel.

'Good morning.' He reined in beside her. 'Don't worry, the dogs aren't savage.'

'Cecil said you went over to the neighbours.'

'Yeah. They were looking after the dogs.' He dismounted as he spoke. 'Come on, I'll walk back to the house with you. That young feller should have breakfast ready by now.'

His dogs crowded about him the moment he stepped off his horse, whining excitedly and vying for his attention. He rubbed their heads with rough affection and then pushed them away. 'Down, Soda. That's enough, Buster. Thought I was never coming home, didn't you?' He grinned at Louise. 'They're just trying to make out they missed me.'

As with Dynamite, the horse, his fondness for the two animals was obvious. Louise imagined him living alone here, month after weary month, with only these four-legged brutes for company. The mental picture of him playing and romping with Soda and Buster touched her, making him seem young and vulnerable.

They walked together towards the homestead, their boots scuffing up small clouds of grey dust from the track. 'Do you see much of the Jamiesons?'

He nodded. 'They've been very good to me. Mrs Jamieson often has me over for a meal, just to make sure I don't starve myself. And they always keep an eye on things for me if I'm away. Jock Jamieson and his boys give me a hand with the mustering and I return the favour. It suits us both.'

'You're lucky to have good neighbours.'

'Yeah.' He slapped at one of the dogs playfully. 'They're a sight better than most.'

Lloyd and Divine were busy for the remainder of the day, cross-branding the cattle in the crush with his LK brand, finally letting them out of the yard and holding them on the river flat until they had settled down to graze. Miss Forrest had asked about washing her clothes, so he'd shown her the wooden washboard he used along with the iron bathtub. When he returned to the house for dinner he wasn't surprised to see her riding habit hanging from the clothesline, a wire strung between two trees. He averted his gaze from the white undergarments next to the habit and then looked back again. Two pairs of his moleskins hung beside them, along with a couple of his shirts. Luckily he didn't usually wear underwear, or they'd probably be hanging there as well.

He had to say something to her when he went inside. 'Thank you, but you shouldn't have done me washing, Miss Forrest. It's not right–a lady like you.'

She looked down at her hands, reddened about the knuckles from all the scrubbing she'd done. 'I'll admit I hadn't washed clothes before today. But I wasn't a drover until a week ago, either.'

'She's sweet on you,' Divine mumbled crossly to him later. 'She never did my washing.'

'No, and do you blame her? By the time you've worn the same set of clothes for a fortnight they're that stinking and stiff with dirt they're only fit for the fire!'

Cecil didn't flinch. 'She'd make a terrible wife. She can't cook and she was too la-di-da to help with breakfast this morning.'

Lloyd stared at him in surprise. 'Who's talking about marriage?' He cheerfully cuffed the boy under the ear. 'Now cut out the cheek, Divine!'

On Sunday morning Louise was still wrestling with her problem. It was one thing to arrive in Banana on the appointed day on the mail coach, accompanied by numerous articles of luggage. To turn up unheralded at the Greenwoods' doorstep almost a week early, on horseback and in the sole escort of a young man who wasn't her relative, with nothing more than a valise and a couple of changes of clothing to her name, was quite another. It was going to involve careful explanation and so far her ingenuity had failed her.

Cecil Divine had left straight after breakfast to return to his home in Banana, so it was a relief not to have to worry about listening ears. She rehearsed several stories for Kavanagh's benefit as they rode down the rough bush track that led to the town. He merely laughed and contradicted her, shaking his head when she asked him for suggestions.

'It's a bit funny asking me, when you haven't even told me why you left the Barclays in the first place.'

She chose to ignore that. 'Perhaps I could say they were called away suddenly to a dying relative and decided to put me on an earlier coach. And then,' warming to this theme, 'my bags were overlooked at the depot at Westwood and unbeknownst to me weren't even loaded onto the coach.'

'And have the Greenwoods try to recover 'em for you and find you were never even on it? You'll have to do better than that, me girl.'

'I'm not "your girl",' she flashed. Drat his impudence!

'And,' he continued, ignoring her outburst, 'it's pretty unlikely that Barclay would shove you off a week early without sending word ahead to have 'em expecting you.'

'Unlikely, but not impossible,' she retorted coldly.

Three minutes later she had cooled down enough to try again. 'Well, perhaps my luggage fell off the top of the coach and no-one noticed.'

'Hmph. If there were the usual three or four coves perched up the top they could hardly have failed to notice.'

She sighed in exasperation. 'Then what do you suggest, Mr Know-it-all?'

He grinned. 'You spun enough yarns to me and now you'll just have to spin a few more. Perhaps it would be better if you put up in Banana for the night while I ride out with a message. At least that way you won't just turn up out of the blue and it'll give you more time to make up your story.'

'Oh,' she exclaimed impatiently, 'now that we've come this far we may as well continue. Since the coach would have arrived on Friday, I shall have to tell them I've been staying at an hotel. I shall just say my bags were stolen at Westwood and the authorities are doing their best to trace them. They'll have to be content with that.'

Kavanagh's face set in a stubborn expression. 'I still think it'd be better if I rode out with a message.'

'Why? Why shouldn't you have offered your services as an escort if you heard I needed one?'

A flicker of a smile touched his mouth. 'I can tell you why I *would* have and that's the very reason Mrs Greenwood isn't going to like it. It's not going to help you, you know, setting her against you like that for a start. You better hope she never finds out what you've been up to for the past week.'

Louise flushed, realising for the first time how much she'd compromised her reputation. It was obvious that even Kavanagh, with his doubtful background, considered her behaviour irregular. Perhaps irregular was putting it mildly.

Shortly afterwards they reached Banana Creek, ahead of them the big lagoon that watered the town and, beyond that, the little township sprawling over an open rise. Today Banana dozed under the hot sun, with only a few pedestrians and a man on horseback moving in the main street, but the crowd of travellers and teamsters camped beside the lagoon hinted this was usually a busy commercial centre.

'What's the population of the town, Mr Kavanagh?'

He glanced at Louise and shrugged. 'About a hundred and twenty, at last count.' He drew rein, adding abruptly, 'Let's get out of here. If anyone who knows me sees us together there'll be talk and the less talk the better as far as the Greenwoods are concerned. I hope to God they don't come to town too often or they'll find out you never came in on that coach.'

So Louise was left with only a fleeting first impression of Banana as they bypassed the centre of town and joined up with the Westwood road. They passed through several miles of scrub wasteland, thick with hopbush and blackcurrant bush, before stopping for lunch in a dry gully shaded by tall gums. They filled their quart-pots with water from canteens on their saddles and made their fire in the shade out of sight of the road. Louise felt awkward, remembering Kavanagh's earlier comments about the Greenwoods' likely disapproval. Had he agreed to take her because of *that*– because she was female and he was male? Had he hoped something would come of it? It was a disturbing thought.

They ate in uncharacteristic silence. Finally Kavanagh rose and poured the dregs from his quart-pot onto the fire, making it sizzle and smoke. He kicked dirt over the embers with his boot and the combination of drifting ashes and dust tickled Louise's nose, making her sneeze. She knew his precautions were necessary, for the hot, gusting winds had only to sweep up a spark and the dry bush would be in flames.

He saddled the two horses and turned when Louise made no move to go. He stood there looking at her, waiting, and suddenly she dreaded their imminent parting.

Emboldened by the fear that he was about to be lost to her, she patted the ground beside her. 'Come here, please.'

He obeyed her, dropping to his heels. 'We have to go. You know that.'

Her gaze fixed on his face and she swallowed the lump of uncertainty in her throat. 'I know. I just wanted to thank you for escorting me this far. You've been very good–I must say it was the greatest piece of good fortune I encountered you at Bauhinia Downs that day.' She uttered a shaky, self-deprecating laugh that was totally unlike her. 'Perhaps you've thought it otherwise, however.'

He continued to regard her intently, saying nothing and she added, 'We should say goodbye now. We shall hardly be able to do so under the eagle eye of Mrs Greenwood.'

She held out her hand to him, which he took, his eyes still holding hers. The expression in them reminded her of the way he'd looked at her a couple of nights ago in his shack and she realized she'd lured him into something more than a simple handshake. This was the moment to move away and forestall him, but anticipation held her captive. Her heart thudded while he edged closer, clasping her hand in his and moving his calloused thumb caressingly on her palm.

Her breath caught in her throat and her eyes locked with his, while the movement of his thumb sent little tingles of delight coursing through her body. Then he twisted her hand so that their palms were together, their fingers entwined. He tipped off his hat and bent his face down to hers to find her mouth.

One hand on the ground supported his weight, the other relinquishing hers to come up and stroke the sensitive skin at the back of her neck. The awkwardness of earlier was overtaken by her body's surging response as his mouth moved over hers. Louise was conscious of nothing but a blurred image of green eyes and light-brown hair, tanned skin and a firm mouth that tasted of pipe tobacco and strong black tea. At last he lifted his head, his hand dropping to her shoulder. Owing to his crouching position their bodies hadn't even touched.

'Louise'– he used her Christian name for the first time, his voice husky–'what the dickens made you leave the Barclays like that?'

She looked at him, startled even in the midst of her desire. 'How did you know my name was Louise?'

'It was on one of your handkerchiefs.'

Of course. She'd dropped a handkerchief beside the campfire one day and he'd retrieved it for her. It had happened to be one that little Sarah Barclay had embroidered, using Louise's first name instead of the more usual initials. It was lucky she hadn't used the initials. That item would have to stay packed away in future.

'I'm generally called Lucy, you know.'

His hand tightened on her shoulder. 'Louise suits you better. But you haven't answered me question. I want you to tell me why you left the Barclays–the truth, that is.'

Her nerves tightened. Suddenly she badly wanted to tell him. She couldn't go on under false pretences like this, letting him believe in Lucy Forrest, the governess. Yet she would have to feel the way, first.

'Lloyd, have you ever heard of the Ashfords?'

'Which Ashfords do you mean?'

'The Harry Ashfords, from Banyandah. They're cousins of James Barclay.'

'Harry Ashford,' he repeated. He jumped to his feet, his face and voice suddenly grim. 'Yes, I know of the family. I didn't know they were cousins of the Barclays, though. James Barclay's a bit too good for 'em, isn't he?'

'Why?' She could hardly breathe. 'What do you know of them?'

He laughed unpleasantly, looming above her in a way that made her heart pound. 'Not a lot. But I do know that Charles Ashford's supposed to be a rake of the worst kind and Harry Ashford's a rotten scoundrel who doubled his money by cheating other people. Me included.'

She gasped. 'Have you met him? But surely—'

'Oh, I've never met him. Don't want to, either. I've seen him once or twice, in the distance. But when I was carrying in Rockhampton, me partner and I contracted to do a few loads for him. More fools us.'

'Why? What happened?'

His mouth was set a tight, angry line. He moved restlessly, not looking at her as she stared up at him. 'He swindled us, that's what. He's just the sort of arrogant, crooked blighter that makes us workers hate the upper classes' guts–excuse the language. Sorry, I know you're upper class yourself, but you're different.' He drew a deep breath. 'I don't mind what the other fellow's got so long as he hasn't lined his pockets at the expense of everyone else.'

Louise digested this in stunned, painful silence. This was a picture of her father that had never been presented to her before. It was difficult to credit. She knew he was arrogant, but she'd always believed him to be respected in the community as a gentleman. She hadn't heard allegations of dishonesty before; but as his daughter, she realized, she would be the last person to hear.

Instinctively, she sensed Kavanagh wasn't lying. Strange to think she would vouch for his integrity before that of her father.

She resisted a hysterical temptation to laugh. Heavens, if he were to know it was Harry Ashford's own daughter that he was addressing! How could she tell him now?

'What made you bring the Ashfords up, anyway?' Kavanagh was asking in a more level tone, looking down at her now. 'Did you meet 'em while you were with the Barclays?'

'Oh, I'd met them before,' she dissembled. 'But Charles was coming to visit and that is why I left. I… I was afraid of him.'

This was at least part of the truth. However Louise immediately wished she hadn't said it, for Lloyd's gaze sharpened, his eyes hard and discerning. She felt her colour heightening again as she realized how he would interpret that statement, knowing as he did Charles' reputation.

He spun away abruptly, untying Shadow and leading the horse to where Louise now stood. He moved to her side as if to help her to mount, but then he paused, looking down at her. The hardness in his eyes faded and Louise met his gaze uncertainly, wondering if he meant to kiss her again. Her heart beat faster; she knew she should move away and put an end to this foolish dalliance. Yet when he dropped the reins to slide his arms around her, bending his head to hers, she was unable to deny herself this new, exquisite pleasure.

There was a difference in this embrace to the previous one. His mouth was more insistent and she opened her lips under his, responding purely by instinct. He pulled her close until their entire bodies were in contact–she could even feel his thighs through the layers of clothing that separated them. That slim strong body that she'd become so aware of, had watched so covertly,this was what she'd been wanting for days now, though she'd scarcely admitted it to herself. Yet even this wasn't enough.

Away from the constraining presence of Cecil Divine, away from the sheer hard work of the past few days, the spark that had flickered between them ignited to a blaze. The kiss went on and on, until he was breathing unevenly and her own breath seemed to have escaped her lungs. Her mind and senses were full of the feel and smell and taste of him. Their embrace was verging on indecent, but she couldn't bring herself to protest.

It was like a dam that had been slowly filling for the past week and now the bank had burst, with the water rushing out of control. How ironic that she'd been so indifferent to Jack Barclay and now had fallen into the arms of this man who was nothing that Jack was and everything Jack was not.

It was this realisation that finally brought her to her senses. She pulled away from him, panicking a little, remembering the family she was supposed to be going to and whom it was holding her so intimately. A man whose loathing for her father could only be equalled by her father's contempt for him. A man who didn't know her real name and would probably hate her for her deception if he found out.

'Oh, Lloyd, this is impossible.' Her voice shook. 'We're worlds apart, you and I. I shouldn't have let this happen.' She knew she should be angry with him, but to be fair she'd invited this.

Lloyd stood there looking at her for a moment, breathing heavily. At last he turned away and busied himself with tightening the girth on his saddle. Then, without another word, he helped her on to her waiting horse and mounted himself. He led them back to the road and they resumed their journey in strained silence.

Miserable and ashamed, Louise watched him covertly. It was as if she'd been living in a dream world these past few days and had suddenly emerged into reality. Hadn't she already done enough to defy her parents without becoming involved with this impoverished selector? She'd mooned over his looks the other night, but the truth of it was that he still looked more the stockman than station-owner in his best clean moleskins, leather leggings, scuffed riding boots and rusty goose-necked spurs.

Certainly she couldn't marry him to put right today's indiscretions–supposing he was of a mind to offer matrimony. That he was attempting to raise himself from the squalor of his origins would count for nothing with her parents.

Lloyd looked up to find her watching him and met her gaze levelly. 'I'm sorry,' he said. 'Sam Naylor asked me to take care of you. I shouldn't have taken advantage of the situation.'

She shook her head, her eyes downcast now. 'I could have prevented it, but I didn't.'

Her honesty did her credit, but did little to ease his shame. It was one thing to kiss her, but he'd taken it further than either of them had intended. He'd wondered about her, true enough, but he suspected now she was more inexperienced than he'd thought. He'd noticed her flushed gaze dropping hesitantly to him and quickly away again, as if this was her first real encounter with the male body. That very innocence and freshness reminded him of his own lack of either. How could he even ask a girl like her to ally herself with someone like him?

He found himself thinking of his old mentor, Mr O'Donnelly, who had lectured him about his attitude to women on several occasions. Lloyd had never hit a woman as his father had hit his mother and he was determined he never would. But at fifteen he'd already learned to drink and had lost his innocence with the type of female O'Donnelly disapproved of. The old bloke had told him any man who couldn't live without liquor and loose women wasn't worth two bob and he'd believed him.

But right now he was impatient of such pious ideals. It was too long since he'd drunk rum with his mates, or enjoyed female company that wasn't oppressively respectable.

Once his errand was discharged Banana would be awaiting him and to hell with behaving himself. If he was too choosy to fraternise with the whores of Banana, at least getting drunk would stop him from thinking about this hopeless attraction that had him tied in knots.

COLONIAL DAUGHTER

Chapter Seven

They arrived at the New Haven turnoff in the early afternoon. Lloyd dismounted to open a set of slip-rails, frowning as he did so. If the Greenwoods couldn't be bothered making a proper gate for their entrance, it didn't bode well for what lay ahead.

The narrow rutted track crossed a deep gully and appeared to lose itself in a patch of brigalow. However it didn't peter out amongst the scrub after all, but continued over the rise and entered a small clearing containing a new weatherboard home. In contrast to the slip-rails, this house suggested a family of some standing.

The outbuildings–a shed of some sort, a meat-house and what appeared to be servants' quarters–were far inferior, all obviously older than the main house, the upright slabs greying and in disrepair. Some of the shingles had fallen from the roofs and a slab hung drunkenly from one of the shed walls, a water-butt disintegrating nearby. The entire appearance of the homestead was one of starkness, for there was no greenery apart from a few native trees. Perhaps any attempt at gardening was discouraged by the fowls scattering in front of their horses' hooves, to say nothing of the small herd of goats watching indifferently from a meagre patch of shade.

As they drew up, two small, grubby children ran out of the house and came to an abrupt halt at the sight of them. One of them turned and sped indoors again, shouting clearly, 'Mama, there's someone here', but the younger, a boy of five or six, stood his ground and stared at them inquisitively. Lloyd dismounted and helped Louise to do the same, then stepped back quickly as his body responded to her nearness yet again. He tied their horses' reins to a hitching rail while Louise asked the child, 'Is your Mama at home? Will you tell her please that the new governess has arrived?'

The boy nodded and turned to obey her, but was pre-empted by the appearance of a middle-aged woman and several children of varying ages at the doorway. The woman was stylishly dressed in a fashionable gown that contrasted strangely with the shabbiness of her children's clothing. Her plump face was set in stern lines of disapproval, the heavy black eyebrows raised suspiciously.

'Who are you? Did I hear you say something about the governess? Surely not–she's not due until Friday.'

'However, I'm afraid you heard correctly.' Louise was at her most charming, smiling and holding out her hand. 'I'm Lucy Forrest and this is Mr Kavanagh, who was kind enough to escort me from Banana. You, I presume, are Mrs Greenwood?'

Lloyd stayed back a little, watching the proceedings with growing amusement. Louise was shameless and he shook his head with wonderment, admiring her polished manners and her sheer gumption in dealing with an impossible situation. It was hard to believe this was the same girl who'd seemed so vulnerable in his arms just a short while before. He suppressed a sigh at the memory.

However, Mrs Greenwood seemed immune to her charm. Her cold gaze flickered to Lloyd and back again. 'But why have you arrived today? Why did you not send us word?' She looked at Louise's riding habit and sniffed derisively. 'An unusual way to present yourself, young lady. Where did you acquire your "escort"?'

He noticed Louise clenching her teeth at the woman's insinuating tone and knowing how volatile her temper could be, quickly stepped in. 'I was introduced to Miss Forrest in Banana, Mrs Greenwood. I have a property on the Dawson and I was in town getting supplies. Seeing as how she was stranded there with no-one come to meet her, I offered to bring her out.'

Mrs Greenwood looked back to Louise, obviously unappeased. 'You haven't explained why you're early. Could it be that we had the dates wrong?'

From her tone, it was obvious she believed no such thing and Louise bit her lip. 'If you'll allow me a moment, Mrs Greenwood, I shall explain. Mr Barclay, my former employer, was called away suddenly with his family to a dying relative. I had nowhere else to go, so I had no alternative but to travel here immediately. Unfortunately my luggage was stolen at Westwood, leaving me with only a valise'– she'd left her swag at Myvanwy – 'and although I notified the police they had little hope of its recovery.'

Lloyd suppressed a grin. It was an unlikely tale at best, yet it was spoken with such candour that Mrs Greenwood was obviously left struggling with the possibility that it might be the truth. She stared hard at Louise for a moment or two and Louise stared unflinchingly back. At last she said ungraciously, 'Since you're here I suppose we may as well allow you to prove your worth, or otherwise. If you'll collect your belongings, I shall show you to your room.' At the doorway she appeared to remember her manners and paused to address Louise's retreating companion, 'If you care to wait a moment, Mr?'

'Kavanagh.'

'Yes, Kavanagh, of course. I can offer you a drink to sustain you on your return journey. A cup of tea, perhaps?'

Lloyd would have preferred to refuse, but he was worried about leaving Louise with this unwelcoming family. He was left waiting outside while Mrs Greenwood hustled her away, so he sat down on the top step, glancing thoughtfully about him at this imposing house, in such stark contrast to its neglected surroundings. He'd heard little of the Greenwood family before and Mrs Greenwood didn't impress him at all, for all that she obviously thought herself far above him.

Louise was ushered through a well-furnished, if untidy sitting room to a bedroom at the far end of the house. It was tiny, containing only a narrow iron bed, a wardrobe and a chest of drawers, the latter also serving as a washstand. Everything was covered in a thick layer of dust. Louise wrinkled her nose in dismay. But she held her tongue–heaven knew she was in no position to complain.

'I hadn't had the room made ready for you, since I wasn't expecting you just yet. I'll send the maid in to deal with it presently. Here, Edith.' The woman signalled a child who was hovering in the background. 'Take the jug and fill it with water so Miss Forrest may wash.'

As Edith obeyed, she continued, 'I shall leave you now. Join us in the dining room when you're ready. It's at the end of the hallway, to the right.'

The child, a girl of about ten or eleven with her mother's dark hair and sharp eyes, returned shortly. She placed the jug on the chest of drawers and stood watching Louise with unconcealed curiosity. 'Your habit's dusty and your hair's all messy. Why'd you come on horseback?'

'Because it was easier than hiring some other conveyance. Mr Kavanagh loaned me the horse.'

'Who's that man with you? Is he your beau?'

Louise was taken aback at the impertinence of this child. She felt herself flushing guiltily. This morning she'd had a clear conscience on that score, at least; now it was difficult to have a clear conscience about anything. 'No, he isn't my beau.'

Edith twirled a lock of her long hair in her fingers, smiling slyly. 'Mama thought he was. I could tell.'

'Could you? Well, I'm afraid your Mama was mistaken.' Louise kept a cool tone, but she'd already formed a distinct dislike of this inquisitive child and her precocious questions, along with her surly mother. 'Will you leave me now, if you please? I'd like to wash.'

Edith accepted the rebuff calmly and departed. Louise washed her face and hands and tidied her hair, before joining Mrs Greenwood and Lloyd at the large polished table in the dining room. She noticed her employer directing doubtful glances at Lloyd over the teapot and could almost read her thoughts.

She was obviously wondering if she should have sent the young man to the kitchen. Considering his dress, it was probably only his mention of owning a property that had saved him. Louise thought irritably how the woman was as much a snob as any Ashford and watched anxiously to see how Lloyd would acquit himself in the way of table manners. However he managed the delicate cup and saucer creditably, due perhaps to the years he'd spent with Mr O'Donnelly, who must surely have been a gentleman.

There was little conversation over afternoon tea and Lloyd didn't linger. Louise made him a little formal speech of thanks in Mrs Greenwood's hearing, as if he was a stranger, and then he was gone, taking Shadow with him as she'd previously requested. It took all her willpower not to call him back and ask him to take her, too. She was left bereft and lonely and more uncertain of the future than she'd ever been.

'Well, well,' tut-tutted Mrs Greenwood as he rode away. 'I cannot say I think much of the way you've been travelling the countryside with that young man. Why, he must be no more than twenty-five. You won't have much reputation left if that's the way you behave. Remember that I'm expected to entrust you with the care of my children.'

Louise gritted her teeth. 'Mr Kavanagh's character was recommended to me. I could see no alternative, unless I was to wait in Banana until Friday and I couldn't afford to stay at the hotel until then.'

'You're never short of a response, are you, Miss? I advise you to watch your step if you wish to remain in my employment.'

With an effort Louise held her tongue. The only thing she would achieve by arguing further was instant dismissal.

After that Mrs Greenwood formally introduced her to all of the children. Maria at fourteen was the eldest but one–her older brother was away at school in Brisbane. Edith was next in age and she was followed by Amy and Julia, seven-year-old twins. The youngest was William, who was five years old.

Maria was very much the young lady. She was tall for her age and physically mature. Louise detected a note of insolence in her manner and suspected she might be reluctant to accept the authority of someone as young as herself. Edith she already disliked and the fair-haired twins looked to be mischievous, lively tomboys, though perhaps more tractable than their older sisters.

There had been no mention of her having the charge of William. He was the most appealing of the five, a sturdy, dark-haired, silent boy with inquiring grey eyes. He regarded her solemnly throughout the introductions and when pushed forward by his mother obediently greeted her with, 'How do you do, Miss Forrest?' They were the first words he'd uttered and Louise wondered if he was often encouraged to speak for himself.

Arthur Greenwood arrived home at dark from a day spent in the paddocks. Louise encountered him in the hallway, a grim-faced man in his mid-forties. He looked at her doubtfully–his wife had obviously informed him of the circumstances of her arrival–but didn't bother to introduce himself, continuing to his bedroom to wash for dinner.

'Ah, Lucy.' Mrs Greenwood descended on her as she entered the dining room. 'You will be taking your meals in the kitchen from now on.'

Louise's mouth dropped open. What had happened to the assurances from the employment agency that she would be treated as a member of the family? About to remind Mrs Greenwood of the fact, she remembered her already precarious circumstances and bit back her retort. Trembling with anger and humiliation, she made her way to the kitchen, holding her head high. The cook and housemaid were busy serving up the family's meals, but they turned to survey her uncertainly.

'I have been told I'm to eat with you.'

'Yes, Miss.' The cook's stern face softened a degree. 'Sit yourself at the table there and we'll have a meal in front of you shortly.'

They were joined by two station hands, one little more than a lad, the other probably forty years his senior. Both were roughly dressed and looked her up and down in an assessing manner, further increasing Louise's discomfort.

'My, we've got a swell here,' the older man observed as the cook introduced them. 'How'd you end up at this blasted place, girlie?'

The young fellow sniggered and Louise turned away, not deigning to answer. How was she supposed to deal with such impertinence? She ate in uncomfortable silence, leaving her companions to engage in desultory conversation amongst themselves.

She excused herself as soon as the meal was over and retired to bed, anxious for some time alone. But sleep wouldn't come. Her indignation and growing unease with her present situation made her toss restlessly and she sought refuge in thoughts of Lloyd Kavanagh and the kisses they'd exchanged. The gentleness of that first interlude had stunned and captivated her, unexpected as it was, in a man of his class and culture. The raw desire of their second embrace had been, if possible, even more exciting and infinitely more disturbing. She had wondered what it would be like to kiss a man—really kiss him, that is, with depth and passion. Now she knew and the memory made her blood surge.

Yet she could hardly have chosen a less suitable partner. She thought miserably of the empty farewell she and Kavanagh had exchanged and wondered if she would see him again. Perhaps it would be best if she didn't. With the attraction between them brought into the open, the easy friendship they'd shared was over. But sadly, in her new life as Lucy Forrest, Lloyd was the closest thing to a friend she had.

The next few days did nothing to improve on Louise's first impressions. Mrs Greenwood continued to treat her as a servant, which was particularly infuriating since in other circumstances the woman would have been her social inferior. There is no snob to equal the social climber and this title Louise mentally applied to Mrs Greenwood. Her husband ignored domestic matters, but the children with the exception of William were dreadful. Edith was cheeky and Maria was lazy, vain and arrogant. The twins would have been tolerable without their sisters' influence and after several days Louise did succeed in exerting some authority over them. However Maria and Edith set out to defy her every order. It was useless for Louise to appeal to their mother for support.

On the second day of lessons Mrs Greenwood brought up the subject of William. 'I hadn't intended to begin William's schooling just yet, but I'm sure he would be little trouble if he sat in on the girls' lessons. If he learns something of the Three Rs, he'll find it that much easier next year.'

The truth, Louise knew, was the woman wanted him off her hands. She agreed only because she wasn't in a position to refuse, but the girls were such a handful that she'd little time to spare for William. The twins' lessons were still of a very elementary standard, but a five-year-old isn't inclined to sit quietly and learn of his own volition particularly when classes were disrupted as often as hers were. Much as she would have enjoyed sitting with William and teaching him his letters, she simply was not able to and his presence put a further strain on her resources.

Meal times continued to be an ordeal. The two women treated her kindly enough, but the men seemed to relish making her uncomfortable. They always sat to dinner in their dirty work clothes and their language was crude and generally disrespectful to the three women. Complaints about the food were usual, although justified, since their meals could only be served after the family had taken their fill. Sometimes there was only a scraping of stew left in the bottom of the pot and they had to fill up with bread and dripping.

'She's a right old tyrant,' the cook complained. 'She don't stint herself at all, but she looks over me shoulder all the time making sure I don't cook too much.'

'A bitch is what she is,' the old man growled. 'Don't know why I put up with it.'

'Yeah, a man should bloody up an' leave,' the younger one agreed.

Louise only wished they would. If she was a man, she wouldn't stay a moment longer.

For two weeks she tolerated the situation. Two weeks of going to bed hungry, feeling alone and ill-at-ease much of the time. Her hours in the schoolroom were an ordeal of constant, purposeful irritation on the part of the two older girls and of high-spirited naughtiness on that of the twins. If she'd had anywhere else to go, she wouldn't have stayed beyond the second day, but as it was she could hardly afford to leave. Without a reference from the Greenwoods it would be futile to apply for further positions.

So she kept a tight control over her temper, until the day when Maria overstepped the mark.

The confrontation was prompted by something as trivial as her shortage of clothes. The Louise Ashford of old had owned a closet full of gowns, but now, as Lucy Forrest, she had two dresses to choose from and a barely adequate supply of underwear. She had to wash her clothing every few days, an unaccustomed burden. However Mrs Greenwood maintained the maid had enough chores to do without taking on the governess' laundry, which was true enough.

Finally, with an air of longsuffering, Mrs Greenwood decided to lend 'Lucy' one of her oldest gowns, until she was able to order new ones from a dressmaker in Banana. Louise inexpertly took in the seams and lengthened the hem, but the result was dowdy and ill-fitting and she hated herself in it. The niggling thought came to her that perhaps life in England would have been better than *this*, but she swiftly discarded the treacherous notion. Her pride wouldn't allow her to admit she might have been wrong after all.

She expected the children to have something to say about her attire when she assembled them in the classroom that morning and they didn't disappoint her.

'Why, Miss Forrest!' exclaimed Maria, all wide-eyed innocence, 'Isn't that Mama's gown?' She began to snigger. 'I never did like it much, but it looks rather ghastly on you. All shapeless, like a black gin's dress!'

Her snigger was echoed by the other three girls, while William stared at her in puzzlement, not comprehending their humour. Louise banged a ruler against her desk and snapped, 'Enough of your impertinence, Maria. You won't speak again unless you are spoken to, is that clear?'

'No,' retorted the girl, openly rebellious now, her smile gone and with it every vestige of innocence. 'It isn't clear. I don't see why I should have to do what *you* tell me. Why, only last night I heard Mama saying to Papa that she wished it were not so hard to get governesses out here, as she'd disliked you from the very first! She said your morals seemed very loose and she wasn't at all sure she believed your story about the missing luggage. She thought Papa should make a few inquiries about you–and find out where you met your *"escort"*!'

Her jeering emphasis on the last word made the insinuation obvious. It was that shaft in particular that struck home. Louise stared at Maria's triumphant, malicious face, a red tide of fury taking her past caution.

'How dare you speak to me like that! If you were really a young lady, you wouldn't understand what you're implying. Come up here and stand in the corner. You may stay there until lunchtime and during the lunch break you will write, two hundred times, 'I must not repeat malicious gossip.' And if I find even one spelling mistake you'll write it another two hundred times.'

Maria was on her feet now, her face white. 'No, I shall not and you can't make me. If you think Mama will side with you, you're much mistaken.'

Louise crossed quickly to the girl's chair and dealt her a resounding slap on the cheek. Maria stepped back, her hand raised to her reddened face.

'How *dare* you? I'm going to tell Mama! You'll be sorry!'

She turned and sped out of the room and Louise stood still for a moment, breathing rapidly. She'd burnt her bridges now, but until she was told otherwise, she'd carry on here. She squared her trembling shoulders and confronted the girls, who were gaping at her. William was grizzling softly into his desk. How she wished he hadn't witnessed that dreadful scene.

She forced herself to speak calmly. 'Let us begin lessons. Edith, you may attempt those sums you couldn't do yesterday and Amy and Julia, open your readers at page fifteen. William, you pay attention with the twins. And please stop crying–everything will be all right.'

As she'd expected, Mrs Greenwood wasn't long in coming. She marched into the schoolroom, eyebrows bristling, disrupting the renewed peace and quiet.

'Miss Forrest, my daughter has come to me with the most incredible story of your conduct. I find it unbelievable. How you obtained a reference from your last employer I shall never know and I plan to write to the agency and complain. Do you have anything to say in your defence?'

'Actually, I have.' Louise faced her defiantly, in spite of a heaving stomach and a growing urge to be sick. 'I've never had the charge of a more disagreeable, insolent child than your eldest daughter. Until she's encouraged to have some respect for authority I think you will continue to have problems with her tutors.'

Mrs Greenwood's face was an angry, mottled red. 'How dare you? Who gave you the right to criticize my daughter? After your behaviour I can only wonder at your impertinence. You give yourself these superior airs, but your actions in using physical violence against my daughter give the true picture of your origins.'

'As does your behaviour,' countered Louise coldly, 'in conducting a brawl with me in the schoolroom. Don't you think we should conclude this interview in private?'

The woman flushed even redder and swept out without a word, gesturing brusquely for Louise to follow. She led her to her husband's study and shut the door, her chest heaving. 'You may leave at once.' She scrabbled in a drawer and finding a pound note, thrust it at Louise. 'Please go and pack. I shall send for one of the men to take you into town. And don't ask me for a reference.'

'I wouldn't dream of asking you for anything.' Louise barely restrained herself from slamming the door on her way out.

Chapter Eight

Charles Ashford paced up and down the Barclay's sitting room, barely restraining the urge to throw something. He could hardly believe his sister's temerity and stupidity in running away as she had, and her complete defiance of his instructions. Then there was her lack of consideration for the Barclay family. Mary Barclay had been so distressed when he arrived at Sherborne, it had been left to James to explain Louise's deceitful flight.

To his credit James had glossed over the worst of it–the things she'd to all intents and purposes stolen, regardless of the money left in payment. Mary seemed not to care about the lost possessions at all. The poor woman was hardly coherent, apart from pleading with him to forgive them for not preventing Louise's rash behaviour.

'What is there to forgive, Cousin Mary?' Charles bit back his anger in an effort to be gracious. 'You've done more than enough for that ungrateful baggage. Why should you have suspected what she was planning? When I find her she'll feel the sting of my whip, I can assure you.'

Mary looked at him, her face pale and pinched with anxiety. She seemed almost afraid of him and he battled to conceal his impatience. Thankfully James seemed to have kept his wits about him.

'Oh, if we could only know that she's safe." Mary was saying. "I could forgive her for behaving so badly, if we could be assured of that. But when I think of her travelling out there, alone and unprotected, with all the ruffians who are on the roads these days, to say nothing of the blacks–and no-one seems to have seen her. It's as if she has disappeared into thin air.'

For James and the two boys had already searched and asked innumerable questions of travellers and townspeople, with no success. Charles could only hope the girl hadn't been raped or murdered, or both. Even if she reached this position she was going to without mishap, she would have compromised her good name by travelling unchaperoned. It was difficult to ask questions without creating a scandal, but he was beginning to think a possible scandal was of secondary importance to Louise's safety.

Charles borrowed a fresh horse from his cousins and rode into Gainsford. James had told him that he'd already asked discreet questions of the townspeople, but he would have to ask them again. Surely someone had seen her.

An Indian hawker was camping beside the river, his bony, overworked horse hobbled beside his overburdened wagonette. This would be just the person to ask, as the hawkers travelled widely and missed nothing and most of them never seemed to forget a face.

'Yes, I remember Missy Ashford.' The man smiled at Charles ingratiatingly. 'I visit Sherborne on Friday. I bring mail from Gainsford–there two letters for Missy Ashford. She take them and go away–she not buy anything.'

'You haven't seen her since then? Travelling on the road, perhaps?'

'No, sir. She has run away?'

'We believe she went riding and got herself lost. I would appreciate it if you could keep an eye out for her. Should you happen to see her send me word at this address.' Charles quickly scribbled his name and address on a scrap of paper. 'I will make it worth your while.'

The hawker looked at the piece of paper slyly. 'If she lost, maybe black trackers find her?'

'We're about to send for the black trackers. But in the meantime, if you see or hear of anything…'

The hawker put the piece of paper in his pocket. 'I will look out for her. I travel many miles, I see many people. I never forget.'

Charles could see he was suspicious of the story, but that was too bad. 'Good man.' He swung into his saddle. 'I hope we find her before it's too late.'

Gainsford yielded nothing. It seemed she hadn't ridden this way, or at least not by road. Charles decided to retrace his steps to Westwood, after buying some food from the storekeeper to replenish his saddlebags. He camped by the road that night and embarked on a similar round of questioning when he arrived at the railway terminus. At last he found a lead, although it was a tenuous one and it made him even more frustrated and angry, for it seemed he'd ridden in the wrong direction.

'I heard a story about a woman travelling alone,' a bullocky camped at Westwood told him. 'I was stopped at Gainsford a week ago and these two fellows rode up to the camp. They'd come from Springsure. They mentioned they'd seen a woman riding sidesaddle, coming down the road towards Bauhinia Downs. They said she was young and dressed swanky-like. Not the sort you'd expect to see on her own.'

'Did they describe her, or her horse?'

The man shrugged. 'I can't remember that they did. I had a couple of me bullocks sick and I was full of me own troubles. I didn't ask no questions.'

'Do you know these men?'

'No, we didn't get 'round to exchanging names. They said they was going on to Rockhampton. Christ knows where they'd be by now.'

With no more information forthcoming he retraced his steps to Sherborne to inform the Barclays of this latest, hopeful lead. He stayed overnight and caught his own horse in the morning, before setting off towards Bauhinia Downs.

In her room Louise sat on the bed for a moment, hands clenched, trying to contain the anger that made her whole body tremble. At last she snatched her valise from the top of the wardrobe and roughly bundled her clothes into it, keeping aside one of her dresses and exchanging it for Mrs Greenwood's gown. She threw the offending garment fiercely to the floor and, gathering her possessions, left the room without a backward glance.

She set her valise on the front step and sat beside it to wait for the station hand who'd been dispatched to take her to town. Gazing about her contemptuously, her eyes fastened on every feature of neglect and indifference. For all Mrs Greenwood's pretensions her husband apparently couldn't afford a gardener and "Madam" was too busy playing the grand lady to exert herself to plant a shrub or two. What hope had those children of ever amounting to anything with a mother like that and a father who ignored them all?

At last Pat, the younger of the two station hands, drove up in the buggy and climbed down to take Louise's valise. She brushed aside his offer of help and stepped unaided into the vehicle. Then she found herself retracing her steps on the road she'd travelled with Lloyd Kavanagh such a short time before.

Pat, ill-mannered at the best of times, seemed to think her status as the dismissed governess made her easy prey. Louise quickly snubbed him and moved as far away from him as her narrow seat would allow. She thought it was typical of Mrs Greenwood to be critical of her choice of escort and then subject her to being alone with this young ruffian, who was more offensive than Lloyd Kavanagh had ever been.

She was still fuming inwardly when they reached Banana. The station hand dropped her off in the main street, outside a hotel named for the town, leaving her to book a room there and transfer her belongings. The hotel was a low, unimposing building, but the room she was shown to was clean and the young maid who brought her water was friendly and pretty in a pert, round-cheeked fashion. Once Louise had freshened herself up she wandered off to look at the town. She knew she must decide what to do with her future. The anger that had carried her through her confrontation with Mrs Greenwood was beginning to ebb, leaving her sick with uncertainty.

Bowen Street was lined with numerous shops and houses: blacksmiths, saddlers, two general stores, a Post Office and another hotel, the Commercial, further down the hill opposite the Police Reserve. Today, being mid-week, it was extremely busy. The main street hummed with people and vehicles of every description–horse and bullock wagons, drays, buggies, buckboards and gigs. She watched a Chinaman sell fresh vegetables from his cart and followed the progress of a man, presumably a horse dealer, with a string of horses of all colours and pedigrees.

With nothing else to do, she strolled down the flat towards the lagoon. The long, narrow waterhole stretched for over a quarter of a mile in length, patches of water lilies persisting in it despite the dry season and the churned, muddy edges. She counted six bullock wagons drawn up around it, along with the campsites of other travellers. Pausing for a moment to survey the scene, her mind worked busily.

What was she to do now? Should she stay in Banana and try to obtain another position with children? It would be difficult, if not impossible, with neither credentials nor references. She bit her lip, realising how easily she could find herself slipping into a less acceptable form of employment.

Louise retraced her steps and as she passed Fitzpatrick's general store she noticed a big creamy horse tied to the rail in front of it. Her pulse tripped.

Stepping closer, she recognised the LK brand on the near shoulder and the splash of white on the off hind pastern. Her heart thumped. She'd thought she wouldn't see Lloyd again, but that was ill-considered, since he still had the care of her horse, her saddle and her swag. She badly wanted to talk to him, to tell him about Mrs Greenwood and the circumstances of her dismissal as she couldn't confide in anyone else. Lloyd at least knew something of her background story.

She waited there beside Dynamite, resting her hands on the hitching rail, her back to the store. When she heard his step behind her she turned slowly, reading the surprise on his face and the guarded pleasure.

'Louise! Er… Miss Forrest.' He glanced quickly about him as if to assure himself that she was alone. 'What are you doing here?'

'Looking for another job.' Her name had never sounded so good as it did on his lips, but it would be foolish to give him leave to use it. She smiled and absently reached out to stroke Dynamite's neck. The big horse snorted and sidled away. 'I wasn't altogether much of a success with Mrs Greenwood.'

'I told you that you wouldn't be.' His tone was sharp. 'I could see she didn't like it one bit, the way you turned up there.'

'Yes, but that was only part of the problem.' Louise shifted restlessly as a couple strolled past them, glancing curiously in their direction, and entered the store. 'Is there somewhere we can talk without interruption?'

He grabbed his horse's reins and took her arm. 'Let's walk towards the lagoon.' As they left the noise and bustle behind them he asked, 'Now, what's all this about? And what are you planning to do?'

She laughed. 'That's a good question. It is precisely what I've been trying to decide.'

'What happened? Did Mrs Greenwood give you the boot?'

'To put it crudely, yes. I had the biggest row imaginable with her. Oh, how I detest that woman. And her precious offspring are worse.' She related the events of that morning, her eyes flashing with renewed fury. Kavanagh listened intently, looking faintly incredulous as she outlined the scene with Maria.

'Crikey, you'll never keep a job at this rate. Still,' he grinned, 'I wouldn't have minded being a fly on the wall. I reckon you'd be a match for old Green Ant any day.'

'Green Ant!' She had to laugh, knowing the fiery sting of a green ant's bite. 'What an apt description!'

Lloyd's eyes glinted as they shared the moment of humour. Then he sobered. 'So–she didn't give you a reference, of course.'

'Of course. That accounts for my present predicament. Without wishing to sound vain, I don't lack qualifications–I thought of setting up as a music teacher. That woman would soon blacken my character, though. And I don't have the finance.' She sighed. 'The trouble is, my temperament isn't suited to being a governess. It's not that I don't enjoy the children, providing they can be disciplined, but I just can't tolerate having to kowtow to women like Mrs Greenwood.'

Lloyd didn't reply immediately. He seemed deep in thought and after a moment he said, 'You know, I've got an idea. I know a family who might have you. The kids are likeable, though I can't promise they're little angels, and their mother is nothing like Mrs Greenwood. The Jamiesons.'

'Your neighbours?' Louise's response was eager. 'Do you think there's a possibility?'

'You never know. They did have a tutor last year, but he left and Mrs Jamieson's been teaching the children herself, with the help of the oldest girl, Mercy. But Mercy's not keen. There's eight of 'em all together. I don't remember all their ages, but Mercy's sixteen and there are two boys who are working with their father now.'

'But there remains the problem of no reference.'

'Look, Miss Forrest, we'll have to tell 'em the truth. This pack of lies you've been spinning will only get you into trouble. I'll tell 'em how I met you at Bauhinia Downs and how you helped with the cattle. Young Cec was there to make it decent. I'll say your job with the Greenwoods didn't work out and when they hear what she was like they'll probably give you their full sympathy.'

'I hope you're right.' But she wouldn't be telling them the whole truth, only the truth as Lloyd knew it and God knew that was fabrication enough.

'And if they won't have you, I really think you ought to go to England, to your family. The bush is no place for a girl like you on her own. You're not likely to meet someone your father would want you to marry around here. I'll lend you the money for the fare if you haven't got enough.'

Louise set her mouth stubbornly. 'Thank you, but I have no intention of going to my family. I've already told you, I don't care for them and I don't want to live in England. This is where I was born and this is where I mean to stay.'

He gave an exasperated grimace. 'You know, for bloody pigheadedness you take some beating.'

She raised her eyebrows haughtily. 'Your language is offensive, Mr Kavanagh.'

'Sorry. But I'm just a rough and ready ex-teamster, remember. Where are you staying tonight?'

'I booked a room at the Banana.'

'I'll walk you back there, then. I'll see the Jamiesons in the morning and if they're interested they can come in and talk to you. Have you got enough money to put up here for a few days?'

'But of course. I can use the time to organise some clothing.' She dropped the arrogant tone and looked up at him uncertainly. 'I hate to put you to so much inconvenience, though. Did you have business in town?'

'Yes, but I've finished it,' he retorted abruptly.

Louise looked at him curiously. His colour was heightened and his eyes shifted away from her scrutiny. To see Lloyd Kavanagh discomforted was something new. Just what was this business of his?

Outside the hotel she paused, looking up at him uncertainly. 'You'll let me know if the Jamiesons don't require my services?'

'Of course I will. It's not far to ride in.'

She smiled wryly. 'Only twenty-odd miles. I hate to ask more favours of you. I don't know how to thank you, Mr Kavanagh.'

He swung into his saddle and sat there looking down at her, smiling into her eyes with his usual confidence restored. 'You can call me Lloyd, like you did the other day.'

Her gaze locked with his and her colour rose with a combination of excitement and embarrassment. She knew he was remembering more than just her use of his Christian name. His eyes gleamed with devilry as he added, 'But not here in the street.'

He turned his horse away and rode off before she could think of a suitable retort.

Lloyd rode over to see his neighbours early the next morning, hoping to catch Jock Jamieson before he left the homestead. He was in luck, for Jock was shoeing a horse at the shed when he arrived.

'G'day to ye,' the Scotsman greeted him, turning from his task of stoking the forge. Sweat ran down the middle-aged man's flushed face and trickled into a heavy, flowing beard that seemed to diminish the proportions of his slight frame. 'And what brings ye over so early, lad?'

'I'd like a word with you if you can spare a moment.' Lloyd dismounted and propped himself against the shed wall, the heat of the forge reaching out to him in shimmering waves.

'Well, out with it! This old nag can wait a few minutes.'

'Jock, it's about a girl I've met back in Banana. She's looking for a job as a governess and I thought of your family.'

Jock stared at him with an expression of incredulity. 'Surely ye don't mean that maid at the hotel that I hear talk ye've been messing with?'

'No, not her.' Lloyd felt himself flushing at the note of censure in the older man's voice. He wished it was possible to do anything in Banana without the whole community knowing about it. 'She's nothing like her. She's a young lady. Her name's Lucy Forrest, from near Rockhampton. She was working for the Barclays of Sherborne and she went to the Greenwood family on the Westwood road, but that didn't work out.'

'Ye seem to be going mad for the lassies all of a sudden, Lloyd. How did ye meet this one?'

Shifting uncomfortably, Lloyd began his story, telling how Louise had asked for his escort from Bauhinia Downs. After describing their trip he paused in his uncharacteristic fiddling with his horse's reins and looked up at his neighbour. 'Crikey, she's a girl and a half—as game as they come. And she can ride like the devil.'

Jock Jamieson's face had registered a number of conflicting emotions during his narrative, but the chief one was amazement. 'Sounds a pretty wild sort of lass—and ye're asking us to take her on to look after our bairns?'

Lloyd shook his head. 'She's a bit headstrong, I'll admit, but she *is* a lady. Her clothes and the way she talks—the family's got plenty of land and money. Her parents have shifted back to England and she won't go with 'em. She hasn't got anywhere else to go now and that old hag Mrs Greenwood didn't give her a reference.'

'So she had a wee bit o' trouble with Mrs Greenwood?'

'Yeah, but if you met the woman you'd know why. I took Miss Forrest out there and it seemed a queer set-up. They gave her a hard time from the start. The kids were spoilt rotten.' He paused and looked at Jock appealingly. 'I wish you'd talk to Mrs Jamieson about it. You said yourself she's been flat out since the tutor left and Mercy would sooner be out in the paddock.'

'That's as may be,' agreed Jamieson, 'but ye're asking us to take on a lass that we know nothing of bar that she spent nearly a week traipsing around the bush with ye. We don't want your floosie foisted onto us, lad. If ye want to do the right thing by her, ye had better marry her.'

'Look, Jock,' said Lloyd, impatience outweighing embarrassment, 'I wish you'd get it out of your head that she's me woman. She's a sight too grand for me–she wouldn't have me if I asked her. And she is a lady, even if it don't sound that way. Hell, I wouldn't ask you to take on some trollop to teach your kids.'

'No, I guess not, at that. But how did she come to be roaming about by herself in the first place?'

'I'm still not sure. She had to leave the Barclays in a hurry, but she wouldn't tell me much about it. I gather she wanted to get away from some rake that was coming to visit.'

Jamieson offered Lloyd tobacco and filled his own pipe. He returned the pouch to his pocket and puffed in silence for a moment. 'Ye know, all this that ye've told me ain't much of a reference.'

'I suppose it isn't. But that's why I'm asking you. At least I can tell you the full story like I couldn't tell anyone else. And I wouldn't ask you if I didn't think she would be a good teacher for your kids. She's had a sight more education than the pair of us put together.'

'Och, I don't know, lad. I'll have to talk to Harriet and see what she's got to say. What did ye say the lass's name was?'

'Miss Forrest. Lucy Forrest.'

'Aye, well.' He lifted the horse's near fore and held a shoe against it, assessing the fit. 'I'm not making any promises, mind ye.' He dropped the hoof and turned to look up at Lloyd under raised brows. 'What about this lass at the Banana, then? She's not the sort to do ye any good. I thought better of ye than to get mixed up with a hussy. Just be careful she doesn't try and trap ye.'

'I'm finished with her now.' Lloyd shrugged away his inner shame. 'I was a fool, I suppose, but I'd had a bit much to drink.'

'Well, I was married by the time I was your age. I hadn't been near a woman afore that.' He surveyed Lloyd gravely. 'Though I suppose I never drank, either. I'd hate to see ye going down the same road as your old man.'

Sometimes Lloyd found himself wishing his neighbour was a normal, fallible sinner like himself. 'Jock, I saw what the grog did to him and just because I had a few the other night doesn't mean I'm about to follow in his tracks.'

Jock regarded him soberly. 'I know ye think it's nothing to do with me, but ye haven't got your family to look out for ye.' He turned back to his horse. 'I'll talk to Harriet when I'm finished here, but don't be surprised if she doesn't like it.'

Chapter Nine

Louise had little to do in Banana but while away the hours in her hotel room. A message that she had visitors had her hurrying downstairs, her stomach squirming in a confusion of anticipation and dread.

A middle-aged couple awaited her in the hotel lounge. The woman stepped forward to shake her hand. 'Miss Forrest, I take it? We are Mr and Mrs Jamieson from Kilbride.'

Mrs Jamieson was a plain, stern-looking woman with dark hair drawn severely back from a center parting. She went on to ask a lot of questions which Louise tried to answer truthfully without revealing too much. Her little, heavily-bearded husband seemed less intimidating, but made no attempt to hide his surprise as he ran his shrewd eyes over her clothing. Her gown, though the plainest Louise owned, was of better fabric and tailoring than anything she had seen in the streets of Banana.

'Ye seem a bit flash for a governess,' he told her. 'No sense us taking on a lass who thinks she's above ordinary folks like us.'

'Mr Jamieson, I shall be grateful for any respectable post.'

'And so you should be, in the circumstances,' his wife interjected. 'But I'm willing to take you on trial. You seem to be well-qualified. I can only wonder why you've compromised your good name with your recent behaviour. I know'—she waved her hand dismissively at Louise's protest —'you've given me a lot of excuses, but I think there's a bit more to it. However, if you can behave yourself, I'm prepared to put that behind us. Perhaps you'll be able to encourage our eldest daughter in some feminine pursuits.'

Louise breathed a sigh of relief. 'Thank you for giving me a chance, Mrs Jamieson. I shan't fail you.' It was an echo of her words to Lloyd and she'd proved them true.

'But be warned, young lady. At the first hint of trouble you'll be out the door.'

Louise soon discovered that Mrs Jamieson had a kind heart under that forbidding exterior. She'd expected to be under scrutiny for the first week or so and conceded the fairness of that in the circumstances. But her new employer was also just, giving credit where it was due.

She wondered why sixteen-year-old Mercy didn't help her mother with her siblings' lessons, until she realized Mercy had a greater interest in animals than young children. The girl was more likely to be found helping her father and brothers with the mustering than assisting her mother with home and family. She possessed a menagerie of pets—a cat, several dogs, a young poddy calf she fed from a bucket, an orphaned kangaroo-rat and a white sulphur-crested cockatoo in a cage. That was to say nothing of her horses.

From the first day, Mercy seemed to dislike her but the other children were less of a challenge. Andrew and Donald, at fifteen and thirteen respectively, were already working and weren't her concern, while little Gertie hadn't begun her schooling. Maggie, Annie, Agnes and Maurice accepted her readily and quickly settled into a routine. They were intelligent, likeable children, sometimes mischievous, but always responsive to discipline. After an initial period of adjustment, Louise found herself handling their lessons with confidence. She would set the older children some sums while she attended to Agnes and Maurice, or alternately busy these two with their copybooks while Maggie and Annie recited their spelling.

On Saturdays Louise often took her pupils on a nature study excursion, accompanied by Mercy and occasionally by Andrew and Donald. At other times the entire family picnicked by the river, near a big waterhole where the young ones caught perch and jewfish and rowed in a small dinghy kept for navigating the river at flood-time.

The Jamiesons lived simply, but they were a happy, close family. Mrs Jamieson told Louise how she'd emigrated from England as a young woman, meeting and marrying the Scottish-born Jock in Brisbane. Jock had selected their property, Kilbride, in 1862, initially stocking it with sheep. Thanks to the ravages of dingoes, Jock had replaced them with cattle in recent years, but an aging Chinese shepherded a small, remnant flock used mostly as "killers", providing meat for the station's consumption.

Even with Louise's help with the children, Mrs Jamieson seemed to be endlessly working, keeping the big slab-house clean and tidy, making bread, jam and preserves and sewing clothing for the entire family. There was only one household servant, a young Aboriginal girl who answered to Elsie, her tribal name forgotten to all but herself. Mr Jamieson employed one stockman, a middle-aged man called Ernie Bates. Louise saw little of him as he always ate his meals in the kitchen with Elsie.

Here, she actually *was* allowed to dine with the family.

One Saturday afternoon when the men folk were out on the run shifting cattle, their neighbour came to visit. Louise noticed Lloyd's arrival from her position near the window where she was helping Mercy with some troublesome needlework, but she said nothing. She had her suspicions as to why Mercy wasn't particularly friendly towards her.

The girl lifted her head as voices floated through the window. She jumped to her feet and hastened to look out.

'Why, it's Mr Kavanagh!' Mercy's eyes brightened, her colour rising as she brought her hand up to her cheek. She came away from the window, giving a little childish half-skip and deposited her embroidery carelessly on her chair. 'I'm going out–are you coming, Miss Forrest?'

'Yes, since there would be no point in remaining here without you. Now, Mercy, walk out like a lady–don't run, please.'

She followed her charge sedately, trying to stifle her own quiver of anticipation. It was bad enough to have Mercy swooning over Lloyd; she was determined not to join her in making an idiot of herself.

Lloyd was standing at the top of the veranda steps and she heard Mrs Jamieson apologise for her husband's absence and invite him to join them for afternoon tea. As they sat about the table drinking tea and eating scones, Mercy added her own invitation.

'Miss Forrest is taking the children for a walk shortly. Will you come with us, Mr Kavanagh?'

Lloyd glanced from Mercy to Louise. 'Where are you going?'

'Donald came across an emu's nest in the horse-paddock the other day. We're hoping to find it.'

'Yes and he said it had nine eggs in it!' Maurice interjected. 'I've never seen an emu's nest. What about you, Mr Kavanagh?'

'Not for a while.' He smiled indulgently at the little boy. 'Since your father's not here, I may as well go with you.'

Except for Mercy, the young Jamiesons seemed to regard Lloyd much as they would a favourite uncle. Louise wondered if he was aware of Mercy's infatuation. Surely he must be; her occasional naive attempts at indifference were as transparent as her usual eager seeking of his attention. And Lloyd was far from obtuse.

They set out, having donned shady hats and stout walking shoes. There had been some discussion on whether Gertie should accompany them.

'She'd better stay with me,' Mrs Jamieson said. 'You could be hours on this wild goose chase. She won't be able to keep up.'

'It's not a wild goose chase, Mother,' broke in Maurice indignantly. 'It's an emu, not a goose.'

'That's just an expression, Maurice. A figure of speech. Now, please don't interrupt me.'

Four-year-old Gertie had meanwhile broken into sobs. 'But I wanna go! Please lemme go!'

'I can carry her if she knocks up,' offered Lloyd. 'She's only a little scrap.'

'I shouldn't give in to her, but, very well. If you don't mind, Lloyd.'

Louise stiffened as Mrs Jamieson turned her penetrating gaze on her. Did she suspect his motives in joining this expedition? She would have to be careful. She couldn't afford to have her employer suspicious of their relationship.

The children ran ahead, searching an area across the gully that Donald had described to them. Louise followed at a sedate speed and Lloyd fell in beside her. Mercy seemed undecided, not running with the children, but obviously impatient with their relaxed pace.

Once Mercy had moved out of earshot, Lloyd turned to smile at her. 'Are you happy with your new job, Miss Forrest?'

'Yes, very.' She returned his smile. 'I'm already attached to the children and Mr and Mrs Jamieson are very kind to me. I haven't thanked you for securing the position for me.'

'Don't mention it. They wouldn't have taken you on if they hadn't liked you. Jock didn't seem to think much of it at first.'

'Thank you, nevertheless. You seem fated to come to my rescue.'

He gave a brief smile. 'I wonder if Mrs Greenwood's got herself another governess yet?'

'If she has, I feel sorry for the girl. I'm not surprised she hasn't found one who'll stay.'

He chuckled. 'Perhaps I should go into business escorting 'em backwards and forwards.'

'Oh, Lloyd.' Laughter bubbled out of her. 'Mrs Greenwood would love that.'

Awareness leapt between them as she met those grey-green eyes, still smiling but suddenly intense. Suddenly she realized she'd used his first name and mentally chided herself. The consequence of such familiarity had been proved to her already.

It was right there between them now, though they kept on walking, not touching despite the memories which still shocked Louise with their intimacy. Her blood rushed hot in her veins as she saw Lloyd swallow, his eyes intent on hers. She turned away quickly to break the rising tension.

Mercy chose that moment to rejoin them, her possessive attitude towards Lloyd apparently overtaking her desire to discover the emu's nest. The girl stared at them with open suspicion. 'What are you two talking about?'

'Nothing much.' Louise smiled at her, relieved at the distraction. 'We were just discussing my former employer, Mrs Greenwood.'

'What was she like?'

She met Lloyd's eyes briefly. 'A dragon. I had better not say any more. I don't wish to set you an example of disrespect for your elders.'

Mercy's colour rose and she looked at Louise as if she wished her far away. It was obvious she'd sensed the undercurrents and perhaps treating her like a child wasn't the answer. Mercy turned away in a huff and almost ran to rejoin the children.

Louise cleared her throat uneasily. 'This is none of my business, Mr Kavanagh, but do you realize how that girl feels about you?'

Lloyd looked uncomfortable. 'I can't help that. She'll grow out of it–she's only a kid.'

'She's sixteen,' she reminded him. 'She's not so much younger than I.'

'She seems much younger. I don't think Mrs Jamieson would fancy me as a son-in-law, anyway.'

Surprised, she darted him a sidelong glance. 'I thought she liked you.'

He shrugged. 'She's always nice to me, but she doesn't approve of me background. Jock doesn't let it worry him, but they're both so religious and strait-laced and I haven't been inside a church in years. I'm a Catholic and they're Presbyterian. Do you go to church, Louise?'

'We used to go, as a family, when we visited Rockhampton.' Her mouth twisted. 'It was the thing to do, to be seen at church. I imagine my parents will be attending Sunday Service regularly now, trying to impress the–'

She broke off abruptly as Maurice ran up and clutched her hand.

'We've found the nest!' The little boy was almost out of breath. 'The emu was sitting on it, but she ran away as soon as she saw us.'

'He, you mean,' Lloyd corrected him. 'The male emu sits on the eggs. Or so they say. How many are there?'

'There's nine. I know, 'cause I counted 'em!'

Lloyd looked surprised. 'Can you count to nine, Maurice?'

'I can count to a hundred!' Maurice stamped his foot indignantly. 'I'm six years old, you know!'

Louise glanced at Lloyd, catching his wink. She suppressed a smile. 'Mr Kavanagh's only teasing you, Maurice.'

But the little boy's attention was already elsewhere. He was tugging at Lloyd's arm. 'Come and look at the nest. It's flat on the ground, in the middle of nowhere! And the eggs are beaut. They're big and blackish-green, with bumps all over 'em! Do you think you could blow one for me, Mr Kavanagh?'

'I'll give it a go. Come on, Miss Forrest. We'd better have a look at this nest.'

The eggs were as Maurice had said, out in the middle of nowhere. There was no evidence that the bird had prepared the spot at all and why that particular spot had been chosen over any other was mystery. The eggs were about the size of a grapefruit, only oval, with a pitted surface.

'Why doesn't the emu make a proper nest?' Maggie asked.

'I don't know. Perhaps the lack of nest is, in its way, a type of camouflage.' Louise picked up an egg and turned it over in her hand, examining it closely.

'Which one do you want, Maurice?' Lloyd crouched beside the little boy, thankfully distracting him before he could ask what 'camouflage' meant.

After inspecting each one in turn and squabbling with Gertie, who thought she should choose, Maurice eventually made his selection. Gertie stood there wailing, her eyes and nose streaming, so to placate her Lloyd threw her onto his shoulder for a ride home. Louise watched him take his hat in one hand and steady the little girl by grasping her sturdy legs, while Gertie clutched his bare head. She was laughing now, despite her tear-streaked face.

As she watched Louise was surprised by Lloyd's ease with the little girl. Of course, he'd had a whole family of younger brothers and sisters, but it hadn't sounded as if he'd known much of the affection and kindness he was showing to Gertie. Perhaps his grandmother had been able to compensate for her downtrodden daughter's neglect.

Something made her look up and she found Mercy staring at her, a resentful expression on her face. Dismayed, she realized she must be careful to hide her interest in Lloyd from Mercy.

Chapter Ten

The end of the year was approaching. Between Christmas and New Year a two-day race meeting and ball was to be held in Banana. Louise found herself caught up in the family's excitement and preparations.

She had ordered three new gowns from the dressmaker in Banana. There was a taffeta and a poplin for the race-meeting and a muslin with trimmings of lace for the ball. When the finished gowns arrived, Louise felt like crying as she compared them to the garments she'd left with the Barclays. But at least the muslin with its three-quarter-length sleeves was suitable for a governess, which was more than could be said of the low-cut sleeveless ball gown she'd worn in Sydney the previous year. It would hardly do to have all heads staring at her.

The children were almost beside themselves with excitement when they set out for the races, Jock Jamieson driving his wife and children in the wagonette while Andrew, Donald, Mercy and Louise accompanied them on horseback. Any excursion to town was a rare event in lives that Louise would once have considered hard and monotonous. Yet she was rapidly realising the novelty of such pleasures added to their enjoyment, making the sophisticated frivolities she'd experienced seem jaded in comparison.

Lloyd's homestead, visible from the road, stood deserted as they passed. Donald commented, 'It looks as if Lloyd's left already.'

Mercy blushed and slid her gloved hand along her horse's mane, playing with the coarse tufts of hair. 'Yes, I think he was riding in yesterday afternoon.' She turned to look at Louise. 'I suppose he's having a reunion with some of his teamster friends. Most of them make a point of being in Banana for the races.'

Louise decided this information was intended to remind her she was the outsider, the newcomer who didn't know Lloyd's habits as she, Mercy, did. She didn't respond, knowing Mercy could wish all she liked, but if Lloyd wasn't attracted to her there was little she could do about it.

While still outside of town, in the shelter of the trees, Louise and Mercy exchanged their riding habits for race-going gowns. Then they squeezed into the wagonette with the others, tying their horses behind. Fortunately it was only a matter of five minutes in the hot, jolting wagonette, cramped uncomfortably amongst the baggage, before they arrived in Banana.

The racetrack was situated on the creek flat, close to the lagoon. Rough bough sheds had been built for shade and to house the bar which was easily distinguished by the noisy crowd of men surrounding it. The carts and buggies, their horses unhitched and tied in the shade, were outnumbered by the saddle-horses, both racehorses and spectators' mounts, tethered randomly to trees and posts. The ladies were colourful in their best hats and frocks, while the men wore either coats and waistcoats or more casual riding apparel. Some of the race-goers placed bets on their favourites and cheered enthusiastically at the winning post, while others sat under the bough shelters and chatted amongst friends.

It was a hot, cloudless day and the thrashing hooves quickly whipped the dry track to dust. It wafted over the heads of the spectators, settling in a thin layer on buggy seats and picnic baskets, coating faces and clothes with grit.

At lunch-time the Jamiesons clustered in the shade beside the wagonette, far from the noisy bar, to eat the food Mrs Jamieson had packed earlier. Lloyd walked up, looking sober and presentable in his good corduroys and blue-striped shirt. It seemed Jock had invited him to eat with them.

Lloyd admitted to losing a crown on the previous race. 'Fool of a horse played up at the start and was going backwards when they dropped the flag. He never did catch up.'

A conversation with Jock followed, concerning Lloyd's teamster friends and the way the railways were pushing the carriers further out. After the initial greeting he paid no attention to Louise and she tried to ignore the niggle of hurt, knowing his neglect was necessary.

Once they had eaten Lloyd disappeared into the crowd and Louise took Maggie and Agnes to the rail to watch the next race, the Publican's Purse. The man standing near her seemed vaguely familiar. Then her fingers gripped the rail as she realized it was Sam Naylor, the Bauhinia Downs head stockman.

He turned and saw her at almost the same moment and approached her, raising his hat.

'Miss Forrest, isn't it? How do you do?'

'I'm well, thank-you, Mr Naylor.' Louise tried to speak calmly, though her body was as taut as fencing wire. She moved away from the girls who were totally absorbed in the event in progress. 'You've travelled quite a distance for the races.'

He smiled. 'It doesn't seem so far without a mob of cattle to slow you down. How did you manage, that trip?'

'It was quite an experience, but we got the cattle there safely.' Louise described the storm and the resulting cattle rush.

'You were lucky to get off so lightly. I saw Kavanagh in the distance before, but I haven't been talking to him yet. And what about yourself, Miss Forrest? Are you still governessing?'

'Yes. I'm with the Jamieson family now, from Kilbride. My first position didn't suit.'

'The Jamiesons...they're neighbours of Kavanagh's.'

She nodded. 'Mr Kavanagh was good enough to secure the position for me. He's been very helpful.'

Naylor looked relieved. Perhaps his conscience had been bothering him at sending her into the bush with such an inadequate escort. 'Yeah, he's a decent young chap.' He glanced about him as if to ascertain there were no listening ears and lowered his voice. 'A fellow came looking for you about a week after you'd gone. I didn't see him–I was away mustering–but he talked to the Boss. A gentleman, a real flash young cove, Mr Dutton said.'

Louise's throat went dry. Her heart hammered painfully and she almost choked over the words. 'What did your employer tell him?'

'He couldn't tell him anything. He'd only just got home and we'd been busy with cattle. I hadn't got around to telling him about you and Mrs Black had got the sickness from that fellow Thompson she was looking after. So she wasn't available for questioning. Mr Dutton couldn't help the man, so he went away.'

'Did the man name me, or say why he was looking for me?'

'No. I don't think so. He didn't even tell the boss his own name. He just gave a description that fitted you.'

That would be Charles all over, Louise thought. He would hardly want to advertise the fact that he was Charles Ashford, searching for a runaway sister. Fortunately for her.

She was silent. After a moment Naylor asked awkwardly, as if the time for minding his own business was past, 'Who's this chap to you? Did you run away, or something?'

Louise ignored the second question. 'He's a man who made something of a nuisance of himself while I was at my last position. I'm pleased he didn't discover my whereabouts. If he should come your way again, I beg you not to tell him the truth.'

'Of course.' Naylor appeared both disconcerted and embarrassed, obviously unable to decide what he should make of her. 'I'll tell Mr Dutton, too. Goodbye, Miss Forrest.'

As he strode away, she turned back to the racetrack. The race was over by this time; she'd been dimly aware of much cheering in the background. An excited group of people were clustered about a jockey on a big grey horse, shaking the man's hand and congratulating him loudly. The horse's nostrils were lined with red, his coat sweat-darkening as he fidgeted and sidestepped restlessly.

Louise let out her breath in a gusty sigh of relief. Her stomach was churning and her heart was banging against her ribs. What a close call! If Naylor had been at home, or if the housekeeper hadn't been ill... Charles had evidently been just as relentless in his search as she'd feared. If he'd ridden as far as Bauhinia Downs, where else might he have travelled? She felt a momentary twinge of conscience. However, he was no doubt safely on his way to England by now.

At that moment Lloyd joined her, smiling down at her. 'Did you see that? A mate of mine rode the winner! A beautiful finish. And damn it, I never even put a penny on him.'

Louise forgot her misgivings about Charles. There was something reassuring about Lloyd's presence that made her choose to ignore his language. Besides, she'd once used the same word in his hearing, so she could hardly afford the high moral ground. 'I'm afraid I didn't even see it. I just met Mr Naylor from Bauhinia Downs and was talking to him while the race was in progress.'

Before Lloyd could respond, Maggie and Agnes joined them, looking for their mother. They declined Lloyd's offer of a lemonade and went on their way, leaving Louise alone with him. He purchased soft drinks for them both and they moved to an unoccupied patch of shade, sipping their drinks and watching the crowd. Just the pleasure of his company was enough, making words unnecessary. When they were approached by a young man whom Lloyd introduced as Clive Beck, a friend from his teamster days, Louise sighed inwardly, resenting the interruption.

As Beck's brother had just ridden the winning horse, he was in a high humour, looking askance at Lloyd's lemonade. 'Don't tell me you're off the grog, Kavanagh. I'll shout us a rum to celebrate.'

'Not just now, Clive. We're in the company of a lady, remember.'

Clive made a gallant bow in her direction. 'My apologies, Miss Forrest. Ladies are so scarce around here, us coves forget how to behave. Oh, here comes the jockey.'

The latest arrival seemed even more intent on celebratory drinks than his brother. Clive was of medium height and build but Fred stood not much over five feet. He made Louise feel like an Amazon with her excess of inches.

She stayed long enough to congratulate the man on his win, but had noticed Mrs Jamieson looking in her direction. The group was unsuitable company for a governess intent on keeping her good name. She excused herself, guessing they'd make their way to the bar as soon as she'd gone.

Her employer glanced at her curiously. 'Was that the head stockman from Bauhinia Downs you were talking to earlier?'

'Yes, Mr Naylor. It was he who assisted me when I arrived there from Gainsford, as the owner was away at the time.'

'I hope he doesn't gossip about you. We hardly want all of Banana knowing how you came here.'

Louise flushed. 'I shouldn't think so. He seems very much the gentleman.'

'I hope so, Louise, for your sake.'

The family had been offered accommodation that night with friends who lived in Banana. Lloyd was camping beside the lagoon as he'd presumably done the previous night, in the company of the Becks, other teamsters and station workers. Louise imagined them carousing into the early hours, earning the disapproval of respectable people like Mrs Jamieson.

The races continued the following day. The crowd was larger and the dust more pervasive. There was one event that jarred Louise's pleasure in the day, troubling her long after she should have been able to put it from her mind.

Probably she shouldn't have witnessed it at all. She seemed to have developed the annoying habit of watching Lloyd, her gaze straying in the hope of sighting him. Most of the time when a race wasn't in progress, she would find him in the vicinity of the bar, in the company of Clive Beck. Not that he appeared to be suffering too much as a consequence. He'd certainly been sober at lunch and surprisingly he still seemed to be more or less so.

Louise was sitting under one of the bough sheds with Mrs Jamieson and some other ladies when her attention was drawn to the nearby bar. A young woman had joined the men there. She was no more than a girl, actually, perhaps Louise's own age and she was plump and round-cheeked, with chestnut hair. Louise had seen her before; her name was Eva and she worked as a chambermaid at the Banana Hotel, where Louise had stayed after leaving the Greenwoods' employment. She was flashily dressed in bright yellow and the pert little hat she wore tilted forward over her eyes was decorated with an excess of ribbon and an unlikely bunch of yellow flowers. Her behaviour was fittingly extroverted as she laughed and flirted with the men. It was obviously Lloyd who held her chief interest, for after a moment she gave him her full attention, moving close to him and whispering something in his ear. Her smile held an invitation that was unmistakable, even to Louise.

Lloyd seemed unimpressed. He laughed at her and bought her a drink, exchanging a few brief words with her before turning back to his mates. However, she wasn't so easily dismissed. She pressed close to him, putting her hand on his arm and apparently entreating him, making play with her eyes. Then she lifted her other hand to the front opening of his shirt, fingering the material and playing intimately with one of the buttons. Louise stared, unable to look away as she knew she should, shock and disbelief coursing through her. Who was this girl to him?

Lloyd brushed her hand away, obviously embarrassed now, while his companions watched the scene with ribald grins. He bent down to her and whispered something in her ear. His meaning must have been clearly expressed, for the girl's smile disappeared and she flounced away, disappearing into the crowd.

Louise jumped to her feet, murmuring something to Mrs Jamieson about the children. She found Maurice and Gertie playing in the dirt near the wagonette, their best clothes filthy, and took them to watch the horses being led around the saddling paddock in preparation for the next race. When Lloyd's voice spoke near her ear, she stiffened, her nerves tangling in disagreeable knots. Looking up at him, she caught a whiff of something on his breath and knew it was spirits of some sort. It was the first time he'd spoken with her that day, but now she almost wished he'd stayed away.

'Are you going to the dance tonight, Miss Forrest?'

'Well, yes, Mrs Jamieson said I may. But I must put the children to bed first and stay with them until the little ones have fallen asleep.' She was pleased with the cool, controlled tone of her voice, betraying nothing of her inner turmoil.

'Can I take you to the hall when you're ready? You shouldn't be walking the streets on your own. There'll be drunks about tonight.'

Remembering the scene between him and that fancy piece she'd just witnessed, she thought she should refuse. But he was right about the drunks and she was uneasy about arriving unescorted at the dance. 'We're staying only a few houses from the hall. But very well, if you wish. I hope the children will be asleep by half-past eight.'

'I'll meet you then. Whose house are you staying at?'

'It's the Britons.'

He nodded, flashing her his quick smile. 'Will you write me name against some of the dances on your card? Make sure there's a waltz or two, if you have some spare.'

She couldn't admit she had most of them spare. Perhaps accepting his offer was preferable to being a wallflower. 'All right, you may have two or three and let us hope it doesn't set the gossips talking. Now you had better go and extract the same from Mercy. It's her first ball.'

He glanced at her sideways. 'Of course I'll dance with Mercy. She's a good little kid.'

'Don't tell her so, or she'll probably do you an injury. It must be difficult to have so many females dangling after you.'

He looked at her quickly, as if surprised at her acerbic tone, then turned to walk away. At the last moment he paused and spoke over his shoulder. 'But there's only one of 'em I fancy.

Chapter Eleven

Lloyd arrived for her at half-past eight. Louise was dressed in her uninspiring new muslin, which in deference to evening was cut to expose her throat and was trimmed with a frothing of lace. The effect was pretty but demure; hardly stylish or elegant like the gowns she had once worn.

She satisfied herself with a last peep at the children tucked safely in their beds before joining Lloyd on the veranda. 'They're all asleep,' she said. 'I'll have to look in on them sometime during the night.'

He'd been smoking, leaning casually over the rail, but now he straightened and knocked out his pipe, returning it to his pocket. It was the first time she'd seen him wear a coat and waistcoat and the effect was surprisingly elegant. 'Let's go, then, before one of the little brats wakes up.'

She had to laugh, in spite of herself. 'I thought you liked them.'

'I do, but they've got their place. At the moment I'm in the mood for dancing.'

He held out his arm to her and she laid her hand on it, accompanying him down the steps. She sniffed suspiciously. 'I didn't think alcohol was served at the ball, Mr Kavanagh!'

'I haven't been there yet. I've been playing billiards for the last hour.'

'Well, I hope you're sober. Don't expect to dance with me if you're three sheets to the wind.'

He looked down at her with a crooked half-smile. 'Louise, I wouldn't insult you like that. You must've been living with the Jamiesons too long. You're beginning to sound like 'em.' He changed the subject. 'You look nice tonight. I see you've been making use of the local dressmaker. Very pretty.'

'Very suitable for a governess, you mean.' She pulled her hand away from his elbow, giving way at last to the indignation simmering inside her. 'Not a bit like that maid from the hotel who was attempting to seduce you today.'

Her words fell into an echoing silence. She stopped in her tracks, aghast, putting up her hands to her flaming cheeks. What had possessed her to say that? Finally she forced her gaze up to Lloyd's, to find him smiling down at her, an intent, suggestive look to his eye.

'*What* did you say?'

'I think you heard me.' Her voice was muffled.

'I don't think Mrs Jamieson would approve.'

'You're a fine one to preach. If Mrs Jamieson had seen the way that girl was making up to you she wouldn't be allowing you to dance with her Mercy.'

His smile faded. 'Hell, Louise, I told her to shove off, didn't I? I wish she wouldn't make a fool of herself in front of everyone.'

'You must have encouraged her in the first instance.'

'More's the pity. It's over and done with now.'

'Yes and I'm sorry I raised the subject. It's really none of my business and it was most unladylike of me to mention it.'

In truth it wasn't prudishness that had motivated her censure, for she was accustomed to Charles and his light o' loves. If she was honest, she knew her outburst had been prompted by jealousy and she had an uneasy feeling Lloyd guessed it.

The band was playing enthusiastically when they arrived and the floor was full of dancing couples. To Louise's ear the fiddle, piano and concertina were played with gusto rather than skill, but the locals were evidently uncritical. The hall itself was primitive, hinting of a recent, more violent past. It had been built with slits in the walls between the slabs, for the purposes of shooting marauding blacks. After all, it was only a few short years since the Aborigines in the area had been hostile. The walls were now lined with hessian and people danced in complete unconcern, forgetting those days when it had been necessary to safeguard against attack.

'May I have the pleasure of this dance, Miss Forrest?' Lloyd spoke with assumed gallantry, smiling mockingly at her.

She looked at her half-empty card, inwardly angry with herself for mentioning a subject that should have been ignored. 'This is useless, since I don't know which set they are starting. Very well, Mr Kavanagh. The alternative is to be a wallflower.'

She quickly discovered that though Lloyd had a good sense of rhythm, he wasn't an accomplished dancer. Of course, he wouldn't have endured hours of instruction as she had in preparation for her Sydney debut. It didn't seem to matter, though, so aware was she of his arm about her waist and his eyes looking into hers, smiling, knowing more than was good for him. His confidence infuriated her, but it was too late to wish she'd refused him. However the music gradually soothed her ruffled feelings and his closeness was intoxicating. By the end of the dance she'd thawed sufficiently to accept his thanks with a gracious smile.

Between dances she sat against the wall with Mrs Jamieson, Mrs Briton and Mercy, while the men talked in groups or strolled outside to smoke their pipes. Some of them, supposedly unbeknownst to the ladies, had planted bottles outside in the grass so they could refresh themselves between dances. Mercy was flushed and excited, for Lloyd hadn't forgotten to claim his dance with her. He hadn't been the only one to seek a space on her card, either. This, her first dance, was beginning to look like a success.

At ten o'clock supper was provided outside, under the stars. Two coppers were tended by a group of ladies, while several men boiled billies for tea over an open fire. Lloyd got plates for himself and Louise, onto which a woman ladled steaming beef curry from one copper and gluey rice from another.

'Have you been to check on the youngsters yet?' He settled himself on his heels beside her seat, balancing his plate on his knees.

'No. I shall have to walk up there shortly.'

'Tell me when you're going, then, if you'd like me to walk with you.' He grinned and lifted a forkful of curry to his mouth, holding her eyes with his as he chewed it and swallowed. 'You know, drunks and all that.'

She smiled. 'Yes, I remember. Drunks. I'm not sure that you're not fast becoming one yourself.'

'Me?' He feigned innocence. 'You know I left the pub a couple of hours ago.'

'You've been drinking since then, Lloyd! I've noticed you wander outside every time the music stops.'

He merely laughed and would admit to nothing.

'It's that Mr Beck. He is a bad influence.'

Their second dance together was a waltz. As the music came to an end Lloyd swung her around with an exuberance that had never been intended for that sedate dance, so that she came up hard against him. His arm tightened. Then the band was no longer playing and she pulled away, afraid someone might be watching them. A governess of all people could not afford to be seen acting with such abandon.

'Don't you think it's time you went up to the house?' he whispered in her ear, his voice husky.

'Yes,' she agreed, desperate to be alone with him, yet knowing in her weakness that he presented more danger to her than a dozen inebriates. 'I shall meet you outside. I'll just tell Mrs Jamieson.'

He waited on the veranda of the Britons' house while she looked in on the children's bedroom. Maggie and Annie were sharing one bed, sleeping head to toe, while Agnes and Gertie occupied the other. Maurice, scorning the need for a mattress, was playing tough and was rolled in some blankets on the floor.

Maggie stirred as Louise surveyed them from the doorway, the kerosene lamp in her hand casting the room into shadow. Louise stepped silently over to the girl's bed, finding her eyes open.

'Is everything all right?' she whispered. 'Gertie hasn't been having one of her nightmares, has she?'

'No, I don't think so,' Maggie murmured sleepily, rubbing her hand over her eyes. 'What time is it?'

'Twenty past eleven, according to the clock in the hall.'

'What's the dance like? The music sounds good.'

'It is. Everyone is having a fine old time.'

'I wish I was old enough to go. Has Mr Kavanagh danced with Mercy?'

'Yes, twice, I think. As have several other boys.'

'What about you? It's you he likes, not Mercy.'

Louise blushed in the darkness. 'Now, now, Maggie. Just go back to sleep.' She tucked the sheets in more securely and brushed her hand over Maggie's hair. 'I shall tell you all about it in the morning.'

She tiptoed outside and settled herself beside Lloyd on the veranda step. He turned to her, smiling. 'Everything all right?'

'Yes. Maggie was awake and wanted to hear all about the dance, but the others are sound asleep.' She laughed. 'Maurice is sleeping on the floor. I think he'll find it a bit hard by morning. He wanted to stay out in the shed with Andrew and Donald.'

'He's a good little fellow. A bit better than I was at the same age, I think.' He paused and suddenly said unexpectedly, his voice sober now, 'Louise, I'm sorry I teased you for bringing that up about Eva. You've got a right to be shocked at the way she carried on. But don't think I'd expect you to be here with me now if I was still seeing her.'

'Oh, Lloyd.' The gentle apology disarmed her more than anything else could have done.

He put up his hand and trailed his fingers along her hairline from her forehead to her ear. 'What would your father say if he knew you were keeping company with a cove like me?'

'It would be brief and to the point.' She laughed breathlessly; his fingers were caressing her neck now.

'Oh, damn and blast!' He pulled her into his arms and buried his face in her hair. 'What are we going to do? I don't want to give you up. Kiss me, Louise.'

It seemed they could do nothing else. They kissed in a way that would have horrified the respectable matrons up at the dance, until the sound of boots crunching in the gravel caused them to pull guiltily apart. A man walked past the front gate, glancing curiously in their direction.

'This is a bit public,' Lloyd murmured hoarsely. 'Are there any dances you have to go back for?'

'Only the one with you. I'm not exactly the most popular girl there tonight, you know.'

'The others are scared of you. They think you're too good for 'em.'

'What makes you the exception?'

'You spent a week in the bush with me, remember. Come on, let's go for a walk. I'll let you out of that one dance.'

They wandered down the road towards the lagoon, stepping out of the moonlight into the shadow of a big bottle tree. Lloyd drew her to the far side of the swollen trunk, out of sight of passers-by. He kissed her again, gently at first and then with escalating passion. Louise allowed him to pull her tight, glorying in the closeness of that lean body that pressed so hungrily to hers. The taste of rum in his mouth, mingled with the flavour of pipe tobacco she remembered from that other time, made it all seem somehow wicked and forbidden. Even in her inexperience she almost matched his desire, responding dazedly to his mouth and restless hands.

She forgot commonsense, duty, morality, putting it all aside as they leaned against the tree-trunk, using its strength to support them while temptation beckoned them one step further. His thigh pressed against her voluminous skirts, finding a space between hers. One of his hands slid to her hip to hold her there, while the other caressed her throat above the neckline of her gown. She murmured encouragingly and as if emboldened by her response he slipped several of the buttons at the front of her bodice, opening it to expose her chemise and tightly-laced corset. His fingers slid under her chemise, stroking the soft rise of her breasts while his mouth dropped to her neck. She tipped her head back and shuddered with pleasure, unable to deny him.

It was like a weakness in her, a weakness born of the childhood that had known so little love and affection; a weakness bequeathed by a family that had seldom concerned itself with morality. Now she couldn't bear to forgo his touch, although she knew the natural ending to their passion would be total folly.

Lloyd lifted his head and held her for a moment, breathing heavily into her scented hair. Then he resolutely put her away from him and re-buttoned her bodice.

'Louise,' he murmured huskily, 'we can't keep on like this. It'll only get us into trouble. I know I'm not good enough for you and I haven't much to offer you, but I want to marry you if you'll have me.'

Louise stared up at him hazily, willing him to come back to her. Didn't he realize that her father would never let her marry him? Couldn't she at least have *this*, if nothing else? If the maid from the hotel could have his body, why couldn't she?

'Oh Lloyd, how can I marry you? I'm under age and my father would never give his consent. It's impossible until I turn twenty-one.' She gave a little quivering sigh and moved back close to rest her face against his coat. 'I never suspected when I first met you at Bauhinia Downs that we'd end up like this. Under normal circumstances we wouldn't have become acquainted, but it has happened and I'm not sorry.'

He clasped her shoulders with his hands, moving her away so he could look down at her face. 'I'm not sorry, either. But if we go too far you'll have to marry me, whether your parents like it or not. If you're worried about that little shack, don't think I'd ask you to live there. I'll build a decent house, get a couple of black girls to help you. How long is it until you turn twenty-one?'

'It is more than two years. I'll be nineteen in February.'

'Heavens, I can't wait two years!' He gave a little rueful, half-laugh and let his hands slip down her sides to hold her at her hips, pressing her close to demonstrate without words how hard he would find the waiting. 'Perhaps we should elope.' He kissed her one last time and loosened his hold. 'Come on. The Jamiesons will be wondering where we are.'

'I don't care what the Jamiesons think.'

'You'll care in the morning when they tell you to pack your bags.'

'I suppose I will.' She sighed again but made no attempt to move out of his arms, enjoying the warmth and strength of him and a sense of security she hadn't known before. 'Oh Lloyd, what are we going to do?'

'We'll find a way. Just not like this, bringing shame to ourselves with the people who've been good to us.'

She stepped back and attempted to tidy her hair, tucking the stray wisps into place. 'Walk me back to the house, please Lloyd. I couldn't face returning to the dance now.'

There was no sign of life when they stepped onto the veranda. The front door was shut as she'd left it and she stole a nervous glance at it as she went into his arms for one last kiss.

'I hope you don't get into trouble over this,' he whispered. 'I'll go back to the dance for a while so it doesn't look so bad.' He rubbed his cheek against hers and she clung to him. 'I'm riding home with you all tomorrow, so I'll see you then. I love you, Louise.'

The words of love didn't come so easily to her. She didn't answer but quickly kissed his cheek before turning to the door. She found a lamp in the hallway and lit it. As she passed the Britons' open bedroom door she noted with a sigh of relief that the room was still empty. She eased open the children's door and peeped in. Maurice muttered once in his sleep and rolled over, then once more silence reigned. She closed the door and tiptoed to the empty room she shared with Mercy, where she undressed, brushed out her hair and slipped into bed. Wide awake, she lay there with her thoughts tumbling confusedly upon each other, until eventually she heard the others return.

Chapter Twelve

The next morning, the sun was high in the sky when Louise was awakened by the children dressing noisily in the room next door. Immediately her mind flooded with recollections of the previous night and the abandoned embraces she'd shared with Lloyd. She cringed inwardly, wondering if he was thinking the less of her for the liberties she'd permitted him and the further, momentous liberty she'd been prepared to grant him had he been of a mind to take advantage of it.

Yet worse was the prospect of the interview with Mrs Jamieson to come. She was sure to question why Louise hadn't returned to the ball after seeing to the children and would no doubt have noticed Lloyd's coinciding absence. His return an hour or so later would have done little to rectify the situation.

Mercy was dressed and gone. When Louise entered the dining room, she found her already sitting at the table with the others. Everyone seemed as normal, responding cheerily to her 'Good morning'. Except for Mrs Jamieson, who glanced up at her and said nothing and Mercy, who looked down at her plate.

After the breakfast dishes had been cleared away, they made ready for the return journey to Kilbride. When Lloyd rode up, the children were settled in the dray and Louise and Mercy, dressed in their riding habits, waited with their mounts. Mrs Jamieson gave Lloyd a sharp look but Mercy's welcoming smile was undimmed.

Louise supposed she was to bear all the blame for having led him astray.

Louise was unable to look at Lloyd or meet his eyes. He'd asked her to marry him, but what must he be thinking at this moment?

At last, after a final visit by Gertie to the "little house" in the back yard, they were ready to leave. Lloyd helped Mercy into her saddle. He seemed withdrawn and uncharacteristically quiet and Louise began to wish the ground would open up and swallow her. That was until he turned to help her to mount and smiled gently into her eyes. The touch of his hand on hers and the warmth of his look instantly set everything right with the world.

Mrs Jamieson delayed the expected interview until after dinner that night, when all Louise wanted to do was retire to the solitude of her room. 'I'd like a word with you, Lucy. Come to the study with me, please.'

Louise followed her employer and waited in rigid silence as the door was shut behind them.

'Why didn't you return to the dance last night? Am I correct in suspecting you were in the company of Mr Kavanagh?'

Louise drew a deep breath and managed to look the woman in the eye. 'Yes, you are. Mr Kavanagh walked with me when I looked in on the children, Mrs Jamieson. I was nervous of going alone when there were so many strange men about, some of them the worse for drink.' She took another breath. 'After I had been to the children's room we sat on the veranda and talked for a while. Then we went for a walk. On our return I was disinclined to return to the dance, so I retired to bed. Mr Kavanagh said he intended to go back to the hall.'

'Yes, he did, eventually. But this was more than an hour after you left. It won't do, Louise, to behave this way. I was worried about you and if you leave a function in the company of a young man and don't return you can hardly blame people for thinking the worst.'

'I'm sorry, Mrs Jamieson. But I didn't actually leave the hall with Mr Kavanagh. He waited for me outside.'

'You may be sure that someone noticed it, nevertheless. What is your relationship with him, Lucy? I know you've already spent more time in his company than is proper for any young girl, but that is an unfortunate situation we cannot rectify. Unless you intend to marry him, you shouldn't be sitting about in the dark with him for five minutes, let alone for an hour. While you are in my house, teaching my children, I expect you to abide by my standards.'

Louise bit her lip, deciding honesty was the best course. 'He has asked me to marry him, Mrs Jamieson, but I can hardly accept. I'm under age and my parents would never consent to it.'

Mrs Jamieson shook her head. 'I'm not surprised. You're obviously a well-bred girl and Kavanagh's background couldn't be much worse. He's a hard worker and a likeable young man, but he has little to offer you besides more hard work.' Her lips flattened in a stern line. 'I find it hard to understand why you've given up the life you had to become a governess. And your relationship with your parents is more of a puzzle, Lucy. You don't write to them, nor they to you.'

'I'm not close to my family, Mrs Jamieson. If you knew them you would understand why.'

'If you've had a disagreement with them, I wish you would try to mend it.'

Louise shifted restlessly. 'I'm sorry, but you've no idea how many of the upper classes live. I hardly saw my parents as a child and if you think they live by the same standards as you do then you are much mistaken. The wealthy make their own rules.'

Mrs Jamieson's eyes were cold. 'Perhaps, but you can't do so now, my girl. I can understand your attraction to Lloyd Kavanagh, for he's a very personable young man, but he has lived by a different set of rules also. He has admitted to us that his father was drunken and it dismays me to see that he still drinks himself. Alcohol is at the root of so much evil. I also believe he isn't above mixing with loose women. I suppose that touch of wildness makes him exciting to you, but physical attraction doesn't last when you're bone-tired with bearing babies and hard work. If you haven't grown up with these hardships, you may end up resenting him in the end.'

'You've forgotten one thing, Mrs Jamieson,' said Louise levelly. 'That is the love and friendship we share. As you've just pointed out, Mr Kavanagh and I have spent more time in each other's company than most young people are ever allowed to do. I find him attractive, yes, but he's also the best friend I've ever had. Perhaps he does drink and has known loose women, but he has a strong sense of decency for all that. Compared to my brother Charles–'

'I don't know your brother, but whatever your feelings, Louise, there can be no future in the relationship without your parents' good will. As I see it, you've no alternative but to put an end to it.'

'I know that.' Louise buried her face in her hands, muffling her next sentence. 'But I can hardly bear to do so.'

Mrs Jamieson's face softened, reminding Louise of her innate kindness. 'I don't know what else to advise, my dear. Perhaps you should join your parents in England and hope that distance will help you forget him.'

Here it was again, the same thing Lloyd himself had suggested not so very long ago. She shook her head decisively. 'I'm determined not to leave Australia. I'm afraid I'd never be allowed to return.'

But Mrs Jamieson didn't know the full of it. There was one further barrier to the young people's relationship she couldn't possibly have guessed at. Louise had still to tell Lloyd who she really was.

How would he react to the revelation that she was Louise Ashford, daughter of a man who had ill-treated him with the typical arrogance of his class? Did he love her enough to accept her in spite of it, in spite of the deceit she'd practised on him? Oh, if only she'd been brave enough to tell him that day when he'd first kissed her. If he'd rejected her then she could have borne it.

After the New Year the dry spell was broken. It rained steadily for five days and the sun struggled with the clouds for another two. The rain had provided a brief respite from the heat but now the sun reappeared with renewed vigour, drawing vapour from the sodden ground in almost palpable waves. The children suffered with prickly heat and Louise found her corset and petticoats almost unbearable.

Just as the ground had dried enough to allow travel on horseback, the clouds opened once more in another deluge. They were all unused to being housebound and during a break in the weather Louise took the young Jamiesons to the river, anxious for any diversion to settle fraying tempers.

The Dawson's peaceful clear waterholes were swallowed by brown, rushing water. The flood carried with it sticks and leaves and blobs of frothy scum which caught and settled against the straining branches of partly submerged tea-trees, trees that a fortnight before had stood tranquilly in the dry bed.

Andrew and Donald amused themselves by throwing sticks in the water. They watched the sticks drift with the current, arguing amongst themselves over the feasibility of swimming it. Louise had no intention of allowing them to find out.

'You boys are just plain silly,' Maggie told them.

'Yes, you'd get drowned for sure,' Annie chimed in, obviously relishing the chance to score one over her older brothers.

Mercy sat alone on a rock, looking quietly down at the water. Louise noticed her with a twinge of compassion. She had been very reserved since the weekend of the races. It was obvious her attachment to Lloyd was no swiftly passing thing. Yet he might never have returned it. Surely it was better for her to put it aside now than waste years in yearning for something that might not eventuate.

When they returned to the house, Lloyd was there, talking to Jock. If they had grown bored during the rain, it must have been doubly tedious for him, alone in that little shack. Not that the men folk were often idle during the wet season. There was always harness to repair, ropes and whips to plait, saddles to counter-line. And when a lull came in the weather, work began on yards and outbuildings, making repairs and additions. Yet labour could hardly compensate for human company.

Andrew suggested a game of whist. He and Mercy played against Lloyd and Louise at the big dining table, while Mrs Jamieson wrote a letter and Jock read from his bible. Annie, Agnes and Gertie played with cutout paper dolls, while Maurice elicited Donald's help in fashioning a shanghai from a forked stick he'd cut with his pocketknife while at the river.

After Lloyd and Louise won the first two games, Lloyd suggested they change partners. He ended up partnering Mercy, but as partners sat opposite that meant Louise found herself sitting next to Lloyd. She wondered if that had been his intention, though perhaps not a wise one with Mercy's intent gaze on them from the other side of the table.

It was bittersweet torment having him there, the brush of his arm against hers as he reached over the table for a card, and the freshly washed smell of him mixed with the aroma of pipe tobacco in her nostrils. She watched his brown forearm, revealed by his rolled-up sleeve, as it rested on the table and his strong fingers as he plied his cards. The memory came to her, unbidden, of those fingers slipping under her chemise and she swiftly thrust it away.

Louise looked down at her cards, willing herself to concentrate. She played badly, but Lloyd did not. He was clever and quick with a good deal of daring. As he played yet another trump suit Louise wondered bitterly how he could be sufficiently indifferent to her to apply his mind to the game.

And then, when she was approaching despondency, his riding boot reached for her own shod foot under the table, entangling with it under her skirt. She trembled at his audacity, glancing quickly at his face. He continued to scan his cards as if nothing was happening, but at least she knew he was thinking of her after all.

With the final clearing of the clouds, the atmosphere lost some of its humidity, making the heat more tolerable. The land was now lushly green and fertile, with lagoons brimming full and tiny, fast-drying pools of water in every gully. Finally shedding the last remnants of their winter hair, the stock grew sleek and fat almost overnight. Now that the breeders were fit and strong Jock set about mustering them to brand the cleanskin calves. The sale bullocks would be allowed to continue fattening until May or June, although the cattle market had become very uncertain since the recent closure of the Lakes Creek Meatworks at Rockhampton.

The children were allowed a few days away from their lessons to help with some of the muster. And Louise, joy of joys, was able to accompany them, making Shadow, whom Lloyd had brought to Kilbride for her, earn his keep at last. Only little Gertie was forced to stay at home with her mother, much to her resentment. Although she could ably manage her fat little pony Jock considered the days too long for her.

There was a bonus for Louise in being allowed to participate in the muster. It gave her the chance to see Lloyd, who was helping his neighbours. In return Mr Jamieson would take himself and his sons to Myvanwy in a few weeks' time to help with the muster there. Such an arrangement appeared to favour Lloyd in terms of numbers, but the older man seemed perfectly satisfied with it and, after witnessing a day's mustering, Louise understood why.

Mr Jamieson, who freely admitted his riding experience in his native Scotland had been limited to jogging bareback astride his father's draft horses, was an unskilled rider and cattleman. And his sons clearly lacked the experience of their neighbour, who could gallop through a patch of scrub with his horse at the shoulder of a beast all the way. On one occasion Louise watched in breathless admiration as Lloyd threw a two-year-old micky with a quick flick of its tail. Before it could rise, he was off his horse and upon the winded animal, unbuckling a bull-strap from his waist.

Not only was Lloyd out riding with the Jamieson men during the day, but he was also sleeping and eating at their house, allowing Mrs Jamieson the opportunity to serve him some good, nourishing food. Louise was given no opportunity to be alone with him and she wasn't shameless enough to seek it. She knew even a single kiss would have broken down the barriers and made it difficult to behave with the respect that was due to their hosts. So well did they play their parts that Mrs Jamieson stopped watching them, much to Louise's relief. Sometimes it was hard to believe she and Lloyd had ever been involved in lustful, uninhibited lovemaking under a certain bottle tree in the main street of Banana.

Chapter Thirteen

One day in mid-February, Mrs Jamieson again called Louise to the study.

'Now that the mustering is done, I'm going away for a few weeks to visit my sister in Rockhampton. I'm taking Maurice and Gertie with me but I'm confident about leaving the other girls in yours and Mercy's care.' She gave one of her rare smiles. 'Maurice and Gertie haven't been further than Banana so it will be a rare treat for them.'

Relieved that she wasn't being subjected to another lecture, Louise tried to hide her surprise. 'Of course, Mrs Jamieson. I'm sure we will manage splendidly. I hope you enjoy the vacation.'

The very next day, Mr Jamieson drove his wife and youngest children to Banana to catch the Westwood coach. Louise watched the departing wagonette with a lightening of spirit. She would be practically her own mistress for the next few weeks, with Mr Jamieson not the sort to throw orders at her. Of course, she and Mercy would have to share her employer's usual workload, but she was determined to uphold Mrs Jamieson's faith in her.

During their mother's absence Andrew and Donald between them began a weekly ritual of riding to Banana to collect the mail as it arrived on the coach from Westwood. When they returned, all the children would crowd eagerly around while their father read aloud the letter from their mother.

Louise tactfully absented herself on these occasions, until one day when her employer called her to join them.

Mr Jamieson's face was ashen, his whole body slumped, the letter shaking in his hand. Mercy gripped the back of a chair with whitened knuckles, staring anxiously at her father, while her siblings looked at each other in dazed disbelief. Except for Maggie, who was the most sensitive of the four girls and who had already begun to cry.

'What is it?' Louise halted in the doorway, looking from one to the other while her heart beat a swift tattoo against her ribs. 'What has happened?'

'Maurice has contracted the diphtheria,' Mr Jamieson croaked, the Scottish accent more than usually pronounced. 'They don't hold out much hope for the lad.' He pushed the letter blindly under a china ornament on the corner whatnot, averting his grief-stricken features. He left the room hastily, leaving the others to stand there in a silence relieved only by Maggie's sobbing.

Diphtheria! Louise knew enough about the disease to appreciate that it was usually fatal. A membrane formed at the back of the throat, obstructing the windpipe and often leading to suffocation. If not the victim was likely to die of other complications. It was a highly infectious disease and Louise remembered an epidemic when she was a child. Isolated at Banyandah from their peers, the Ashford children had escaped the illness, but she knew of others who had died.

With Mercy's assistance she consulted Mrs Jamieson's medical book. Following its instructions, she fetched a shovelful of hot coals from the stove and sprinkled sulphur over them before carrying it from room to room. The fumes were supposed to act as a disinfectant. It seemed certain that Maurice had contracted the disease in Rockhampton, but she took comfort in doing something positive. That was the worst of it for everyone; feeling so helpless, with nothing to do but wait for further news.

The week passed in a fever of anxiety. When the mail coach was due to arrive, Mr Jamieson saddled up and rode into Banana himself. He returned looking grey and defeated, his hands trembling as he fingered a crumpled envelope.

'Maurice seems to be pulling through,' he told them heavily, 'but Gertie took sick the day after Mother last wrote.' He looked at them all as if searching for a way to break it to them gently. 'She died on Tuesday.'

After those first moments of dazed shock they all went through the motions of normality, milking the house cows, feeding the fowls, sweeping, dusting, washing and cooking. Yet all the tasks were done in a sort of haze and afterwards Louise could hardly remember actually doing them. It was difficult to absorb the fact that poor Gertie would never be returning from that special treat, a visit to the coast.

Louise was forced to adopt the role of surrogate mother, comforting the girls when they broke down in tears. The family's grief distressed her and since it was her first immediate experience of death, she struggled with her own reactions to it. It was hard to believe the small, warm body that had curled up to her at story time now lay lifeless in a cold grave, the happy, affectionate spirit forever quenched. Death was appalling at the best of times, but obscene when it involved a child.

Andrew rode to Myvanwy with the sad news and returned accompanied by Lloyd, who looked pale and shaken. Louise remembered how he'd carried Gertie home on his shoulder after they had searched for emu eggs and suspected he was feeling the shock as keenly as she.

'I'll help the boys keep an eye on things if you want to go to Rockhampton, Jock,' he offered.

But Mr Jamieson shook his head. 'I don't want to risk carrying the infection back here. I think it's best if I stay where I am, lad. Harriet's got her sister and brother-in-law to look to. I dare say she won't be coming home for a while now.'

The following week they received better news. Maurice was recovering, though very slowly. According to the doctor his heart was weakened, but if he took care not to over-exert himself he should be able to lead a normal life.

'A normal life,' Mr Jamieson exclaimed angrily. 'What sort of normal life is it for a boy who can no' exert himself? That does away with living in the bush. He'll have to set his sights on a desk job in the town. He'll no' think too highly of that. And how do ye tell a lad like Maurice to take it steady?'

No-one had an answer for him.

Mrs Jamieson intended to remain in Rockhampton with Maurice while he convalesced. They would not be able to return home until there was no danger of infecting the other members of the family and the boy had the attentions of a doctor there. Louise could only guess what a difficult time it must be for Mrs Jamieson, having to endure sickness and the death of her youngest child. On top of that, there was the enforced separation from the husband whose comfort she must be longing for.

Louise was no longer the decorative but functionless young society lady of her days at Banyandah. In the past twelve months she'd become a children's governess and had briefly experienced the life of a drover. Now she found herself having to neglect the girls' lessons at times as she lent Mercy a hand with the cooking and housekeeping.

The task of cooking for ten people, including the stockman Ernie Bates and the Aboriginal maid, was a big responsibility for someone of Mercy's age and inexperience. So Louise found herself suffering the sweltering heat of the wood stove, learning to tell when the corned beef was done, or keeping an eye on the leg of mutton that was roasting in the oven. She followed Mercy's directions on the making of blancmanges and rice puddings and put jellies to set in a safe hung with cooling wet hessian.

She also supervised Elsie, the dark housemaid, wielding a broom or a duster herself on occasion. On washday she helped Elsie lift clothes with an old broom handle from the steaming copper, leaving them to drain in a slatted wooden box before rinsing and pegging on the line. If there was nothing else to claim her attention she helped the younger girls in Mrs Jamieson's vegetable garden. Louise supposed her mother would be horrified to see her with dirt on her hands, ingrained under her chipped fingernails, but that old life when such things had mattered seemed remote. This was her life now; this was the sort of life she would be leading if she married Lloyd.

No wonder Mrs Jamieson had seemed busy. Louise had never really understood before the extent of her duties. How great a contrast was her life to that of Mrs Ashford, who now was no doubt living an ever more indulgent lifestyle at Fenham Manor. Yet only when Louise was at her most exhausted, when the day had been insufferably hot and the children had been quarrelling, did she ever think wistfully of having nothing to do.

One day Lloyd rode over to see Jock. An Aboriginal stockman from Bauhinia Downs had carried a message to him, informing him they had a number of cattle from Myvanwy and Kilbride at one of their mustering camps. Because it was such a large station, the stockmen at Bauhinia Downs held the cattle from outlying areas in an open camp to brand and draft instead of bringing them all to the homestead stockyards. After the calves were branded, the fat bullocks and any other stock that were to be separated from the main herd were drafted out of the main mob on horseback.

Jock and Lloyd set off together at daylight the next morning to collect their cattle, light swags strapped to the cantles of their saddles. They rode briskly and came onto the now brimming waterhole in Roundstone Creek in two hours. Here Lloyd was surprised to find that the tribe of AAborigines, who'd been camping here when he came through with Louise in October, had departed.

'They must've gone walkabout,' he commented to Jock. 'They were still here before the Wet. Or perhaps they've shifted for good. The fleas might've got a bit thick for 'em.'

'Aye. Or it might be just that their gunyahs were falling down on top o' them and they thought it simpler to build a new lot elsewhere.' Jock eyed the flimsy structures critically. 'If we get another good storm there'll be nowt left of this lot.'

They watered their horses and continued on their way. Some three miles distant Lloyd suddenly drew rein in the midst of a thicket of brigalow. He held up his hand for silence as Jock began to speak. 'Listen!'

'Sounds like a beast bellowing.' The noise was more distinct now and they looked at each other, startled.

'What the buggery...?' Lloyd muttered. For it wasn't a cow calling her calf, or a lone beast merely separated from its mates, or even a bull on the rampage. The bellows were those of a grown beast and they carried the unmistakable gutwrenching tones of extreme pain or fear.

Lloyd shoved the spurs into his horse's belly and set off at a controlled gallop through the scrub, Jock following more cautiously at the rear of his crashing progress. Lloyd checked Dynamite momentarily at the edge of a slight clearing. Ahead of them, partially obscured by the leathery grey leaves of the brigalow, was a group of Aboriginal huntsmen. Some of the men stood back with spears poised while their companions stabbed ruthlessly at the unfortunate animal kicking and writhing at their feet. Its tortured bellows were a thousand times more dreadful than those of the most strident calf at branding.

Lloyd swore and set his horse towards the natives at a wild gallop. Behind him Jock gave voice to a less obscene profanity, in temper riding as recklessly as Lloyd. The Aborigines, normally so acute of hearing, were deafened by the cries of their prey. At the last minute they turned to the sight of two yelling, furious horsemen threatening to trample them. They scattered in terror, some of them even dropping their weapons in their haste. One man, however, younger and more impetuous than the rest, paused long enough to obey an instinctive, panic-stricken impulse.

Perhaps the Aborigine would have thought better of it in a saner moment. At any rate he didn't wait to see the outcome as he fled with the rest of his companions. They doubtless knew how terrible the white man's vengeance could be.

Lloyd felt the spear whistle past him, almost brushing his sleeve, before he heard Jock's cry. He pulled his horse up violently, causing Jock's mount to collide with him. He grasped its rein and dragged it to a standstill, controlling his own excited horse one-handed. Jock was clutching the pommel of his saddle, ashen-faced, the other hand gripping the quivering shaft of the spear that protruded hideously from his left thigh. Already the blood was beginning to form a dark stain on his trousers.

Lloyd checked a horrified exclamation and slid from the saddle, dropping Dynamite's reins and steadying Jock's mare. Jock was crouched forward over her withers now, the breath wheezing through his clenched teeth, his face contorted.

'Get the bloody thing out, Lloyd! Quick, before it kills me!'

Lloyd obediently grasped the wooden shaft of the spear and, gritting his jaw, wrenched the weapon from its bed of flesh and muscle. Blood gushed freely and Jock uttered a sharp, agonised cry, before toppling from the saddle into his companion's arms. Lloyd carried him away from the horses and gently laid him full-length on the ground. He tore the blood-soaked trousers away to expose the wound.

It looked ugly to his inexperienced eye. As far as he could see, the barbed spearhead hadn't touched the bone, but had gone deep enough to cruelly lacerate the flesh. After that first gush, the blood was pulsing steadily. He knew if he didn't stop it, his friend could bleed to death.

In Jock's pockets he found a clean handkerchief, still folded, which he placed over the wound to act as a pad. Then he tore the tail off his own shirt and wrapped it tightly around Jock's thigh, knotting it securely with the aid of his teeth. Jock was beginning to come round and opened his eyes as Lloyd straightened.

'Did I go out to it?' he asked weakly.

'Yeah. Just for a couple of minutes.'

'Ye got the spear out? How does she look?'

Lloyd hesitated. 'Not too bad.' He thought he had the bleeding under control, but now he was more concerned that wounds like this always went bad. He knew men had died in agony from lesser injuries. He helped Jock to a seated position. 'We'd better get you home. Do you think you can sit on a horse?'

Jock grimaced. 'Aye, it hurts like the devil, but I'll manage. That blasted black fellow–if I ever get me hands on him he'll be sorry.'

It was an effort to get him into the saddle. At last it was accomplished and he hung there, trembling, heavy beads of perspiration standing out on the greyish pallor of his face.

'What about the beast?' Jock managed.

'He's buggered.' Lloyd glanced briefly in the direction of the stricken steer, which was moaning softly, the blood bubbling from its nostrils. He took the revolver he always carried on his saddle and walked over to it, dispassionately putting it out of its misery.

That was the last attempt at conversation Jock made until they arrived back at Roundstone Creek nearly an hour later. Lloyd carried water to him in his quart-pot. 'Would you like to stop for a spell?'

Jock shook his head. 'Just keep going.'

As the miles drew by, they travelled with ever-increasing slowness. Jock grew feverish and dizzy and Lloyd was forced to dismount and walk beside his horse, supporting him in the saddle. This made for awkward progress in the heavy timber, until Lloyd, in a fit of exasperation, tied the reins around Dynamite's neck and allowed him to follow at will. Then the gelding upset matters by pushing past them and trotting ahead, disturbing Jock's normally quiet-natured mare.

They didn't stop at all, for any advantage gained by allowing Jock to rest was outweighed by the difficulty of getting him into the saddle again. He was growing steadily more feverish and Lloyd knew it was imperative to bring him home and into bed as swiftly as possible.

It was well into the afternoon when they finally reached Kilbride. Andrew, Donald and the station hand were away from the house working on a new fence-line, so only the females of the family were there to greet them. The sight of their father hanging slackly in the saddle, flushed and drifting on the edge of delirium, shattered even Mercy's composure. Surely there had been enough sickness and tragedy in the family without this.

Mercy stood there, stunned into immobility and it was left to Louise to help Lloyd carry the injured man to his bedroom. Yet after they had laid him on the bed, Mercy appeared in the doorway with a solution of Condy's Crystals to bathe the wound and strips of sheeting to bandage it, apparently once again in possession of her wits.

'Good girl,' responded Lloyd tersely. 'I hope you've got a strong stomach. It looks a bit of a mess.'

Wordlessly Mercy did what had to be done, her face set. When fresh bandages had been applied and the covers had been drawn over her barely-lucid father, he stirred himself enough to say, 'Don't ye write to Mother about this. Don't want her worried.'

'No, Father.' Mercy patted his calloused hand. 'Don't fret yourself now–just hurry up and get well.'

Lloyd drew Louise aside. 'Do you think you could get me something to eat?'

She looked at him swiftly. Jock had left at five, so presumably Lloyd had breakfasted earlier than that. Although they'd carried food in their saddlebags he would hardly have stopped to eat. 'Of course. Come to the kitchen if you don't mind eating there.'

The three younger girls were hovering outside the door. Louise noted their white, anxious faces and her heart twisted. 'You may sit with your father if you like, but don't talk to him. He must be allowed to sleep.'

Maggie shook her head, on the verge of tears. 'We'll be as quiet as mice, Miss Forrest.'

In the kitchen Louise set cold meat, pickles and bread in front of Lloyd and sat across the table from him. He looked tense and dishevelled, his clothes blood-spattered, but just being alone with him again after all this time made her pulse beat faster.

'Do you think Mr Jamieson will be all right?'

'God, I hope so.' Lloyd sighed and dragged his hand through his sweat-matted hair. 'The wound itself should heal if it doesn't go bad, but that fever doesn't look too good. Those poor kids. Fancy this on top of everything.'

'Do you think we should let Mrs Jamieson know?'

'No. There's no point. She'd only fret and not be able to do anything.'

He ate rapidly and gulped down several pannikins of hot, sweet tea. As he chewed his last mouthful, he pushed back his chair. 'Thanks, Louise. I'll take another look at Jock and head off.'

'Where are you going?'

He didn't answer and she followed him into Jock's study, where he took one of the rifles from the rack on the wall and pocketed a handful of cartridges.

'What are you doing?'

'I'm going to see where those black fellows have got to. I'll hunt 'em off if they're still about. I won't have 'em on Myvanwy if they're gunna be spearing cattle. We can't let 'em get away with this.'

Alarm rushed through her at the hard note in his voice. 'Lloyd, you're not going to shoot them!'

He looked quickly at her and gave a tight smile. 'No, I won't do that. But if I went to the traps, that's just what would happen.

They'd put the Native Police onto 'em and they'd slaughter the whole tribe. There's no need for that–I just want to scare 'em off.'

'What if Mr Jamieson takes a turn for the worse?'

'There's not much we can do. There's no doctor in Banana, so it's no use taking him there. The trip'd kill him, anyway. You'll just have to do the best you can for him.'

'Lloyd,' she could only whisper, afraid to put it into words. 'Do you think he'll die?'

'God, I hope not. But it doesn't look too good. If he does...'

'Don't do anything silly, for God's sake. I wish you'd stay here.'

'No, I can't let 'em get away with this. If they think they've got us scared, they'll be eating our cattle whenever they feel like it and throwing spears at us into the bargain. Besides, I couldn't stand to hang around here doing nothing. Can you get some food together for me?'

'Why don't you take one of the boys with you?'

He shook his head. 'You might need 'em both here. I don't want 'em mixed up in any trouble, anyway. The Jamiesons have enough problems right now.'

'What about you?' she demanded fiercely, angry that he should place less value on his own safety. 'Do you think no-one cares about you?'

He smiled tiredly. 'At least me mother and father don't.'

'They may not, but *I* do! And you know the Jamiesons do, too.'

She spun away from him before he could respond and returned to the kitchen, where in some agitation she packed meat and bread into a sugar-bag. Lloyd didn't follow her and she guessed he was visiting Mr Jamieson. When he reappeared with the rifle in his hand she thrust the bag at him and turned away without a word, waiting until he'd gone outside before she gave way to her tears.

Chapter Fourteen

Lloyd didn't bother returning to Myvanwy to change his horse. Dynamite had rested sufficiently on the long, slow trek home with Jock to regain whatever energy had been expended on the brisk morning ride.

He strapped the rifle in a scabbard under the flap of his saddle and tied the sugar-bag to the dees on the pommel. Maggie and Agnes had saddled their ponies and ridden off to fetch their brothers. He considered waiting for their return so he could enlist the help of Ernie Bates, but decided against it. It was better to have at least one mature adult at the homestead in case Jock's condition deteriorated.

He rode his horse at a trot and canter most of the way, shortly before dark reaching the area where the beast had been speared. At first he had trouble finding the spot in the thick timber, but after a short delay he came upon the little clearing in the brigalow. Dismounting, he took the time to inspect the beast properly. It was a roan steer, at least two years old, with his LK brand on the ribs. The body had stiffened but hadn't yet begun to swell and apart from the many spear wounds the carcass was still intact. Obviously the Aborigines hadn't dared to return for any of the meat.

Lloyd compressed his lips. In another two or three years this animal would have grown into a heavy sale bullock. He hated to think of raising an animal past the age where it was likely to succumb to drought or dingoes, only to have it fall prey to the blacks. At this stage he couldn't afford to lose too many of his bullocks. Perhaps he should have adopted the practice of some station owners of killing a lame or otherwise defected beast for the Aborigines at intervals in the hope that they'd leave his more valuable animals alone. But their natural game had seemed abundant and this tribe hadn't shown signs of hunger.

However the killing of his cattle mattered little when he thought of Jock lying in his bed at Kilbride, fighting the fever and the poisons in his blood. If he died, after the tragedy the poor family had already suffered, the natives would have a lot to answer for. It wasn't as if either he or Jock had ever treated them badly.

And Louise...he remembered her bravely taking charge of the household and something softened inside of him. He pictured her at Bauhinia Downs on the first day he met her, all haughty and conscious of her superiority and realized how much she'd changed. Unbidden, the memory of her in his arms, pliant and willing, came to disturb him. He gathered Dynamite's reins and swung impatiently into his saddle, tired of the wanting and waiting for their chance to be together.

He could have had her the other night. He'd considered fetching his swag and taking it to some dark, secluded spot. No-one would have known, but his sense of shame had held him back. The Jamiesons trusted him, had been kind to him. If they had guessed he was out there in the dark with their governess...

He'd never met anyone like Louise and couldn't understand why someone from her class would consider shacking up with a rough cove like him. She was so much of a mystery to him and he suspected that was part of the fascination.

He turned his horse in the direction of a nearby gully where he knew there would be water. Although it was fully dark when he arrived, there was sufficient moonlight to see that the Aborigines had been camping there. It was evident they'd vacated the spot in a hurry, for close to one of the gunyahs was a possum-skin dilly-bag, apparently dropped in haste. Dismounting, he struck a match to examine the contents:several birds' eggs, a few yams and a handful of fat, white grubs–obviously one of the women's gatherings for the day. Well, the eggs–if they were fresh–and the yams would supplement his supper, but he discarded the grubs with a grimace of distaste.

Daylight found him once more on his way. He followed the Aborigines' trail over the Myvanwy boundary and into Bauhinia Downs and still they seemed to be well ahead of him. It appeared they'd been thoroughly frightened by the outcome of yesterday's encounter and needed no encouragement from him to spur them on their way. In the south-west, a heavy cloud of dust indicated the presence of the Bauhinia Downs mustering camp. He decided to go ahead and collect the stray cattle, knowing it would be another year before they were mustered again and meanwhile he and Jock would risk losing their calves to the neighbour's brand.

The men were cutting out bullocks when he arrived. They were holding two lots of cattle while Sam Naylor, mounted on his best stock-horse, camp-drafted selected animals from the main mob to another which, Lloyd guessed, would later be taken to a paddock close to the homestead. The head stockman paused in his work, directing one of his men to take over and walked his blowing horse to meet Lloyd.

'G'day, Kavanagh. How are things with you? I was expecting you yesterday.'

'They're not too good.' Lloyd spoke bluntly, forgoing a greeting. 'We would've been here yesterday, but we ran into a bit of trouble.' He went on to tell Naylor the whole story, adding, 'Looks like the blacks have cleared right out of it and just as well for them. I wouldn't have minded putting a few shots behind 'em if I'd run into 'em today.'

'Christ, that's bad luck for Jock.' Naylor took out his pipe and thumbed fresh tobacco into the bowl. 'Those spear wounds are rotten things. It was lucky you could get it out'

Lloyd grimaced at the memory. 'It wasn't easy. Jock went out to it in the process, poor bugger.'

'He was lucky. Plenty of blokes have died with a spear still in 'em.'

'He might still die.' Lloyd looked away, his eyes scanning the endless scrub. 'Do you know this tribe I'm talking about?'

Naylor nodded. 'I certainly do. We have one of 'em here. A young fellow we took in at the homestead when he was a bit of a kid.'

'Could I have a yarn to him?'

'Yeah, I'll get him.'

He signalled to one of the riders blocking the face of the camp, a dark boy on a scrawny, brown horse. The youth came promptly, his eyes wide and scared in his black, dusty face.

'Billy, you know 'bout wild-feller blackfellers bin spear 'em white man yesterday?'

The Aborigine's eyes widened further. 'Me no wild blackfeller. Me good blackfeller. Me brand 'em calves, chase 'em cows all longa day. Me no spear 'em white man.'

Naylor laughed and turned to Lloyd. 'He's heard about it, all right. God knows how the hell they do it. These black fellows know what their mates are up to from twenty miles away. I didn't see any smoke signals yesterday, but I might've been too busy to notice.'

'He looks bloody worried,' Lloyd agreed. He frowned at the black. 'Billy, you bin tell 'em blackfellers, no more spear 'em white feller, no more spear 'em bullock. Big boss policeman he bin come shoot 'em blackfellers dead. You tell 'em blackfellers, they hungry,' rubbing his belly, 'they come longa see me.'

Billy nodded, trembling. 'I bin tell 'em, Boss. Other white feller, he all-same die?'

'No, but he all-same plurry crook.' Lloyd injected a note of grim warning into his voice. 'Might be he die, bye 'n bye.'

Naylor gestured to the terrified Aborigine. 'When you see 'em blackfellers, Billy, you tell 'em clear out plurry quick. You tell 'em whitefellers plenty cranky.' He watched after the stockman's retreating figure, grinning a little. 'That'll put the fear of God into 'em.'

'Yeah, but if Jock dies it won't be much help.'

'No, it's a rotten business.' Naylor puffed his pipe in silence, reflecting. At last he stirred. 'Well, I'll help you get your cattle out of the mob. There're two cows and calves of Jamieson's and a dry heifer and four steers of yours. Will you stop and have some smoko with us first?'

'Thanks, Naylor, but I want to get back as soon as I can. Mrs Jamieson's away–they lost their little girl to diphtheria the other day. There's just a houseful of kids and the governess.'

Naylor cleared his throat uneasily. 'That's sad news about the little girl. But I think you're reaching a bit high with that governess, Kavanagh.'

Lloyd felt himself flushing. 'What do you mean?'

Naylor watched him steadily. 'Someone saw you together at the race ball. I think you're riding for a fall. She's a wild girl, but remember what I told you when I first asked you to take her with you back at Bauhinia Downs.'

Lloyd squirmed inwardly. Perhaps she was a bit wild, but her male relatives were a safe distance away in England and he was too smitten with her to just walk away while there seemed to be a chance for him. 'She's not a trollop, if that's what you mean.'

'I wouldn't know about that,' Naylor retorted. 'But I also don't know what a girl of her class was doing wandering about the bush on her own and I wonder if you do.' He shrugged. 'I've got a bad feeling about it, but it's your business and I'll keep my nose out of it. Let's get these cattle.'

Lloyd carefully threaded his horse through the herd, looking for the strays that belonged to him and Jock. He found a red steer with his earmark and set about cutting it out. Old Dynamite watched the beast with pricked ears, muscles quivering, swinging with each turn of the beast with a rough, choppy motion that would have unseated a lesser rider.

At last he had them together. The cows and calves had taken considerable time and patience to separate from the herd, as it was essential to bring a cow and her offspring out together. A lone calf was usually impossible to handle on horseback.

'I'll send someone with you to see you on your way,' Naylor told him. 'I hope you don't have too much trouble with 'em. I'm sorry now I couldn't spare another man the other day to take them over for you and Jock, but we were pretty flat out. I wouldn't have trusted 'em to the Abo on his own.'

'That's all right, Naylor. What happened to Jock could have happened at any time. Thanks for your help.'

'I just hope Jamieson gets over it. He's too good a man to die.'

Louise was dreaming. Andrew and Donald had brought Lloyd's broken, bloodstained body home. The tattered, filthy clothes hadn't hidden the spear wounds in his body and his skull had been hideously crushed by a nulla nulla. The familiar, beloved features were barely recognisable under a layer of dried, encrusted blood.

She jerked into wakefulness, shuddering and crying with the horror of her nightmare. Still under its spell, it all seemed too real to be dismissed. Trying to divert herself, she threw back the sheet and buttoned her robe over her nightgown. She put a trembling match to the kerosene lamp that stood on the duchess beside her bed and glanced at the clock beside it. It was only half-past ten. She felt as if she'd been sleeping for hours.

Holding the lamp in her hand, she trod softly along the hall to Mr Jamieson's room. The flickering light revealed Mercy asleep in a stretcher beside her father's bed, curled up on her side with the bedclothes thrown back. Mercy had insisted on staying, rejecting Louise's suggestion they both look in at intervals during the night.

Mr Jamieson was neither asleep nor awake as he fought a war of entanglement with the blankets. He was muttering deliriously, his forehead hot and fevered under Louise's hand and her stomach churned with sickening apprehension. When they'd last changed the bandages, the wound was red and festering, inducing them to pack it with a mixture of sugar and soap to draw out the infection. Louise was dreadfully afraid there might be another burial in the family.

She straightened the covers and took the empty water jug to the kitchen to fill, using the lamp to light her way. As she retraced her steps along the landing that connected this building to the main part of the house, she heard a sound that made her pause, heart thumping. It came from somewhere near the saddle-room–a horse blowing wearily through its nostrils, a voice murmuring some soft, indistinguishable word. She set the jug on the railing, hurrying back through the kitchen and down the steps.

'Lloyd, is that you?'

'Yeah.' His voice came from inside the saddle-room, accompanied by the clinking of stirrup irons. Louise gave a sob of relief and abandoned the lamp, running towards the building in complete heedlessness of the dark. She bumped into him coming out the doorway and clutched at him, crying. Hard to believe that he was here under her hands, living and breathing flesh and blood, when that vivid nightmare had convinced her he'd met with some gruesome fate.

'Oh, Lloyd, thank God you're back!'

He hugged her briefly, his voice anxious. 'Is Jock all right?' It was obvious that he'd misconstrued her tears.

Her moment of pleasure dissipated. 'It's bad news, Lloyd. He's extremely ill. Mercy's sleeping in the room with him. I just looked in and he's very feverish.'

'I'll take a look at him.'

She retrieved the lamp and the jug and accompanied him, bypassing the kitchen this time. 'How did you manage?' she asked. 'Did you find the Aborigines?'

'No, they've cleared out. I went and got those cattle from Bauhinia Downs. I left them on Roundstone Creek. There were a couple of cows and calves of Jock's that couldn't come any further. At least they're a bit closer to home. The calves made it slow travelling and I had to make a bit of a yard to hold 'em all last night.'

'You must be exhausted.' In the bobbing lamplight Louise looked anxiously at his whiskered face. 'I'll make up a bed for you on the veranda.'

'No, don't bother. I've got me swag. I'll sleep in the saddle-room.'

Mercy stirred as they entered Jock's room, hastily pulling the covers over herself when she saw Lloyd. She watched them silently as he bent over the sick man. 'How do you think he is?' she whispered at last. 'I didn't mean to go to sleep.'

'You can't stay awake all night, Mercy.' Louise spoke as gently as she could. 'You did your share of the vigil last night, too.'

Suddenly tears were streaming down the girl's face. 'But if he were to die while I was asleep...'

'Oh, Mercy.' Lloyd crossed to her in one swift, compassionate stride, sitting on the edge of her bed to hold her against him, stroking her hair. 'Shush. Your father's not going to die. He's as tough as old boots.'

He sat there with Mercy, holding her and soothing her, while Louise tried to stifle her irrational jealousy. She knew Mercy's need was greater than her own, but somehow that didn't make it any easier.

She moistened Jock's mouth with water and bathed his face and arms to cool him. At last Lloyd got to his feet and pulled up chairs for himself and Louise, side by side. 'We'll stay here and help you watch him, Mercy.'

And then, while they watched, there was a change in the sick man. His fever seemed to abate and he roused enough to drink from the glass Louise held to his lips. Eventually he slipped into a restful sleep, the delirium easing at least for the moment.

Lloyd pushed back his chair, yawning. 'I think that's the worst of it over. Go back to sleep, Mercy and don't fret. He's going to be all right. I could do with some sleep meself.'

Anxious to be alone with him, Louise followed him out of the room and he turned to face her. 'Could you fetch me a pillow and another blanket, Louise?'

She went to the linen cupboard and followed him out to the saddle-room, where he was laying his thin swag on a pile of old sacks. He took the bedding from her and set it down, pulling her into his arms and holding her so tight she knew he must feel the thud of her wildly beating heart. As he held her, she sensed the weariness in him begin to ebb. Obviously he also needed the comfort and closeness of another human being, but the way he was holding her was very different from the way he'd held Mercy.

'Will you stay with me, Louise?'

She nodded and pressed closer, knowing what he was asking, but the emotions surging through her were too strong to be denied. The events of the last weeks had shown her how quickly life could be snatched away, making the moral issues seem less relevant.

He lifted her face with his fingers so he could look into her eyes. 'Do you mind waiting while I have a wash?'

Behind the kitchen was the dray with the iron ship's tank Mr Jamieson used to carry water from the river. The men often washed here before entering the house and a towel and cake of soap lay beside it in readiness. Louise stood and watched, holding the lamp, as Lloyd removed his shirt and bathed under the trickling water. She was fascinated, her eyes riveted in open flagrance of modesty. She hadn't seen him without a shirt before, despite those nights in the bush when they'd slept in the same droving camp. As she'd envisaged, his body was lean but well-muscled, with a light growth of hair on his chest glistening wet in the shadowy light.

Then he bent to slip off his boots and socks, balancing himself with one hand on the shaft of the dray. He looked up at her and grinned.

'I'm going to strip right off now. Turn your back if you want to.'

Louise's blood rushed to her face, her heightened senses responding with an unnerving blend of arousal and embarrassment. She set the lamp on the bed of the dray and swung away, trembling. She was still standing rigidly with her back to him, long after all sounds of splashing water had ceased, when his hand fell on her shoulder.

'Louise...'

She turned nervously, her eyes dropping in spite of herself. To her relief he'd replaced his trousers but was carrying his boots and shirt in one hand. He drew her to him with his free arm and kissed her, his bare chest damp against her robe.

'Don't be scared. I love you, Louise.'

Louise hesitated, caught between desire and inexperience. Briefly she wondered what she was letting herself in for, if she was ready for this. But that was absurd after the way she'd tempted him at the Race Ball.

Back in the saddle-room, she slipped off her outer robe and let him draw her down to his meagre bed. The odour of leather and neats-foot oil from the saddles mingled with dusty chaff and the scent of his bare skin, smooth under her quivering fingers. He raised himself above her to kiss her, exploring her mouth with his tongue, while his calloused hands stroked and gentled her. Then his fingers were at the front of her nightgown, slipping the buttons, and nervous anticipation held her enthralled.

She wore nothing but a chemise beneath the garment; there were no corsets and petticoats this time to deter him. As he cupped her bare breast in his hand for the first time he seemed to momentarily lose control, uttering some soft, unintelligible exclamation. Then his mouth was there where his hand had been while she ran her fingers restlessly through his hair, moaning with pleasure.

He touched her in other places she hadn't anticipated, reassuring her in her uncertainty, taking her past her natural shyness into a state of abandoned sensuality. In a haze of desire Louise clung to him, caressing the smooth play of muscles on his back and shoulders but afraid to explore further. He left his trousers until the last moment, unbuttoning himself to take her with her nightgown bundled above her breasts and her dark hair spread over the pillow.

Louise had expected pain, but her desire almost took her beyond it as she surrendered to his pleasure and hers. At last he shuddered against her and was still, growing heavy as his languorous body lay over hers. Then he rolled her to her side with him, still joined with her, whispering words of love and stroking the damp tangled hair back from her face.

Lloyd was the first to sleep, but he was also the first to wake in the dim light of dawn with Louise's head pillowed on his shoulder. The memories of last night rushed in as he gazed at the soft sleeping face, Sam Naylor's warning disregarded. He'd never taken a virgin before and he'd been nervous of hurting her, but mostly afraid that she might change her mind and stop him at the last moment. But she'd given herself bravely, responding to him with a mixture of eagerness and innocence that he'd found curiously touching. The whole encounter had moved him in a way he'd never experienced before.

He moved cautiously, easing his arm which had grown numb. She was instantly awake, turning her head to look at him after the first moment of disorientation. Lloyd saw the morning-after uncertainty and guilt reflected in her face and decided not to give her too much time for reflection. He kissed her and slid his arm about her waist to pull her tightly against him.

This time he was a little bolder, drawing her nightgown over her head and slipping off the remainder of his own clothes. He felt irresponsible and careless of the consequences, almost overwhelmed with excitement as he enjoyed every detail of her slim, firm body in the dim light. He admired it as he'd never admired the plump, dimpled curves that were considered fashionable. That brief hesitation past, Louise was passionate and eager, readily obeying his gentle instructions. She wrapped her legs around him and held him to her as if she might never let him go.

For a few moments Lloyd forgot the threat of death and sorrow and found relief from the strain of the past weeks. Later, they drifted in a satiated haze until he murmured drowsily, 'I heard the other day that the Catholic priest was in Banana on his rounds. He's probably still in the district somewhere. Once Jock's well, we should try an' track him down.'

Louise hesitated, her voice husky. 'I couldn't leave the Jamiesons just now, Lloyd. Not until Mrs Jamieson comes home. And unless I lie about my age, I'm sure he won't marry us without my father's permission.'

'Perhaps he might. If he knows your parents are on the other side of the world. And if we hint that we've...well...jumped the gun.' He kissed her and smoothed her hair away from her face, smiling a little. 'Anything to stop us living in sin.'

Louise didn't return his smile. He felt her body tense and for an instant he wondered if she planned to marry him at all. But that was ridiculous, after the way she'd just responded to him.

'We'll see when Mrs Jamieson arrives home,' was all she said.

When the first rays of sun peeped through the open door, Louise knew she could stay no longer. She reached for her nightgown and slipped it over her head, looking away uncertainly in the half dark as Lloyd stood to pull on his trousers. His male body was still so new to her. He smiled at her covert glances and pulled her to him to kiss her one last time.

'You'd better go quickly, before the house wakes up.'

'Yes.' She sobered. 'I must see how Mr Jamieson is.'

When she looked in Mercy's bed was empty, but Jock was sound asleep. His skin was clammy to the touch, but the burning heat of fever had gone. Perhaps it was too early to celebrate, with the possibility of a relapse; but for the moment they could be a little less anxious.

She took the jug from the washstand in her bedroom and went to the kitchen to fetch hot water from the tank on the side of the stove. She found Mercy there, beginning the preparations for breakfast. Mercy was the last person she wanted to face now, so she quickly filled the jug and escaped to her room. Here she stripped off and washed herself all over, looking apprehensively in the small mirror at her duchess, wondering if the evidence of the night's lovemaking was there for all to see. Her face and lips were reddened from the abrasive effect of Lloyd's unshaved beard, but fortunately the soreness of her body was something only she need know about. Otherwise she looked the same and she wondered how that could be so, when she felt irrevocably changed.

Perhaps Lloyd was right and a priest would marry them now, with or without her parents' permission. In the eyes of the world she'd ruined herself and her parents would surely wash their hands of her if they knew. But before they could wed there were certain confessions she had to make. Confessions that had only become harder with the passing of time.

It was difficult to face Lloyd at the breakfast table. His hair was damp and he'd shaved with Jock's razor, but he looked exhausted, with dark smudges under his eyes. That wasn't surprising, for she knew how little sleep he'd had. She wondered if he was reacting, as she was, to this houseful of innocent children which made the intimacies of last night seem indecent.

But he managed to eat hugely, demolishing a full plate of porridge and four or five chops before sending Maggie back to the kitchen to toast more bread over the fire. 'I haven't had anything to eat since yesterday dinnertime,' he said.

Louise looked up quickly, her cheeks flaming. 'You should have asked me to fetch you something last night. I didn't realize you hadn't eaten.'

He brushed aside the suggestion, smothering a yawn as he leaned back in his chair. He smiled at her, a touch of mischief in his eyes. 'I wasn't that hungry for food last night.'

She hastily began gathering plates to take to the kitchen, clattering the china noisily in her confusion. She knew the children would be oblivious to his double meaning, but perhaps Mercy would be suspicious and Louise hardly needed to be reminded of their transgressions right now.

Andrew, from the other end of the table, looked up at her and gave a little crow of delight. There'd been precious little laughter in this household lately, but with the easing of the boy's dreadful anxiety about his father he obviously needed some lighthearted relief.

'Miss Forrest's as red as a beetroot! She's sweet on you, Lloyd!'

In spite of herself she met Lloyd's eyes across the table. He kept on looking at her, smiling, while he answered Andrew. 'All the girls are sweet on me, Andrew.'

Louise quickly made her escape to the kitchen. As she stacked dishes in the sink she heard him farewelling the children and then he was there on the landing as she returned to finish clearing the table. He didn't speak but paused a moment, looking solemnly into her upturned, indignant face. He lifted his hand and gently trailed his fingers across her cheek in a caress that said more than any words. Then he stepped past her and, with a brief 'goodbye' to Mercy who was waiting in the doorway, watching, he was gone.

By lunchtime the improvement in Jock's condition was noticeable and the next morning he was able to sit up in bed and take a little food. As they were finishing breakfast, Lloyd arrived to ask after the patient.

'He's as bad-tempered as an old bull!' Mercy sniffed. 'He won't eat anything I cook for him.'

Lloyd laughed. 'He must be better if he's well enough to complain.'

He visited Jock's room and found the invalid propped up in bed with several pillows, picking with distaste at the eggs Mercy had placed on his breakfast tray.

'Och, this flaming egg's raw!' Jock greeted him irascibly. 'If they'd send a man something decent to eat. I'm that weak I can hardly lift the spoon and they give me something that turns me belly to look at it! What were they having in there?'

Lloyd told him, at length.

'Chops,' Jock growled. 'Aye, I might have known it. Now, if the lassies had cooked me a chop, it might have tempted me appetite. Something to put a bit of strength back into a man.'

'It's good to see you looking better,' Lloyd said, grinning. 'How's the leg?'

'Pretty sore. I'm as sick as a black fellow's dog and that's a sight better than I was yesterday. But enough about that. How did ye manage with those cattle? Mercy told me ye'd gone and got them.'

Lloyd stayed long enough to tell him and then, seeing that he was tiring, carried the unfinished breakfast away. Mercy looked at it anxiously.

'How does he expect to get better if he won't eat?'

'Perhaps you should try him with something else. Those eggs were nearly raw. He might prefer something he's used to, like a bit of good old mutton.'

Mercy looked at him in open horror. 'He can't be expected to eat *meat* when he's had nothing for days. He needs something that's easily digested. Mother's recipe book has a section on invalid cookery and it suggested coddled eggs. But I've got some broth boiling on the stove, that might tempt him.'

At least soup should be less nauseating than raw egg. 'I wouldn't worry too much. He'll eat when he's hungry.' He paused. 'Where's Louise?'

Mercy's thin little face stiffened. 'Miss Forrest is in the schoolroom with the girls.'

'Oh, in that case I'd better not disturb her. I'll come over again in a couple of days to see how your father is. But in the meantime send one of the boys over for me if you need help, won't you?' He looked in concern at her pale, drawn face and added in a different, gentler tone, 'It'll be all right, Mercy. Soon your mother will be home and things won't seem so bad.'

She nodded mutely and he turned from her and left the house. He badly wanted to see Louise, but he wouldn't intrude on the schoolroom. He didn't regret their night together; the very memory of it made his blood quicken with excitement and his longing for a repeat performance made his lonely bed at the shack oppressive. But he was acutely aware of how shocked and dismayed Jock would be if he knew, which made it more difficult than ever to pursue his relationship with her in her employer's house. Their plans would have to wait for a better time.

Chapter Fifteen

If it had been difficult before to conduct their relationship under the Jamieson's watchful gaze, their own guilt made it even harder now. Louise found their separations painful and their brief meetings tantalising and frustrating. It seemed Lloyd felt the same way, for one day while visiting the Jamiesons he slipped her a note when no-one was looking. Louise made some excuse to leave the room so she could read it.

It was brief enough, but as she perused it her stomach muscles clenched with a mixture of nerves and excitement. She hadn't seen his handwriting before, but although the hand appeared a little childish the spelling was better than she would have expected of someone who hadn't had a formal education.

Louise, can you make up some excuse to go riding and meet me at the boundry gate on Sunday morning? About ten o'clock? I love you. Lloyd.

She managed to signal the affirmative with a nod, accepting their relationship had gone beyond what was sensible or circumspect. After he'd gone, she folded the note carefully and hid it in her drawer amongst her underclothes, before spending the remainder of the week in a fever of anticipation.

It was usual for her to go riding on a Sunday. Mr Jamieson, who had left his bed and was sprawled on the front veranda in a squatter's chair, didn't even comment when she announced her intention of saddling Shadow that morning. Thankfully the children didn't clamour to accompany her. She trotted and cantered her horse, wondering if Lloyd would be waiting for her, fearing that perhaps he would be late.

He was there however, mounted on the chestnut mare she had ridden on that droving trip from Bauhinia Downs, with his dogs Buster and Soda at his horse's heels. He opened the gate for her without dismounting and kneed his horse close enough to kiss her, while their mounts fidgeted restlessly. His eyes were dark with desire as he smiled down at her.

'Where are we going, Louise? Back to the shack?'

Louise's heart did a quick pitter-pat. She knew what they would end up doing, wherever they were, and staying away from his shack would be no more than a futile and uncomfortable pretence at decency.

She nodded and he swiftly turned his horse about. With one accord they set up the road towards his homestead. At the horse-yards they unsaddled and turned the horses loose before she fell into his arms.

It was so different now to that night at Kilbride. Their mood was light-hearted, carefree, without the threat of death hanging over them. At the doorway to his shack he scooped her up and held her to his chest, laughing down at her as she squealed in mock terror, grunting a little at the weight of her.

'Crikey, you're heavy!'

She laughed back at him. 'You're full of compliments today, sir.'

'Heavy, but beautiful,' he amended, his eyes glinting mischievously.

He kicked the door closed behind them, carrying her to the other room where she'd slept once before, so long ago it seemed now. She briefly remembered that time, thinking she would have been aghast if she'd known then that she would one day be here with him like this.

The old makeshift bed had been replaced with a wrought-iron bedstead and horsehair mattress, much to her relief, as she feared the original contraption might not have supported them both. There were even sheets under the rough grey blanket, crisp and cool against her bare skin.

She commented on the addition to his furniture later as they lay in each other's arms. 'When did you acquire the bed, Lloyd?'

He smiled at her, trailing his fingers contentedly across her breast. 'Just after New Year. I ordered it up from Rockhampton. Just in case.'

'Just in case… of what? That I visited you here?'

He nodded, watching for her reaction. 'I needed it anyway. But the sheets were just for you. First time I've ever slept in sheets.'

Heat rose to her cheeks. 'You're shameless, Lloyd Kavanagh.'

'Look who's talking.'

'I know. I feel most awfully sinful.'

Lloyd looked at her searchingly. 'Louise, I love you and I'm going to marry you as soon as I can. I wouldn't want the Jamiesons to know about this, but I'm not ashamed of it. I know we should have waited until we were married, but I've seen people do a lot of worse things.'

'So have I.' She thought of Charles and the pregnant girl he'd cast aside. 'Once Mrs Jamieson comes home we can make our plans.'

She put aside her misgivings then, allowing him to arouse her again. She hadn't known it was possible to feel this way about a man, to enjoy or want his body so much. Perhaps she was immoral and certainly unladylike, but she couldn't help thinking a marriage that encompassed this much pleasure must have a fighting chance of success.

They left the bed eventually and made themselves a cosy lunch, eating it with her sitting on Lloyd's lap at the rough table. Louise wore her chemise, with the frilly legs of her drawers peeping out beneath it, while he'd abandoned his shirt and was clad in nothing but his trousers. A certain wickedness about it all only added to her excitement, but there was also an atmosphere of loving closeness that enchanted her. The rapport between them was so intense that she couldn't bear to spoil it with unwelcome confessions, so the words she'd planned to say to him remained unsaid.

The intimate meal rekindled their desire and they retired to the bedroom again. At last Lloyd filled the tub in the corner for her and she made herself respectable.

It was so hard to leave him; it was as if he'd become a part of her. When he finally farewelled her at the boundary gate it was early afternoon. Louise rode forlornly back to Kilbride, stepping quietly past Jock who was snoring in that same chair on the veranda. The voices of the older children, apparently engaged in a game of cribbage, drifted from the sitting room. She entered the house through a side door, going straight to the privacy of her room, where she spent the rest of the afternoon reading and dreaming, needing the solitude of her own thoughts. Please God Mrs Jamieson would be home soon so she and Lloyd could make their plans. She was tired of being furtive, tired of feeling guilty. She wanted to announce their love to the world so they could be together for more than just a few stolen hours.

Mrs Jamieson returned a month later, travelling on the train to Westwood and then on the coach to Banana. Jock insisted on driving in himself in the wagonette to meet her, limping because his leg still hadn't properly healed. It plagued him constantly by, as he put it, 'itching like the devil', but he'd been lucky to survive the blood poisoning and to escape tetanus, a possible complication that had secretly worried Louise. She could only guess the profuse way the wound had bled had helped to cleanse it of infection.

Mrs Jamieson appeared very drawn and tired, with a new look of sorrow on her face. She was also obviously with child, much to the surprise and even shock of everyone excepting Jock and the younger girls. Of these, even Maggie who was twelve years old, didn't appear to realize the significance of their mother's protruding stomach. The older ones had been told nothing and even now everyone preserved a discreet silence, pretending to be unaware there would soon be a new addition to the family.

Maurice was thin and pale and still weak. It would be a long time, if ever, before he regained his old exuberance. He'd been too ill to know when his sister died, but he'd been closer to the tragedy than the other children and it had obviously affected him deeply. After all, he'd only narrowly escaped the same fate himself.

When a hawker drove up to the homestead one day in a covered wagonette, Mrs Jamieson seemed unenthusiastic. But the children were excited at this rare novelty so she took them outside to greet him. Louise followed them out of the schoolroom, thinking of few personal items she needed to buy.

The man was standing with his back to Louise, sorting through a battered suitcase, when she joined Mrs Jamieson. Then he turned, holding up a length of dress fabric. Louise went very still. The blood drained from her face and she stood there mutely staring at him.

She couldn't help but recognise those smooth dark Indian features and the greasy black hair, even though she'd only seen him once before and briefly at that. This was the same hawker who had plied the Barclays with his wares some seven months ago, two days before her flight that had been precipitated by the letters the man had carried to her. Oh God, if he should remember her!

But it was too late to hide. 'This muslin, Missus Jamieson, would make very charming frock for one of your lil' girls.' He held it up for closer inspection. 'See quality , an' colour! Such pretty shade, don' you think?' He glanced towards Louise as he spoke and paused abruptly. A startled expression lit his eyes, to be replaced by a slower one of pure cunning. He smiled blandly. 'Why, Missy – Ashford, isn' it?'

Louise stared coldly back at him, hoping he couldn't read her dismay. Surely he shouldn't have remembered her name. Beside her she sensed Mrs Jamieson start and heard one of the girls give a soft exclamation.

'You must be mistaken.' She kept her tone cool, interjecting just a faint note of surprise. 'I'm Lucy Forrest. Have we met before?'

'At first I think…' The man considered her, his lips still spread in that sly smile. 'But no, perhaps not. As you say, I make mistake.'

'You must meet such a lot of people in your travels,' observed Mrs Jamieson calmly. 'It wouldn't be much wonder if you confused a few faces.'

'Very so,' responded the hawker smoothly. 'It has happened before. My apologies, Missy Forrest.'

Louise heaved a sigh of relief. Heavens, he'd startled her there for a moment. But he appeared to have accepted her denial. She made a few small purchases but didn't linger, fearing that her continued presence may serve to jog his memory further. She was relieved he didn't stay long enough to be offered accommodation for the night, but continued on his way with his larder replenished by some fresh mutton. As usual he would make camp by the roadside when it grew dark.

That night she lay awake after the others had retired, worrying about this unexpected development. For the first time she realized she could not hope to remain undetected for much longer. It was disconcerting that the man had known her name, for there had been no introductions made that day at Sherborne. He obviously had learned it somehow and remembered her more than superficially–possibly because he'd heard the story of her disappearance.

The incident had also brought home to her the likelihood of encountering some day, perhaps in the streets of Banana, a past acquaintance who would know Charles had been searching for her, or who would unwittingly betray her to the people who had become important to her. The answer was to be done with the pretence and marry Lloyd as soon as possible, for what could Charles or anyone else do then?

There was another, more urgent reason for not delaying their marriage plans. Unlike many girls of her age and class she knew one didn't have to be married to have a baby. Seeing Mrs Jamieson's evident pregnancy had brought home to her the realisation that the same thing could happen to her. She didn't want the shame of an infant born a few months early, knowing how people whispered and stared. Her behaviour had been both foolish and wanton and she'd given Lloyd a power over her that would have been frightening if she'd trusted him any less. She had no doubt of his love for her, but she would have to test that love to the limit before they could become man and wife.

There was no chance of seeing him during the week, but she resolved to ride over to his shack at the weekend even if it meant taking Mrs Jamieson into her confidence. But then something happened that made all her plans come to naught.

Louise was reading aloud to the children on the Friday afternoon, seated on a rug in the cool of the front garden, when Agnes stood up, looking down the road.

'Miss Forrest, there's someone coming!' She pointed excitedly at a puff of dust. Visitors at Kilbride were not frequent and two in a week were certainly the exception.

Louise twisted to gain a better view, watching as the lone occupant of the buggy grew gradually distinct. As she sat there her heart began to thud and muscles spasmed in her stomach.

'Oh, God,' she whispered under her breath. She looked down at her hands clenched together in her lap. They were trembling. Suddenly she was filled with a mad, fear-filled impulse to run and hide. But what was the use?

She stood slowly and turned to face the visitor. He reined his horses at the gate Maurice had already opened and stepped down. In the casual manner of one who was accustomed to having such services performed for him, he handed the reins to Maurice. He stretched his slim, elegant form and turned to smile easily at the governess as if he'd seen her only yesterday.

'Why, good afternoon, Louise.'

She could only stare at him, speechless. He raised his eyebrows.

'What is this? Haven't you a warmer welcome for your brother? I thought you'd be pleased to see me after all this time.'

Like a sleepwalker, she moved to him and presented her cheek for his kiss. He clasped her very briefly, his lips cool on her skin. She was stupidly aware that the children were gazing at them both in amazed fascination.

She jumped at the sound of Mrs Jamieson's voice at her elbow. Mercy was just behind her. 'Who have we here, Lucy?'

It was rare for Louise to be bereft of words, but now she found herself barely coherent. 'Mrs Jamieson, th…this is my brother Charles.' She put her hand on the woman's arm in a panic-stricken plea. 'Could I have a word with you in private, please?'

'No.' Charles Ashford's voice cut in, hard and emphatic. 'You've had months to make your explanations, Louise!' He'd already removed his hat and now he held out his hand to Mrs Jamieson, smiling briefly. 'You must be Mrs Jamieson. I apologise for this intrusion, but our parents have asked me to take Louise to England. I'm Charles Ashford.'

Mrs Jamieson, staring dumbfounded from one to the other, took his outstretched hand. But at his last words she started and dropped it. 'Did you say–*Ashford*?'

'That is correct.' He grinned maliciously at Louise. 'I'm afraid my sister has been practising a small deception on all of you.'

Mrs Jamieson gasped. 'Then that hawker was right!' She turned to stare at Louise with sudden hostility. 'So you've been using a false name all this time?'

'Yes.' Louise retorted fiercely, stung to anger by her brother's deliberate cruelty. 'I'm Louise Ashford. If Charles would only allow me to explain –'

'You've had six months to explain.' Charles cut in. 'You've left it a bit late, my girl. Right now you're going inside to pack your bags. Come along.' He turned to Louise's employer. 'Once again, my apologies, Mrs Jamieson. I hope this doesn't inconvenience you too much. But my sister should never have been here at all.'

They left the others gaping after them, the children looking bewildered, Mrs Jamieson and Mercy wearing expressions of incredulous anger.

'Which is your room?'

'In here.'

Charles propelled her inside and shut the door behind them. He glanced about him and grabbed a portmanteau from the top of the wardrobe, throwing it onto the bed. 'Now, pack.'

'No!' She glared at him. 'I'm *not* going with you. I can't leave them like this.' She laughed harshly, mimicking him. '"I hope it doesn't inconvenience you too much.' A jolly lot you care.'

'You're right, dear sister. I don't care. Exactly what you think you, an *Ashford*, is doing working for middle-class settlers like these I can't imagine.' He looked about him disdainfully. 'Good solid farming stock, I daresay. But the sort of people we normally would have working for *us*.'

'I don't care what you think of them, but they're my very good friends. You may cast me off if you like, but I'm staying here. I intend to marry a young man from the neighbouring property.'

'Ah, yes,' he drawled. 'I think I heard a whisper of a romance. Full of gossip, are these people in Banana. I believe his name is Lloyd Kavanagh. An enterprising young chap, from all I can gather. Perhaps he thinks a wife like you will assist him on his way up. I must take a look at him before we leave.'

'Before *you* leave. I shan't be accompanying you.' Louise's words were bravely spoken, but her heart was a lead ball in her chest. Charles was so implacable; she knew there would be no moving him.

'But yes, you shall be.' Charles opened the wardrobe and grabbed the hanging garments, then threw them onto the bed.

'But I *can't*!' She turned from him and sank down on top of her dresses, in desperation saying the only thing that was left to her now. 'I can't *not* marry him now.'

'What are you saying?' Charles loomed over her. He grasped her arm in his hard fingers, squeezing until it hurt. 'Don't tell me you've let him seduce you?'

She trembled and swallowed, but then she nodded, her face averted. Suddenly she dared not look up at him. 'He wants to marry me as soon as we can find a priest to do it.'

'Well, well, well.' That hateful drawling note was back in his voice, making her body quiver uncontrollably. 'It seems this Kavanagh is even more enterprising than I thought. I'm becoming more anxious to meet him by the minute.'

She jerked her head up, fear cramping her stomach. 'What are you going to do? Please, Charles, it wasn't his fault! At least, it was mine just as much. Just go away and forget all about us, *please.*'

'You're a little fool,' he said contemptuously. 'Don't you know that men never marry what they've already had?'

She flinched. 'Speak for yourself. I know Lloyd is different.'

'He'd marry you if I stayed to hold a gun at his head! Otherwise he'd do as he pleased. There are plenty who get away with it.'

'You should know! What about that wretched servant girl you ruined? Don't you ever think of her and the poor nameless child you fathered? Don't you ever wonder if they starved in the gutter?'

His eyes blazed and Louise shrank back, realising how close he was for an instant to striking her. 'Pack your clothes,' he ground out. 'You're not going to marry that bloody Irishman. You're coming to England with me.'

She stared at him hopelessly, trembling. 'But what future can there be for me in England? What other man would want me now?'

'They won't know about it and you won't tell them. Now hurry up!'

He left the room, slamming the door behind him. Louise heard him striding down the hall and then his voice.

'Ah, Miss Jamieson, is it? Perhaps you could assist my sister to pack?'

The sobs came without warning, convulsing her body. She turned away as Mercy opened the door without knocking and entered, stung to shame by the curiosity and contempt in the girl's eyes. In desperation Louise began bundling clothes into the portmanteau.

'I can't believe what you have done,' Mercy said. 'You've lied to us all, including Lloyd. He doesn't know who you are, does he? With a brother like that, what are you doing here?'

Louise said nothing, wiping her streaming eyes and nose on her sleeve.

'Hasn't Mother been through enough without this? You've picked a fine time to leave us, with the baby coming.'

Again. Louise didn't respond. She could have pointed out that she hadn't picked the time of her leaving.

But what was the point?

Chapter Sixteen

That night, locked by her brother in her bedroom at the Banana Hotel, Louise cried herself to sleep. She could hardly bring herself to believe that now she was to be dragged off to England. Her bid for freedom and the happy months in between had achieved her nothing but heartache. And what of Lloyd? Charles hadn't allowed her to see him. She imagined the Jamiesons telling him what had transpired and cringed inwardly. Heaven knows she hadn't wanted to hurt him and now he would learn her true identity in the most hurtful way possible. She would write to him once they arrived at Banyandah, but she wondered if he would ever forgive her. It was immaterial, she supposed, as she would probably never see him again.

Charles was late in coming to her room in the morning. When he did so his boots were dusty and his breeches saddle-stained, as if he'd already been out on horseback. In her despondency it barely registered with her. But she did notice that Charles was no longer angry; in fact he appeared to be extraordinarily good-humoured.

'Are you coming out for breakfast, or are you still sulking?'

'I shall join you,' she retorted stiffly. It was no use protesting and making a fuss that might be overheard. She may as well resign herself to her fate with as much dignity as was left to her. She'd always known there was no swaying Charles.

He'd allowed her nothing more than a brief goodbye to the Jamieson family yesterday and a stiff apology which hadn't been well accepted. Who could blame them? Someday, perhaps, she may be able to make amends to them. Mrs Jamieson had handed her a cheque for her wages, which Charles had promptly taken and handed back.

'Keep your money, Mrs Jamieson. We have no need of it, I can assure you.'

She'd gone with Charles without further protest, unwilling to suffer the degradation of another scene. It was bad enough to think the children had witnessed as much as they had. She'd become so fond of them and they of her. She'd hugged the girls and little Maurice, but she hated to think of the confusion they must be experiencing now.

Breakfast was a hurried affair, with Charles anxious to be on his way. There were few people in the street to see them leave when he handed her into the Banyandah buggy, but those present stared at her curiously. Charles began to whistle as they set out on the rutted, pot-holed coach road and turned to smile at her in the old, charming way she remembered well.

'Cheer up, dear girl! It would never have done to have married that fellow, you know. You'd be nothing but a household drudge inside five years, with as many brats swarming at your feet.' He idly took one of her hands and removed the glove from it. 'You're already on the way to it, by the look of this. Did that Jamieson woman set you to scrubbing the floors? I thought you were supposed to be a governess.'

'I *was* a governess!' she snapped, snatching her hand away. 'But Mrs Jamieson has been away and Mercy needed help with the cooking and housekeeping.'

'Is Mercy that little sharp-faced urchin? She looks as if she's been in the sun too long.'

Louise flinched at his derisive tone. 'Some people have to work for a living.'

He smiled. 'But you don't have to, do you, Louise?'

She turned away from him, refusing to rise to his bait.

After a long silence she said coldly, 'I thought you would have been in England long since, Charles. Why didn't you sail without me?'

He looked at her, his expression incredulous. 'Did you really think I would leave, not knowing where you were or what had happened to you? By heavens, you've led me a merry chase.' He laughed without humour. 'When I arrived at the Barclays' last year to find you gone, I spent days in the saddle, making inquiries. The Barclays were in a terrible state. I think they've long since decided you were probably murdered, or raped, or both. Somehow I never thought so, though. We Ashfords know how to look after ourselves. Not,' his mouth twisted, 'that you've been doing such a good job of it lately.'

She was silent and after a moment he continued, 'I suppose you've guessed it was the hawker who finally set me onto you. He was in the Gainsford district when you disappeared. I remember asking him if he'd seen you. He recognised you the other day and sent word to me when he reached Banana. He succeeded in dunning me for two quid, the cunning little bastard.'

'Charles, I may be a fallen woman, but no-one of my recent acquaintance has subjected me to that sort of language.'

'If you had married that Kavanagh chap, you would soon have grown accustomed to it, no doubt. And to being beaten every day, most likely.'

She laughed scornfully. 'I'm sure your wife–should any girl ever be deluded enough to marry you–would be in more danger of being beaten. Lloyd is not a violent person.'

'Meaning that I am?' Her implication seemed merely to amuse him. 'Then hadn't you better watch your tongue?'

She barely heard him. Talking of Lloyd had caused a fresh wave of desolation to wash over, making her drop her head into her hands. 'Oh, God, Charles, why did you bother? Why didn't you give up on me long ago?'

Charles lightly flicked his long buggy whip across the backs of the pair of horses. 'Why? Because I was determined to find you. Do you think I could have greeted our dear parents with the news I'd left you behind here, living in God knows what penury? You might have been starving for all I knew.'

Louise snorted. 'Our "dear parents" have never overly concerned themselves with either of us. You know that as well as I do.'

Charles shrugged. 'I've always been happy to go my own road without interference from them. I thought you felt the same way.' He turned to smile at her. 'But you're my favourite sister. I care what happens to you and I don't believe they're as indifferent as you suggest.'

'If you really cared for my happiness, you would allow me to stay and marry Lloyd.'

Charles, however, was obviously tiring of the argument. 'One day you'll thank me for getting you out of this mess.'

'Do you really think so? It may please you to pretend you're fond of me, but it's only for as long as it suits you. You've never cared for anyone but yourself.'

He laughed harshly. 'Don't try to tell me you're any different, Louise.'

'I believe I am different. This past year has shown me that.'

'Pray enlighten me.'

She tilted her chin. 'I've learnt riding roughshod over others isn't the only way to succeed. I've seen how it is to be a member of a happy, united family and I believe that's more important than position and money. We Ashfords may be able to trace our ancestors back to William the Conqueror, but does that make us better people when all is said and done?'

'You're talking rot,' Charles sneered. 'Of course it does. Acting as governess to all those brats has turned your brain. And you're a hypocrite, besides. Didn't you ride roughshod over the Barclays when it suited you?'

'I'm sorry for that. I realize now just how badly I behaved.'

'Such humility. Perhaps you would have suited your Irishman after all.'

'He's not an Irishman. He's an Australian.' Just talking about him was a comfort. She hugged the words to her, like a child with a favourite toy. Whatever happened she had her memories and no-one would be able to take them from her.

'What difference does it make?' Charles sounded bored. 'Not to worry–a few months of the good life in England will have you forgetting all these small-time selectors to whom you've become so partial.'

Louise bowed her head, refusing to reply. She would never forget Lloyd – how could she? Perhaps the pain would ease in time, but right now the hollow, yearning ache threatened to consume her.

Charles started to whistle again, refusing to allow Louise to spoil his good mood. She'd snap out of her doldrums soon enough. He was still congratulating himself on the way he'd handled Kavanagh.

Charles had been taught boxing in his college days and it had been surprisingly easy. There would be no interference from that quarter, no danger that the upstart might attempt to pursue Louise. Louise had made it possible by virtue of her deceit.

Early that morning Charles had hired a saddle-horse from the hotel-keeper and ridden out to Kavanagh's place, while Louise slept. The sun was rising above the tops of the gum trees when he forded the river and turned right towards Kavanagh's homestead.

Guided by the unmistakable sound of an axe splitting wood, he found Kavanagh working at the woodheap behind his shack. The hard physical work showed off his sister's lover to advantage, accentuating the strong shoulders and muscular thighs braced sturdily against the swing of the axe. Charles sat his horse unobserved and watched for a moment, taking in the primitive shack and the rough dress of the man before him. He imagined the fellow and Louise in bed together and his anger built.

Lloyd looked up, startled, at the horseman's approach. He set down his axe and wiped his sweaty face with his sleeve. Still mopping his face, he advanced towards the man, squinting a little into the rising sun. It wasn't every day a well-dressed silver tail came riding up to his homestead, but he hid his surprise and greeted the stranger with his usual friendly civility.

'What can I do for you?'

'Are you Kavanagh?'

Lloyd nodded. The visitor said nothing, looking him over leisurely and then he leaned forward on his horse's neck, lifting a lock of mane in his long fingers and smoothing it to the other side. At last he smiled, a pleasant, friendly smile that somehow made Lloyd's gut tighten with apprehension.

'So you're the bastard who's been having a go at my sister.'

Lloyd stared at him, speechless, the blood draining from his face. Shock turned to dismay, mingled with recognition. So this was Louise's brother. Wasn't he supposed to be in England? But how did he know that he and Louise had–

Now was the time to tell him he wanted to marry Louise, but instinct told him to be silent. Somehow he didn't think that information would mollify this debonair stranger who looked so much like Louise and who was yet so different. So alien.

'Well, have you anything to say for yourself?' Charles was still smiling, but the pleasantness was an illusion, fast disappearing. 'Louise says you intend to marry her. Is that so?'

Lloyd swallowed and nodded. 'We would have been married by now but for circumstances.'

'So meanwhile it's been a case of have your fun while you wait, is that right?'

Guilt and the beginnings of anger made the heat rush back to his cheeks. 'What do you know about it?'

'Louise told me.' Charles casually felt in his coat pocket and withdrew an envelope, tossing it to Lloyd. 'She sent you this.' He paused and raised a sardonic eyebrow. 'You do read, I presume?'

Lloyd ignored the taunt, catching the envelope and opening it with suddenly unsteady fingers. The white page within was inscribed with a stylish, flowing script which looked like Louise's, but he'd only seen it once or twice. As he slowly read it, talons of dread and disbelief clawed at innards.

My dear Lloyd, the note said.

I apologise for leaving you like this without explaining in person. I have been deceiving you, as you will see. But you must realize that I could never have married you. I'm sorry I allowed you to entertain that hope. I'm going with my brother Charles and shall sail to England on the first available ship. It is doubtful if we shall meet again and probably as well that we should not. Perhaps it will amuse you to discover that I am not Lucy Forrest, but Louise Ashford, the daughter of Harry Ashford formerly of Banyandah.

Regretfully yours,

Louise Ashford.

When he reached the reference to her name and saw the signature he started. He stared at it for a moment, dazed and barely comprehending.

'Louise *Ashford?*' he repeated, incredulous.

'That is correct.' Charles was grinning down at him, clearly enjoying it all. 'I'm Charles Ashford. And it doesn't do to play around with the Ashford women, you know.'

Lloyd hardly heard him. He was still staring down at the letter, his brain whirling. 'She didn't write this.'

Charles's face hardened and he straightened in the saddle. 'Oh yes, she did. She has been rather leading you down the garden path, old chap. Not to worry, she gave me the devil of a time too, trying to find her. She's an inconsiderate little hussy.'

Lloyd looked at him levelly, though his heart was beating a death march in his chest. 'I still don't believe she wrote it.'

Charles laughed at him. 'What makes you so sure of her? Why didn't she tell you who she really was, if she planned to marry you?' He swung lithely out of the saddle and dropped the reins. 'Before I go...'

He turned towards him and then moved so suddenly, Lloyd didn't see it coming. His fist smashed into Lloyd's face with a force that rocked him partially off his feet. An equally vicious left followed swiftly, driving into the belly. Given no chance to retaliate, Lloyd doubled up and sank to the ground, moaning. An elegant, highly polished riding boot caught him in the groin, driving him backwards. He screamed in agony, rolling swiftly to his side and drawing up his body in an effort to protect himself. He began to dry-retch, shock and pain making him violently nauseous.

Charles stood over him, his eyes glinting dangerously. 'I'll leave it at that. I'd hate to spoil a good-looking chap like you for the ladies. I don't care who you screw, so long as it's not my sister. Just don't bother coming after her.'

He caught his horse, which had shied away at this sudden eruption of violence and now stood snorting. Through a red-rimmed haze Lloyd watched him mount up, ruthlessly controlling the frightened animal, and ride away without a backward glance.

Lloyd moved his tortured body, his moans giving way to a string of profanities as he struggled to a sitting position. Burying his head in his arms, he let wracking sobs of grief and humiliation shake his frame. But he didn't cry for long–he hadn't done so since his tenth birthday when his father had beaten his mother and him in a drunken rage. He wouldn't continue to abase himself over a woman so fickle and deceitful.

When at last the pain had eased enough to allow him to rise, his eyes were dry. He staggered to the woodheap and sat on an uncut log, holding his bleeding face in his hands. It was unbelievable, but it had to be true. That had undoubtedly been

Louise's brother, for the likeness was unmistakable. And he'd behaved just like an Ashford, after all.

For a foolish, angry moment he entertained thoughts of revenge, but he quickly thought better of it. Vengeance was useless and gained a man nothing but his pride. Pride was of little use to someone who was rotting in gaol, which is where he would most likely end if he tangled with Charles Ashford.

Images of Louise filled his mind. Mounted arrogant and aloof on old Shadow that first day out from Bauhinia Downs. Clinging to him dazed with passion on the night of the race ball. Coupling with him in the saddle-room at Kilbride; and again here in his own bed. He remembered her dodging the marriage issue with the agonising realisation that she'd never intended to marry him at all. She'd lied to him and amused herself with his body. But the incredible part of it was, she'd given him her virginity in the process.

He thought of his life and of the few people who had ever loved him. Louise had meant the world to him, a new and better future, and he hadn't doubted her commitment. Now his dreams were in ruins and the pain was tearing him to pieces.

Gingerly he rose to his feet and staggered into the shack, rummaging in one of the cupboards for a bottle of rum. He sat at the table with it, drinking steadily, until at last oblivion overtook him and he slumped there in the chair with his head pillowed on his arms.

Chapter Seventeen

Two weeks later at Moreton Bay, Charles and Louise Ashford boarded a sailing ship bound for England. Charles hadn't wanted to wait for a passage on a steamship, which would do the journey in half the time. Louise suspected it was because, once they were at sea, it would be impossible for her to run away again.

He'd engaged a companion for her, a middle-aged Englishwoman who had been widowed in Rockhampton and was now returning to her homeland. During the journey by steamer from Rockhampton to Brisbane Louise had been miserably ill with seasickness and hadn't enjoyed sharing the cramped confines of her cabin with a stranger. Her companion, Mrs Souther, was a dour-faced woman with whom she found it difficult to converse. She wished Charles had dispensed with convention and allowed her to travel without a female chaperone.

As Louise stood on deck and watched the shores of Moreton Bay recede before her eyes, despair lodged in her throat, making her gasp for breath. Would she ever see again the familiar Queensland coastline or the man she loved? Above her, the giant sails filled and billowed with the breeze, while the rigging groaned and the wooden deck creaked protestingly as the ship rolled with the swell. Lloyd was already separated from her by hundreds of miles. By now he should have received the letter she'd written to him from Banyandah. She wondered if he was still angry with her and if he was missing her.

Tears stung her eyes despite the proximity of her fellow passengers jostling for space at her elbow. Turning her face to the breeze to dry them, the familiar queasiness began to stir her stomach at the increasing motion of the ship. She brought her handkerchief to her mouth and hastened below.

As the weeks went by Louise's sickness didn't ease. Unable to eat more than the lightest of meals, she spent most of her time in her cabin. Instead of losing weight as she would have expected, her gowns seemed to be growing tighter at the waist. As the days went by her fear increased.

The ship's doctor, whom Charles had summoned to visit her on more than one occasion, must have suspected something. He asked if he could examine her and gently probed her stomach.

'When did you last have your monthly bleeding, Miss Ashford?'

Louise paled. 'Not for more than two months. Probably three. Is that significant?'

'I'm afraid so.' The doctor, a middle-aged man with wise, gentle eyes, looked at her compassionately. 'Is it possible you could be with child?'

Louise flushed and bowed her head. 'Yes, it is possible. I have been afraid of this.'

'I take it the baby's father is no longer in your life.'

She nodded. 'Not from my choice, or his. My brother didn't consider him a suitable husband for me.'

'What a pity. If he's back in the Colonies it is too late for second thoughts on your brother's part. But Mr Ashford will have to be told. Would you like me to talk to him?'

She nodded, knowing Charles would be appalled and angry, though there was nothing that could be done about it. They could hardly ask the ship to turn around and take her back to Brisbane. She was going to England, child or no.

Charles looked grim and pale when he came to see her. Thankfully he didn't lecture her or moralise. From Charles of all people she couldn't have taken that now.

'It seems I took you away too late. The damage has already been done.'

'You were so determined to take me,' Louise responded bitterly. 'If only you had left me there.'

Charles ignored this comment. 'We'll find a way out of this. If you keep to your cabin once it begins to show...heaven knows you've been doing that already. When we disembark, you'll be wearing your cloak; you can keep that wrapped around you. Once we arrive at Fenham Manor you can stay in seclusion until the baby is born. No-one need know.'

She stared at him incredulously. 'But what of the baby? How do we hide its existence?'

'We'll find a good home for it. There's sure to be a childless couple around who'd keep their silence.'

'I'm not about to give it away! How can I give it away? You speak as if it were a stray puppy!'

'Louise.' Charles sat on the chair opposite her and looked at her levelly. 'You've no choice. If you keep it you ruin yourself and disgrace the entire family. You can hardly raise an illegitimate child at Fenham Manor and expect society to accept it. You'll have to play your part in this for everyone's sake.'

She hadn't the strength to argue. What was the use? What else could she do but miserably reconcile herself to whatever plans they had in store for her?

The weary weeks went by. They had long since rounded the southerly tip of Western Australia and entered the vastness of the Indian Ocean. At least the seas were calmer now. Louise had grown weak and pale with constant sickness and a disinclination for food, much of which she was unable to keep in her stomach. Her feelings about the baby were ambivalent. She was shamed and humiliated at her pregnancy, yet the child was Lloyd's and as such could not be rejected. She worried about the infant's welfare, but at around four months she felt the first strange, fluttering movements and was reassured.

Day after endless day she lay in the lonely saloon-class cabin that she shared with Mrs Souther, usually seeing no-one but the widow, the doctor and the stewardess who brought her meals. She even began to look forward to Charles's visits. Living as she was in a state of emotional and physical apathy, she found her resentment towards her brother fading and Charles was willing to be kind.

Perhaps he regretted his decision to take her away. Perhaps he felt responsible for the pale wraith she had become, but it was too late for second thoughts. When the vessel lay becalmed in the torpid heat of the Tropics for several days, so helplessly at the mercy of the winds, she suspected he also wished he'd waited for a passage on one of the steamers.

Mrs Souther had become aware of Louise's condition and the woman's shocked censure added to her misery. Charles bribed the widow to silence and found a dressmaker on board who was able to make over Louise's gowns that no longer fitted. Since she wasn't appearing in public it hardly mattered what her clothes looked like. At least the calmer seas enabled her to recover from her nausea and eat heartily for the first time since boarding ship. Then at last the winds came to their rescue, blowing them into the Gulf of Aden and the Red Sea and finally through the Suez Canal.

England at last! As they docked at Portsmouth, Charles was in high spirits but Louise viewed the grey, grimy town with indifference. It was early autumn and raining, with already a damp cold that seeped through her many layers of clothing and made her shiver. And this in the south of England. It was fortunate for Charles that he didn't expect to drag her into the north. Sunny Devon, her mother had used to say. Well, let her only be right.

As they disembarked, Louise drew her cloak more firmly about her, covering her loose dress. Her pregnancy wasn't particularly obvious, even without the cloak, as she wasn't large for six months gone. With her hood pulled over her hair she was a drab, insignificant figure, scarcely recognised by her fellow passengers who hadn't seen her for the last two months of the journey. They'd been told that Miss Ashford was confined to her cabin with illness and her present appearance did nothing to contradict that story.

The Ashfords passed the night at an uncomfortable hotel that wasn't usually frequented by the upper classes. In the morning they took their leave of Mrs Souther, who would be returning to her old home in Sussex, and boarded the train which would take them through Southhampton to Dorchester.

Louise paid little attention to the varied beauties of Dorset, with its valleys and down-lands and long coastline. Charles was in a better humour and inclined to be interested in the scenery despite an outward bearing of nonchalance. Louise, though now free of the acute nausea that had plagued the early months of her pregnancy, was tired, dispirited and unbearably homesick for Australia and the man she'd left behind there.

In Dorchester they exchanged the train for a hired horse-drawn carriage and as each jolting, uncomfortable mile brought them closer to Devon she began to dread the approaching confrontation with her parents. They would be expecting them, for Charles had managed to send a letter ahead of them while their ship was waiting to dock in Portsmouth. But she guessed he hadn't entrusted to letter the delicate matter of her condition and that he was dreading the interview with their father almost as keenly as she. Louise suspected their parents wouldn't have chosen to jeopardise the family's good name for the sake of their elder daughter. Charles was likely to be out of favour for bringing her to England.

Charles enthused over the extreme age of such Devonshire townships as Exeter, with its cathedral dating to the Norman occupation in the twelfth century. To one who had never been out of Australia, where even the first settlement at Sydney wasn't yet a hundred years old, these centuries of history were something to marvel at. But Louise barely glanced at the historic buildings in the streets of Exeter.

It was only a few hours' journey from here to Fenham Manor, so Charles gave the coachman orders to proceed straight through town. Once out of the metropolis they passed through some of the most picturesque countryside they had yet seen. The green hills and valleys wooded with oak and beech, the farmlands with sheep and red Devon cattle, the many quaint villages with their cottages of cob and thatch; this was what Mrs Ashford had enthused over. Yet Louise, staring blindly out of the coach window, was unmoved by the beauty of it all.

Dreading the approaching interview with her parents, she longed to be back in the comfort of Lloyd's arms, unencumbered by this embarrassing pregnancy. If she closed her eyes she could almost hear his voice murmuring endearments and feel his hands stroking her hair, with the coarse weave of his shirt rough under her cheek and the smell of horses and saddle-leather in her nostrils. The physical desire for his body was gone, quenched by the dragging weight of her stomach and the tenderness of her swollen breasts. But she seemed to have succumbed to an emotional weakness that made her need of him stronger than it had ever been. What had begun so recklessly and thoughtlessly had ended dismally, in shame and misery, with the child within her the innocent victim.

It was almost dusk when she was roused by the horses' hooves clattering noisily on the cobblestones of yet another village street. Charles's voice intruded on her misery. 'This is the local village. Buck up, old girl. We're nearly there.'

Louise had barely time to register the sign on the ancient inn– featuring the head of a huge black boar and appropriately titled – when the coachman turned up a narrow country road. After a mile or so they came to a set of wrought-iron gates, opened for them by a gatekeeper even before the horses drew up. She stared apprehensively down the short driveway, bordered by a sweep of emerald-green lawns, to the manor.

It was a large stone house of two floors with a tiled roof and countless chimneys. She shivered, finding the stark aspect of the house grey and forbidding in the waning light. As she descended stiffly from the coach the massive front door opened and an important-looking individual stepped out.

'Mr Ashford, Miss Ashford,' the man said formally, inclining his head in a slight bow. 'Welcome to Fenham Manor. I'm Dawes, the butler. I trust your journey was comfortable?'

Dawes was very civil and correct, but Louise no longer felt at ease with servility. She merely nodded her head and left the responses to Charles.

'As comfortable as could be expected.' Charles spoke tersely. 'However we're both tired. If you could send someone to see to our luggage...'

'Of course, sir. Mr and Mrs Ashford are waiting in the library. They are most anxious to see you and Miss Ashford.' He led them through the door and into a sparsely-furnished entrance hall, with medieval tapestries hanging on the otherwise bare granite walls. 'If you will allow me to take your coats I will show you to the library. Dinner has been held back until nine o'clock.'

Charles allowed the butler to help him out of his overcoat but restrained him when he made to take Louise's cloak. 'Could you have Miss Ashford shown to her room right away? She isn't well and must rest. I shall see our parents now.'

'Certainly, sir.' Dawes rang a bell for one of the maids and on her prompt arrival instructed her, 'Show Miss Ashford to her room and see that she has brought to her whatever luggage she requires.'

The maid, a thin, pale-faced girl with wispy hair escaping from her cap, swiftly did as she was bid, leading Louise up a magnificent oak staircase. She took her down a long hallway, past a number of closed doors, finally pausing at the end of the passage.

'This is to be your room, Miss.' The girl spared her a nervous, yet curious sideways glance as she swung open the door. 'Mr Ashford will have one of the rooms at the other end of the passage.'

Louise stepped inside, staring in surprise at the elegant interior. There was a four-poster bed with silken hangings, a beautiful mahogany dressing-table in the much-decorated contemporary style, sumptuous wallpaper, a thick carpet and heavy velvet curtains.

'This room has the best view of all,' the maid was saying. 'It looks over the back gardens and the woods, as you will see in the morning. And this doorway leads to your dressing room and beyond it is the bathroom.'

The bathroom was fitted with a large tub and hot and cold taps, all very modern. It appeared this part of the house had been recently renovated. Louise knew the building itself dated from the sixteenth century and the draughty hallways had done nothing to dispel the exterior impression of almost Spartan starkness.

Louise closed the dressing-room door and turned back to the maid. 'Could you have my trunk brought up, please?'

The girl directed her a quick look and Louise remembered belatedly that her family didn't say please and thank-you to servants.

'Of course, I'll see to that right away, Miss. Would you like me to take your cloak? Mrs Ashford's maid will be along to help you change.'

'No, that won't be necessary. I'm accustomed to dressing myself. I shall not be coming down to dinner. Could you have a tray sent up to me?'

'Very well, Miss.' The girl looked at her strangely but went obediently to the door. 'Please ring if there's anything more you need.'

Louise heaved a sigh of relief as the door closed behind her and quickly slipped out of her cloak. She left it on the floor where it fell and went to the bathroom to wash. While she was there she heard her trunk being deposited in the dressing-room, but decided not to change for bed just yet. Should either of her parents decide to confront her tonight she would be better equipped to face the interview fully dressed.

The maid had turned back the covers on the bed but she didn't get between the sheets, merely laying on top and drawing the hangings about her. She closed her eyes in the comforting darkness, succumbing to an exhaustion that was as much the result of emotional strain as of the rigours of travel. It was surprising to reflect that she'd once ridden almost as many miles on horseback as she'd travelled by train and coach since arriving in England. Of course she hadn't been six months with child then, but on the contrary had been in the best of health and spirits. How much her life had changed since that day she'd ridden away from Gainsford almost a year ago.

She was unable to sleep, tired though she was. Instead she lay there with her thoughts drifting again to Lloyd and fleetingly to the Jamiesons. Mrs Jamieson would have given birth to her infant long since. She wondered bitterly if Lloyd had turned to Mercy for consolation and how he and the Jamiesons had responded to the letters she'd written from Banyandah. Had they accepted her excuses for deceiving them? In Lloyd's letter she'd included the address of Fenham Manor and had asked him to write to her there. If he did so and presuming his letter wasn't intercepted by her father, would she tell him about the baby? There was little he could do but agonise. But if he didn't write she would assume he hadn't forgiven her and so he would never know of the existence of his child.

The thought depressed her further, making the tears smart behind her heavy eyelids. Her own predicament was distressing enough, but her anxiety for the future of her child outweighed even her yearning for the babe's father.

A dinner tray was brought to her and she forced herself to eat for the infant's sake. When the long-awaited knock came at her door she leapt off the bed and went to the mirror to compose her dress and hair before opening it.

It was her mother, slim and still attractive, elegantly attired in evening dress but with more grey in her fair hair than Louise remembered. It was approaching two years since they had seen each other but there were no glad cries of welcome. Mrs Ashford swept into the room without a word, her well-bred face showing only cold anger and contempt. Louise, though faint with tiredness and trepidation, was strengthened by a surge of the old defiance that had so exasperated her mother in past times.

'Well!' Mrs Ashford surveyed her daughter. 'I found it hard to credit Charles with the truth at first, but I can scarcely disbelieve the evidence of my own eyes! How many people have seen you in this disgusting condition?'

Louise flinched. 'Only Mrs Souther, the companion Charles engaged for me, and the stewardess who came to my cabin aboard ship. And the doctor, of course. I was careful to keep my cloak wrapped about me whenever I had to appear in public.' She heard the defensive note in her own voice and despised herself for it, so added derisively, 'So with any luck you may yet be able to keep this dark family secret. The Ashford skeleton in the closet, no less!'

Her sarcasm did nothing to improve Mrs Ashford's humour. 'Louise, did it ever occur to that rebellious head of yours that being allowed to stay behind in the colonies was a privilege? Did it ever occur to you that perhaps you shouldn't have abused that privilege? No, I suppose not,' she continued when Louise made no reply. 'But having put Charles and the Barclay family through a great deal of anxiety and inconvenience–to say nothing of us, when we finally heard from Charles–and having found a responsible position with a hopefully respectable family, need you then have acted like a woman of the streets? Charles says your lover was a humble selector of convict stock! An Irish Catholic, no less! One could be forgiven for thinking you were deliberately *trying* to hurt us and dishonour the family name!'

Her words were meant to sting and sting they did. Louise was mature enough now to see the truth of them and to appreciate her mother's point of view. Yet it was Mrs Ashford's contemptuous dismissal of Lloyd that fired her anger.

'No, I wasn't deliberately trying to hurt anyone,' she retorted through set teeth. 'I merely fell in love with a man who is honest and decent and loving in spite of his origins. If Charles had let me alone we would be married now and my baby would have a father and a name. That is all I have to say for myself.'

'It won't be enough to satisfy your father, young lady! He was too angry tonight to even think of seeing you. You say this man was decent, but your relationship obviously went beyond decency. You may be thankful if your father ever forgives you.'

'His forgiveness or otherwise is a matter of complete indifference to me. Now if you please I wish to retire to bed.'

'I wish instead you would learn some respect,' Mrs Ashford snapped. 'How a daughter of mine could grow into such a tramp I shall never understand! You look a disgrace–where on earth did you get that terrible gown? At least you used not to be a sloven. You look as if you haven't been eating properly–but if the baby is sickly and doesn't survive it will be a good thing. Now, don't answer me back; I'm tired of your impertinence. Your father will be up to see you in the morning.'

With that she left, closing the door none too gently behind her. It was an indication of her state of mind, for normally any lapses in good manners were unknown to Mrs Ashford. Louise guessed that the shame of her predicament was hitting hard at her mother's pride. She supposed she should feel sympathy for her, but the callous reference to the baby's health made that impossible.

The interview with her father in the morning was no better. Her hands were already shaking when she opened the door to him. He was the same as ever, large, grey-haired and swarthy with the tan of Queensland summers that so far the English climate hadn't managed to fade. He looked angry and forbidding, his expression hardening even further as he took in her appearance.

'I have very little to say to you, Louise,' he stated grimly. 'But I would like to make two things clear. First, that the only two members of the household who are to know of your condition will be Mrs Evans, the housekeeper and Brown, your mother's maid. Mrs Evans will bring you your meals and Brown will attend to your clothes and any other personal needs. You will remain in your room except for occasions when it can be arranged for you to walk in the grounds without being seen. The remainder of the household will be told and must believe that you are ill.

'Secondly, you must know what is to be done with the infant. The coachman and his wife have no children. If they show interest in adopting a child, it can be arranged without them knowing whose it is. Jones is a trustworthy fellow and would keep his silence even if he suspected. The child could grow up as the Jones's own and need never know differently. Hopefully it will be born before Christmas so you are free to join the family festivities. Then at Easter we will go to London for the Season and you and Caroline will be presented.'

Louise laughed bitterly. 'I'm to be presented? Dressed in purest white to make my curtsy to Royalty? What a sham!'

'You will do as you are told,' Harry Ashford snapped. 'Think yourself lucky we're doing this much for you, for I can assure you that you don't deserve even the roof above your head! I should have laid my whip about your sides when you were younger, instead of leaving you to the discipline of that foolish governess. If you make any sort of marriage at all you should be thankful. And stay away from Caroline, do you hear? The less she knows of this the better.'

Louise didn't answer and he glared at her in silence before turning on his heel and leaving the room. Louise flung herself across the bed, raging silently.

'Oh God, I hate him. I hate him. They shan't take my baby away from me!'

But in her heart she knew they would and even that it was the only solution.

Chapter Eighteen

By the next day Louise was stricken with a severe head cold. Charles, who had visited her briefly the previous day, stayed away and she saw only Brown and Mrs Evans, the maid and housekeeper who had been assigned to look after her.

When her health improved she asked Mrs Evans to obtain some cambric and lace so she could fill the tedious hours by sewing for her child. If this was the only thing she would be able to do for the poor little mite, at least he or she wouldn't be foisted onto the world without a wardrobe. It gave her a sense of purpose into the bargain. She stitched until her fingers were sore and her eyes smarted, but she was very proud of the resulting, beautiful collection of gowns and bonnets.

She didn't see her sister Caroline for two weeks. Finally she encountered her one day when returning from her walk in the grounds via the little-used back stairway.

Louise, her pregnancy disguised by the cloak, paused and looked at her startled sister without speaking. Caroline would now be almost seventeen. She was both the fairest in complexion and the smallest of the three siblings, resembling their mother rather than the Ashfords. Her soft brown hair and wide-eyed, pink-skinned prettiness would win her many admirers when she made her come-out next season. She was plumper than Louise, with a softer, rounded figure. Louise begrudged her that.

'Louise...' Caroline hesitated and then spoke with a rush, her words tumbling over one another. 'I would have come to see you, but Mama said not to since you were ill and she thought it might be contagious. Are you feeling better now?'

'Yes, thank you.' Louise's tone was dry. 'It seems a long time since I saw you last. Quite grown up, aren't you?'

'Mama is presenting me next season, as I suppose you know. I can hardly wait. Mama says you will be making your come-out, too.'

They spoke of trivialities for a few moments before Louise pleaded exhaustion and made her escape. Caroline was obviously ignorant of her situation and she wondered if her sister would be gullible enough to swallow her mother's excuses for keeping them apart for the next two months. Probably; she was a simple-minded, obedient girl, nothing like her brother and sister.

One cold, frosty night in early December, Louise went into labour. She was attended by a doctor from Exeter, a taciturn bachelor who Harry Ashford knew and trusted. Louise found herself in a terrifying world of fierce contractions, seeming to merge into each other until there was no respite. She hadn't known it was possible to endure such pain. The doctor refused to administer chloroform, even though Queen Victoria had made the use it of fashionable.

'God intended women to suffer in childbirth,' he said. 'Why should you be the exception, young lady?'

When at last it was over and Louise heard the infant's cry, she was trembling with exhaustion. Somehow she mustered the strength to query its sex and Mrs Evans, who was aiding the doctor, smiled at her compassionately.

'It's a boy and a fine, healthy lad at that. It's surprising, Miss, considering how poorly you've been much of the time.'

Louise lapsed against the pillows and after a moment whispered, 'Can I see him, please?'

The housekeeper looked at her doubtfully. 'I don't know that it's for the best, Miss.'

'Please! I must see him.'

Mrs Evans reluctantly carried the little, blanket-wrapped bundle to the bed and laid him beside her on the pillows. The infant's face was red and wrinkled, his head covered in a shock of dark-coloured hair. Louise could detect no likeness to either his father or herself in his tiny, unformed features. Opening the blanket, she assured herself of his perfection and that he was indeed male.

'Are they usually so small and wrinkled?'

'Why, aye, Miss.' The woman sounded surprised. 'He's a fine-looking little chap and a lusty set of lungs he's got, too. I'll take him away now so you can get your rest. It's better so. We can't have you getting attached to him.'

Louise was too exhausted to protest. She dropped off to sleep, awakening at last to find Brown sitting beside her bed, mending a torn stocking. The maid declined to bring the baby to her and when Mrs Evans was summoned, she also refused to yield.

'We've had our orders, Miss Ashford. You're only torturing yourself. You couldn't possibly keep him, you know. This is the best way for everyone. We'll be taking him away tonight to a wet-nurse in the next village. He'll stay there until a home's found for him.'

Louise berated them, but to no avail. They left her sobbing in her pillow, desolate and bereft, her arms aching to hold that tiny bundle. The focus of her emotions had changed. Her yearning for Lloyd was quite overtaken by this fierce, unfulfilled desire to hold and suckle Lloyd's child.

It was even worse when her milk came in on the third day. Mrs Evans bound her breasts, yet the pain was excruciating. She became feverish and at one stage hoped she might die and so find an escape from her suffering. It was only milk fever, Mrs Evans told her, dosing her with a herbal infusion. The medicine relieved her symptoms and at last her body seemed to comprehend that there was no infant to nourish. As her milk dried up the swelling and pain in her breasts began to ease. Her torn body was also healing, but the depression didn't leave her.

She kept asking the housekeeper about the child, but the woman could only tell her that, the night after his birth, Charles had driven herself and the baby in the landau to the next village. The wet-nurse with whom he'd been left was a woman whose good character had been recommended.

'He's safe there and well-looked-after. Never you fret now. You must be after putting this behind you.'

And then Mrs Ashford came to see her.

'We decided you should know what is to be done with the child,' her mother informed her briskly. 'Your father mentioned his hope that Jones, the head coachman, would agree to take him. Jones and his wife are childless and although they are now middle-aged they are delighted with the scheme. Your father has told them the child was born to a cousin from Somerset. There is no need for them to know the truth. However they will give out the story that the mother was a niece of Mrs Jones, who died during childbirth. The Joneses are kindly people who will care for the child just as they ought. You need have no fears on that score.'

Louise merely nodded and turned away. She was seated on a chair by the window, a robe over her nightgown. It was her first day out of bed and she knew she looked dreadful, her eyes circled with dark shadows. At least once she began to go about in the normal way, her appearance would lend credence to the story that she was recovering from an illness which had confined her to her bed for the last three months.

'I assume you will shortly be fit to leave your room. You may do so openly now, of course, but you must create the impression that you are convalescing. You need not come down to meals for a week or so yet. We must be careful that your recovery doesn't appear to coincide too closely with the infant's arrival at the Joneses', or people may put two and two together.'

Mrs Ashford's tone was coldly unemotional. Louise said, 'Yes, Mama,' and resumed her contemplation of the scene outside her window. She thought she would almost prefer her father's anger to her mother's lack of warmth, but Harry Ashford hadn't been to see her since that first time.

Charles had visited her twice since the birth. In her desolation she'd reached out to him, the only member of her family whom she held in any degree of affection. Her brother's casual, shallow attentions and the kindly concern of Mrs Evans were all she had to sustain her.

As the weeks went by Louise's physical health improved, but she continued to be depressed and lethargic. In keeping with her "convalescence", she began to assume the normal life of a young English lady living in the country. The approach of Christmas had Caroline and her mother decorating a huge tree and directing the servants to hang holly and mistletoe. A light snowfall made the manor and the village look like the pretty Christmas cards they had used to send people back home, incongruously, while heat shimmered the brown paddocks of Central Queensland. Christmas dinner was more appropriate to the climate than it had ever been at Banyandah; the sweet mince pies, the roasted goose and joint of beef and the heavy, rich plum pudding with brandy sauce were a welcome defense against the cold. Louise participated in it all but her mind and heart were with a man far away in Australia and a baby close by in the coachman's cottage.

Louise made her first public appearance on Christmas morning, accompanying her family to the village church. She endured the curious, yet friendly stares of the villagers and her father's tenant farmers, conscious of her own and her family's hypocrisy as they piously sang carols and offered praise to the Lord. She was no longer an unthinking girl just out of school and she realised as never before that not one of the Ashfords in reality practised the Christian faith.

They had been joined by Mrs Ashford's brother, his wife and two daughters for the Christmas season. Louise was not in a convivial mood. Her cousins obviously thought her a little odd, the outcome, no doubt, of living all her life in the colonies. Charles behaved in his usual selfish manner, charming them and ignoring them in turn, according to his whim. Caroline, whom they already knew, was the only one with whom they seemed at ease.

It was a relief for Louise when the festivities were over and the visitors left. Now that she was sufficiently healed she took comfort in the stables, riding every morning when the weather permitted. Sometimes she was accompanied by Charles and Caroline, but more often she rode alone when Charles was otherwise engaged and Caroline wasn't inclined to brave the cold. Yet she was never completely alone, for a groom would be expected to accompany her. Young ladies didn't go about anywhere in England without a chaperone of some sort.

In the afternoons she was expected to rest for two or three hours, reading, writing letters and playing the piano. This was the worst part of the day, when boredom overtook her and allowed her too much time for reflection. It was better when she retired to her bedroom to begin the critical business of dressing for dinner. Then Jane, the cheerful maid who had been assigned to her, would chat and laugh with her as she laced her corset and arranged her hair.

Dinner itself was always stiff and formal, as relations with her parents were strained. Her father ignored her completely and her mother was coldly distant. Only Charles was able to keep the conversation flowing, but he was seldom present and Caroline seemed to have nothing of importance to say. Louise applied herself to enjoying the rich, plentiful food, the like of which she'd never seen before, even at Banyandah.

It wasn't only the horses that drew her to the stables. There was also her desire to know Jones, the coachman. To her relief she found him to be a gentle, friendly man, patient with the horses he obviously loved and admired by the grooms and stable boy in his command. Jones was particularly courteous towards her and she wondered if he'd guessed she was the mother of the child he and his wife had fostered. Louise knew she must never mention the infant, but it tormented her to have her babe so close, yet so inaccessible to her.

She had yet to meet Mrs Jones, although she'd seen her at a distance, working in the garden of the little thatched cottage where she and her husband lived. Mrs Evans had described her as a kindly soul and Louise wanted very much to believe that, knowing the welfare of her son was in her hands.

'They're having him christened at the village church next Sunday,' Mrs Evans told her. 'Matthew Stephen, they're calling him. They're naming him for Mrs Jones's grandfather, or so she told me.'

'And what are the gossips saying?'

Mrs Evans chuckled. 'She's a wily one, is Mrs Jones. She's not mentioning the baby's father, so they're all putting two and two together and guessing her poor dead niece was an unmarried mother. That's enough scandal to keep them happy and they're not looking further than that.'

Certainly not to the occupants of the Manor, who managed to absent themselves in Exeter at the time of the christening.

It snowed in earnest after Christmas, after a week of heavy frosts that set the ground hard underfoot. The weather kept all but the farm workers indoors, heavily clothed against the cold winds that penetrated the draughty corridors of the old house. The snow was enough of a novelty to Louise to intrigue her at first. She stirred herself to make a snowman with Caroline and they even threw a few snowballs at each other, but she quickly lost interest. Once the novelty of looking at the pristine landscape wore off she grew restless at the enforced inactivity. Having contracted another of her head colds, she spent much of the time rugged up in the chair beside her bedroom window with a book, snuffling and sneezing, while a fire crackled in the grate and roared up the chimney.

But she soon discovered snow was far preferable to the sleet following a few weeks later, driving everyone indoors and turning the ground to slush. Even the miracle of spring was tempered by showery, overcast weather. She longed for some hot, Australian sun to banish the pervading damp. Oh God, how she hated England!

Yet it *was* a miracle to see the stark skeleton trees begin to bud and then suddenly burst forth into new leaf, to see the first spring flowers creep through and the brown earth begin to assume a sparse carpet of green. And to witness the joy of the cattle and sheep as they were released from the barns that had housed them for the winter. Even the staid old dairy cows frisked and galloped like newborn calves.

With the coming of more clement weather the family's social life was resumed. Mrs Ashford took her two daughters to Exeter to purchase the basics of their Season wardrobes. Additional gowns would be ordered from a more fashionable Regent Street dressmaker when they reached London.

Caroline was full of her coming out. After all those dreary years in the schoolroom the anticipation of the balls and dinner parties ahead had her in a state of perpetual excitement. She delighted in the shopping sprees with her mother and was forever persuading her maid to arrange her hair differently, often with ridiculous results. Louise grew tired of her sister's insipid prattle. Caroline made her feel world-weary and jaded and the three years that separated them in age often seemed more like thirteen.

At least it was easier now she was finished with the secrecy and humiliation of her pregnancy. Although the loss of her baby son was a nagging ache inside her, she no longer fretted as much over his day-to-day welfare. She'd grown to trust Mrs Evans' reports that he was being nurtured with as much love and care as any natural mother might show her child.

Even her memories of Lloyd had dimmed. Thinking of him was like trying to recapture a dream, shadowy and insubstantial. She would try to recall the exact timbre of his voice, the way he sat his horse, the way he smiled, or the way he walked...and find it all eluded her. It was almost a year since she'd last seen him.

Harry Ashford had rented a house in London for the Season. It was situated in a fashionable area and although comfortably furnished and roomier than its narrow facade suggested, was overshadowed by the town houses of the nobility in the next street. They had taken only a few servants with them from Fenham Manor, but these were enough to keep the household functioning smoothly.

London was dirty, smelly and oppressive. Louise had always preferred the country and in the time she'd spent with the Barclays and the Jamiesons, she'd grown more rustic than ever.

Her whole being rebelled at the formality that governed polite society. The tedious business of leaving calling cards, the stilted calls on the ladies her mother considered it beneficial to know, the continual fostering of the right connections–she abhorred it.

Before she and Caroline could appear in society, they were presented to the Prince and Princess of Wales at one of the four Drawing Rooms at Buckingham Palace. The Queen, still mourning her beloved Prince Albert, seldom appeared in public these days. As Louise waited for what seemed hours with her train draped over her arm, she was thankful this was something she would only experience once in her life.

After curtsying to the stout, bearded Prince of Wales and his longsuffering Princess Alexandra, she was required to retire backwards out of their presence without tripping over her train. The difficulty of performing this feat was exacerbated by her fear that someone must see through the facade of purity and innocence and recognise her as an imposter, a fallen woman. It would require only a whisper of the truth to ostracise her from society and destroy Caroline's chances of making a good marriage.

Louise wasn't an instant success at her first ball. She was different from the other debutantes; at twenty –years-old a young woman midst the girls just out of the schoolroom. Fortunately two or three of the young men seemed to admire this tall, grave-faced girl from the Colonies and she wasn't quite abandoned to that humiliating fate of becoming a wallflower.

'It is your complexion, Louise!' her mother complained in the carriage on their return. 'Too much Australian sun...oh, I know you're as white as a ghost now, but the damage has been done. Why, there are even freckles on your nose and with your dark hair. I purchased some creams yesterday for you to try. I shall bring them to your room later.'

Louise sighed. 'I doubt if they will be of any use, Mama, any more than the lemon juice and rose-water were. Besides, you know that isn't the true problem.'

'If you would only smile a little more...'

'What is there to smile at?'

Mrs Ashford glanced at Caroline, flushed and triumphant at the conquests of her first outing and seemed to bite back the retort she'd been about to make.

Caroline looked at her older sister pityingly. 'You're too tall and thin, Louise. No gentleman wants to dance with a girl as tall as he is. Besides, you're older than the rest of us and everyone thinks you've been left on the shelf.'

'And what would you know about it, Miss? You've been cosseted and protected all your life; you know nothing of the outside world. I received two proposals of marriage before I came to England, so I certainly don't consider myself left on the shelf.'

'I think it's time we ceased this conversation,' cut in Mrs Ashford coldly. 'Shame on you, Louise, for mentioning a past we would all prefer to forget.'

Louise didn't attempt to reply. She turned her face to the window of the closed landau, staring out at the grimy street. It was raining–again–but the thoroughfare was as busy as ever, with barouches, broughams, phaetons, hackneys, carts and a brewery wagon all jostling for space in the narrow street. As she watched, a ragged boy snatched an apple unnoticed from a greengrocer's cart and dived through the traffic, narrowly avoiding the hooves of a high-stepping pair in a gentleman's curricle. Good luck to him, she thought. She was used to seeing hardship in the bush, but the abject poverty of the London street dwellers distressed her.

Ironically, she realised she would have been better to have come to England with her parents two years before. At eighteen she would have doubtless adapted to the social whirl and made a good marriage. The interlude in Australia had gained her nothing but much heartache and a dislike for the frivolity of the rich.

She was tormented by guilt whenever she thought of the child she and Lloyd had recklessly brought into the world. Looking back, she was appalled at her behaviour in running away from the Barclays and at the risks she'd taken. She'd written to Cousin James before leaving Australia, attempting to apologise for the way she'd treated him and his family. The forgiving reply she'd received from him recently was probably more than she deserved.

Her ex-lover and the Jamiesons had apparently not been so generous. From them she hadn't heard one word.

Chapter Nineteen

As the weeks passed Louise adapted to her new life, despite the strict etiquette that governed the life of a young lady. On the one hand she was supposed to attract the attention of eligible suitors and on the other it was necessary to behave with stifling decorum or risk being considered fast. It was as if she was walking a tightrope from which she must surely stumble.

She would never forget her first dinner party. The courses seemed countless and began with the customary soup and fish and included stuffed quail, venison, truffles, roast beef and duck, savouries and cheese and finished with ices, *gateaux* and fruit. The table decorations were elaborate and ostentatious and included at each setting a menu handwritten in French. Guests gorged themselves with little regard for the starving paupers in the East End.

Fortunately there were other, simpler pleasures to compensate, such as morning rides in Hyde Park, where the gentlemen and more adventurous ladies exercised their horses on Rotten Row. In the afternoon it was fashionable to drive a carriage instead. Louise enjoyed visits to the opera and the theatre, where it was possible to relax a little without the need to make polite conversation. She gained some weight from all the rich food and although her mother's remedies had done nothing for her complexion, the return of her old vitality brought a healthy glow to her cheeks.

Charles appeared to be enjoying the Season immensely. With his adventurous, sporting nature he'd made many friends among the young blades. At one of the balls they attended he introduced Louise to his favourite companion, an attractive young man whose brown eyes smiled into Louise's as he clasped her hand.

'I would like to introduce Mr Richard Langley. My sister Louise, Richard.' Charles laughed then and cast formality aside. 'Just be careful of him, Louise. He's the son of a vicar, but he doesn't let that bother him.'

Louise returned Langley's smile, intrigued in spite of herself. 'I'm pleased to make your acquaintance, Mr Langley. Is your father really a vicar?'

'He certainly is, Miss Ashford. I grew up in a country vicarage in Sussex and I couldn't wait to escape the confounded place.'

Louise laughed out loud for the first time in many months, genuinely amused by Langley's irreverent honesty. 'Surely you don't mean that, Mr Langley!'

'I'm afraid I do.' Langley's dark eyes held a glint of appreciation and she was human and fragile enough to be flattered by it. He made a striking figure in his cutaway coat with its long tails, elegant waistcoat and narrow trousers. He looked fit and athletic, with dark curls that sprang around his face despite the application of Macassar. Instinct told her to tread warily, but the promise of a little excitement was enough to entice her out of her indifference.

'Would you do me the honour of writing my name on your card, Miss Ashford? Meanwhile, may I fetch you a glass of punch?'

'If you'll excuse me, there's someone I must see,' interjected Charles at this point, apparently sensing he was fast becoming superfluous. 'Just remember that I warned you, Louise.'

That night, Louise genuinely enjoyed herself for the first time since her debut. She had to admit it was Langley, with whom she shared several dances and who escorted her to supper, who made the difference. Anyone less likely to have originated in a religious household Louise couldn't imagine, for he was impudent and unconventional, with an amused contempt for stuffiness that struck an answering chord in Louise.

Her mother filled her in with all she could not have guessed in the carriage on the way home.

'I noticed you enjoying yourself with Richard Langley tonight.'

Louise looked up, unable to read Irene Ashford's expression in the darkness. 'I danced with him, yes.'

'Be careful, Louise. He's twenty-six-years-old and he's not the marrying kind. His mother had money of her own and he resigned a commission in the army when she died last year. He's been living off the proceeds of her will ever since. But he has expensive tastes, so the money isn't likely to last him long.'

'I believe his father is a vicar,' Louise responded coolly.

'And his grandfather's a Viscount, but don't let that fool you into thinking Mr Langley respectable or a good catch. He's reckless and irresponsible and as the youngest son of a youngest son his prospects are not bright. I can't forbid you to see him, for he's Charles's friend, but I would prefer you kept him at a distance.'

'I enjoyed his company, but I'm not about to be taken in by an accomplished flirt, Mama.'

Louise noticed her mother keeping Caroline out of Langley's way, but after that first warning Mrs Ashford didn't intervene in her friendship with him. She probably had no hopes now of Louise making any sort of splendid marriage and any marriage at all was better than none.

In some ways Richard was different from Charles, who had a shrewd head for business and never allowed himself any unnecessary extravagance in his pursuit of pleasure. Richard lacked Charles's calculating nature and his uncertain temper. But in their determination of what their pleasures were, they were very much in agreement.

Louise cared for nothing but the fact that Richard made her laugh and laughter had been lacking in her life for many months now. With Charles to act as chaperon– though the idea of Charles being considered a fit person to chaperone anyone secretly amused her–the two enjoyed a great deal of each other's company. Charles seemed pleased to see her behaving like her old self again and did nothing to discourage a friendship that under normal circumstances he would have been unlikely to foster.

Harry Ashford, watching them dance the polka together at yet another ball, swore under his breath and determined not to concern himself with his elder daughter.

At least Caroline had managed to fulfill his expectations. She'd attracted the interest of Sir Samuel Barton, a young, wealthy baronet and the announcement of their engagement would shortly be appearing in the Times. They would be marrying towards the end of the year when Caroline was eighteen. It seemed her future was assured.

Louise had no illusions about Langley. She knew he was anything but a saint and she didn't trust either him or herself enough to allow him any liberties. She supposed that lack of trust was the major difference between her relationship with him and her previous relationship with Lloyd. She wondered if he asked her to marry him, if she would accept him. Life with him would be full of uncertainties, not the least of them knowing where their next meal was coming from. Perhaps he would be unfaithful to her and that would bring loneliness. But nothing could be lonelier than her present situation.

She wasn't like the other debutantes; innocent, compliant young girls who expected to marry men of their families' choosing while understanding nothing of what marriage entailed. She knew the importance of physical attraction and she found Langley extremely attractive. Surely it was preferable to have a little worry and heartache mingled with the pleasure than no pleasure at all.

Another thing Richard could give her was children. Another child might ease her restless yearning for the infant she'd left behind at the coachman's cottage at Fenham Manor.

At the end of August when the Season was over, the Ashfords returned to Fenham Manor, accompanied by several house guests. Charles had asked Richard Langley to accompany them, so he could enjoy some of the good hunting and shooting to be had in the Devonshire countryside. Harry Ashford had invited an old college friend of his, Mr William Howard and his beautiful, younger wife Agatha. Caroline's fiancé also was to be staying over for a time.

Sir Samuel Barton was a plump, shy, twenty-one-year-old who, except for his schooldays, had lived all his life at the family home in Yorkshire. He was more interested in farming than in the delights of London and Louise wondered what had prompted him to propose to a girl with such opposing interests. Yet he seemed devoted to Caroline, who basked happily in his admiration. Louise wondered if her fun-loving sister would persuade him to leave the rustic life of Yorkshire for the London Season each year, or if she would eventually go alone.

She mentioned her misgivings about the match to Langley but he only laughed. 'Your sister will twist dear old Sam around her little finger, you'll see. I wonder if he's even kissed her yet? He's such a dashed Puritan it's boring.'

Louise's colour rose. 'Surely...they are betrothed, after all.'

'Oh, a chaste peck on the cheek, no doubt. There is more to the art than that, as I would willingly demonstrate if you weren't so evasive.'

His eyes were laughing down into hers, his mouth mere inches away. Louise wasn't sure how he'd come to be so close. He was about to put his intention into practice when Charles walked into the room. Caught between disappointment and relief, she stepped back hastily. She imagined Richard's notion of kissing would go further than was sensible or circumspect. Already she was too vulnerable.

Charles was standing with raised eyebrows, having missed no detail of this little scene. 'Sorry to interrupt, old chap, but I must remind you that my sister isn't one of the kitchen maids.'

Louise flushed and was about to withdraw from the room when Langley put his hand on her arm to restrain her. 'I can assure you that I hold your sister in every respect, Charles.'

'I should have known better than to trust you,' muttered Charles softly.

'If I may have a word in this matter,' put in Louise icily, 'I have no intention of allowing myself to be seduced.' She turned on her heel and left the room, closing the door purposely behind her. But then curiosity overcame dignity and she paused with her ear to the door, straining to hear Charles's next words.

'You had better make up your mind, Langley. Either marry her or leave her alone.'

'Don't rush me, old boy.' Langley sounded bored. 'I'm not ready to leap into matrimony just yet. But don't fret yourself. I'd not seduce the sister of my friend.'

'Not in that friend's house, at any rate,' agreed Charles on a note of amused cynicism. 'Your father may be a clergyman, but I've never known that to inspire your conscience.'

Louise decided to retreat, before one of them opened the door to find her eavesdropping.

Caroline and Sir Samuel seemed to have one thing in common and that was a dislike of foxhunting. They preferred to keep sedate company with Mrs Ashford while the remaining members of the house party attended the local meets. Louise and the adventurous Agatha Howard shocked the older men by riding enthusiastically to hounds, keeping pace with the men despite their sidesaddles as they galloped over field and ditch. Most women, if they participated at all, preferred to follow at a more dignified pace.

Louise relished the excitement of following the baying hounds in the crisp morning air, but preferred to distance herself from the kill. She was too practical to become sentimental over a fox or deer and had seen cattle and sheep butchered for meat, but still she rode for the thrill of the chase rather than from any ghoulish delight in the outcome. She supposed foxhunting was as mindlessly frivolous as any of the pleasures of the wealthy, but it was enough for her that she found it enjoyable.

Agatha Howard rode even more fearlessly than she did. Louise could see that Charles was fascinated by her and Agatha encouraged his attention. When there was no hunting to be had the young people often made an excursion on horseback, enjoying a picnic lunch carried by one of the grooms. Agatha left her indifferent husband to discuss politics in the study with his host while she accompanied them, and Charles's obvious interest in her developed into an open flirtation.

Langley seemed amused by the developing affair but Caroline and Sir Samuel were obviously embarrassed and dismayed. Perhaps they were not familiar with the morals of the Marlborough House Set, of which Louise had heard whispers. To the Prince of Wales and his friends, romantic intrigue and affairs with other men's wives were the order of the day.

Louise's suspicions of an affair were confirmed when she surprised Charles leaving Mrs Howard's room early one morning. Charles seemed unrepentant, laughing at his sister's shocked face. 'Aren't you being a bit hypocritical, my dear?'

She flushed. 'I don't think so. I have never stolen another woman's husband.'

'Howard should be aware of the facts. If he can't keep her happy, someone else will,' he retorted cynically.

'And what if it had been Mr Howard who surprised you just now? Or Papa, for that matter?'

'The Pater wouldn't dare say a word. I know too many of his own secrets. As for Howard, I shall cross that bridge if I come to it.'

At the end of October the Howards left. Louise, relieved to see the end of that potentially explosive situation, wondered if William Howard was blind, or if he just preferred to pretend to be. Everyone else had clearly noticed the flirtation, even if they had affected not to. Perhaps Howard ignored it for the sake of his friendship with Harry Ashford, or possibly he'd long since resigned himself to his wife's infidelities.

Sir Samuel also announced his impending departure. Langley made noises about leaving too, causing Louise to wonder about his intentions.

One morning he asked her to walk with him in the garden and took her to a spot amongst the roses. He took both her hands in his, for once looking serious.

'Louise, I've just spoken to your father. Will you do me the honour of becoming my wife?'

Her breath caught in her throat. 'Oh, Richard.' In that instant she made up her mind. It was time to make a new life away from Fenham Manor and its wretched memories. She firmed her chin and met his intent gaze. 'Yes, I'd love to be your wife.'

He smiled his triumph and released her hands to slide his arms about her waist, drawing her close. He bent his head to kiss her and she submitted briefly.

'Richard, please.' She pulled away, afraid of giving in to her own excitement, for he was very appealing and obviously very experienced. 'We must discuss this seriously. Where shall we live? I couldn't abide London, you know.'

He smiled. 'What have you in mind? I must warn you I have more debts than money.'

'I'll be receiving a sizeable sum when I turn twenty-one in February. Do you fancy purchasing a house and some good farmland in the country somewhere? Papa would probably assist us and we could repay him later. We must be independent, Richard; we cannot exist on the charity of your family.'

'And nor shall we live on the charity of yours,' he said quickly.

'Of course not. Anything Papa might give us would only be a loan. As for my own money, I would prefer to spend it on farmland than anything else.'

He grinned. 'So you fancy turning me into a farmer, do you? I don't intend to rusticate completely, you know. I'm not like our worthy Samuel. Farming has never interested me greatly.'

'We must live, Richard. Have you any other suggestions?'

He shook his head. 'Not unless I rejoin the army and you wouldn't like being a soldier's wife. Would you prefer I followed in my father's footsteps and entered the church?'

Louise laughed at prospect. 'You're teasing me, Richard! I'm sure farming must be the lesser of the two evils. Besides, I would make a shocking vicar's wife.'

'We would both of us loathe it.' He drew her close again. 'Now for another kiss. And you aren't about to escape me this time, my dear.'

To her surprise he was gentle and circumspect. He held her close for a time, stroking her hair and Louise relaxed in his arms. It felt so good to be held again. Perhaps she would find happiness with this man after all.

'When would you like us to marry, Louise?'

'Do you think April would be a good month? It will be a little warmer then.'

'Of course, if your parents agree.'

As Langley was due to leave in a couple of days, he asked Louise to take an early morning ride with him. They left the stables before the others had breakfasted, dismissing the groom who would normally have accompanied them. After a short gallop they drew up, laughing, at the fringe of a wood. Richard led the way through the trees and paused in a grassy clearing where a fallen oak tree made an inviting seat. He eyed Louise's sparkling face.

'Let's stop here for a while,' he suggested.

He dismounted and helped her out of the saddle, fastening their horses' reins to a branch and guiding her to the moss-covered log. 'Once your sister's wedding is over you must visit my family in Sussex. My father will be most anxious to meet you. I wrote yesterday to inform him of our engagement. No doubt he'll be gratified to hear that I'm settling down at last.'

'Had you mentioned me in your previous letters?'

'Of course.' He smiled and drew her hand into his. 'I'm sure Father will like you, even if he does disapprove of your prowess on the hunting field.'

'Will he be shocked, do you think?' She laughed up at him, allowing herself to be provocative with him for the first time.

His fingers moved caressingly on her palm and wrist, sending shivers down her spine. 'Very likely.' He kissed her, at first with his previous gentleness. As he drew her to her feet she moved instinctively close to him, her mouth opening under his. The kiss deepened and what had begun as a comparatively innocent embrace was suddenly not innocent at all. His tongue explored her mouth and he moulded her body into his. He was so vital and compelling, very different from Lloyd and yet for all his sophistication and class not so different after all if she closed her eyes. She found herself matching his passion, her defences down, her previous evasions having perversely added to her desire.

At last he stopped kissing her long enough to murmur in her ear, 'Will you leave a plate of sandwiches outside your door for me tonight, Louise?'

She pulled back, dismayed, unaware of the significance of the sandwiches but in no doubt as to his meaning, all the same. 'A plate of sandwiches?'

He watched her keenly, his breathing quickened, his face flushed with arousal. 'That's what Mrs Howard used to do, when she wished Charles to visit her at night. It's the usual procedure amongst the Marlborough House Set.'

She moved away from him and bent to pick up her discarded whip. 'If it's an affair you're seeking I wonder that you bothered to speak of marriage. I think it is time for us to return home.'

'Louise.' He caught her hand, staying her. 'I do wish to marry you and I apologise for making such an improper suggestion. Let us say I was carried away with the passion of the moment. I'm truly sorry.' He clasped her face in his fingers and kissed her gently. 'It's just that April seems so far away.'

'Perhaps we shouldn't ride alone in future. It was foolish of me.'

He smiled so charmingly that it was difficult to maintain outrage. 'Then I shan't be able to kiss you again. Somehow I don't think you would even want me to be respectable and boring like Sam is.' He helped her into the saddle and then paused, his hand still holding the rein. 'You did know that Charles and Mrs Howard were lovers, didn't you?'

She nodded. 'I did, although I suppose I should not have done. Correctly speaking, we shouldn't be having this conversation.'

'Louise, it is because you are no simpering Miss that I was first attracted to you. You know more of the ways of the world than your sister. You must tell me about your Colonial experiences sometime.'

Louise eyed him warily, knowing there was six months of her life that she could never tell him about. 'Those experiences were mostly boring. I'm sure you don't wish to hear about my time as governess to my cousin, James Barclay's, children.'

'One of your hardy pioneers is your cousin James, I believe,' Richard murmured. He took her gloved hand and kissed the exposed skin of her wrist, his eyes darkening and never for a moment leaving hers. 'I'm quite impatient for the day you become my wife, Louise.'

The combination of his touch and caressing words was very erotic. Louise signalled her mount to move off, knowing she would have to tread very carefully over the next few months. She was determined not to risk being an unwed mother a second time and if that meant keeping Richard at arms length, so be it.

Chapter Twenty

It seemed fate was against her that day. Perhaps she'd never been intended to marry Richard Langley and the events that transpired were not coincidence at all, but an integral part of her destiny. Looking back, it was strange that she should see her son today for the first time since his birth. She had on many occasions ridden past the thatched stone cottage that housed the coachman and his wife, hoping for just such an eventuality. On these days she hadn't caught a glimpse of the woman or the child, yet today Mrs Jones was walking up the path to the front gate as they approached, the baby bundled in her arms in a rug.

Louise drew rein abruptly, hardly conscious of her actions or of her companion beside her. Her heart pounded as her gaze riveted on the face of the little boy. Her mare, perhaps sensing the tension in her body, began to fidget and she checked it mechanically, aware of nothing but the approach of woman and child.

Mrs Jones, clearly recognising her, stopped and clutched her adoptive son more closely, an expression of alarm crossing her face. She hesitated for a moment but then continued through the gate, nodding her head deferentially towards them. 'Good morning to you, Miss Ashford. Sir.'

She would have slipped past them, but Louise put out her hand in a restraining gesture. 'Mrs Jones, isn't it? May I see the baby?' She slid from the saddle and dropped her horse's reins to step closer to the woman. 'I trust he has been keeping well. How old is he now?'

Louise had no need to listen to Mrs Jones's reply; she knew well enough. He was ten months and one week old. She drew the blanket away from his face, noting that his hair was still dark, like hers. Otherwise, the likeness to Lloyd was unmistakable. The mouth, nose and chin were a softer, more rounded version of Lloyd's. He was a beautiful child; only the hair and the blue-grey eyes that regarded her with solemn curiosity were hers. A sweet shaft of pain pierced her heart and her voice trembled.

'May I hold him for a moment, Mrs Jones?'

The woman couldn't refuse, though her reluctance was obvious. Louise took the baby awkwardly, surprised at his weight. He twisted in her grasp, looking at the horses, then returning his steady gaze to her face. Louise's throat constricted, the pain a physical thing stabbing at her chest. Opening the blanket slightly, she noted the sturdiness of his body under the warm clothing, but he was turning in her arms, not crying but restless and discontented. He reached out to the woman who was to all intents and purposes his mother.

Mrs Jones moved forward. 'I think it's best if I take him back, Miss Ashford.'

Louise relinquished him unwillingly, trembling and beyond speech.

'We called him Matthew, you know.'

Louise nodded. The compassion and understanding in the woman's eyes stung her to respond. She *knew*…

'He's a bonny child,' she croaked.

'Aye, he is that. I'll be on my way now, Miss. It's a hefty walk to the village.'

Louise stood mutely looking after them, the fierce ache in her chest and throat taking her back to the days immediately following his birth. Oh God, he was so much like Lloyd!

She sensed Richard moving to her elbow and remembered his presence with a start. She averted her face in an attempt to hide her misery.

'Shall we continue, Louise?'

Louise nodded and accepted his help to remount. As they rode back to the stables her dazed thoughts winged across the miles to Lloyd. She pictured his face in her mind, recapturing it vividly as she hadn't managed to do for some time. A sob welled up in her throat and she choked it back. She glanced at the man beside her. Had she really agreed to marry him, this irresponsible charmer with the laughing eyes that were not laughing now, but were disturbingly sharp and observant?

His vigilant expression alarmed her. Could she pretend to be one of those maternal females who were obsessed with babies in general?

'I must apologise.' She managed a light laugh. 'I warn you that I have a weakness for babies.'

'I'm surprised. I wouldn't have thought it of you, Louise.'

'We're all full of surprises, Richard.'

When Langley returned to his room to change out of his riding breeches, he took the opportunity to interrogate his general manservant and valet, a trusted employee of many years.

'Johnson, since we have been here have you heard any gossip concerning Miss Ashford?'

The man looked startled. The engagement hadn't been officially announced, but Langley was sure his servant had a fair idea of what was being planned. 'Why no, sir. Not gossip, as such.'

Langley smiled. 'Yet you have all engaged in a great deal of speculation about her, I don't doubt.' He laughed at the man's expression. 'Come, Johnson. I know the talk that goes on below stairs. Miss Ashford was very ill when she first arrived here, I believe.'

'Yes, that is what I was told. She didn't leave her room for more than three months.'

Langley's eyes narrowed. 'Was she seen by the servants in that time?'

'I believe most of them didn't see her, sir. She was attended by Brown, Mrs Ashford's maid, and by Mrs Evans, the housekeeper. I know Barnes, Mr Charles's valet, told me the first time he set eyes on Miss Ashford was shortly before Christmas.'

Langley laughed to himself. 'Well, old chap, you nearly got yourself hoodwinked good and proper.' He looked up at the obviously bewildered valet. 'Johnson, I want you to discover if anyone else saw Miss Ashford while she was ill. Also I would like you to ask a few discreet questions about the child I saw today with a woman called Mrs Jones. She must be the coachman's wife. Find out if it is hers and when it arrived on the scene. She looks too old for childbearing.'

Johnson wasn't stupid. He stared at his master, open-mouthed. 'Sir, do you mean...?'

'It doesn't matter to you what I mean, Johnson. Just do as I ask you and be discreet about it. There is no need to tell the rest of the world.'

'Very well, sir.'

The man hung Langley's discarded clothing and directed an anxious glance at his employer before departing. Langley's mouth twisted and he walked restlessly to the window, opening the curtains to look down at the gardens. Louise had surprised him this morning with her response to that damned kiss. No protected and cosseted young lady should know how to kiss like that. He'd already suspected her of an unconventional upbringing and had thought she would be more fun to bed than most of the naive girls his parents had wanted him to marry. It was no wonder men had affairs when their wives were encouraged to think of marital relations as nothing but an unpleasant duty. Yet if she wasn't a virgin. He'd been prepared to overlook so much, but was he prepared to accept sullied goods?

And now it seemed she was more than just sullied. The mother of another man's child, perhaps. Of one fact he was certain: if his suspicions proved to be correct, he would not–could not–marry her.

It was provident that the engagement hadn't yet been announced. It was a shame, for he was genuinely fond of her and now he would never have her in his bed. After this morning he wanted that very badly.

During the usual buffet luncheon Langley found himself discreetly studying Louise, noting that the sadness had returned to her face. This theory of his would explain a lot and he felt a pang of conscience at having to add to that sorrow. After the meal was over he returned to his room for a prearranged rendezvous with his valet, whom he found sewing a button on one of his shirts.

'Well, what did you discover, Johnson?'

'It does seem to fit, sir. I believe Miss Ashford was seen by the butler and one or two other servants when she first arrived. However she was wearing a heavy cloak and the chambermaid who escorted her to her room says she didn't take it off in her presence. She did look ill at the time, according to the maid. Later it was given out that she was confined to her bed and she wasn't seen again until mid-December, when she began to leave her room. She didn't dine with the family until just before Christmas.'

'Did the doctor visit the house in all of this time?'

'He did pay one visit that I can be sure of, sir. And one of the maids thought she heard someone being let in late one night. This was at the beginning of December.'

Langley nodded. 'Did you question the two women who attended Miss Ashford?'

'I didn't care to, sir.'

He smiled. 'Formidable old characters, are they? And what about the Jones infant? When did it make its appearance?'

'That was in the second week of December. It was given out that his mother was Mrs Jones's niece, who died in childbirth. No-one appears to suspect any differently.'

Langley nodded. 'Well done, Johnson. I can't believe though that you were able to ask all of these questions without arousing suspicions.'

'I did the best I could, sir.'

'I suppose you did. Very well, you may go. We're to be leaving first thing in the morning, remember.'

That afternoon Langley once again requested an interview with his host. Harry Ashford led him to the library with its high, book-lined walls and enormous fireplace, in which a blazing fire tried to dispel the creeping cold of evening. But even the fire could not allay the coldness that was within him.

Later that afternoon, Louise received a message from her father to join him in the library. He was seated by the fire when she opened the door, staring sightlessly into the flames with an unread book in his hands. She quailed at the expression on his face.

'Come here, Louise,' he commanded grimly, rising to his feet.

She moved hesitantly closer, afraid and a little bewildered. What had she done now? Had he heard that she'd seen the child?

'One would think you'd be satisfied, Louise,' he began through clenched teeth, 'with disgracing yourself and bringing shame to your family without telling the world about it. Don't you care at all?'

She stared at him, stupefied. 'But I haven't told a soul!'

'You've done the next best thing! Damn you, haven't you any discretion? Langley's no fool! It's a pity you didn't pick someone a bit less sharp than he is if you wanted to wear your heart on your sleeve!'

'Richard?' She paled. 'Has he been to see you?'

'Yes he has, the impertinent young swine. It seems you've set your fate at spinsterhood, my girl, for he politely declined the pleasure of marrying you!'

'Oh, God!' She groped for a chair and sat heavily. 'How can he have guessed?'

'I suppose it wasn't very difficult.' Her father's face was an ugly mottled colour and he clenched and unclenched his fists as if struggling to contain his anger. 'You made yourself jolly obvious when you saw the child this morning and he set his valet to ask a few questions amongst the servants. You're determined to ruin us all, you little harlot. Why you had to go near that bastard of yours I'd love to know.'

'No, you wouldn't know, would you?' Stung to anger, Louise's derision matched his, now. 'You wouldn't know what it's like to love your own flesh and blood! All that concerns you is the family honour and if you want to preserve that perhaps you should look to Charles for a change! I didn't ask to leave Australia and since I seem to cause you so much embarrassment why not let me return there?'

'Once Caroline is safely married I don't care where you go, but if you leave before the wedding it will set the gossips to wondering. Now get out of my sight and don't ask to see Langley, for he's already left.'

'Without a word to me?'

'I told him to go. Now leave me, if you please.'

Louise did so, hurriedly, slamming the door behind her. She ran up the stairs to her room, in her pain and fury taking them two at a time as she hadn't done since being severely disciplined by her governess when she was a child. Luckily there were no servants around to see it. She locked her door behind her and paced aggressively about the room for a moment or so before slumping in her chair, her anger giving way to grief. Well, that was her second future in ruins. Was there anything she could salvage from either of them to make a third?

Wildly she imagined snatching her baby in the middle of the night and making off with him to carve a living for herself far away from all the Ashfords and their kind. Yet enough sanity remained to her to question this idea. How would she live? She and the baby would most likely starve, or worse, be driven to depths that only the street-dwellers knew about. That would spite her father, but she wouldn't sacrifice them both for that.

Her throat ached and tears of self-pity welled to her eyes, but although she wanted to give way to them she couldn't. It seemed she'd cried too much in the past eighteen months and all her tears were exhausted.

It was some time before she noticed the envelope on her dressing table. She opened it with shaking fingers and took out the sheet of expensive white paper with the Langley crest at its head. At first she hardly dared to read the familiar careless handwriting, so totally in character with Richard Langley.

> *My dear Louise,*
>
> *I apologise for leaving without so much as a word to you, but your father ordered me off the premises. No doubt he has apprised you of his reasons.*
>
> *It is with regret that I am forced to withdraw my offer of marriage. There is very little I can say, but you have my word as a gentleman that this story will go no further from my lips. There are others whom I cannot speak for, however and if I am indirectly responsible for the exposure of this affair I am sorry for that. If it does become public, Australia would be an advisable retreat.*
>
> *It is fortunate that you gave yourself away this morning, as I would have discovered the truth eventually. A secret like that is difficult to keep. I was prepared to be tolerant, but I could not be that tolerant.*
>
> *I am quite distressed about this as I have become extremely fond of you, but I am sure you will*

understand why I had to come to this decision. If we meet again, I hope it may be without embarrassment.
Yours,
Richard Langley.

Louise viciously tore the letter into little pieces and threw them in the grate. The cad. Little he cared what became of her. It seemed no-one cared.

At church in the village next Sunday Louise was aware of curious glances and whispered words. Richard Langley's abrupt departure had obviously aroused speculation. She held her head high and bravely sat through it all, although she longed to be elsewhere.

She suspected the servants were talking about her. It was there in their averted gazes and measured words. But the good rapport she'd already established with them must have stood her in good stead, for she sensed an undercurrent of sympathy and they continued to treat her with respect.

Miraculously Caroline's wedding passed without a hitch. It was a grand affair, with several titles on the guest list and for Caroline, beautiful in white satin with orange blossom in her veil, it was a glorious success. It was an ordeal for Louise, who was subject to a few snide remarks about the absence of Richard Langley. Her mother wore an air of harried nervousness. Louise knew Irene Ashford was wishing her far away and for once she had every intention of obliging her.

Charles had decided to return to Australia immediately after Christmas, to reassume the managership of Banyandah. Louise wondered if their father had encouraged the decision, in order to separate him from Agatha Howard. She also suspected the sedateness of farming in Devonshire dissatisfied Charles. It was a world away from the excitement and danger of mustering half-wild cattle, of working with his men with sweat and dust on his clothes and blood on his hands.

Louise obtained her parents' permission to accompany her brother. She would have gone with or without their approval, but their readiness to see the back of her stung. They had done what they considered to be their best for her, but it had been out of duty, not love.

The voyage home, by steamer this time, was swifter and far more pleasant than their opposing journey eighteen months before. Louise didn't suffer so much from sickness and her anticipation of seeing again the box-tree flats of Banyandah took her mind from the distressing circumstances of her departure. Leaving Fenham Manor without seeing her son again, and accepting that she may never do so, had twisted the dagger a little deeper into her heart.

Her only solace was a promise from Mrs Evans to write and keep her informed of Matthew's progress.

Chapter Twenty-one

Banyandah hadn't changed in her absence. The wet season had finished early and the grass held only a hint of green, but the familiar landscape reached out and enveloped Louise like a comforting blanket. The acting manager had opened and readied the house for them. It was so good to be back, to see and smell and feel all the familiar things–the blue skies and open spaces, the gum trees, the scent of eucalyptus in the early morning, the hot sun that struck to one's very bones with warmth. And yet, the time when this house had been home to her, a naive young girl with a yen for adventure, seemed like a distant memory.

Louise accompanied Charles on horseback as he inspected the property, checking the cattle and the fences, the water and grass. It occupied her time and was preferable to some stuffy London drawing room, but there was an ache inside of her that wouldn't let go. She thought wistfully of Lloyd Kavanagh, wondering if he'd found someone else by now. Had he married Mercy Jamieson?

With Charles as head of the household, life at Banyandah was more informal than it had been in her father's day. He employed few indoor servants and Louise spent her days as she pleased. Charles had thrown himself wholeheartedly into work on the property and seemed content for the moment with little socialising. Those dissipated days of his London Season were far away.

One day the mailman with his laden packhorses brought a letter for Louise addressed in Mary Barclay's small, neat hand. The two had corresponded while Louise was in England and Louise had written again when she arrived in Australia. At the dinner table, she mentioned Mary's letter to Charles.

'Cousin James and Mary have invited me to visit them. I would love to go. Have you any objections?'

Charles smiled ironically. 'It's a wonder they'll have you, after the hullabaloo you caused before.'

'I hope they realize I have grown up a little since then.'

His companionable attitude disappeared. 'I hope so, too. No more consorting with the lower classes, I trust?'

She glared at him. 'Charles, I'm of age now. You shan't dictate to me anymore and I consider Papa and Mama no longer have the right to do so.'

'And I'll say be damned to you! Just don't get yourself into the mess you did the last time.'

She ignored that, applying herself to her plate of roast beef and Yorkshire pudding. 'In that case, I shall go.'

'For how long?'

'For as long as I am welcome.'

'Perhaps you'll find yourself a husband there.'

She smiled humourlessly. 'Jack Barclay asked me to marry him once. He may still be interested.'

'Jack is the oldest boy, isn't he? Poor innocent chap–I daresay you'd have no trouble fooling him.'

'I wouldn't deceive him, Charles.'

He regarded her mockingly. 'Do I gather that you would tell him? You're a fool if you think any man would still have you.'

She didn't respond to that. She supposed Charles was right, but nor would she risk being found out in her deceit. There was only one real solution and she'd spent many hours pondering the possibility of bringing it about. But Lloyd hadn't replied to the letter she'd written him before leaving for England. If he hadn't forgiven her lies…if he was already married or entangled with someone else… No, it was impossible that she could approach him. To do so would only invite further hurt and humiliation.

It was a little over three years since Louise had first made the journey from Rockhampton to Gainsford and there were many changes. The Great Northern Railway that had for many years not advanced beyond Westwood, had made startling progress since 1873. Now that the bridge over the Dawson was completed, the most recent extension had opened at Duaringa, seven miles west of the river, in March. She wasn't travelling that far–James was to meet the train at Boolburra, four miles from Gainsford.

Considering the circumstances of her departure from the area, Louise was anxious about meeting her cousins again. When she stepped from the train the first thing she saw was the buggy from Sherborne with James and Mary standing beside it, Sarah between them straining to catch a glimpse of her.

They approached her eagerly, Mary and Sarah embracing her, while James took her hand, saying in his quiet manner, 'It is good to have you back with us, Louise.'

Mary and Sarah were exclaiming over her clothes and her hairstyle, Sarah at twelve being of the age to notice such things. 'You're more sophisticated than ever,' Mary commented. 'I feel so dowdy in comparison.'

'It is I who am out of place,' responded Louise, relieved and gratified by their welcome. 'Most of my new clothes are unsuitable for the heat. Not that I'm complaining, mind you. It's wonderful to be able to enjoy the sunshine and be properly warm again.'

'What did you think of England?' Sarah asked.

'It's very pretty, Devon especially, but I'm too countrified to like London, I'm afraid.'

'But it must be very exciting to see where the Queen lives and to be presented to the Prince of Wales and Princess Alexandra, as you wrote to us.'

Louise smiled at the girl's enthusiasm. 'That was more intimidating than exciting, Sarah.'

As the horses slowly walked the buggy down the rutted road, Louise leaned back in her seat and sighed. 'Oh, but it is good to be back with you! Thank you so much for inviting me. It was generous of you, considering how I treated you last time.'

'We were more worried than angry,' Mary responded quietly. 'It was such a dangerous thing to do and I used to lie awake at night wondering if you were safe. We were so relieved to hear at last that you were unharmed and well and on your way to England with Charles.'

'Cousin Mary, I'm so sorry.' Suddenly Louise was choking back tears. 'I wanted to write, but a letter would have betrayed my whereabouts. What a futile, senseless exercise it turned out to be.'

She noticed Mary's penetrating glance and quickly changed the subject, injecting a lighter note into her voice. 'How is Jack?'

'Very well and looking forward to seeing you. He's busy fencing at the moment.'

'And Lindsay is at school in Brisbane. Does he enjoy it there?'

Mary nodded. 'He seems happy enough. He was at home at Christmastime and so pleased to be back with the cattle and horses. This will be his third year away.'

As they bypassed Gainsford on the opposite bank of the river, James commented that one of the hotelkeepers had already departed to set up his business in Duaringa.

'The town will soon be abandoned,' he said. 'The wagons won't be coming this way anymore; the goods will go as far as Duaringa by train. But for the big flood we had in the river in March last year, the line would have been completed sooner. It washed Boolburra away and did a lot of damage to the freshly laid tracks.' He gestured with his pipe to the big gum trees that grew on the banks of the river. 'Notice the flood rubbish, high up in the trees. It was a tragedy for the teamsters who were waiting at the river. They lost most of their teams in the flood.'

Louise stiffened, thinking immediately of those living upstream at Myvanwy and Kilbride. 'How dreadful. Did you lose cattle too?'

'Yes, probably a hundred head. But there are others much worse off than us. If only the market for beef would improve.'

'Charles mentioned the Lakes Creek Meatworks hasn't reopened yet.'

'No, it's been closed since the beginning of '74, after the slump in the London market. The price of tallow is good, but I hate sending cattle to the boiling down works and having good meat dumped into the river. If refrigeration can be brought in it will make a big difference to the beef industry. There isn't much market for canned beef, but frozen product will be a different proposition.'

'The world is changing fast,' Louise said. 'Let us hope some of those new ideas will happen sooner rather than later.'

Although the homestead at Sherborne hadn't changed, it was as if Louise saw everything with new eyes. She'd experienced so much since she was last here. She'd sampled life in a droving camp, sleeping in her swag; and had attended balls in some of England's greatest mansions. Perhaps it was the contrast between the two that made her a misfit, with nowhere to really call home.

When Jack arrived he greeted her eagerly. He was more mature and self-confident than she remembered. Louise found his attentions flattering, distracting her from painful memories.

Sarah was already under the care of a governess, so there was little for Louise to do but help Mary with the lighter household duties. She filled the remainder of her days as she pleased, riding, walking, reading or sewing. But she'd become accustomed to the life of upper class idleness in England and the lack of activity didn't make her as restless as it once had. Jack was forever plying her with offers to take her riding and seeking excuses for her company, so she had no reason to be bored. She wondered if he intended to propose to her again and if he did, what her answer would be.

One day she took a book to the river, to the same old spot where she had used to sit and daydream in those carefree days of her innocence. Gazing at the brown water, she thought of Lloyd living not so very far upstream, or so she still assumed. It was easy to feel close to him, to recapture him, here in his own environment. She remembered that last day she'd spent with him at Myvanwy, picturing it vividly in her mind, and found herself crying for him and for the consequences of their folly as if it was only yesterday that they'd been separated. Suddenly it seemed incredible that she could even consider marrying Jack, whom she neither loved nor wanted. It would be better to die an old maid with her memories than settle for second best.

She was cool with Jack after that, refusing some of his invitations and putting a distance between them. Jack was obviously puzzled, probably wondering if he'd done something to offend her. But she knew the small hurt he was suffering now was nothing to the pain she would bring him if she married him.

May was unusually cool that year, with a promise of early frosts. The summer rains hadn't been heavy and with the prospect of a dry, cold winter ahead of him James sent a large consignment of bullocks by train to the Laurel Bank meat-works at Rockhampton. With the mustering over, he received an inquiry from a horse-dealer asking if he had any surplus horses for sale. James Barclay's thoroughbreds had a reputation locally for quality and endurance, both on the track and as stock-horses.

Louise didn't realize that the horse-buyer was based in Banana until Mary made a chance remark on the day of his visit. Even then his name, Ted Weatherby, wasn't familiar to her. She was relieved, for she preferred not to meet anyone who had known her as Lucy Forrest.

She was dusting Mary's best china on the sideboard when the buyer rode in shortly after lunch. She was vaguely aware of male voices outside, of James mounting a horse and riding off with the buyer to the stockyards.

The entire afternoon must have been spent in haggling, for it was late when James returned. Mary told Louise that Weatherby was camping overnight by the river and had been invited to stay for dinner.

'It will be nice to have company,' she said cheerfully. 'We so seldom have visitors that even a horse-dealer makes a pleasant change. James said he had a young chap with him, too.'

The two men walked up to the house at dusk. They stood talking to James and his sons on the front veranda while Louise helped Mary put the finishing touches to the table. Then James appeared in the doorway of the dining room with a portly, florid-faced man who greeted Mary jovially and was then introduced to Louise. For a moment Weatherby took her full attention, but it was the name James next uttered that made everything spin out of control.

'And I would like you to meet Mr Kavanagh, Mary. This is my wife, Kavanagh. And this is my young cousin, Miss Ashford.'

Louise's gaze flew past Weatherby to the tall, young man who now stood in the doorway beside James. The blood drained from her face and her mouth fell open in a soundless 'Oh'. He was obviously as startled as she, standing rigid with shock. She swallowed and put her hand to her throat, the words of greeting she'd been about to utter frozen to silence. Mary was looking from one to the other of them and Louise pulled herself together enough to murmur, 'How do you do, Mr Kavanagh.'

She stepped hastily aside and James and Weatherby, laughing together over some joke, entered the dining room. The younger visitor followed slowly and, in a daze, Louise heard Mary asking him if he lived in Banana too. His answer was lost in the roaring sound that seemed to have filled her ears. Jack made up the rear and Mary directed everyone to their places.

Louise couldn't remember experiencing anything as ghastly as that meal. She thought she might faint, but all the while she was forced to make polite conversation, responding when spoken to, keeping the muscles of her face in place when they threatened to crumple with the strain.

And Lloyd... oh God, this was Lloyd Kavanagh sitting across the table from her, like a stranger. She kept stealing furtive glances at him over the food she could not eat. He seemed not to look at her at all but ate doggedly, saying little. But as he raised his fork to his mouth she noticed how his hand trembled.

He was hardly changed at all, at least not in ways that were visible. Perhaps his mouth was set a little harder and she'd seldom seen him look so unhappy, but he was only subtly older. He would be twenty-five now, almost twenty-six and he was just as brown and slim as she remembered.

This man that she'd loved too well. After all those months of longing to see his face again, she had to sit opposite him and pretend he was a stranger. Her heart threatened to thump its way out of her ribs and her throat was so heavy, she could scarcely breathe. And she could see it was hurting him just as much.

Oh, for a moment alone with him. It was impossible now to let the matter rest as she'd resolved to do. Perhaps he was already married to someone else, but she couldn't let him walk out of her life without finding out.

The meal seemed interminable. It was obvious Lloyd was longing to be elsewhere. She wasn't surprised when he excused himself as soon as he decently could, leaving Weatherby, who seemed in no hurry to leave, to accept James's invitation to stay and enjoy a glass of port.

Louise was in turmoil. Every instinct, every shred of upbringing rebelled against following Lloyd out there in the dark, but this wasn't the moment for discretion. If she didn't seize her opportunity now she might not be granted another and the prospect of watching him leave in the morning without having exchanged a single meaningful word with him was intolerable. Waiting until Mary signalled her to retire from the table, she excused herself, lit a kerosene lantern and slipped outside by way of the kitchen.

Lloyd had disappeared and would doubtless be already at his campsite. She knew he and Weatherby were staying by the river so she hurried down there, the flickering lantern lighting her way through the long grass.

He had stoked up their fire and was sitting on a log staring into the flames, his face lit into angles of misery. He didn't look up at first, obviously expecting Weatherby. Louise paused, heart thudding, and murmured his name.

Lloyd leapt to his feet and stood looking at her with his back to the fire and his face now in darkness. She couldn't read his expression, but when he spoke his response was painfully clear.

'Jesus, what are *you* doing here?'

She flinched at the harsh, derisive note in his voice. 'I want to talk to you–please, Lloyd!'

'Well, I've got nothing to say to you. And if it's a roll in me swag you were thinking of, I'll say no to that too.' He was hateful, jeering—a hostile stranger. 'Isn't Jack Barclay man enough for you? He couldn't keep his eyes off you tonight.'

Louise stood transfixed, hardly grasping the full horror of his words.

'Well?' he sneered, after a moment's silence. 'It's not like you to be stuck for words, Miss *Ashford*!'

It was the loathing with which he spoke her name that struck through her disbelief. What had she done to make him hate her so much? She'd followed him in the dark like a shameless trollop but surely that didn't warrant these insults.

Suddenly the full impact of everything she'd lost burst upon her. Her child, the respect and acceptance of her parents–a poor substitute for the love she'd always craved from them, but better at least than nothing–the affection of Richard Langley. Throughout it all the memory of Lloyd's love had helped to sustain her and in the space of a few words he'd shattered that.

There was nothing left.

She uttered a choked sob, turning from him and running into the night. She stumbled over a clump of grass and nearly fell, weeping bitterly. Slowing to a walk she kept on, her breath coming in choking gasps. She was heedless of the danger of snakes in the dark, unsure of her destination but unable to return to the house to face her cousins' stares and probable censure. Angling towards the river, she eventually stopped beside a low bush. The ground beneath it was worn bare by sleeping kangaroos, but she hardly noticed the musty odour. She dropped under the bush, sitting with her knees drawn up and her face pressed into them, her whole body racked with great, gulping sobs.

Lloyd looked after her helplessly, immediately regretting his crudity. Her forgotten lantern fluttered forlornly next to a pile of saddles and swags. He could hear her crying as she ran and in his guilt it hardly seemed right to let her go. Yet every instinct told him that he must. Whatever mess she was in now was probably of her own making. He couldn't let her destroy him again.

He was still sitting there beside the fire when Weatherby joined him an hour later. 'You left early, Kavanagh. You weren't very sociable tonight.'

Lloyd didn't reply and he added in a different, curious tone, 'Did you see Miss Ashford? They were looking for her when I left. Apparently she left the house not long after you did and she hasn't come back.'

Lloyd looked at him quickly. 'Are they worried about her?'

'Yeah, they are a bit. I don't think they're sending a search party just yet, but they asked me to keep an eye out for her.' He paused and surveyed his companion. 'I think they were afraid I might find her down here with you. Mrs Barclay seemed to get the impression you'd met before.'

Lloyd flushed and shifted restlessly. He didn't want to talk about Louise, but guilt gnawed at him. He couldn't just ignore the situation. If she was still out there somewhere he owed it to them all to search for her, since it was him she'd run from.

'I know which way she went. I'll go and look for her.' He took the lantern she'd left behind and quickly departed before Weatherby could ask any questions.

It was the sound of her weeping that eventually led him to her. Crouching beside her he set the lantern on the ground, looking at her impotently as she hunched under that scrubby bush. In her grief she seemed oblivious to his presence. Nothing in his previous knowledge of Louise had prepared him for this. He was shocked and dumbfounded, his guts curled into a hard painful ball. He'd spent the last two years hating her and now her crying was shredding him into pieces.

'Louise, stop it!' He gave her a little shake. 'What's happened to you?'

Her body jerked and she shrank away from his touch without lifting her head. 'Just leave me alone.' Her voice was a broken whisper. 'I never dreamed you would hate me so much.'

'I'm sorry, Louise. I shouldn't have spoken like that. Let me take you back to the house.'

She shrugged his hand off her arm. 'No. I can't face them now.'

'You have to, Louise. You can't stay out here all night. They're worried about you.'

She shook her head and blew her nose. She seemed to gather herself a bit, but still she didn't look at him. 'I'm sorry for that, because I caused them enough trouble before. God, what am I going to do?'

The despair in her voice was more disturbing even than her tears. 'Louise, I'm sorry for what I said–it was crude and uncouth. But surely I don't matter to you? When your brother came you left me without a second thought.'

'How can you say that?' She turned to stare at him, the note of incredulity in her voice making him pause. Ashford had made him believe she hadn't cared, but he supposed that was the bastard's intention.

'Louise, I think we have some talking to do, but we can't do it now, out here, while your relations are out looking for you. I'll take you back to the house and in the morning I'll come and see you.'

Sensing her capitulation, he helped her to her feet and brushed off her dress. She wiped her eyes with her handkerchief and pushed back her dishevelled hair.

'Oh God, what a sight I must look! They'll all think I've run mad.'

Certainly she presented a dejected figure in the lantern light. Just a short while before she'd sat across the table from him in her evening gown, looking elegant and untouchable despite the revealing nature of that same gown. It was a garment no Banana woman would dare to wear unless she was a barmaid or a whore. He supposed it must be acceptable dress for the fashionable English gentry, but when the decent women he knew wore necklines buttoned to their throat and long sleeves to their wrists, it was a shock to see her bare shoulders and arms. Even now, as she bent to dislodge a stone from her shoe, he could see the shadowy swell of her breasts revealed by the low neckline and he dragged his eyes away. It was disconcerting to find that even in her disordered state, she had the power to stir him still.

He slowly walked her back, bypassing Weatherby at the camp. It would be soon enough to answer questions there when he returned. For now the situation with the Barclays was going to test his inventiveness.

There was silence between them until Louise broke it, her voice and manner more composed now. 'So James and the boys have been out searching for me?'

'They just took a look around the house and outbuildings, I think. Weatherby told me they were worried about you.'

She bit her lip, looking mortified. 'I seem to make a habit of this. I ran away from here two-and-a-half years ago, you know, when I was trying to escape from Charles. They searched high and low for me then and it was only the purest luck that Charles didn't uncover my tracks at Bauhinia Downs.' She turned her face away. 'If only he had found me then.'

Lloyd flinched at her bitter tone. 'Looks like we're both sadder and wiser. I must've got the wrong impression, but I thought when Ashford took you off to better things you'd have put all this behind you. What's been happening to you, Louise? I've never seen you cry like that before.' His voice caught as he remembered the only other time he'd heard her cry, that bittersweet night when he'd made her his. And yet she'd never been really his, as it turned out.

She cast him a sideways, resentful glance. 'Oh, if only you knew.'

There was no chance to say more, for James had seen their approach and was hurrying to meet them, carrying his own lantern.

'Louise, thank God you're all right! Where have you been?' He glanced at her companion, his tone anxious and more than a little shocked. 'Was she with you all the time, Kavanagh?'

'No sir, she wasn't. I just found her down by the river. But can you leave the questions until the morning, Mr Barclay? She's very upset.'

James looked at Louise searchingly in the lantern light. 'What happened to upset you, Louise? I was unaware you and Kavanagh were acquainted.' He paused, glancing from one to the other, his voice growing heavy with irony. 'I'm beginning to suspect there is a lot more to this than meets the eye.'

'Please, Cousin James.' Louise's embarrassment and contrition were there in her voice. 'I'm sorry to have made such a stupid display of myself. It's an unhappy story, but I'll try to explain in the morning.'

'Mr Barclay, will you let me call on Louise–Miss Ashford– tomorrow? As you've guessed, we aren't strangers, far from it. It looks like we've got some sorting out to do.'

James stared at him dubiously. 'I'm not so sure...unless Louise wishes it.'

She gave Lloyd a wavering glance. For a moment he thought she would refuse him, but then she said, 'I do wish it.'

'In that case,' James responded ironically, 'there's no more to be said. I'll bid you goodnight, Kavanagh and thank you for finding her. Let us hope we can resolve this situation in the morning.'

Weatherby was sitting before the fire, drinking from an enamel pannikin when Lloyd returned to their camp. He held up a flask with an inquiring look. 'Would you like a drop? You probably need it.'

Lloyd duly splashed a quantity of rum into his own pannikin and added water before sitting on the other side of the fire.

Weatherby regarded him curiously. 'You having petticoat trouble?'

'You could say that.'

'Where'd you meet a girl like that?'

'It was before you came up here. I haven't seen her for two years. She was governessing for the Jamiesons for a while.'

Weatherby's eyes widened. 'I think I heard something about her. She sure don't look like a governess. To be frank, she don't look like your type, either.' And then, when no more information was forthcoming, he added, 'What happened?'

'Her brother took her away. As far as I know she went to England.' Lloyd spoke shortly, hoping to dissuade Weatherby from further interrogation. The firelight flickered over his companion's questioning features and Lloyd abruptly changed the subject. 'Do you mind waiting for me in the morning, Weatherby? We've got to thrash this out.'

He guessed Weatherby had hoped to get away early, but the horse buyer merely commented in a bantering tone, 'Hell, I never thought I'd be getting mixed up in your affairs of the heart when I brought you along. I'll think twice next time.' He grinned. 'But we can't let it be said I stood in the way of true love.'

Lloyd smiled without humour. 'It's over. But I suppose I owe it to her to hear her side of the story.'

The other man sobered. 'There were rumours flying around when I first came to Banana. How you'd been unlucky in love and gone on the spree to forget her.'

'And you thought, "That'll be a Kavanagh," I'll bet.' Lloyd stared at the flames, remembering that futile time and the stupid way he'd set the town talking with his drinking and shacking up with Eva. It was amazing that Eva had taken him back after the way he'd dumped her the first time.

It still hurt to remember how he'd drunk to stop thinking of Louise and his dread of going home again. And when at last he did go home, the cool reception he'd got when he finally plucked up the courage to visit the Jamiesons.

Not that Jock had ever entirely deserted him, good old Jock– and when tragedy struck the Jamiesons again it had shocked Lloyd out of his self-pity. Jock had needed him then. He had got himself back on track and even eventually found himself planning for the future.

But here was Louise threatening to destroy his hard-won peace of mind once more. If he had any sense he'd leave in the morning without even seeing her.

Chapter Twenty-two

Breakfast at the Barclay house was an awkward affair, with Jack looking hurt, bewildered and disapproving, while James was grimly silent. Louise had filled Mary in with the basic details of her relationship with Lloyd, but had yet to speak to James.

They hadn't finished eating when Louise heard Lloyd call from the front step. She pushed her plate of steak and eggs aside, her appetite gone. James went to the veranda to greet him and her throat constricted as she listened to Lloyd's broad Colonial accent. It was one of the many things she'd missed while in England.

'Sorry to bother you so early. Weatherby wants to get away as soon as he can. If you'd let me speak to Miss Ashford in private, I'd appreciate it.'

'Certainly. I'll call her.'

Louise nervously joined them on the veranda. Her heart flipped at the sight of him, standing there with his hat in his hand, looking so dearly familiar in his moleskins and Crimean shirt. During all those months in England his image had become blurred, without substance, and the flesh and blood reality evoked an emotional response that was disturbing in its intensity. Something inside her began to ache and she knew if he left her today she would have to begin the slow road to acceptance all over again.

'Would you like to use the sitting room?' James was saying. 'I'll make sure you're not disturbed.'

'If we could take a walk down to the river...?' Louise offered hesitantly.

'Yeah, that sounds better.' Lloyd flicked his eyes to Louise's face and away again, his expression uneasy. He returned his hat to his head. 'Come on, Louise, before Weatherby goes without me.'

She led him to her favourite spot, where the river gums cast dappled shade on the water and a patch of green grass provided an inviting seat. She sensed him studying her as she settled her skirts about her and tried to hide her mortification, clutching her hands together in her lap to stop them shaking.

'I know I said some pretty rough things to you,' he began slowly. 'It was rotten of me–there was no need to be so crude.'

'You seem to have been left with a low opinion of me, Lloyd.' She shook her head, confused and bewildered. 'I know I was wrong in not being totally honest with you, but as for leaving, I had no choice. The Jamiesons could have told you that. Charles allowed me no opportunity to see you or explain.' She added hesitantly, 'I was extremely...foolish...and indiscreet...in my dealings with you, but I didn't think at the time that you thought less of me for it. It appears I was wrong.'

He drew in a sharp breath. 'Christ, girl, at the time I loved you too much to think any wrong of you! I was in no flaming position to judge you, anyway. At least you came to me pure, which is more than I can say for myself. I wouldn't like to tell you some of the things I've done.'

Her gaze flew to his face. 'What sort of things?'

'Never mind. It makes me a bit sick to think of it now. Me mate Will and I–we knew a couple of girls who were as wild as they come. That was before Connal O'Donnelly got hold of me.' He seemed to notice her shocked face and paused. 'I told you me upbringing was pretty rough.'

'Yes, but...you were only fifteen years old when you went to Mr O'Donnelly!'

He smiled without humour. 'That's old enough, Louise.'

She supposed this was a frank, even crude discussion to be having with a man she hadn't seen for two years, but she was too tired and exhausted to care. 'I can't think even Charles began his sinful career so young.'

At the mention of Charles his face closed abruptly. Turning away from her, he stared out over the river. 'Let's not talk about your brother, eh?'

Louise looked sideways at his profile, wondering at the sudden change in him. A moment ago he'd seemed contrite and approachable, yet now the barriers were up and he was angry again. As she watched him, the emotional longing surged within her, but he showed no sign of sharing it. Agonisingly, he seemed to be lost to her. There was an implacability about him that she hadn't seen in the old days.

'Lloyd, you haven't forgiven me for deceiving you, have you?'

His expression became even more guarded. 'Should I have?'

'But I wrote to you. I thought, when you read my letter you would realize—'

'That bloody letter!' he cut her off, jumping to his feet. 'I'm surprised you'd mention it! It made a joke of everything you'd said to me! You say Charles forced you to go, but it sure didn't sound like it to me.'

'How can you say that?' She was incredulous, her voice shaking. 'I told you how sorry I was for deceiving you and how devastated I was at leaving.'

He stared at her. 'Are we talking about the letter Ashford gave me?'

'But... when did you see Charles?'

It was his turn to look confused. 'The morning after he took you away from the Jamiesons. Surely you knew he'd ridden out?'

She shook her head.

'But he gave me your letter then!'

'Lloyd, I hadn't even *written* a letter, at that stage. I didn't write until we arrived at Banyandah.'

'Well, I never got that one. I daresay I wouldn't have read it if I had, after the first one.' He took a deep breath and shook his head. 'Which you say you didn't write? You know, that fits. I remember thinking at the time it didn't ring true.'

'What on earth was in it?'

'Ha! Something about it being funny I'd been courting Harry Ashford's daughter all this time and hadn't even known it!'

'That diabolical brute!' Louise trembled. 'I might have guessed he'd make sure you didn't attempt to follow me. What did he say to you?'

Lloyd turned quickly and walked away a little, not answering. Louise noticed the tense set of his head and her stomach churned. 'Lloyd, what did he do?'

He didn't look at her. 'He just made bloody sure I'd never want to set eyes on any of you Ashfords again.' Abruptly, he changed the subject. 'Did he take you to England, then?'

'Yes. I've been back here only six weeks.'

'I'm surprised you were allowed back.'

'It's a long story. The man I was about to become engaged to changed his mind and I was out of favour with my parents. Charles was returning here and in the end they were glad to be rid of me. Besides, I came of age in February and am now presumably old enough to be allowed out of their care.'

She heard the bitter note of sarcasm in her own voice and he swung around quickly. 'What happened with your beau?'

She met his gaze levelly. 'He found out about us.'

His eyes flickered. 'How?'

'Does it matter?'

He eyed her searchingly for a moment, but let it pass. At last he said, 'So you were twenty-one this year? I suppose that fits, but was anything else you told me ever the truth?'

She flushed. 'Most of it was. It was just my actual identity that was false. The rest of it wasn't so much lies as omissions. I explained everything when I wrote from Banyandah. If you didn't receive the letter, Charles must have intercepted it. There was one for the Jamiesons, too.'

'I'm sure they didn't get theirs, either.'

Her mouth twisted. 'Lloyd, I don't suppose you'll believe this, but I was going to tell you who I was very early in our acquaintance, on that day you took me to the Greenwoods. But you seemed to despise my family so much that I'm afraid I lost my courage.'

'Yes, I remember that. I remember you talking about the Ashfords.' His gaze probed her face. 'And so you left the Barclays just to get away from Charles?'

'I was young and foolish, Lloyd.'

'You can say that again! God, I wish you'd just gone to England and none of this would ever have happened. If we'd never met it would have been better for both of us.'

That stung, even though she'd said much the same thing last night. She turned away blindly, on the verge of tears. 'Do you really mean that?'

He sat beside her again, hesitating, his voice gentle. 'Yes, I do. Look at the mess I got you into last night. I wasn't in any better shape after your brother took you off to England. It ended between us for me then, Louise. I can't go back now.'

Her voice was so choked it was an effort to speak. 'It may have ended for you, but it certainly didn't for me.'

'What do you mean? I thought you said you nearly got engaged to someone else.'

Oh God, should she tell him? Much better to let him remain in happy ignorance. And yet, perhaps it was important to make him appreciate how much she'd suffered. The knowledge of the child was the only thing that might bring him back to her now.

'Lloyd, what we did was wrong and you may think it had finished when Charles took me away, but in truth it had only just begun. There's a little boy back in England who won't escape the consequences of it, ever.'

There was a dawning fear on his face, along with denial, as if he preferred not to comprehend her words. 'What are you talking about?'

'I'm talking about our son. You see, when Charles took me to England I was carrying your child.'

He paled, his face and body stiffening. His obvious distress made her want to take her words back. Better to have kept that particular agony to herself. But it was too late now.

The silence stretched on, interminably. Lloyd had turned away from her and sat mutely, unmoving except for the stalk of grass he kept twisting in his strong brown fingers. She watched anxiously as he stared at some indistinct spot on the far bank of the river, as if he might find an answer there–something to help him adjust to this disclosure that had just turned his world upside-down. At some stage his lips moved as if he was talking to himself and his Adam's apple rippled his throat as he swallowed.

When at last he spoke aloud his voice was strained, the question abrupt. 'So what happened to the baby?'

'My parents took him away and gave him to the coachman and his wife at Fenham Manor. Don't worry; no-one could care for him more dearly than they do. They hadn't any children of their own, you see.'

'A little boy! Poor little bastard!' He turned to stare at her, as if trying to read her thoughts. 'Did you want to keep him?'

'Oh yes, I begged and pleaded for it.' Her voice was flat and lifeless. 'He was all I had left of you.'

Lloyd put his hand to his brow and bowed his head, wincing visibly. 'God, Louise, I'm sorry. To think I put you through that. I've always despised blokes who went around fathering nameless brats. Looks like I'm no different. I never even tried to be careful with you.' He rested his elbows on his bent knees and buried his face in his hands.

At last he looked up at her again. 'Are they poor, these people he's with? Does he get enough to eat?'

'Yes, I'm sure he does. There's plenty of fresh, wholesome farm food. He won't have money, but he'll be given the chance to work his way up in the stables as his foster father did. As long as there are Ashfords at Fenham Manor he's assured of a position there.'

'Yeah. Me son working for Charles Ashford. That's fate for you.' He plucked another blade of grass and shredded it into tiny pieces, his mouth twisting. 'I suppose I'll never see him.'

'Since the day he was born, I've only seen him once myself. He has my colouring, but he looks like you, Lloyd. He's a beautiful little boy.'

He managed a brief smile at that. 'If he looks like me he could hardly be beautiful.'

She echoed the smile. 'Nevertheless, he is beautiful and he does look like you, so make of that what you will.'

Lloyd reached for her hand and clasped it in both of his. 'How did your parents take it?'

She uttered a short, mirthless laugh. 'They despised me, of course. But I suppose they did what they considered was their best for me. Other girls in the same situation have been thrown out, so I was lucky to escape that. They gave me another chance, but I spoiled it all in the end.'

'What do you mean?'

She shrugged. 'The baby was the best-kept secret of the century and they even had me presented to the Prince and Princess of Wales. Just as my engagement was about to be announced, the man in question discovered everything. As you can imagine that put an end to it.'

'Who were you going to marry?'

Her mouth twisted. 'Mr Richard Langley, the youngest son of a vicar from Sussex.'

He stared at her. 'The son of a *vicar*?'

Louise almost smiled at his expression. 'He wasn't in the least religious, Lloyd. As a matter of fact, if my parents hadn't been so anxious to be rid of me I wouldn't have been allowed near him. Richard had little money and he was irresponsible and not particularly moral, but he was intelligent and attractive and very amusing.' She didn't add he had aristocratic connections; that hardly seemed relevant.

'Did you care for him?' Lloyd's tone was jealous.

She remembered Richard's careless sophistication and his polished, artful courtship, so different from the earthy sincerity with which Lloyd had wooed her. She didn't need to reflect on it to know who would make the better husband.

'I was fond of him and I found him attractive, but I'm sure he would have made me miserable,' she said at last.

He turned away from her. 'Why don't you marry Jack Barclay? I saw the lovesick way he was looking at you last night. He has more to offer you than I have.'

'I think he's had second thoughts about me already. I'm sure he wouldn't have me if he knew the truth.'

'You wouldn't have to tell him.'

She shook her head. 'I couldn't live a lie like that for the rest of my life. I'm through with lies. You've no idea what a nightmare it was, hiding myself from the world for all those months so no-one would see my condition. Besides, I don't love Jack.' She looked at him bravely, sacrificing her pride. 'I love you, Lloyd. I have always loved you and oh, how I wish I'd married you when you first asked me. I was such a coward, procrastinating because I didn't have the courage to tell you who I really was. Richard Langley was a poor substitute.'

Lloyd stirred restlessly. 'How can you possibly still want to marry me after associating with all the aristocracy of England? Last night sitting across the table from you, I wondered that I'd ever dared to touch you. You looked so different, so much the grand lady.'

'I fell down in the role shortly afterwards, as you know.'

'Not without reason.'

She looked at him searchingly, suspecting a further reason for his reluctance. 'Are you involved with anyone else?'

He went very still. 'What makes you ask that?'

'I just guessed. It was in my mind that I might find you already married.'

'No, but there's Mercy–I've been seeing a bit of her, though I haven't asked her to marry me yet.'

'Is she expecting you to?'

His lips twitched. 'You know Mercy. I wish she'd outgrown her fancy for me, but she hasn't. And she's become very...fetching.' He paused and Louise knew it was her turn to look jealous. 'I've started building a new house, but I've kept putting off asking her. I was tired of being on me own, but I wasn't sure...' He sighed. 'I feel like a cad for encouraging her at all, now. If only I could have married you two years ago–you were broken-in to the life then. But when I think about the places you've been and the life you've lived...'

'That life is finished for me now. I never chose it and even if I wanted to, I couldn't go back. There's been too much gossip.'

'So I'm the best prospect that's left to you? You *have* come down in the world, Louise Ashford.'

'It was you who brought me down, Lloyd Kavanagh.'

'You're right, it was. I owe it to you to marry you if that's what you want.'

She bowed her head at his lack of enthusiasm and his voice softened. 'I'm sorry, but this takes a lot of getting used to. I've spent the last two years hating you, but I can see now it was your brother's plan. Damn, he's a clever, cruel bastard.' He lifted his hand to brush the hair away from her face. 'How can you be an Ashford and still be the person I thought you were?'

She shook her head. 'I don't know. All I know is, I don't fit in with them. I think I was always a little different, but the time I spent away from them changed me irrevocably.'

'There's something else I should tell you, Louise. Ted Weatherby comes from Grenfell, where me family is. He's only been up here for eighteen months or so. I asked him for news of them and it wasn't a pretty story. One of me brothers is doing time in Bathurst Gaol for highway robbery.' He snorted derisively. 'He must fancy himself as a bushranger, the silly b... Most of the others haven't turned out much better.'

'What of your parents?'

'Ma's living with one of me sisters and Dad died of consumption two years ago. I bet Ma's pleased to be rid of him.'

She was silent for a moment. It repelled her to think Lloyd's brother was a felon, but she wasn't particularly proud of her own brother. 'I'm sorry, Lloyd, but you can't be held responsible for the rest of your family.'

He smiled. 'I don't deserve such loyalty. But if we're going to get married we'd better do it quick, before Charles gets wind of it.'

'What can he do? I'm twenty-one. Papa said he'd washed his hands of me and Charles told me I could do what I liked and be damned to me.'

Lloyd regarded her pensively, his thoughts troubled. It was typical of Louise that she should reappear and in less than twenty-four hours turn his world completely upside-down. In all decency he couldn't do anything else but marry her. What he'd suffered was nothing to what she'd been through and if he walked away from her today he knew he would be of no use to Mercy or any other woman. Even now the urge to hold her and do a lot else besides, threatened his determination to keep a cool head.

On the other hand the grief Charles Ashford had caused him could not be erased so easily. And he dreaded hurting Mercy again. It was all such a mess and had been ever since that day Ashford came into their lives and disrupted all their plans.

'Louise, I think we'd better go back and talk to your cousins now.'

'Yes, we should.' She let him help her rise and brushed off her skirt. 'I know they're worried.'

'They'll think it's a bit sudden, but I don't trust Charles, no matter what he said. And how can I court you from Myvanwy? It's more than a day's ride. I'd have to take three days off to visit you and I don't have that much time to spare right now. Besides, we did our courting two years ago.'

'Just how soon are you thinking?'

'I'll go home and finish the house. Then I'll take you to Rockhampton and we can be married there.'

Chapter Twenty-three

Leaving Lloyd to wait on the front step, Louise went in search of Mary. She found her in the garden, weeding her geraniums. The older woman put down her trowel and stood up, stripping off her gloves.

'Come and sit on the back veranda, where it's cool.' Mary seated herself on one of the homemade chairs, facing Louise. 'You look much happier than you did this morning. Did you and Mr Kavanagh reconcile your differences?'

'Eventually, yes. Once we realized how much of the misunderstanding was due to Charles's meddling.' She looked Mary squarely in the eye and briefly outlined their plans. 'Since there's no hope of obtaining my parents' blessing I hope you and James will give us yours.'

'Oh, Louise.' Mary seemed at a loss for words. 'This seems hasty, after two years apart.'

'We bided our time before and gave Charles the opportunity to separate us. Lloyd doesn't want to risk that happening again.'

'I know there's no love lost between you and your parents, but there is love for you here, my dear! You don't need to betray your class to find it. This Kavanagh...the name's Irish. Is he a Catholic?'

'Yes, he is. Not that it matters.'

'It does matter, I'm afraid. Mixed marriages cause all sorts of problems. And what will Charles think if we condone your relationship with a man he's tried so hard to separate you from?'

Louise bristled. 'After the unscrupulous, domineering way Charles treated us, I really don't care! Besides, he can't blame you. I shall write to them all once we're safely married.'

Mary looked horrified. 'Don't you intend to tell them first? You owe them that much courtesy.'

'No.' Louise was adamant. 'Papa is too far away to stop us, but I shan't risk interference from Charles! I won't have him told while there's a chance of him trying to prevent the wedding.'

Mary twisted her hands together in her lap, obviously distressed. 'I shall see what James has to say. If he thinks he should write to Charles I shan't dissuade him.'

'Not Charles, I beg of you.' Louise jumped up and paced to the edge of the veranda, her heart racing. 'He would be sure to come here and cause trouble. He's a devil–you don't know what he's like.'

'I do know that no-one could have tried harder than he to find you when you ran away from here. You'd better talk to James.'

But James was even less receptive than his wife to the proposed marriage.

'Why, Louise? You've lived without him for two years and you seemed happy enough before this.'

'I may have appeared happy to you, Cousin James, but you haven't seen the tears I've shed in private.'

'Louise, your father is squire of Fenham Manor. You have both looks and character. You could have your pick of the eligible men in this area, young men of good family. Why throw yourself away on a struggling selector like Kavanagh?'

'Because, as I said to Cousin Mary, I love him. Besides, I wouldn't describe him as struggling. He owns a good-sized property on the Dawson.'

James waved his hand dismissively. 'I've been talking to Weatherby this morning. True, he does own a good property, but his father was a drunkard and his brothers and sisters don't sound any better.'

Louise paused and drew a deep breath. 'Lloyd can't be held responsible for his family.' Perhaps there was only one way to convince him. 'You won't dissuade me, Cousin James. It so happens that he's the only man whom I have any right to *expect* to marry me.' There, it was said now and she couldn't be sorry, in spite of James's narrowed, measuring gaze on her. 'Lloyd is waiting to speak with you and I ask you please to invite him in and treat him with courtesy. This is Australia, after all, not England.'

James smiled thinly. 'I never thought to hear an Ashford speak for class equality. But don't worry, Louise. I have no intention of showing him the door. It seems it's too late for that. Unless I misunderstand you it sounds as if your morals are no better than the rest of the Ashfords. And Kavanagh's aren't so different from his family's, after all.'

Coming from the usually mild-mannered James, it was a pungent criticism. 'I make no excuses for myself, Cousin James. But I do know that Lloyd's morals are a good deal better than those of many supposed "gentlemen".'

'That doesn't say much. We may be out of touch with things here, but I do know the Prince of Wales set has all of England scandalised.'

'Needless to say Lloyd doesn't have the money or the time to waste on their sort of frivolity.'

'No, I don't imagine so. Weatherby says he's a hard worker. There'll be plenty of hard work in it for you, too, my girl.'

She shrugged. 'Cousin James, I experienced the lifestyle while I was working for the Jamiesons and I adjusted well to it. Idleness isn't all it's supposed to be.'

'I agree with you wholeheartedly on that score.' James rose to his feet with a weary sigh. 'I'll be civil to Kavanagh. If your mind's made up there's no point in being anything else.'

She found Lloyd still sitting on the steps, smoking his pipe, but fidgeting restlessly. He looked up at her, his smile a little tense. 'How did they take it?'

She shrugged. 'Cousin James is waiting to have a private word with you.'

He paused at the top of the steps, looking down at her. 'From your expression I gather they weren't too happy.'

'I won't pretend they think you're the ideal husband for me, but they'll reconcile themselves to it once they become better acquainted with you. They are very kind people, you know.'

'Yeah, so I've always heard.'

James appeared at the doorway then, greeting Lloyd civilly and inviting him into his study. Louise smiled encouragingly at Lloyd and lightly touched his hand, then left them to it.

Louise was flicking indifferently through a book when Lloyd rejoined her. She looked up anxiously as he sank down beside her on the sofa. 'What did James say to you?'

His mouth twisted. 'Why'd you let him guess what'd been going on between us?'

Her eyes dropped and she found herself looking at his moleskin-clad thigh, only an inch or two from hers on the sofa, and his bare brown forearm almost brushing hers. 'There seemed no other way of convincing him not to oppose us.'

'It didn't impress him much. He doesn't seem to think too much of me as it is.'

'Nor of me. But perhaps he'll decide we deserve each other.'

Lloyd grinned. 'I think he's already decided that.'

The chiming clock on the wall struck the hour and he jumped to his feet. 'Crikey, look at the time! Weatherby was chomping at the bit–he'll be packed and gone if I don't get back soon.' He pulled her up and into his arms. 'Louise, I promise I'll write as soon as I know what I'm doing.' He looked down into her eyes, his hands at her waist pressing her close. 'Are you happy?'

She nodded. 'I can't quite believe it, yet.' She lifted her face in invitation, drinking in the familiar smell of horses and saddle leather that clung to him, her body thrilling to his touch. 'Kiss me, Lloyd, so I know it's real.'

It was like old times. They seemed to fit together as if they were made for each other and it was gratifying to sense the passion in him as strong as ever. Perhaps it would work for them, after all.

'Oh, Louise, I used to try to stop myself thinking about this.' His voice was tense with desire. 'I've never felt like this with anyone else, ever.'

'Have there been so many others?'

He moved back a little, looking down at her. 'You've never asked me that before.'

'I know, but...you shocked me a little yesterday. It made me realize there's a lot I don't know about you.'

'There haven't been so many and no-one at all since just after you left. Unless you count Mercy and don't worry, I haven't slept with her.' He grinned down at her with a touch of his old mischievousness. 'And I can tell you, two years is a long time.'

'Oh, Lloyd. If James or Mary were to hear you...' Blushing, she moved away from him and took a sealed envelope from the top of the piano. 'Will you deliver this to Mrs Jamieson for me? I must write some explanation and apology to replace the letter they didn't receive. I shall feel very awkward about meeting them again.'

She paused and eyed him anxiously. The humour had disappeared from his face and he'd turned very pale. 'What is it? What did I say?'

'I won't be giving any letters to Mrs Jamieson.' His voice faltered. 'She's dead, Louise. She died having the baby–three months after you left.'

Louise stared at him in dismayed silence, wishing she could bite out her tongue. He'd turned away from her, trying to hide his grief in typical masculine fashion and she remembered how Mrs

Jamieson had looked after him and cooked meals for him as if he were her own son.

'Oh, Lloyd.' Louise went to him and put her arms around him, pressing her face against the warm skin of his throat. Tears pricked at her eyes. 'What a lot you've been through–life is so cruel! That poor family must be heartbroken. But what happened to the baby?'

'She's doing well. Mercy's like a mother to her. Poor Mercy, she's held that family together, doing her mother's work and looking after the baby. God, I hate to hurt her, Louise.'

A shudder ran through him and he drew her closer, stroking her hair. As he bent his head to kiss her the sound of someone clearing his throat made them break apart. James was at the door, his eyes carefully averted.

'Weatherby's waiting outside, Kavanagh. You'd better go.'

Chapter Twenty-four

Back at Myvanwy Lloyd set to work to complete his house. So determined was he to finish it in the next two weeks that he didn't spare the time to visit the Jamiesons, though he knew he must. He was on the roof one day fixing shingles when he saw Mercy ride up. His heart sank.

It wasn't the first time Mercy had visited him like this. Her calls were ostensibly to view the progress on the house, which Lloyd suspected she hoped to share with him one day. He also knew her visits were made without her father's knowledge, when she was supposed to be checking their own paddocks.

Lloyd had tried to persuade her against coming, for her visits worried him. He owed Jock too much to risk compromising his daughter and compromised she would be if she were discovered here alone with him.

It hadn't been so bad before she enticed him into kissing her. Until he was ready to commit himself to marrying her, he'd hoped to avoid that. But she hadn't made it easy for him.

Mercy had brought a billy of tea over to him one day when he was laying the slab floor of the house. She'd sat beside him on a log as they sipped the hot tea and ate slices of fresh-baked brownie, smuggled in her saddlebag. Watching him when she thought he wasn't looking, she reached across him for a piece of brownie, allowing her breasts to brush against his arm. His body responded and he smiled grimly at her bent head as she nibbled the cake, but didn't make the desired move. After a moment she looked up at him, her face flushed.

'Lloyd, don't you care for me at all?'

Her innocence made him feel very gentle and protective. 'I care for you too much to treat you lightly, Mercy.'

'You used to care for Miss Forrest and you slept in the saddle-room with *her*.'

'Miss Ashford.' His voice was suddenly harsh.

'Miss Ashford, then. I don't care what her name was; she was a liar and impostor. I hated her for what she did to you. You aren't still in love with her, are you?'

He shook his head numbly. 'You weren't supposed to know she'd stayed with me that night. The last thing I wanted was to expose you lot to that.'

'I got up to get a drink of water and saw her come out of there.'

'Oh, Mercy. I'm sorry.'

She put her hand up and touched his hair. Her eyes were very tender. He bent his head to lightly brush her lips with his, and then attempted to draw back.

'No,' she breathed. 'Kiss me properly... please, Lloyd.'

So he kissed her as thoroughly as she was begging for, until he felt his self-control ebbing. He wrenched away from her and stood up, angry with himself. The worst of it was, when his blood was running hot he hadn't been thinking of Mercy at all. All he wanted was a female body to enjoy and comfort himself with and he knew she wouldn't have stopped him, not from any lack of morality but out of her love for him and her eagerness to please.

'Now you know why I didn't want to kiss you,' he said, trying to keep his voice level. 'Your father trusts me and we shouldn't be alone together like this.'

He knew this was the moment to ask her to marry him, but he couldn't bring himself to do it. For even after all this time, in that moment of passion he'd found himself thinking of Louise.

He'd told her not to come again, but she'd done so. And inevitably he'd kissed her again. Mercy had grown up a lot in the past two years and she could be very tempting. He was terrified that one day he might lose control and he knew he would never be able to look Jock in the face afterwards. It wouldn't matter if their act was undiscovered and even marrying her wouldn't be enough to put things right. For he feared he wouldn't take her with the gentleness and respect he owed her, but with the unresolved anger he still felt towards Louise.

She would make him an easy, comfortable wife and her presence here would put an end to the loneliness and frustration he presently endured. He wouldn't remain a bachelor for the rest of his life because the one girl he'd wanted had treated him badly. Yet it would hardly be fair to Mercy unless he was sure he loved her. So he kept putting it off, telling himself he'd ask her once the house was finished and everything was in order.

Now, as he set down his hammer and stepped across the roof to the waiting ladder, the only comforting thought in his mind was the blessed relief that he hadn't become engaged to her. For it was going to be bad enough, by all accounts.

Mercy sat her horse, smiling down at him as he approached. She held out her hands to him and unhooked her leg from the saddle-horn, sliding down into his arms. She lifted her face to his, expecting to be kissed, but he stepped back, releasing her abruptly.

Her smile disappeared and she looked up at him with an anxious expression. 'What's wrong?'

'I have some news for you, Mercy.' He took off his hat and fiddled with it, unsure how to tell her. 'I'm sorry about this and I hate hurting you, but I can't change the way things are.'

She'd gone deathly pale as she stared at him. 'What is it? What's wrong?'

'Nothing's wrong, really. I just met someone I didn't expect to see the other day, when I was at James Barclay's. Your ex-governess, Louise Ashford.' Noticing her eyes widening with shock and disbelief, he added slowly, 'It's not so surprising. She's their cousin, you know.'

'What of it?' Mercy's voice trembled slightly. 'Of what interest is it to me if you did meet her?'

'Mercy, I'm going to marry her.'

For a moment, there was deathly silence. Then she uttered a sharp cry of pure protest.

'Heavens, Lloyd, you can't mean that. She deceived you and led you a merry dance last time and then left you flat.' She stared at him in pleading silence and he looked down at his hat, saying nothing. At last she let out a little sob of despair. 'So she's got her hooks into you again. Oh, be blowed to the pair of you. I hate you both!'

She swung away, bursting into tears and he watched her helplessly, painfully, wishing there was something he could do. But there was nothing. He'd known it would be like this. His and Louise's happiness at the expense of hers.

'Mercy, don't take it so hard,' he said at last. 'I'm not worth it. I can't help the way I feel about Louise and I found out I've been wrong about her all this time. You see, her brother forced her to go with him and he pinched the letters she wrote to us. She suffered more at the separation than I did.'

Mercy turned back to him, a strange expression crossing her face–whether it was guilt or something else he couldn't be sure. Suddenly a suspicion came to him. 'You knew Louise didn't want to go.'

Mercy faltered, brushing at her tears with the back of her hand. 'Well, yes, she was upset when her brother took her away. I could have told you that, I suppose, but we've never discussed her.'

Lloyd made no response. It was true–they had never discussed Louise and the other Jamiesons had known as much as Mercy, he supposed. Yet he couldn't help thinking of the sorrow he and Louise might both have been saved if he'd been given any reason to believe Ashford was lying.

Still, Mercy's admission did little to lessen his remorse. It was like having history repeat itself as he was reminded of how Mercy had silently watched his budding romance with their governess. It wasn't his fault she'd initially become infatuated with him, but he was responsible for allowing that infatuation to strengthen over the past few months.

'I'm sorry about all this, Mercy. But if I don't marry Louise now I'll be no good to you, anyway. All this time I've been telling myself that she was a lying hussy and I was better off without her. But she did care about me and she still does, more than I deserve.'

'I'm sure I wish you happy, then.' Mercy held her head proudly despite the tears glistening in her eyes. 'Don't upset yourself on my account, Lloyd–I'll survive.'

She threw the reins over her horse's head and he moved swiftly to help her mount. 'Louise gave me a note to give your father. I won't give it to you now–we don't want him to know you've been here. I'll ride over tonight and see him.'

'Whatever you like.' She kicked her mare in the ribs and shot off at a fast canter without bothering to say goodbye, balancing effortlessly in the sidesaddle. Lloyd stood there for a long time, motionless, watching her dust gradually drift and settle, before he got back to work.

Jock Jamieson made him feel worse than ever when he arrived at Kilbride just on dark.

'Come inside, Lloyd. It's grand to see ye. How did ye fare with your horse-buying trip?'

'Pretty good, thanks Jock.' He stood his ground, ignoring Jock's gesture to enter. 'I got a grey two-year-old filly–looks like she'll be able to gallop. She was cheap, but I've got nothing against the colour.'

'Aye, I'll have to come over to see her. I suppose you'll be taking her to the races next year. But come in, lad. Ye'll be staying for tea, won't ye? The lasses have cooked plenty.'

'Thank you, but not tonight. I've got some news for you, Jock and you probably won't think much of it.'

Jock frowned. 'What might that be?'

Lloyd took a deep breath and plunged head-first. 'I know this is a bit sudden, but I wanted to tell you that I'm getting married. D'you remember Louise Ashford? Forrest, as we knew her?'

'Aye.' Jock's face was suddenly guarded behind the heavy beard. 'My memory's not that short.'

'I ran into her the other day, at the Barclays. She's a cousin of theirs, you know.'

'She told us she'd been governessing for them before she came here.'

'Yeah, that's right. She was staying with 'em when her family went to England. Anyway, I've got a letter here for you which should tell you everything.'

Jock took it and eyed it dubiously. 'This is a wee bit late, ain't it?'

Lloyd flushed, whether for himself or Louise he didn't know. 'She wrote letters to us when her brother took her away, but he must have got hold of 'em. She didn't know we'd never got 'em.'

'Aye, but I'd be inclined to take most things she told me with a grain of salt. 'Lucy Forrest', indeed!'

'She was trying to hide from her brother. If I'd known then what I know now I'd never have let him take her.'

Jock's eyes narrowed and he stared at Lloyd thoughtfully, sizing him up as if he were a beast for sale. 'So she's got her clutches into ye again,' he said at last. 'And what of our poor wee Mercy? She's been to thinking ye was going to wed her at last. Are ye going to be bringing this other lass to this fine new house of yours instead? Just what is this hold this Lucy has over ye?'

Lloyd's face heated. 'Louise,' he corrected automatically.

'Louise, then. We used to think it had all blown over between ye and then she ups and leaves with that brother of hers. The next thing we know ye were in a worse state than we'd ever seen ye, spending your time between the bar of the Banana and a back bedroom. And it seems only our Mercy knew all the time just how things were between ye and that governess.'

Lloyd started. So Mercy had told her parents what she knew about his relationship with Louise. Jock hadn't said anything before this. This made things more difficult, for Jock was less likely to accept and respect Louise as his wife now. He might excuse Lloyd's own part in it, but Louise was supposed to have been responsible for his children.

'Jock, you don't have to approve of everything we did, but I'll thank you to remember what a tower of strength Louise was to your family during all your troubles. Hell, if it hadn't been for her wanting to stay here while you needed her, we'd have been married before her brother found her. Perhaps it seems like we were sneaking around behind your back, but we couldn't be together any other way.'

'That doesn't excuse it. But I suppose she had her good points. She worked hard and probably did things she'd never had to do before. It was a tough time on all of us and it only got tougher.' Jock's voice broke, but then he collected himself and forced a brighter note. 'So what's she doing back here? Was it pure chance ye met up the other day?'

Lloyd nodded, relieved the awkward moment had passed. 'She's only been back here a couple of months.'

'Well, it's your bed and ye are the one that's got to lie on it. I hope ye'll be happy. I'm disappointed in ye, but it's our Mercy I'm most worried about.'

'I'm worried about her too, Jock,' he rejoined harshly. 'Jesus, don't think I like it. I wish she didn't care for me, but I can't change that.'

'For a newly engaged man ye don't sound too excited about it all.'

'Oh, Christ, I've never stopped wanting Louise, never been able to forget her. She's the only woman for me, Jock. I just hate hurting Mercy. She's been through enough, poor kid.'

'It's a wee too late for that, lad. It was a bad day for our Mercy when she took crazy over ye.'

Lloyd stirred restlessly, kicking the dirt with the toe of his boot. 'Yeah, well...it's getting late. Now you know why I didn't want to stay for tea. I'd better get home and cook myself something.'

He mounted up and rode away, loneliness and uncertainty eating away at his resolve. It would never be quite the same with the Jamiesons again. The relaxed, happy meals he'd shared with them were already a thing of the past. Jock might outwardly forgive him for his cavalier treatment of his daughter, but Lloyd would always be conscious within himself that he'd hurt her. And Louise...how could he flaunt her in Mercy's face? How would the rest of the family react to her?

He wondered if he was really being a fool, as Jock obviously thought. Louise had certainly lied to him and nothing would alter the fact that she was an Ashford, the daughter and sister of two men he had reason to hate. He'd once thought the person he'd known as Louise, the girl he'd loved, had been nothing but an empty shell. But their one meeting had brought back the reality of her, the knowledge that he really hadn't been deceived. Oh, perhaps as to her identity, but not as to her character, her true self. Besides, as the mother of his son, his debt to her was greater than his debt to Mercy.

The mailman brought Lloyd's promised letter to Sherborne a little over two weeks later. It was the first real letter Louise had ever received from him and she opened it uncertainly, remembering the note he'd written to her once arranging an illicit meeting at the boundary gate. She still kept that note, folded up amongst her underclothes–the only memento of him she'd possessed.

His handwriting was as she remembered, neat but unformed, the sentence structure unpolished.

Dear Louise,

I trust you are well as this leaves me. I have almost finished bilding the house and will leave here on Monday, taking the coach to Westwood and arriving at Bulbra on the train on Wensday morning. Dont worry about getting someone to meet me. I will borrow a horse in town.

We will have to look at furnature in Rockhampton as I have not got much as you know, apart from the bed and the table and I hope to make a few more chairs. We can get it sent out by train to Westwood and by wagon from there. We will have to make do until it arrives.

If we fix it with the preest when we get to Rockhampton we should be able to get him to marry us in the next couple of days. I am sorry, but I do not think I will be able to give you much of a honeymoon.

Until Wensday,

Your obedient servant,

Lloyd

Louise had to smile, particularly at the mention of the bed. She wondered if it was intended as a subtle reminder. She hadn't expected a love letter from Lloyd and this was certainly not that, yet it was in its way a commendable effort from one who had never been to school.

She turned to Mary, who was eyeing her dubiously, an unread letter of her own in her hands. 'Lloyd is arriving on Wednesday. He says not to meet him, however, as he will hire a horse in Boolburra.

At least,' she laughed, 'those aren't his exact words. His letter-writing is quite endearing. He didn't go to school, you see. It's amazing how literate he is, in the circumstances.'

'I only hope you don't ever grow to be ashamed of him, Louise.'

'Ashamed?' Louise lifted her head defiantly. 'I'm proud of him. Besides, his lack of education isn't unusual in the bush and is certainly no disgrace amongst the people with whom we will be associating.' She widened her eyes in appeal. 'Cousin Mary, will you look through my gowns with me and help me decide what I should wear to my wedding?'

Mary's face softened and Louise felt a little rush of relief. There was no-one else to share these feminine details with her. Heaven knows her wedding was going to be unremarkable enough, without Mary and James detracting from her pleasure with their disapproval.

Chapter Twenty-five

The day before Lloyd's expected arrival, Louise was reading under a shady tree in the front garden when the dogs ran out, barking. Looking up the track she saw a lone horseman approaching. Her first instinctive, joyful thought that it was Lloyd quickly gave way to a plummeting sensation in the stomach. She dropped her book and ran inside, her skirts bundled out of the way.

She found Mary in the kitchen, rolling pastry for an apple pie. Mary paused with her rolling pin in midair, her eyebrows raised. 'Whatever's the matter, Louise? You look as if you've seen a ghost.'

'It's worse than that!' Louise paused, trying to catch her breath. 'Did one of you write to Charles?'

Mary coloured. 'Yes, I'm afraid your Cousin James did. He thought it was his duty, in the circumstances.'

Louise struggled to control her indignation, knowing James's action was probably justified. 'Well, you had best wash your hands and remove your apron, Cousin Mary. He has just arrived.'

Louise didn't make herself one of the welcoming party. Slipping away to the sitting room, she sat at the piano, playing a tempestuous piece to relieve her frustration. She didn't look up when she heard Charles's footsteps.

He came to the piano and rested against it, contemplating her. 'My dear Louise, you are looking well.'

She stopped playing and returned his gaze. The same could be said of him; he was brown and healthy-looking, impeccably dressed as always. 'Life in the country agrees with me, Charles,' she retorted levelly.

'Yes, I remember you were always convinced of that.' He paused, tracing his fingers along the carved edge of the piano. 'I hear you are about to be married.'

'You heard correctly.'

'Weren't you intending to invite your brother to the wedding?'

'We're inviting no-one to the wedding.'

He raised his eyebrows. 'As hole-in-the-corner as that? It need not be, you know. You could pretend to be the virginal bride and no-one here would know the difference.'

'Stop taunting me, Charles. You know very well why we're being married quietly. I don't believe you've come all this way to inform me that you'll provide a lavish reception.'

'No, not exactly. The problem is, who would we invite? If the Barclays are willing to associate with this Kavanagh chap there are others who might not be so broad-minded.'

'It matters not one whit to me what they think. The people I once knew are of no concern now. Lloyd and I shall be living a different life.'

She turned back to the piano and resumed playing, this time choosing her favourite piece, 'Greensleeves'. Charles grasped the lid and dropped it down with a snap, narrowly missing her hastily withdrawn fingers. Her gaze flew up to his, startled and angry, but she flinched when she saw the hardness there.

'You've forgotten one thing, Louise. I haven't given my consent.'

'I thought we'd agreed that I would go my own way and 'be damned to me'.' Her temper was rising swiftly. 'I'm twenty-one, you know.'

'We'll see, my dear, we'll see.' He smiled mockingly. 'I hear this lover of yours is due to arrive tomorrow.'

'Yes and you can keep away from him with your lies this time, you swine.'

He stepped swiftly closer to her, grasping her arm in his strong fingers, squeezing it until he saw the anger on her face replaced by pain and fear. However, she didn't cry out.

'I'm warning you, Louise. You may be my sister, but I don't take to being called names by anyone.' He paused for effect, glaring down at her. 'Actually, I didn't come to take you home again, as it happens.'

'Why did you come, then? To gloat over me?'

He ignored that. 'You know, when I took you to England I thought you would be thanking me for it in twelve months' time. As it happens it would have spared us all a lot of worry and trouble if I'd left you here. I'm certainly not about to make the same mistake a second time. I merely wish to make it clear to you, if you marry this Kavanagh chap you may as well forget you were ever an Ashford. You will starve in the streets before you receive a penny from us. And if the pioneering spirit deserts you don't come crawling back to Banyandah for a roof above your head.'

Louise eyed him coldly. 'I see no reason why I should ever feel impelled to apply to your charity, Charles.'

'So long as you understand the situation.' He turned to go. 'I shall leave you to your music. I don't suppose there'll be a piano where you are going, so you had best make the most of it while you may.'

At the dinner table Charles was at his most charming. To Louise's disgust James and Mary seemed to like him. Sarah, who was excited about Louise's impending wedding, was clearly fascinated by this sophisticated older cousin. Jack however was morose and withdrawn, as he'd been ever since Lloyd's appearance on the scene. He was obviously not in the mood to be impressed by Charles.

Lloyd and his imminent arrival weren't mentioned at all. This aggravated Louise, who almost felt compelled to introduce him into the conversation. However she had the sense not to do so, knowing Charles was likely to say something unpleasant and embarrass everyone.

She wished Jack wouldn't act the part of the wounded suitor, since nothing had ever been declared between them. She didn't believe he was genuinely in love with her, but it was convenient for him to think so, since she was the only personable girl of his age and class within a radius of fifty miles.

When Lloyd arrived the next morning they were all outside to welcome him, if inadvertently. They were taking morning tea under the shady gum tree in the front yard as Mary liked to do when the weather wasn't too hot. In honour of Charles's presence, the men hadn't gone off to work in the paddocks. Instead they'd spent the morning looking at horses; the brood mares and foals and the yearlings to be sold the following year.

As Lloyd dismounted at the gate James and Jack stood up, looking awkward, but Charles lounged back on the rug with an expression of detached amusement. Only Louise walked to the gate, smiling at Lloyd and murmuring a private greeting. She led him to the group, her hand on his arm in a defiantly possessive gesture, though uneasily conscious of Charles in the background. James greeted him stiffly, Mary reservedly. Then Lloyd's gaze fell on the reclining figure and she felt his entire body tense.

'So we meet again, old chap,' drawled Charles, not bothering to rise. 'You know, when I last saw you I really didn't think we would. I hope you didn't suffer any...ill-effects.'

They were all staring at Lloyd with startled expressions. Louise registered the loathing on his face with a sickening jolt to the stomach. But then he seemed to struggle for self-control and turned away without having addressed a single word to Charles. Not that Charles appeared to regard the snub. He merely looked more amused than ever.

The next half-hour, during which Lloyd accepted a cup of tea from Mary and nibbled without apparent appetite at a scone, was fraught with embarrassed silences and uncomfortable attempts at conversation. Only Charles appeared at ease and indeed he seemed to be enjoying himself hugely, though he didn't contribute at all to the conversation. Louise glared at him when no-one else was looking, but he only grinned insufferably. James glanced at him strangely once or twice, but Lloyd didn't look Charles's way at all. It seemed to Louise that he couldn't do so for fear of losing control of the anger within him.

'When do you leave, Kavanagh?' James asked at last. And then flushed, as if thinking the question might be taken as a desire to be rid of him.

Lloyd glanced at Louise. 'This afternoon. We'll go to Rockhampton on tonight's train. Have you packed, Louise?'

She nodded, smiling at him. 'I've been ready for several days now.'

'Hasn't it occurred to you, Louise,' spoke Charles mockingly behind her, 'that I should by rights be giving you away at the altar? I mean, our dear Papa isn't here to do it.'

Louise swung on him, infuriated. 'I wish you would go away, Charles and leave us alone. We shall do very well without you.'

Mary rose to her feet hurriedly. 'Please help me take these things inside, Louise. I'm sure everyone's had sufficient.'

As the women disappeared inside, James cleared his throat and knocked out his pipe on the trunk of the tree. Carefully tamping fresh tobacco in the bowl, he turned his sober gaze on Lloyd. 'How are you going with the filly you bought from us? Did you get the horses home without any trouble?'

Lloyd nodded, looking up from a careful study of the ground. 'We had a good trip. I haven't had time to even put a rope on the filly, though. I've been flat out finishing off the house.'

'It's ready to move into, I take it?'

'It's livable. There's not much in the way of furniture, but we'll be able to buy some in Rockhampton. Louise will manage until it comes. She's a lot tougher than you'd think.'

'You would know about that,' observed Charles smoothly. 'No doubt she had to be, in your company.'

Lloyd gritted his teeth, looking directly at Charles for the first time since his arrival. 'I didn't ask her to come with me when she turned up at Bauhinia Downs with nothing but a swag and a horse and a valise full of clothes! It was *you* who drove her to that.'

'I was only doing my duty, old chap. Following the Pater's orders.'

Lloyd turned away from him, not answering. His hands were clenched; with an effort he opened his fingers and followed James's example in taking out his pipe. He yearned to smash his fist against that grinning, malicious face, to spoil those handsome features a little. Charles was so like Louise and yet so unalike. The difference was human decency, or the lack of it, in Charles's case.

He longed to just grab Louise and go. They could wait at Boolburra until the train came in. The hours would pass tediously in the half-deserted siding, but a little tedium was preferable to the company of this Ashford bastard.

The shifting shade prompted James to rise, gathering up the blanket on which the ladies had been sitting. 'We may as well proceed to the veranda.' He gave a little, ironic smile. 'We can continue this amicable conversation in the cool.'

Jack quickly rose to follow him, obviously grateful for any distraction from the tension emanating from their two visitors. Lloyd was about to mount the steps in their wake when Charles caught him there.

'So you fancy yourself as a horseman, Kavanagh?'

Lloyd paused and looked at him coldly. 'I don't fancy myself as anything, but I can ride and break-in a horse with the rest of 'em.'

Charles laughed and said in an undertone, 'Let's hope that little bastard of yours takes after you, then, if he wants a place in my stables when I'm squire at Fenham Manor.'

Lloyd's tight rein of control snapped. Swearing obscenely he lunged at his prospective brother-in-law, his fist taking him on the side of the jaw. Charles rocked back with the force of it but retained his feet, the grin wiped from his face. He came swiftly back at Lloyd, raining punches around the other's head and face.

Louise heard the commotion from the kitchen and ran to the veranda, Mary close behind her. James and his son stood back, watching, while Charles and Lloyd fought furiously, disregarding any of the accepted rules of boxing. As they watched, Lloyd's fist caught Charles in the stomach and the latter dropped back a step, grunting with pain. Mary gasped and Louise, gnawing anxiously at her fingernails, moaned, 'Oh, how could they be so stupid.'

'Mother, what are they doing?' Sarah had followed them out and stared incredulously at the fighting men, her eyes wide and frightened.

Mary turned and grasped her arm firmly. 'Come on, Sarah, this is no sight for ladies. Come away, Louise and leave them fight if they must.'

But Louise didn't heed her. She stood there at the veranda rail, grasping it convulsively. Mixed with her dismay and shame that they could behave in this brutal and ill-bred fashion, was her fear that Lloyd may be badly hurt. If he did some serious injury to Charles it would be almost as bad. And suddenly it wasn't because Charles's welfare concerned her, but because she knew what a man of his position could do in the law courts to his social inferior.

They had each other in a wrestler's grip now. Lloyd tripped Charles with his foot and they toppled together to the ground. They rolled over and over in the dirt, grasping each other's arms, grappling together in a way that was reminiscent of lovers, except that there was nothing lover-like about the emotion that drove them. Charles brought his knee up, aiming for the groin and Lloyd jackknifed his body away. He wasn't quite quick enough to avoid the second attempt and the knee caught him in the stomach. He drew back, gasping, relinquishing his grip. Charles followed up his advantage, jabbing him in the chest and face, but he managed to roll out of reach and came back again, breaking through Charles's guard with a particularly savage punch to the ribs.

'Oh God, can't someone stop them?' Louise appealed to her cousins, horrified. 'They'll kill each other!'

James seemed to notice her for the first time. 'Go inside, Louise. We won't let it come to that.'

Yet she stayed, shocked and fascinated, unable to move. They were evenly matched, Charles slightly taller but Lloyd of sturdier build. Charles was well versed in the science of boxing, but Lloyd had learned to fight in a hard, tough school as a boy and his taut body was fit from physical work. Charles was hardly less stalwart, but they were both panting heavily by now, their breaths coming in short, painful gasps. Their clothes were grey with dirt, which looked less out of place on Lloyd's moleskins and striped shirt than on Charles's tailored breeches and tweed jacket. And there was blood on their faces, mingled with the sweat and grime.

'I think they've had enough,' said James. 'Come on, Jack.'

Jack looked hesitant and with good reason, for both combatants were larger than either him or his father and, judging by their present display, far more aggressive. But he bent to grasp Lloyd by the arms, dragging him back, while James constrained Charles.

As James had anticipated, both men were too exhausted to protest. Lloyd rolled onto his back and lay motionless in the dirt, fighting for breath, while Charles struggled to a seated position, gasping with pain. James said not one word but retired to sit on the edge of the veranda. Jack followed his example and Louise, who had come down the steps, was left standing alone in the sun.

At last Lloyd rose slowly to his feet, holding one hand to his stomach as if it pained him. He picked his hat from the dust where it had fallen and crossed to Louise. A trickle of blood ran from the corner of his mouth and already a bruise was beginning to develop on his right cheek bone.

Louise stared in dismay at the picture he presented. 'Oh Lloyd, how could you behave this way? Did you start it?'

It was James who answered her, his voice very calm. 'No, Charles did. At least, it was something he said, which unfortunately for him I happened to overhear.' Lloyd looked quickly at him and he met the younger man's eyes with a sympathetic regard. 'Louise, take Kavanagh inside and help him clean up and then I'd like him to join me in the study for a chat.'

'I think Louise and I should just go, before there's any more trouble.'

'There's no need.' James turned to Charles, who had pulled himself up against the gum tree and was engaged in brushing off his clothes. James's voice hardened. 'You're the one who is leaving, aren't you, Charles?'

Charles looked at him swiftly. He shrugged his shoulders and straightened his tie. 'If that's the way you want it to be, Barclay.'

'I'm afraid it is. Just wash and fetch your things and then I would appreciate it if you went.'

'Certainly.' Charles bowed mockingly and disappeared inside. James sent Jack to catch and saddle Charles's horse and had it waiting for him at the gate when he reappeared. As Charles mounted up he glanced to the front door, where Louise and Lloyd now stood, arm in arm. Sister and brother exchanged looks for a long moment. For Louise this was to be the final cutting of ties with her family. But suddenly she realized that it didn't hurt her to think she might never see Charles again–the older brother whom she'd loved as a child and had continued to love in spite of everything, until the last few weeks.

Charles reined his horse and rode off without a word. James watched after him in silence for a few minutes before turning to the young couple in the doorway. 'Come on, Kavanagh. I think it's time we got to know each other a little better.'

In the study James motioned to Lloyd to sit across from him on a hard, upright chair. He came straight to the point. 'From what Ashford said to you, I gather there was a child.'

Lloyd nodded, looking down as a quick shaft of shame and anguish stabbed him.

James studied him, rolling a pencil between his fingers. 'Did you know at the time?'

He shook his head. 'I had no idea until Louise told me the other day. Poor girl...she had to go through it all on her own. They took the baby away from her, you know.'

'That was to be expected, I suppose.' James's face twisted. 'No wonder Louise broke down the other night. Where is he now?'

'He's with the coachman and his wife at Fenham Manor. Louise says they're good people and he's well-taken care of. But it hurts like hell to know I'll never see him. And I can't stand to think of him working for that bastard when he's older.'

'Whatever their faults, I've never heard that the Ashfords mistreat their servants. I think Charles was merely taunting you.'

'I hope so. God, what a mess we made of everything.'

'It is too late to change that, Lloyd.' James's face softened. 'What's done is done. Just look to the future and concentrate on making it a happy one. You'll have other children and if your little boy is well provided for you'd do best to try to put him out of your mind.'

He hesitated. 'You know, I wasn't happy about Louise marrying you before, but I'm beginning to think I was wrong. I always knew the Ashfords had a streak of rottenness in them and Charles certainly has it. Louise is the best of them by far. Suddenly I can see it all very clearly and I can see what Louise has been looking for that she never had at home.' He rose to his feet and held out his hand to Lloyd, who hastily stood up and clasped it. 'I hope she has found it with you. My very best wishes to you both. I hope you will keep in contact with us and look on us as family.'

'I'm sure that would please Louise very much.' Lloyd met James's eyes gratefully. 'She's very fond of you and Mrs Barclay and her brother made it clear the Ashfords would cut her off if she married me.'

'Perhaps that won't be much loss to her. Come on, then. We'll rejoin the others and I must explain to Mary why I sent Charles off with such lack of ceremony.'

'Before we do, I apologise for making a spectacle of myself with Ashford.'

James smiled grimly. 'You're lucky I heard what he said, or I might not have been so tolerant. I think Jack is still trying to make sense of it, but I won't be enlightening him.'

Louise made an emotional farewell to Mary later that afternoon. James was driving her and her luggage to Boolburra in the buggy.

'Write to me, won't you, dear,' Mary said, hugging her. 'And visit us, if you can spare the time. I hope you'll be very happy.'

Mary was still reeling with the shock of it all; first the fight and then James's revelation. She wondered that anyone could have spoken the way Charles had. She managed to farewell Kavanagh with a tentative warmth, although just looking at him with the bruise on his face and the dirt stains on his clothes made her recoil slightly.

Jack seemed embarrassed by the entire business. Louise didn't prolong her goodbyes to him, but kissed Sarah and promised to have her to stay sometime, before stepping up into the buggy. Then James drove her away, with Lloyd riding ahead on his borrowed horse.

After James left them at Boolburra they had a couple of hours to fill in before the train departed. Walking to the river, they scrambled down the bank to the edge of the water. Lloyd took off his shirt and shook the dirt from it while Louise took her fill of his naked torso, captured by her memories even as she noted the darkening bruises. He glanced at her and she saw his eyes darken as if he read her thoughts. But he merely sat beside her to re-button the shirt and then lay back, wincing as he eased his body into a more comfortable position. He cupped his hands behind his head and stared at the sky, while the slowly stirring leaves of the river-gums made drifting patterns of light and shade across his face.

'Your cousin James is a decent bloke,' he commented thoughtfully. 'He could've very easily blamed me for starting the fight.'

'It's fortunate he overheard Charles, or the outcome would have been different. Not that I wanted anyone else to know what he now knows. Oh, how could Charles have been so indiscreet?'

'Indiscreet? I would've found another name for it.'

'It was worse than indiscreet, I agree. But I didn't think you were one for brawling.'

'I suppose if some bloke seduced a sister I cared about I'd want to belt him up, too. But not the way your brother did.'

'What do you mean? What are you talking about?'

And so he told her then, in a flat, expressionless tone that gave away little of his true feelings. Yet Louise glimpsed his agony and mental anguish in the stark description of brutality and knew she wasn't the only one who'd suffered.

Tenderness rose up in her and she reached across to stroke his cheek. 'I'm glad I didn't say goodbye to Charles today.'

She didn't know it, but the fight with Charles today had begun the real healing for Lloyd, the ending of bitterness. It had excised the humiliation of his beating in a way nothing else could have done, for though he hadn't been the victor in the struggle he'd extracted his revenge. Charles wouldn't take him lightly again.

Chapter Twenty-six

It was just on dark when the train left Boolburra. They shared a compartment with two stiff, middle-aged ladies who looked disapprovingly at them and frowned severely when Lloyd took her hand. Lloyd presented a raffish appearance with the purple bruise on his face and although he'd changed into clean clothes, he was saving his only suit for his wedding day.

They laughed together at the ladies' frigid censure and Lloyd even kissed her as they passed through the dark tunnel in the Gogango Range, his battered mouth making him wince. But there was excitement in that stolen kiss, along with the knowledge they'd soon be married and subject to no-one's disapproval. Louise pulled away just in time to escape the censorious stare of their companions as the train chugged into moonlight once more.

Eventually the rocking carriage and clacking wheels lulled them to sleep, despite the hard, unaccommodating seat. When the train pulled into Rockhampton, Louise awoke with her head resting on Lloyd's shoulder and quickly moved to put a respectable distance between them.

It was shortly after midnight. They left the bulk of Louise's luggage at the railway station and walked to the nearest hotel, shivering, for though it was only May it was cold at this early hour. In the lobby Lloyd asked for two rooms, while the clerk behind the desk looked at them suspiciously, raising his eyebrows at Lloyd's battered face. The rooms he allotted them were obviously set well apart. Louise knew it would have been more circumspect to have stayed at separate hotels, but the hour was too late to be bothered with such niceties.

'And what names will it be, sir?'

'L. Kavanagh and Miss Ashford.'

The man looked up, startled. The name of Ashford was well known in Rockhampton, although her family had never been in the habit of patronising this hotel. Louise wondered if he recognized her as one of them, even though she hardly looked the part with her crushed skirt and hair escaping from its chignon.

She held her head high and made a dispassionate survey of the lobby, wrinkling her nose at its faded wallpaper and worn carpet. The attendant hastily jingled some keys and left his desk, carrying their luggage up the stairs himself. He ushered Louise into the first room with a gracious display of manners, before departing along the corridor with Lloyd's case without waiting to see if he was followed.

Lloyd paused, smiling, obviously aware that he was being snubbed. 'I'll knock on your door before I go down to breakfast. Sleep well.'

At eight o'clock she was dressed and ready when she heard his knock, and waited for a discreet interval before joining him in the dining room. After they'd eaten they paid a visit to the priest. To Louise the Saint Joseph's church in Alma Street seemed foreign and almost sinister with its confessional and statue of the Virgin Mary. Lloyd hardly seemed more at ease, confessing he'd seldom been inside a church of any sort. He appeared to be disproportionately nervous of all the trappings of religion.

The French priest was reluctant to marry them at such short notice, seeming to think Louise should receive instruction in the Catholic faith first.

Lloyd grew impatient, casting off his diffidence. 'We're down from the bush, Dean Murlay and we can't afford to stay for more than a few days. If you won't marry us we'll find someone else who will.'

The Dean was a friendly, approachable man, not the sort of person to inspire the fear in which Lloyd seemed to hold his religion. He looked at the bruise on Lloyd's cheek and smiled. 'Did you have to fight for Mademoiselle, then?'

Lloyd glanced quickly at Louise. 'You could say that.'

Fortunately Dean Murlay seemed to be as broad-minded as he was congenial. 'Then, if you've put yourself to so much trouble I won't send you away. But you have family who would wish to be present, no?'

'My family's in New South Wales and Miss Ashford's is in England. And we're both of age.'

'Oh, in that case…I travel much through the outer reaches of my parish and I perform marriages and christenings as I go. I only regret it will cost you extra for a special licence.'

The time was set for eleven o'clock the following morning and after only a short sermon on the sacredness of marriage and the inadvisability of entering into it lightly, they were able to make their escape.

'Well, that wasn't so bad.' Lloyd squinted a little in the glare of the street. 'And now for a wedding ring.'

After purchasing the ring they spent the rest of the day shopping for household goods and furniture. Louise had money of her own in a bank account in Rockhampton, the inheritance she'd received on her twenty-first birthday. She decided to purchase a few luxury items, including a piano, a bookcase and a sofa.

'It's still a let-down to what you're used to,' Lloyd observed glumly.

She looked up into his eyes and smiled impishly. 'Have you forgotten it was me who went chasing after you the other day, not the other way around?'

'I said you must be desperate.' But he was smiling back at her, as if he knew full well what lured her, this compelling emotion they shared that transcended class and creed.

After dinner at the hotel that night they went for a walk down the street, since the prospect of retiring alone to their separate rooms didn't appeal. They sat on a park bench until a drunken derelict ambled towards them, begging for money in a hoarse croak. Lloyd thrust a few pennies at him and drew her away, turning back to the hotel. When they reached her door he opened it and swiftly checked the deserted passage before stepping inside with her.

She gave him a startled look. 'You shouldn't...if anyone were to see you...'

'There was no-one about.' He locked the door and smiled at her, hoping to soothe her misgivings. 'There's so much I need to ask you, where no-one can hear.'

While she sat on the only chair he perched on the edge of the bed. He asked questions he hadn't asked her before–about her journey to England and then, tentatively, about the time before and after the baby was born.

'It was dreadful when they took him away from me,' she whispered. 'That was the worst part of all, harder even than giving birth to him and I won't even begin to describe the pain of that.' Her lower lip trembled. 'I try not to think of it. I've tried to forget him–but I can't.'

'Why should you?' he remarked grimly, rising to his feet and pulling her into his arms. He held her close for a long moment, his lips against her hair. 'Oh, Louise, I'm so sorry. When I think of what you've suffered–and there I was, feeling sorry for myself, calling you every filthy name I could think of. I wish there was something I could do to make up for it, but I guess I did all the damage long ago.'

He felt her shake her head, with the soft, warm skin of her face against his throat. 'Don't blame yourself.'

But he did blame himself. Perhaps they'd been equally guilty of the original sin, but he'd indulged in that sin before without fathering a child. He'd known what to do. With Louise he hadn't done it, and not from any conscious decision. Possibly it was because the intensity of their union had taken him beyond his usual control; and possibly his desire to marry her and see her bearing his children had done away with his usual caution.

He drew her down to sit beside him on the bed. 'The poor little bloke, I suppose he'll grow up thinking he's a Pom. He'll even talk like one.'

She smiled. 'Is that so bad? The Joneses are pretending his mother was their niece, but I wonder if he'll learn the truth one day. Quite possibly, thanks to the investigations of a certain Mr Richard Langley.'

'He'll know he's a bastard, the poor little beggar.'

'Perhaps, but I think the local people will accept him regardless. They're a close-knit community and I can't see them ostracising the Jones's adopted son.'

'What about your family?' His voice sharpened as he remembered how Charles had taunted him. 'How will they treat him?'

Louise shrugged. 'I imagine they'll ignore his existence as much as possible. But they won't ill-treat him, Lloyd. Whatever his faults Papa has the sense to value his servants. Oh, he rants and raves, but they are used to that. If Matthew likes horses he'll have a good life and it's in his blood, after all. He will have to work hard, but,' she smiled up at him, 'no harder than his father does.'

He put his hand on her stomach, tentatively, tracing through her clothing the soft swell of it where once it had been firm and flat. He tried to imagine her big with child, his child. Even now he found it difficult to accept that she'd given birth to his son on the other side of the world while he remained oblivious to her need of him.

He tried to picture a little boy with Louise's dark hair and his features, imagining him tottering on chubby bow legs. He would be eighteen months old now. Just thinking about him hurt, reminding him of Gertie, who had died. He remembered holding Gertie on his shoulder one day while her grubby hands clutched at his hair and the knowledge that he would never hold his own son made his heart clench.

Louise distracted him from his thoughts with questions about his own life in the last two years and about the Jamiesons. 'Mrs Jamieson...' she hesitated. 'Did she die in childbirth?'

Lloyd looked down at the floor, finding the subject difficult even after all this time. 'She died a few days later. Of infection, they said. She had the baby in Banana with a midwife. She refused to come back here like Jock wanted her to, after the business with the diphtheria and losing Gertie. The sad part of it is, perhaps if she'd come to Rockhampton she might still be alive. Jock says a doctor might have saved her.'

'And the baby? You mentioned it was a girl.'

He nodded, his sorrow fading as he pictured the child who'd helped heal the grieving Jamiesons. 'Isabella. She's a fat, happy little thing. I don't think she misses not having a mother. The girls all make so much of her. And she's the apple of Jock's eye.'

'Every cloud has a silver lining,' she murmured softly. 'What of Maurice? How is he?'

'He's pretty good, but he'll never be quite what he used to be. He tires easily.' His arms tightened and he kissed her cheek and then her mouth. 'Louise, let me stay, please?' He pressed her back on the bed and moved his hips against her, whispering huskily against her ear. 'It's been so long and this is starting to drive me crazy.'

'No, Lloyd.' She put her hands on his chest and pushed him away, though her own breathing had quickened. 'We'd be thrown out of the hotel if they realized you were in here. Besides, I would feel dreadful standing up before the priest afterwards.'

'I'm sure he thinks it's a rush job, anyway. If only he knew it's two years too late for that.' Lloyd's disappointment was a nagging ache inside him, but he sat up, trying to stifle his need. He envisaged the gloomy, overwhelming atmosphere of the little church and the all-seeing, tolerant eyes of the priest–eyes that had seen much of human frailty. 'But you're right. I can wait until tomorrow night. Then you won't be getting rid of me so easily.'

In the morning they booked out of the hotel. Lloyd carried their cases to the railway station and visited a barber's shop to have his hair and whiskers trimmed while Louise looked in shop windows. Then they visited a tea shop and drank tea until it was time to go to the church.

Louise had dressed for the occasion in a fashionable dark blue gown with a high bustle and buttoned cuirasse bodice that had come from England, her dark hair neatly arranged in coiled plaits under a tiny, matching hat tilted over one eye. Lloyd was unusually formal in a coat, waistcoat and bow-tie. With his hair and side whiskers newly barbered he looked more like a middle-class grazier than the stockman she'd first met at Bauhinia Downs.

It was all over very quickly. Lloyd had enlisted two businessmen of his acquaintance to act as witnesses and once the register was signed they were man and wife.

As they walked out into the street arm in arm, Lloyd looked down at her and grinned. 'Well, Mrs Kavanagh, how about that?'

She laughed. 'It's hard to believe. I kept expecting Charles to burst in at any moment and put a stop to the proceedings.'

'He won't be able to come between us now. How does that bit from the Bible go?'

'"What God hath joined together let no man put asunder"?'

'Yeah, that's it. He'd better remember it.'

Their next visit was to a photographer to record their wedding day. The photographer tactfully didn't mention the bruise on Lloyd's cheek, which was beginning to fade and turn yellow at the edges. He posed them with Louise sitting stiffly in a straight-backed chair, her hands folded in her lap, while Lloyd stood behind her grasping the back of the chair with his face slightly averted to hide the bruise.

They purchased sandwiches and bottles of lemonade and took a horse-drawn cab to the new Botanic Gardens. Sitting close together on one of the garden seats, they ate their lunch before wandering down the pathways arm in arm.

Later, after arranging the transport of their furniture, they strolled down Quay Street, looking at the ships anchored in the broad, muddy Fitzroy River. One of them was being unloaded at the dock and they watched the cargo in barrels and tea-chests being transferred to a horse-drawn wagon, its destination a nearby warehouse. When this began to bore them, they moved to a park bench and shared a newspaper, saying little. Lloyd was restless and impatient, barely absorbing what he read, his senses full of his new wife beside him, the clean smell of her hair, the light scent of lavender. The night couldn't come soon enough for him.

It was already dark when they left the train at Westwood. The best hotel in the town was full, forcing them to seek accommodation at a shabby establishment with flimsy walls and peeling paintwork. The shifty-eyed attendant at the desk wore a shiny waistcoat over a shirt that had long since ceased to be white and his languid manner implied indifference as to whether he found them a room or not. But he helped them carry their luggage up the stairs and directed them to the dining area for their dinner.

After a meal of the ubiquitous corned beef, potatoes, cabbage and onions in white sauce, they retired upstairs. Lloyd looked ruefully at the dismal little room. 'I'm sorry. I never meant to bring you to a place like this for our wedding night.'

The bed was sagging and lumpy, the only furniture a washstand and a chipped chest of drawers. Lloyd drew down the bedcovers and tested the mattress under his hand. The springs creaked alarmingly.

Louise's heart sank. She knew what was coming next and how the regular protestations of rusty springs would advertise their activity to anyone within earshot. From one of the adjoining rooms they could hear male voices in murmured conversation and in the other a man was rambling in a drunken monologue, punctuated by occasional outbursts of off-key singing. The interior walls were obviously every bit as thin as the outer ones appeared.

'Lloyd, we can't–they'll hear us.'

He muttered something under his breath and directed her towards the corner. 'If you think I'm waiting any longer...stand over there.'

She obeyed him, wondering what he was about. He picked up the mattress, bedclothes and all and dumped it on the floor, where there was just enough space between the bedstead and the wall to accommodate it. 'Now,' he said, 'that won't creak and it doesn't sag, either.'

Louise shook her head at him, torn between embarrassment and excitement. But there was something about his single-minded determination that was curiously moving and the intent look in his eyes made her body tremble with anticipation. She began to pull the pins from her hair and when it lay loose over her shoulders he came to her and kissed her, unbuttoning her bodice with hard, calloused fingers. She undressed him in her turn, helping him shrug out of his coat and waistcoat, unfastening his shirt and running her hands over his bare skin. By this time they were both breathing hard. As Lloyd dispensed with the rest of his clothes and hers, they sank together onto the bed on the floor.

Later, Louise lay in her new husband's embrace, her face pillowed on the firm muscle of his shoulder, the weight of his arm heavy across her breasts. She'd wondered if it was possible to recapture the joy and emotion of their earlier relationship, but her doubts had been put to rest. For the first time in two years she knew close to perfect happiness, except for that sad little place inside of her that still ached like a rotten tooth.

She would never be free of her memories of Matthew, the son she might not see again. Already she'd missed hearing his first words, seeing him take his first step. His life in England would shape him differently and his foster parents would raise him to their standards and ideals, not her own. Growing in that cool, damp climate, his cheeks would be rosy, his skin unblemished. Hopefully he had inherited his parents' love of horses and would enjoy working in the stables at Fenham Manor as he grew older. It was not a bad life and Jones would be a good mentor.

James Barclay had advised her to put the past behind her and she knew she must do just that. Matthew was in safe hands and she would only compromise his happiness and their own future if she tried to take him back now. With Lloyd alienated from the Jamiesons, they had few enough friends.

So she gave voice to the need that had been eating away at her ever since Matthew's birth. She held her husband to her and whispered, 'I hope we have another baby soon, Lloyd. I want one so much.'

A deep sigh shuddered through his body as he stroked her hair away from her face. 'So do I. I love you, Louise.'

It was the first time he'd spoken the words, this time around, and they were all the sweeter to Louise for knowing they weren't lightly uttered. 'And I love you, too. I realized just how much after we were parted.'

It was a long time before they slept. At last Lloyd slumbered while Louise lay curled into him, lulled by the sound of his regular breathing. There was comfort in his lean, hard body and a sense of security that had been lacking in her life for a long time now.

Tomorrow they would take the coach to Banana and the following day they'd travel to Myvanwy. She remembered the night she'd once spent in his little shack with its chinks in the walls, all the sounds of the bush close at hand. She tried to picture the new house, envisaging a rambling structure with wide verandas and raw, unweathered slab walls. It would be up to her to transform the empty shell of it into a home.

But the prospect did not daunt her.

She turned her face into the pillow and slept.

Heather Garside grew up on a cattle property in Central Queensland and now lives with her husband on a beef and grain farm in the same area. She has two adult children and two beautiful granddaughters.

She has previously published four historical and rural romances and has helped to write and produce several compilations of short stories and local histories. The Cornstalk was a finalist in the 2008 Booksellers' Best Award, Long Historical category, for romance books published in the USA. Breakaway Creek was a finalist in the QWC/Hachette Manuscript Development Program and was released by Clan Destine Press in 2013. It is a rural romance with a dual timeline.

Heather works at home on the farm and for many years helped produce a local monthly newsletter, amongst other voluntary activities. She enjoys patchwork and sewing and regularly attends a local craft group.

For more information about her books, please visit her website at www.heathergarside.com